MW01133028

Daughter
of the
Dark · Moon

BOOK 3 OF THE TWIN MOONS SAGA

By

Holly Bargo

HEN HOUSE PUBLISHING

Holly Bargo

HEN HOUSE PUBLISHING
www.henhousepublishing.com

Cover photograph by Lawrence Green.
Cover design by Karen M. Smith.

Also by Holly Bargo

The Twin Moons Saga
DAUGHTER OF THE TWIN MOONS
DAUGHTER OF THE DEEPWOOD
DAUGHTER OF THE DARK MOON

The Tree of Life Series
ROWAN
CASSIA
WILLOW

The Immortal Shifters
THE BARBARY LION
TIGER IN THE SNOW

The Russian Love Series
RUSSIAN LULLABY
RUSSIAN GOLD
RUSSIAN DAWN
RUSSIAN PRIDE

Other Novels
THE DRAGON WORE A KILT
THE FALCON OF IMENOTASH
PURE IRON
THE MIGHTY FINN
ULFBEHRT'S LEGACY

Short Stories
BY WATER REBORN
SKEINS OF GOLD: RUMPELSTILTSKIN RETOLD

Acknowledgments

Gratitude goes first and foremost to my husband, David, who has learned that the voices in my head really do need to find expression. I also thank my two sons, Matt and Brian, for their tolerant acceptance: Yes, boys, Mommy really does need to write these stories, no matter how embarrassing you find it.

I also thank my editor, Cindy Draughon. Her eagle eyes and insight improve my manuscripts immeasurably. I'm glad she also enjoys what I write.

Further thanks go to the friends and family who offer moral support and encouragement. That means the world to me.

I also thank Dee Owens, my marketing guru, whose expertise in social media eclipses my own and who helps keep me and my books from disappearing into ignominy.

Finally, I must thank you, dear reader, for allowing me the privilege of entertaining you. I hope you enjoy this story.

CHAPTER 1

Tiny biting insects hovered nearby in the sultry summer air, but resisted the temptation of his skin as he moved like a shadow, soundless and unnoticed, through the thickly wooded state park. The very idea of reserving tracts of wilderness amused him, even though this was not his native realm. The fishy scent of fresh water nearby tickled his nose. He adjusted his direction accordingly, and then his flared nostrils caught another, more desired fragrance.

He paused at the forest edge, observing the woman who sat on the old concrete boat ramp as she reeled in a fish with expert skill.

"Y'all can come out now," she called over her shoulder without looking behind her.

He obeyed her beckons and quietly took a seat beside her as she cast her line again. They sat in companionable silence, inches apart, never touching. He did not quite know her reason for the studious avoidance of physical contact and did not question it. He simply enjoyed the soft sounds of her breathing, the rustle of her clothes, the splash of water, the rustling of leaves, and the chirps of birds. It reminded him of his home in midsummer.

She caught another fish, deemed it inadequate for her purposes, and released it back into the water after extracting the sharp hook from its mouth. She glanced at the horizon and noted the sun's descent and the vivid flare of color across the western sky.

"I've got enough to feed both of us tonight if you're hungry," she invited him as she hauled up the day's meager catch. She gathered her cooler and tackle and began the hike back to her tiny cabin. He fell into step behind her, feeling protective and watching for danger.

"Nothing but the occasional black bear or badger around here," she said, her voice quiet in the rustling wilderness.

He said nothing, but shadowed her nonetheless. He knew park visitors occasionally tramped through what she considered her territory and that some of them had less than benign intentions. He'd killed one of them not three days past.

The elimination of a tainted soul did not disturb him. After hundreds of millennia, little actually disturbed him. He glanced at the slender hips swaying with each step, the lure to masculine interest unintentional. Desire surged, a heady sensation he hadn't enjoyed since his mate died.

Had been killed.

Murdered.

That was the last time he'd seen the Erlking, who had avenged the wrong, but the Erlking's justice had not been enough. His mate's death shattered his soul.

The icy fury that always followed that bitter memory sent chills up and down his spine, but did not overwhelm the sanity that most of his world believed he lost long ago. And he had for a short time, until the pull of his son, his only child, had restored him to rational thought. But now Marog, too, was dead and Mogren ruled the Unseelie Court. So, he had finally left the chill, dusty environs of his libraries and laboratories.

He preferred it that way. He mourned Marog's death; any father would. However, the crown prince had chosen his fate, and Uberon, the deposed Unseelie king, believed in free will if he believed in nothing else.

Except where this one woman was concerned.

She was his.

The oracle confirmed it.

CHAPTER 2

Corinne could not help but wonder at the tall man whose shadowed presence she'd felt like an itch between her shoulder blades for the past several days. She knew the disconcerting feeling of being watched. She knew she'd been foolish to invite him to join her. Perhaps, she thought, she was simply gullible and had read far too many fluffy romance novels in which the dangerous killer had a heart of gold. Regardless, she could not force herself to endure that silent presence watching her and had called him out.

Her self-control impressed her when he'd taken a seat beside her on the old boat ramp. She'd maintained her composure, though the sight of his odd clothing identified him as either having wandered off a distant movie set or just plain weird. The supple leather of his trousers molded over hard, defined muscle. The close-fitting shafts of soft-soled boots extended to his knees. The deep ruby of his shirt caught the humid summer breeze and plastered the billowing fabric over well-defined muscles on a tall, lean frame. Covert glances gave her the impression of above average height, supple strength, pale skin, and raven hair. If she'd had an image of a fallen angel, this man matched it.

His failure to make a sound as she walked back to her cabin both unnerved and annoyed her. She considered herself quiet, moving along the narrow footpath without crashing through overhanging branches or stumbling over exposed tree roots and loose rocks. She breathed easily as she lugged tackle and cooler and a line with two good-sized fish. If her shadow, hovering behind her like the Grim Reaper, hadn't followed her, she would have cleaned the second fish and set it aside for the next day's chow. As it was, she'd have to walk to the local farmer's market to stock up on food to feed them both.

Corinne hoped her bank account could withstand the expense of feeding more than one person, the second of whom surely boasted a big appetite. She'd grown up the youngest of six, the other five being brothers, in a family with a penchant for survival training, primitive camping, and bow hunting. Having been impressed into household service by her mother, she grew up knowing how much "growing boys" ate. She considered the tall, broad-shouldered man walking behind her. He'd have a healthy appetite. She resigned herself to cooking both fishes and eating only half of one.

The two-mile hike ended at her remote cabin, formerly a park cabin on park land, but sold off by the park service during the recession of the late 1980s to raise funds for continued operation. Her folks had jumped at the chance to purchase a vacation hideaway in the Appalachian foothills near Salt Fork Lake. Setting down the cooler and tackle box, she wiped the sweat from her forehead and fished the house key from her pocket. A moment later, the Grim Reaper prowled her tiny cabin, too big for its cozy dimensions.

Corinne ignored him and got to work stowing her belongings in their proper places. In such a tiny space, organization and tidiness were mandatory. He followed her back outside to the stump of an old oak leveled off and sanded smooth after the remnant gales of a southern hurricane had toppled it. Cleaver in hand, she lay one largemouth bass on the stump and raised the blade. Another hand wrapped around her wrist, holding it. She looked into the silver eyes of the stranger. He raised one finely drawn eyebrow and, without speaking, gently extracted the cleaver from her hand. With his other hand, he drew her away from the stump. He gave her a pointed look that needed no words to explain he would clean the fish.

"Whatever," she muttered and shrugged her shoulders before going back inside. It was, she mused, quite possibly the most idiotic thing she'd done that day, leaving a strange man outside with a cleaver. What if he happened to be an axe murderer?

Cleaver murderer.

Kitchen killer.

She snorted and giggled at her own absurdity as she pulled a cast iron skillet from the cupboard and set it on the stove. A twist of the wrist, a hiss, and a *whoosh*, and blue flame rose from the burner. Corinne found some dill-infused olive oil and drizzled it into the pan. A heady scent quickly rose. She grabbed a bundle of asparagus and rinsed the spears, cut a lemon in half, got out the salt and pepper and retrieved yesterday's leftover rice pilaf. She loosened the lid on the rice and popped it into the small microwave oven for reheating.

Corinne's guest slapped down two perfectly cleaned and filleted fish on the countertop beside her. Without speaking, the man turned on the spigot and washed his hands and the cleaver in the sink. Corinne found her gaze drawn to those hands, large but not crude, the fingers long and elegant and capable looking. When he finished, she rinsed the fillets, patted them dry with paper towels, dredged them in seasoned flour, and lay them in the skillet. The flesh sizzled. She dumped the asparagus spears into the skillet, too. Knowing she had a few minutes—not many—she pulled down two of her four plates and retrieved the necessary silverware.

"Thanks for cleaning the fish," she said and held out the plates and silverware. "You can set the table. Cups are in the upper cabinet left of the sink. Napkins are in the drawer below the silverware."

The man looked down his straight nose at her, faintly horrified, but he took what Corinne handed him and obeyed her order. With a spatula, she checked the underside of the fish and, satisfied with the golden brown color, flipped it. She turned the asparagus spears to ensure they cooked on all sides, squeezed the lemon over the contents of the skillet, and sprinkled everything with salt and pepper. The correct buttons pressed, the microwave hummed and the old turntable rattled.

She placed a potholder on the table and transferred the skillet from the stovetop to the table. A moment later, she transferred the reheated rice to the table and extracted a serving spoon from a drawer.

"*Bon appétit*," she said in her best imitation of Julia Child as she seated herself and gestured for her guest to take the seat across from her.

He looked at her with a puzzled frown.

"I'm not a good mimic," she acknowledged with good cheer. "You should hear my Jacques Pépin imitation. It's even worse."

He blinked at her. She sighed, crossed herself, folded her hands, and bowed her head to quickly murmur a rote prayer over the food on the table. She crossed herself again and gave him a determinedly bright smile.

"So, tell me about yourself, like your name," she said as she used a fork and spatula to transfer an entire fillet and several asparagus spears to his plate. He simply looked at her. "You've been watching me for the last few days. I know you have. Mind telling me why?"

She spooned rice onto his plate and he picked up his fork. She waited with an expectant attitude as he sampled her cooking.

"Oh, I forgot drinks," she exclaimed and jumped up to retrieve a pitcher half full of iced tea. She poured and set the pitcher on the table.

"Will you at least tell me your name?" she begged as she filled her own plate. "You look like the Grim Reaper frowning at me."

Her guest met her gaze, his unblinking, and he finally replied in a low, somewhat rusty baritone, "Uberon."

She gifted him with a polite smile and said, steel lacing every syllable, "Thank you. Now please tell me why you've been shadowing me."

"You're mine."

Corinne choked on the tea she attempted to swallow. Setting the glass down, she said, "What do you mean by that?"

"You're mine," he repeated, his voice low, quiet, and calm as though he declared nothing more momentous than the state of the weather. He gestured at his plate with his fork and added, "This is good."

"Glad you like it," she replied in a dry tone and wondered why she felt no danger in his presence, especially following his strange declaration and understanding her own vulnerability alone with a stranger in a remote cabin. "You do realize that I have rights and freedom of choice. You can't just claim me as your property."

"You're weary," he said between bites as though she'd not spoken. "When you've finished eating, go to bed. I shall clean up."

Directing an annoyed glare at the handsome brute, Corinne said, "*You* are sleeping on the sofa."

He nodded, not seeming at all disturbed by her assertion of personal autonomy. A frisson of excitement—or terror—tingled up her spine. She met his mysterious silver gaze and, strangely again, felt no fear. This man meant her no harm, despite the weird and disturbing claim of possession.

"Uberon?"

"Yes?"

"Why are you here?"

"Because you're mine."

They finished the simple meal in silence. Uberon ate the other half of her fillet.

CHAPTER 3

When his woman had disappeared into the washroom, Uberon exerted a whisper of power to clean and tidy the kitchen. What would have taken an ordinary human minutes to do took him a mere few seconds. When she emerged from cleaning herself, her freshly washed hair bound in a loose braid and her body graced by short cotton pajamas decorated with yellow cats and pink teapots, the former king of the Unseelie Court nearly swallowed his tongue as the urge to take her as his mate slammed into him. She looked and smelled fresh and clean and absolutely delicious.

He exhaled slowly through his nose, imposing stern control upon himself.

"Bathroom's yours," she said. "I'll fetch a blanket for you."

He nodded and rose from the chair in which he'd been sitting. He watched as she retrieved a blanket and spread it over the sofa cushions.

"You're a bit tall for that sofa, but beggars can't be choosers and you're not sleeping with me," she said with the hint of a snarl.

He nodded, keeping his expression mild. If he climbed into her bed, she'd not get sleep. Nor would he. He approved of her caution and the distance she seemed determined to maintain.

"Oh, and if it gets cold—" she said and waved her hand. Fire ignited on the hearth. She waved her hand again and the fire vanished. "—feel free to light a fire."

The corners of Uberon's lips curled upward in a faint smile at her small display of power. He should have known that fate would not pair him with an unworthy, unequal female. She had power of her own, small power in this blighted world tainted by so much iron, but power nonetheless.

Corinne frowned at his utter lack of astonishment. She'd meant to intimidate him, to let him know that she could protect herself if he decided to attack her. After all, most humans— ordinary humans—couldn't will fire into existence and dismiss it with a thought. She focused and a cooling breeze flowed through the open windows, the fine mesh screens preventing most insects from entering the cabin.

"Thanks for cleaning up," she said and walked into her bedroom, half expecting Uberon to follow her.

In the absence of an invitation, he allowed her privacy. Her second small display of power amused him and he wondered how quickly her power would grow and flourish away from the dampening taint of iron that surrounded people in this mundane dimension. He made his way into the washroom and availed himself of human technology. Using Corinne's soap, he imagined the press of her warm, slippery flesh and his body responded. He stroked his thick, heavy erection once, twice, then turned his soapy hands to cleaning other body parts. He refused to give himself release. The passion of his body belonged to Corinne.

After drying off, he wrapped the towel around his lean hips and crossed the small cabin. Easing the door open, he stepped outside. The whine and buzz of hungry insects swarmed around him for a second, then disappeared. Even insects knew better than to feast upon fae flesh, or at least this fae's flesh.

Probably equal to the Erlking and Enders in age, power, and capability, Uberon, the deposed king of the Unseelie Court, was the second most dangerous living creature on Planet Earth while he deigned to visit.

"I wondered why you gave up the kingdom so easily," came the dry remark from the most dangerous creature on Earth.

Uberon looked at the spiral ivory horn and the flashing opal eyes. "The kingdom was Marog's and he is gone. I have no further need of the crown."

The sleek head swung to look at the dim cabin, then back at Uberon. "What have you need of then?"

"Her."

The unicorn chuckled, but Uberon did not smile. "I never thought to see the day when mighty Uberon whose veins flow with ice succumbed to his libido."

"*Mate,*" he corrected.

"Mate?" The razor point of the horn bobbed. A cloven hoof stamped once. "You were already once mated."

"Aye."

"The fae get but one true mate each, if that."

"Aye."

The unicorn's laughter rang out, inaudible to the ears of mundane humans who did not believe in such mythical creatures. "You want us to transform her for you."

"If you won't, I will."

"Do you really think you have that power?"

"Aye." Uberon knew he did. All those thousands of years of scholarly immersion gave him the knowledge to access and exploit the power he'd need to effect the metamorphosis necessary for his mate to live in his world. Whether she would consent to it was another question, and not one that bothered him all that much.

The unicorn eyed the calm, assured male standing unafraid before him and understood that the former king of the Unseelie Court most likely did have the power to convert his little human into fae.

"We have never had two moon-borns at the same time. They are catalysts. The result may be unpredictable and possibly catastrophic."

"She need not be moon-born, merely fae. She has her own power."

"A human with power? How extraordinary."

"Bring her to us at the dark of the moons."

"No. I will bring her to you when she consents."

"You dare defy us?"

"I will persuade her; but she will come at her decision, not yours."

The beast shook his heavy mane. "You play dangerous games, Uberon."

His lips curled in a smile that offered neither joy nor humor. "I'm a dangerous fellow and I don't fear you."

And that, the unicorn decided, was the problem. Uberon respected little and feared nothing. The Unseelie king turned his back on the dawn swift and returned to the cabin, his elegant bare feet making no sound on the naked wood floor.

Hearing the creak of the door open and shut, Corinne lay awake, covered only by a light sheet due to the heat of a summer's night and the lack of an air conditioner. When she'd bought the cabin from her parents, she'd not thought of such mundane considerations as heating and cooling. Lying on her bed beneath an open window, she wondered if she ought to take out a loan and hire a contractor to insulate the thin walls. Winters in Ohio could get brutally cold and the fireplace in the center of the cabin provided the only source of heat.

That thought brought to mind a brother's naughty suggestion of "plugging in" to his fiancee on a cold winter's night and the attendant vision of what she imagined Uberon looked like without his weird, medieval fantasy costume. He wouldn't have appeared out of place alongside Viggo Mortensen in *The Lord of the Rings* trilogy.

A shiver ran through her body. It felt like thrill, not fear, certainly not cold.

When the hinges creaked again, she rose and padded barefoot across the bedroom floor. She pulled open the door a mere inch or two and goggled at the sculpted male beauty standing in her cabin. As though he heard her soft intake of breath, Uberon turned to look at her and met her gaze. His eyes narrowed, the corners crinkling, and he smiled. Another shiver rippled through her. That smile had nothing to do with humor and everything to do with lust. Heat pooled low in Corinne's belly and the tissues between her thighs felt swollen and somehow achy. She took another breath and found herself suddenly and acutely aware of the gentle rub of her hardened nipples against the loose fabric of her pajama shirt.

This, she knew, was arousal.

Uberon's thin nostrils flared as he inhaled, taking in the scent of her. He caught a hint of uncertainty, a fragrance of innocence. By the twin moons, his fated mate was innocent. How she had remained untouched both puzzled and delighted him, feeding his possessiveness and the urge to protect her from every inconvenience, every hurt, every ill.

"You're a virgin," he whispered into the darkness, just loudly enough for her to hear.

"Don't remind me," she retorted in a sour tone, belatedly remembering to close her mouth after speaking.

"There is no shame in that."

"Says you," she sighed with envy. How anything so utterly masculine and gorgeous could entertain an interest in her was bewildering. Of course, having five overprotective brothers and her father around hadn't exactly encouraged romantic relationships. Hence, the cabin. Dad and her brothers trusted her ability to take care of herself more in relative isolation than if she were plopped in the midst of a busy city teeming with the dregs of humanity—or so they assumed.

"It means you respect yourself," he whispered, pride and possessiveness thrumming through every syllable of his charming, foreign accent. "It means you did not not waste yourself on an unworthy male."

"And you're worthy, I suppose?" Sarcasm dripped from her words.

"More than you know," he answered as though stating mundane fact. The utter lack of pride puzzled her. "But you will understand."

She sighed and shut the bedroom door.

Arrogant man thinks he can have me at the crook of his little finger, just because he looks like God's gift to women. Her own grouchiness surprised her. Corinne attributed it to PMS and a history of watching her own handsome brothers reel in woman after woman with seemingly no effort at all. The frequency with which women threw themselves at her brothers disgusted and exasperated her, as did the cocky pleasure they took in taking advantage of what those women offered.

"They'll settle down when they find the right girls," her mother had tried to reassure her. "Your father was the same way."

"Ugh," she muttered and climbed back into bed.

Uberon paid no mind to the closed door and his mate's displeased reaction to his certainty that she would give herself to him, body, mind, heart, and soul. Fate exerted an influence nothing could escape. One might dodge fate for a limited time, but not forever.

That was a lesson every immortal learned.

He dropped the towel and lay down on the lumpy sofa. As Corinne had predicted, his height and the sofa's length did not match. He paid that no mind either. Nothing as ancient as he endured life without learning to ignore minor annoyances. Pleased to be ensconced in his mate's home, however temporarily, Uberon drifted off to sleep.

When dawn sent its pearly light through Corinne's bedroom window, she woke and again lay in bed and contemplated the man who had taken up residence in her living room. With the grumpiness that accompanied early morning and a lack of caffeine, she hoped he'd passed an uncomfortable night and woke up with aches and pains from having endured that lumpy sofa. With a groan, she levered herself off the bed and padded from her bedroom to the bathroom. A peek at the mirror had her grimacing. She washed her face and ran a brush through her hair and did not see a marked improvement.

"Huh."

Corinne gathered her hair and wove it into a tight braid, securing the stubby end with a rubber band. She tilted her head to one side as she considered her appearance, then frowned with disappointment. Why did she care? Why was she suddenly worrying about how she looked just because a weird man in a fantasy medieval costume had shared a meal with her and spent the night on her couch?

"I must be desperate," she murmured to her reflection. With a sigh, Corinne squared her shoulders, stiffened her spine, and headed for the kitchen. She glanced at the sofa as she passed by. He wasn't there. The blanket had been folded and set aside. But somehow she knew that he hadn't left, not really.

Years of experience lent her a certain economical grace as she filled a kettle with water and set it on the burner, took two mugs from the cabinet, and found her tin of tea bags. She pondered the limited selection of tea, then decided that Uberon could either accept what she gave him or get the hell out of her cabin and not let the door hit him on his very fine ass on the way out. She shook her head, bemused at her unwonted preoccupation with the man's physique.

Soon, the kettle whistled. Corinne poured the boiling water over the tea bags, turned off the burner, and set the kettle back on the stove. The water would keep hot for a while longer. While the tea steeped, she sliced some bread and popped the slices in the toaster. She pulled out the smaller of her two skillets and set it on the stove. A few minutes later, she had two plates of scrambled eggs and buttered toast.

"Your timing is impeccable," she said as the cabin door closed behind her guest.

Uberon raised an eyebrow at her carefully neutral tone and took a seat at the table.

"There's honey for your tea, if you want it," she said, gesturing to the mason jar half-filled with honey—the wax comb still in it—that she'd purchased off a local beekeeper. "I've got milk and grapefruit juice if you want that."

"This is excellent, thank you," he replied and helped himself to the honey.

She nodded and poured herself a glass of juice, emptying the carton. Its acidity offset the sweetness of her tea with honey. They ate in silence.

While clearing the dishes, Corinne said, "I'm headed to the market today."

Uberon nodded and silently helped with washing and drying dishes and putting them away. She wondered why he didn't ask where anything went, then decided that he'd probably snooped through her cupboards while she slept. No matter. She had nothing valuable to steal, except for her computer.

If he touched that, she'd kill him.

She retreated to her bedroom to change into her usual summer attire: khaki shorts, short sleeved shirt, and gladiator style sandals. She liked that style: they didn't slip off her feet and were comfortable to wear.

"You're going to swelter in those leather pants and boots," she remarked.

He glanced down at his clothing and shrugged. Before her eyes, his clothing changed to a masculine version of her own outfit. Corinne gasped and felt faint. Warm, strong hands grasped her upper arms and steadied her wobbly self. She felt the heat of him behind her and practically melted into his body.

"You're not the only one who has a few special talents," he

whispered, his breath blowing softly past her ear.

Corinne concentrated on slowing down her shallow, rapid breathing. After a moment she sighed, once again having collected her wits, and said, "That's a handy skill."

"Indeed," he agreed and released his grasp on her arms.

She immediately missed his touch and silently berated herself for acting like a ninny. Taking a breath, she said, "I usually ride my bike to the market, but since you don't have one, I'll walk."

Uberon liked her correct assumption that he would accompany her. She was his, and where she went he would go, too. Any creature, human or otherwise, that dared accost his mate would suffer. He liked knowing he could protect her, keep her safe and all to himself.

Corinne fetched some cloth shopping bags and her wallet, stuffing the latter into a front pocket. She set off at a brisk pace that he easily matched. Because they walked, she took a shortcut through the forest. She couldn't help but shoot covert glances at him as he moved with nimble strength, the impressive muscles in his legs flexing. When they came to a wide, shallow creek, he scooped her into his arms and carried her across.

"You didn't need to do that," she laughed after a surprised shriek.

"You're mine," he replied.

Corinne made a rude noise in her throat and shook her head. She continued on her way and he walked beside her. The trail spilled out onto a two-lane road.

"Winterset's just another couple of miles east," she said and wiped her forearm across her forehead. The day's heat had already settled in. "We need a good rainstorm to cool things down."

Uberon said nothing.

"There's a diner in Winterset. We can get lunch there. They've got a mean BLT."

Uberon didn't exactly know what a BLT was, but simply nodded and kept a wary eye out for careless drivers and speeding vehicles. Some aspects of this young woman's culture never made sense to him no matter how many times he visited.

He had to admit, though, he found humanity's zest for life fascinating. He supposed that if the fae had such short lifespans, they, too, would suffer less ennui and embrace a more strongly spiritual philosophy. He knew some of the more discontented and self-absorbed fae had enjoyed the adoration of ancient human cultures. Zeus had been particularly needy and exploitive of that adoration, the conceited, bombastic, lecherous imbecile.

Uberon didn't miss him.

However, he did find himself rather … libidinous … lately.

"Corinne," he murmured and halted her steps with two fingertips set lightly upon her shoulder. He noticed her responsiveness, even if she did not.

She glanced up at him, lips opening to ask a question. He stalled the words with a tiny shake of his head. Corinne watched as he tilted his head sideways and listened. A moment later she, too, heard the murmur of voices accompanied by laughter. Three men soon tromped into view.

"Well, if it ain't little Miss Corinne," the oldest of the three greeted with a tobacco stained smile nearly buried in his long, gray beard. "You off to the market this morning?"

"Well, hello, Mr. Silas. Good morning, gentlemen," she greeted, smiling and taking a few steps forward. The younger Mr. Silas smiled at her, eyes gleaming with appreciation. The youngest of the three who looked barely old enough to shave gave her a broad smile and a shy wave. "Yes, I am headed to the market."

"We're glad to see ya, Miss Corinne," the boy volunteered. "Mom's got eggs fresh gathered this morning. I'll run ahead and have her set back a dozen fer ya."

"That's very kind of you, Joey. You let her know that I hope she'll have brought some of her little pies, too."

"Yes, ma'am!" the boy said and jogged ahead.

"Boy's got a crush on you," his father commented. He jerked his head at his father and added, "So does he."

"If I was forty years younger …" the older man began and waggled his bushy eyebrows.

"Who's that with you, missy?"

"Oh, this is Uberon. He's a friend," Corinne answered, not quite ready to explain just what he was, because she didn't know herself.

"He don't look too friendly," Silas commented and glared at the Unseelie king. "You do right by little Miss Corinne here, or you'll answer to us. We're real fond of her. Ya hear?"

Uberon nodded, a regal move. "Aye. I am glad my Corinne has such devoted protectors."

"You hear that accent?" Silas Sr. commented to his son. "What country d'ya think he's from?"

"Well, it's lovely to see you, but I need to move on before I melt in this heat," Corinne said and started walking.

"We'll walk with ya," Silas Jr. volunteered and fell into step beside her. "Bears've been extra active this summer and Joey saw a rattler just t'other day. Somethin's got the animals riled up, and you don't carry no firearms."

His father nodded in approval. "Gladdie's cousin Chester shot a bear two weeks ago. Bear meat's too sweet for my taste, but mebbe you'll like it. I'll send Junior over with a roast."

He glanced at Uberon and recognized an elite warrior. He'd seen their like in 'Nam. He had a granddaughter who'd married one of them Army Rangers. Boy strutted like he owned the world, but he had that same alert air of readiness and danger about him. He also noticed that the tall man with the funny name—what the hell kind of name was Uberon anyway?—never moved more than six inches away from the pretty young woman who lived all alone in the cabin way over yonder. The old man caught the stranger's gaze and held it without fear, assessing the danger he possibly posed to Corinne.

"You watch over her," he murmured as Corinne and Silas Jr. carried on a lively conversation centered on his and Gladdie's eight children and fourteen grandchildren with another one on the way any day now.

"She'll come to no harm while in my care," Uberson replied in a quiet undertone, according the old man a measure of respect he seldom gave anyone, much less a human. He decided to be grateful for the family's extension of protection over his mate. They knew not what treasure they guarded from evil.

Silas Sr. nodded, satisfied.

The distance passed without incident. Father and son veered off to join Gladdie and Joey. Corinne paused to gulp some water from the thermos she carried and offered it to Uberon, who accepted it with a murmured word of thanks. He turned the canister so that his lip touched the exact place on its mouth as had hers. But she wasn't watching.

Wiping her arm across her sweating forehead again, Corinne said, "Vegetables and fruit first. Then baked goods. Then herbs, eggs, dairy, and meat. We'll get lunch before I buy anything that needs refrigeration."

Because she seemed to expect a response from him, Uberon gave her a small nod. He followed her from stall to stall and waited patiently as she examined tomatoes, summer squash, onions, peppers, corn, and other summer vegetables. As she filled each shopping bag, she handed it to him to carry, saying, "If you're going to accompany me and eat my food, then you might as well carry the groceries."

He voiced no objection. No wild animal would accost her while he was near. Only evil men would fail to recognize his protection, and he could easily deal with them.

She led him into a diner and paused to enjoy the blissfully cool air conditioning before sliding into a booth.

"Well, hey, if it ain't our resident author," the waitress greeted them, cracking her gum between her teeth. Her bright eyes turned predatory upon examining the handsome elegance of the man accompanying Corinne. "And who's this? Ain't one of yer brothers, is he?"

"No, Tansy, this is Uberon," Corinne answered with a laugh. "He's just visiting."

Ignoring the cool look the tall man gave her, the waitress tapped Uberon's shoulder and said, "Well, y'all can visit me any time, good lookin'."

An unaccustomed feeling of jealousy surged through Corinne, spurring her to respond, "Get your own man, Tansy. This one's taken."

The waitress laughed and leaned forward. "You let me know if he's got any brothers." She winked and got to business. "Y'all know what ya want?"

Corinne shook her head and relaxed, not quite knowing why she'd staked her claim to Uberon like that. It simply wasn't like her. So, she placed a generous order that included a slice of the coconut cream pie that was the diner's specialty. Tansy looked expectantly at Uberon who simply replied, "I'll have the same."

"Sure thing, handsome." She winked at Corinne with irrepressible good nature and sauntered off to place the order.

"Forward woman," Uberon commented in an undertone.

"Tansy wants a husband so badly she can taste it," Corinne explained with empathy. "She barely managed to finish high school and good jobs are scarce around here. But she's good-hearted; there's no malice at all in her. She'd make some farmer a devoted, hardworking wife."

"You are kind."

Corinne shrugged. "Her prospects aren't good. She deserves a man who will love her and treat her well—and there just aren't that many eligible bachelors in Winterset. Most kids here grow up and leave for college and never come back. Those who don't leave either can't or they're tied to family farms."

She looked around the diner, silently noticing that most of the patrons were a generation or two older than she. She returned her gaze to Uberon's and held it. "This village is dying. It's too far from Athens to catch the university crowd."

Uberon listened as his mate explained.

"About six or seven years ago, the village council decided to sponsor a farmer's market to capitalize on what this area does have, a lot of vegetable gardens, farms, and old-fashioned handicrafts. The Christmas fair gets in some regionally acclaimed folk artists and visitors from a pretty large area, but it's not enough to sustain a hotel or do more than add a temporary boost to the local economy."

Corinne paused and realized she'd been lecturing him. Blushing, she took a breath and apologized. "Sorry, Uberon. I got a little carried away there."

"You care about these people as a good queen should," he replied.

"Queen?" she spluttered and shook her head. "I am no queen."

His eyes took on a far-away look and he added so quietly she had to strain to hear the words, "I lost the caring of my people and left them to my son, who never cared at all."

"Your son?" she echoed.

"Marog. He is dead."

Overcome by sympathy as well as confusion, Corinne reached across the table and covered his hand with hers. "Oh, Uberon, I am so sorry. I didn't mean to bring up bad memories."

He turned his hand to curl around hers. He lifted it and leaned forward to press a kiss to the knuckles. "You bring me naught but joy."

"Oh, that's so romantic," Tansy commented as she set plates on the table's Formica surface. She smiled without envy and bade them to let her know if they needed anything else. Leaning over, she whispered to Corinne, "He's a keeper, that one."

Feeling charitably toward the young woman, Uberon murmured a few words of incantation in his native language and exerted a wisp of his formidable will. Feeling the cool shiver of power waft through the air, Corinne's eyes widened and then focused on the tall, handsome man seated across from her.

"What did you do?" she hissed.

"I blessed her," Uberon replied.

"You blessed her?"

"Aye. By this time next year, she will fall in love, marry, and have a child."

Corinne's eyes narrowed. "And will her husband love her? Will he treat her well?"

"Of course," he replied with equanimity. "Otherwise, it wouldn't be a blessing."

He read her worry. "Don't fret. She will be happy."

Corinne took a bit of her bacon, lettuce, and tomato sandwich, chewed, swallowed, and finally asked, "What *are* you?"

"Yours," he answered and took a bite of his sandwich. He made a note to have another sometime. It was really quite good, the simple ingredients combining for a tasty meal.

CHAPTER 4

Corinne poured two glasses of iced tea, one for herself and the other for Uberon, and carried them to the miniscule front porch of her cabin. He thanked her with grave courtesy as he accepted the sweating glass. Sitting in her favorite deck chair, she flexed her aching bare feet.

"I should have worn sneakers."

Uberon reached over, long arms extending to capture one of her feet. He pulled her foot into his lap and began massaging it. Corinne moaned with pleasure and took a drink of her tea.

"I want you to come with me," Uberon said, his voice easing into the late afternoon heat as though it belonged amid the sounds of birds, insects, and the occasional yip of a coyote.

"Mm, where?"

"To the Unseelie Court."

"The Unsee—*what?*"

He met her shocked gaze with equanimity.

"You have got to be kidding me," she muttered and averted her eyes. "You cannot expect me to believe you're an evil fairy."

"Not evil, dark." He did not mention that the distinction had more to do with the fair-haired characteristics of the Seelie Court than with any tendencies toward evil.

"Evil, dark, what's the difference? And do *not* tell me you're a fairy."

"I am fae, what humans once called sidhe or sith."

"This is insane."

"Why should it be insane?" He released her foot and picked up the other one.

"B-because that's just *myth*. You know, *legend*. Fairy tales!"

He shrugged, the movement of those broad shoulders capturing her attention. "And you are a witch. Why cannot I be fae?"

"I am not a witch," she muttered, disliking his logic. "I have some extrasensory power that most people don't. That's all."

"The fire-haired women in your matriarchal line each had such power. The talent skips a generation or two, but runs true back to the ancestress who took a fae lover and bore him a daughter."

"What do you know about it?"

"I know the Erlking is your ancestor, for 'tis his fiery hair the daughters of his talent bear."

"Erlking."

"He is mated, has been for the past several centuries."

"No more bastard children?" she scoffed.

"He would never betray his mate, nor she him." He fixed her with his own mysterious silver gaze. "Nor I you."

"This is preposterous," Corinne protested and pulled on her foot. He held it with easy strength. Rather than engage in a futile struggle, she huffed and turned her head away to stare into the wooded darkness.

"There are more things in heaven and earth, Horatio, than are dreamt of in your philosophy."

"Don't quote Shakespeare at me, Uberon."

"He was a human of great insight."

She huffed again. "Okay, let's say you're really what you say you are—"

"Fae."

"—and you want to take me to your home, the Unseelie Court." She finished the sentence and turned her head to glare at him. "How do we get there?"

His mouth curled in a slow, sexy smile. "Magic."

"Don't even go there," she warned.

"I can wait until you're ready."

She leaned her head back and groaned. "This is impossible.

You are impossible."

"I am not impossible," he rebutted. "How could I be and hold your foot in my hands? You see me, you have touched me. I have eaten food in your sight. What about me is not as real—as *possible*—as you?"

"Uberon, I don't have the energy to deal with your sophistry right now," she muttered and closed her eyes. "And you're cooking tonight."

She felt rather than heard his movement. Her eyes flickered open to see his face mere inches from her own. His silver eyes gleamed brightly with ageless intelligence and banked power. She inhaled sharply as he leaned down and pressed his lips against hers.

Corinne expected a quick buss on the mouth, but he brushed his lips against hers once, twice, three times. Each fleeting touch made her blood sizzle. He changed the angle and pressed tiny kisses to the corner of her mouth. His hand came up to slide through her sweat dampened hair and tilt her head so he could kiss and nibble an erotic line along her jaw. She began to tremble beneath him, her mind and body assaulted by a delicious passion which she'd never believed existed outside the pages of a lurid romance novel. She realized her back arched, thrusting her breasts toward him in search of a more intimate touch from the hand that lightly stroked one arm from shoulder to elbow. The soft, delicate kisses sent excitement skittering to her core only to shatter seconds later in a shower of brilliance.

She gasped and shuddered beneath his hands and lips, then slumped stunned and limp in the Adirondack chair. Uberon pressed a lingering kiss to her mouth, then drew back and gave her a small smile filled with triumph, controlled lust, and fierce purpose.

"You are *mine*," he whispered. "But I can wait until you are ready."

He straightened to his full, imperious height and let the glamor fall. Corinne's eyes widened and her jaw dropped at the naked male standing before her.

His long black hair shifted gently in the light breeze. His pale skin gleamed, flawless over the lean, muscular physique she'd admired the night before. Her gaze locked on the wide, intricate pattern of silver that draped from one collarbone to the other and appeared to flow over his shoulders, except the metal did not rest upon his skin but was embedded within it. Another wide band of patterned silver filigree highlighted the deep vee of the Adonis belt that arced down to the heavy testicles hanging below a long, thick, rigid, heavily veined cock.

She squeaked in alarm, having never before seen a man so endowed. The naughty movies she'd peeked at in college hadn't prepared her for *that*. Uberon reached forward to stroke her cheek and reassure her. The movement drew her gaze away from his rampant arousal to his hand, and she noticed the sharp, black claws extending over his fingertips.

She squeaked again and shrank from him. She squeezed her eyelids shut.

He withdrew his hand and replaced the glamor, but she nonetheless felt the echo of formidable power emanating from him, too strong for even the glamor to fully conceal. She wondered why she'd not noticed it before even as she trembled and feared what those sharp claws would do to her.

"You shall never come to harm at my hand or while under my care," he vowed. "My touch will give you only pleasure."

She trembled and said nothing as she felt the movement of air that indicated he had walked away. Still shaking, she opened her eyes and exhaled.

No one would believe this. No one.

Even if he did have a damned fine ass.

Her mouth opened, but words stalled in her throat. She closed her mouth, swallowed, and tried again, remembering that she had already asked him *who* and *what* he was and that he had answered. She supposed he could have lied to her, but didn't see why he would have. She inhaled and caught the sweet, musky scent of her own liquid arousal, something she'd never smelled upon herself before.

Corinne averted her gaze to ponder what she had just learned, just experienced. When she looked back at him—or, rather, where he'd been just a moment ago—he was gone, of course. Vanished. Disappeared.

"I should call Great Aunt Helen," she murmured under her breath, thinking of the only living relative she had who possessed *talents* like hers. "Maybe she knows something about the fae."

She listened to herself and shook her head.

"This is crazy. No way is Uberon some short, chubby elf who lives in trees and makes cookies. And no way is he some manifestation of Tolkien's imagination."

Her words dissolved into the sultry summer night. Corinne heaved herself from the chair and walked inside the cabin. She rolled her shoulders and inhaled deeply.

"God, I stink." She looked across the room and headed for the bathroom. "Shower. I need a shower. A cold shower."

The cold water made her yelp when it hit her skin, but then she acclimated and enjoyed it. Her cabin had no air conditioning, which made cool showers a necessity in southern Ohio's humid summer heat. She ran her hands down her body, from the elegant, fragile sweep of her collar bones over her modest breasts and down her flat belly to the tops of her thighs for no other reason than doing so felt good.

"What am I doing?" she wondered aloud, having never succumbed to such indulgence before.

With a huff of annoyance at herself, she grabbed the soap and lathered up. In minutes she found herself stroking the sensitive swollen tissue between her thighs, exploring herself as she'd never done before. She simply hadn't been all that curious, usually disregarding her sexuality except for menstruation when that part of her body gave her more problems than not. *Fucking cramps.* She felt slightly scandalized as the thought ran through her head, although she honestly acknowledged the truth of the sentiment. She rather resented the imposition of her gender, the pain and the mess that turned her into a sniveling, whining wreck every month or so. Or so. She huffed again, remembering that golden year when she was fourteen and her period skipped three whole months. Of course, she'd paid for that reprieve when her next few periods came hard and heavy and in quick succession.

Female biology sucked. Men had it so easy.

She rinsed and concentrated on washing the rest of her body without undue deliberation over any specific part, except to shave. She supposed she was lucky in that she didn't have to shave her legs as frequently as her college roommate had. The poor girl's Italian heritage meant that her body hair grew thick, dark, and fast. Alessia had gone through razors like nobody's business. She chuckled, remembering that her roommate had prevailed upon her family for a loan and gone into partnership with a dermatologist and plastic surgeon to open a medspa offering laser hair removal—and that Alessia had been its first patient.

Alessia. That's whom she'd call. Alessia never judged her. She always listened.

Turning off the cooling spray and stepping from the shower, Corinne dried her body and wrapped her sopping wet hair in the damp towel. She shrugged on her bathrobe, kept hanging on a hook on the bathroom door. She walked to her bedroom, kicked the door closed behind her for privacy, and picked up the phone, an old-fashioned landline. Cell phone signals were seldom reliable in the Appalachian foothills, so she didn't bother with a cell phone. The satellite connection for her computer was expensive enough.

"Hey, Corinne! How's it going?" Alessia's bright, cheerful voice answered on the fourth ring. She seemed slightly out of breath.

"Oh, hi, Alessia. Did I catch you at a bad time?"

Her friend laughed in her usual breezy fashion. "Oh, no, I was outside with Gio and Sal."

"Gio *and* Sal?"

"Yeah, you met Giovanni when you were here last. Sal's his best friend. He's in the Coast Guard, too."

"Oh, so you've got *two* hot soldiers with you?"

Alessia laughed. "Sailors, baby. These guy are sailors."

"And?"

"A lady never tells."

"Since when are you a lady?"

Alessia's laughter reverberated down the line, followed by a squeal and a "Gio, not *now*. Corinne's on the phone."

Corinne heard a deep, masculine chuckle and a shouted, "Is she pretty?"

"Corinne's not your type, Sal. She's intelligent and respectable," Alessia shouted back. "Sorry, Corinne. Sal's a real playboy and thinks everything with a vagina is his to exploit."

"Except you, because you're with Gio, right?"

"Oh, honey, Sal and Gio share *everything.*"

"You—" Corinne gulped, then squeaked, "*Both* of them?"

"Oh, honey, you've got to get out of the stuffy Midwest and

come down to Miami. Think of it: no snow. It's sun, sand, and sea and hot, hot, hot sailors." She took a breath and her tone of voice changed. "Now, what's up, buttercup? You never call on a weekday unless you need a sounding board."

Corinne groaned. "Am I that transparent?"

"Oh, honey, that's what I like about you—no artifice. Talk to Mama Bonetti."

Corinne chuckled and, haltingly, began, "I met someone."

"You did? That's wonderful! Wait ... your brothers hate him, right?"

"My brothers haven't met him."

"Well, that makes it easier."

"Makes what easier?"

"The decision to sleep with him. What the five jolly green giants don't know won't hurt *you*."

"I'm not sleeping with him."

"Okay." Alessia paused and didn't push her to jump into bed with anything sporting a penis just to give away her V-card. "Tell me about him."

"Well, he's gorgeous and older than I am—"

"Older? As in his thirties older? Or even older than that?" Corinne pictured Alessia's dark eyebrows arrowing downward in a frown. "You haven't fallen for some middle-aged dad with a couple of teenaged kids, have you?"

"Um ... I know he had a son—"

"*Had* a son?"

"His son was killed."

"Oh, that's terrible," Alessia responded with genuine sympathy. "Wait, is he married? Divorced? A widower?"

"He's not married or divorced. I think he's either a single father or a widower. I haven't asked and he hasn't said anything about the mother."

"That's suspicious, Corinne."

"It would be if ..."

"If what?"

"Well, if he were ... normal."

Alessia's pause before speaking resonated with the heaviness of a gong. "You've met one of *them*, haven't you?"

"He's not a warlock."

Corinne's friend sighed with relief. "Good, 'cause you can't trust them." Another pause. "What is he, Corinne?"

"He says he's fae."

"Fae."

"Yeah. Fae."

"They supposedly died out a couple of centuries ago. Too much iron around for them."

"Well, he says he's not from here."

Another pause.

"Alessia?"

"Yeah?"

"Why is it you believe in stuff like this when even my Great Aunt Helen doesn't?"

"I knew you'd ask me eventually," Alessia muttered. She heaved a breath and answered the question that had been a long time in coming. "My mother's Wiccan, my dad claims his mother's father was a selkie. And—you promise you'll say nothing to anyone?"

"Of course."

"I've seen them. Remember that summer I visited Italy with Dad?"

"Yeah?"

Alessia's voice lowered to a whisper. "We stayed for a couple of weeks with his mom in the village where she grew up. It was ... educational. And I saw a man walk in from the sea. He was beautiful ... and ... he promised me gold if I would marry him and bear his children."

"You obviously said no," Corinne said.

"Um ... no, I didn't. Dad saw me and confronted him. It wasn't pretty, but he agreed to give me some time."

"Some time?"

Alessia sighed. "I was twenty-one, infatuated with paranormal romances, and the whole thing seemed so amazing, incredible, and romantic."

"You're twenty-four now."

"And I go back to Italy in October."

"Your twenty-fifth birthday."

"Yeah."

"What will you do?"

"I'll go back to Italy. I can't hide from him ... he said my soul called him from the sea." She sighed, paused, then continued. "As much as I'm enjoying Gio and Sal, I'm not sure I want them, like, you know, *forever*."

"A selkie, Alessia."

"Yeah. They're said to treat their women well."

Corinne thought back to a book Alessia had shared with her during their senior year, *A Kiss of Shadows* by Laurell K. Hamilton. The heroine had an intimate relationship with a selkie who didn't unleash the force of his pure nature upon her until after she'd been doused with Bronwyn's Tears. Corinne shivered, thinking about Uberon and the way he'd given her a tiny glimpse of his nature.

"He claimed you, didn't he?" she asked in a small voice.

"Oh, honey, once one of *them* decides you're his, there's no escape. Make the best of it. I intend to." She hesitated and asked, "Look, if I go to Italy earlier than planned, he'll come to me. Maybe he'll figure out who your guy is."

"Unseelie Court," Corinne whispered. "Enjoy your freedom while it lasts, Lessi. Don't cut it short for me."

Alessia gasped, obviously remembering Hamilton's Merry Gentry series. "Unseelie?"

Corinne licked her suddenly dry lips. "He doesn't feel evil. I don't get those vibes from him."

"But he's not all sweetness and light, either, is he?"

"No. He's pretty intimidating."

"I'll bet," came the dry response. "And what rank does he occupy in the Unseelie Court?"

"King," Corinne whispered, her voice hoarse with dread.

"You realize that Hamilton's books are fiction, right?"

"But they feel pretty accurate."

"Yeah, they do, but ..."

"Yeah. I know."

"You know, Corinne, I still read paranormal romance. There's a general consensus among them that if one of them claims you as his mate, then he's pretty damned serious. There's a lot of writing about mates sharing souls and stuff like that. It's unlikely he'll treat you badly."

"That's fiction, Lessi."

"But it's pretty much all we got."

"It's said the fae can't lie. That much I remember. Get your Unseelie king to vow to cherish you and he'll keep that vow."

"That's the best I can hope for, isn't it?"

"Honey, 'There are more things in heaven and earth, Horatio, than are dreamt of in your philosophy.'"

Corinne's giggle carried the sound of hysteria. "That's what *he* said."

"Fucking Shakespeare."

They ended the call on that ominous note. Corinne placed the receiver in its cradle and stared at the phone, wondering just what she'd gotten herself into. She rubbed her face, then rose as though every joint ached. Pulling the damp towel from her head, she gazed at her reflection in the mirror while working a comb through the long, damp tresses. As was common for gingers, her fair skin burned quickly, so she kept her exposure to the sun at a minimum, wore wide-brimmed hats, and used sunscreen with religious fervor. Even so, her complexion had a light golden hue right now at the apex of summer. She contemplated braiding her hair to keep it tidy, but dismissed the thought and decided to leave it loose. After all, why bother to have such long hair if she kept it bound all the time?

Corinne took a deep breath, smelled the mouthwatering fragrance of supper, and gathering her courage to confront the tall, powerful male in her kitchen.

She wished she could go backward a day when she thought him merely an unusually tall and handsome man. When she had confidence in her small magics to protect her. When she met his gaze without trepidation. When she thought she had a choice.

The hinges squeaked when Corinne opened the bedroom door.

"Your friend is correct." Uberon's deep voice floated to her. "The selkie will treat her well. They make devoted mates and fathers."

Anger sparked.

"That was a private conversation."

"I have excellent hearing." He turned off the gas burner and moved the skillet to the table where he set it upon potholders. "Sit. Eat while the food is hot."

She obeyed, unable to think of any reasonable objection not to do so. He poured them both glasses of water and took a seat across from her.

"Ask your questions. I shall not lie to you."

Myriad questions raced through Corinne's mind, but she voiced on the one of utmost importance: "Do I have a choice?"

"For as long as I can give it to you," came the evasive answer.

"What does that mean, Uberon? Either I have a choice or I don't."

He met her gaze without flinching. "Free will is sacred to me."

She nodded, understanding from what he did not say that free will was about the only thing that he held sacred. "But?"

"But there are ... compulsions ... that even I cannot resist indefinitely."

"Compulsions?"

"I lost my son because I allowed him to act of his own free will. I split the fae realm because I refused to coerce my own people."

"Why would that split your realm?"

"Law and its enforcement has limits if it is not to become tyranny: national defense and protection of property."

"I don't understand."

"I gave my people leave to make their own choices, to govern themselves, except for violation of one another's property and to protect their country. They often made poor choices, and those choices brought darkness and hardship to them. That is one reason why my realm became known as the Unseelie Court."

"What has that to do with me? Us?"

"Mogren, king of the Seelie Court, currently works to reunite the Unseelie Court with the Seelie. We shall once again be one nation, one race, one people."

"And?"

"And I shall have no place there. But I cannot linger here for long, nor do I wish to do so. This realm is ... tainted." He picked up his fork and gestured to her. "Eat. You are weary and need to rebuild your energy."

Corinne wished she could argue. With a small sigh, she stabbed a piece of sausage and brought it to her mouth. She chewed, swallowed, and said, "I still don't see what that has to do with me or us."

"Your denial will ... pressure me until I must succumb." He blinked. Corinne could have sworn his eyes flashed red. "If that happens, the aftermath will not be pretty."

"You'd rape me?"

"No, I would destroy myself before doing that. I vowed never to harm you and nothing—*nothing*—could make me break that vow."

"So, either I accept your claim or you die," Corinne said in a flat tone as she jabbed her fork at a green bean. It rolled away from the tines. She jabbed at it again.

"Yes."

"You can't put that kind of responsibility on me."

"I will not force you to accept me."

"Don't you think that telling me that you'll self-combust if I don't accept you is a form of coercion?" she snapped.

"Would you rather I prevaricate and mislead you?"

"Yes!" Corinne sighed and shook her head. "No. No, I don't want you to lie—hey, you're not supposed to be able to lie."

"Myths aren't necessarily true."

"So, you *can* lie. Huh. I'll have to let Alessia know." She put the evasive green bean in her mouth, chewed, and swallowed. "What happens if I die without accepting you?"

"If you die without accepting me, then, assuming I have not already 'self-combusted' as you term it, I will eventually do so."

"So, you don't know how long you have?"

"No."

"Then you can't give me, say, twenty-five years to make up my mind?"

"There is no standard time table or schedule for this, at least none that I have ever discovered."

"Damn. That's not helpful." She looked up from her plate. "And you won't just go away until you're ready to explode?"

He gave her a shark's smile. "No."

"Figures."

The conversation died for a moment. Corinne forced a few more bites down her throat before she voiced another question: "Will I be able to come back and visit?"

"Unfortunately, no. In order to make the transfer to the fae realm, you will need to be transformed. The transformation disallows your return here."

"That's hardly fair."

"I can ask a boon of the swifts. Perhaps they could assist."

"The swifts?"

"The dawn and midnight swifts, the most ancient and most powerful beings in my world."

"Swifts? Like birds?"

"Unicorns."

"Unicorns," she echoed. "You have got to be kidding me."

But he didn't look like he was joking or pulling her leg.

"You're serious."

Uberon nodded.

Corinne sighed and set down her fork. Raising her gaze to his, she asked, "Is there anything else you want to tell me tonight?"

"Your hair looks beautiful left loose like that. I cannot wait until I see you wearing nothing but those tresses."

Heat immediately blossomed between her thighs and a rosy flush rose from her upper chest to spread over her neck and face. Her heartbeat quickened and her breasts suddenly felt swollen, heavy, and aching. Her center throbbed. Her breathing turned shallow. The scent of her sudden and powerful arousal filled the air. Corinne watched Uberon inhale deeply of it. His silvery eyes glittered and he seemed to expand and coil at the same time. The sharp musk of his arousal rose in the sultry air. It made her mouth water and played havoc with her need for independence.

"Ask the swifts. I won't abandon my family. I need to come back, to visit with them," she rasped, unable to deny the compulsion to accept this male as her mate and equally unable to simply yield to their reciprocal need.

He nodded and shimmered into nothingness.

"I will have your answer tomorrow," came the soft whisper. "And then I will claim you."

She bowed her head and pressed her lips together to keep from answering with a needy yes.

CHAPTER 5

Corinne did not see Uberon until the next evening. She spent the day working and taking care of her clients' projects, glad to have the flexibility and opportunity to work on a remote basis. Otherwise, she would have been stuck in a cubicle farm or department store floor somewhere regretting every minute of her employment. Working remotely, clients neither knew nor cared about her young age: they only cared about the results of her efforts on their behalf.

At the end of the day, she logged off all social media, closed her web browser and software, and shut down the machine. Rolling her shoulders and head to work out the stiff kinks, she rose from her small desk and padded barefoot to the kitchen. Glancing at the clock on the wall, she took a moment to decide whether she wanted to wait for a roast or whether grilling made the better option. A waft from a cookout rose from a neighbor's yard over the next hill decided for her: grilling it was. Corinne pulled out a couple of pork chops, figuring Uberon would show up sooner or later and bring his appetite with him.

After seasoning the chops, she lit the grill and then walked back into the kitchen to chop vegetables for a salad.

"Damn it!" she muttered as a radish rolled away and the knife nicked her index finger.

A newly familiar masculine hand covered hers and raised it.

Corinne wanted to lean back into the male heat she suddenly felt behind her, but Uberon moved aside and brought her bleeding finger to his mouth. Eyes gleaming, eyelids heavy, he sucked on it. Corinne gasped at the rough velvet of his tongue against her skin combined with the heat of his mouth and the pull on her finger. She watched open-mouthed as his Adam's apple bobbed with each swallow and thought that, surely, he couldn't be sucking that much blood from her finger.

Corinne shivered as electricity zinged from her hand through her body. Uberon pulled her finger from his mouth and gave the wet tip a slow lick.

"All better now," he murmured and turned her hand so that she could see the healed wound.

Corinne's throat worked, but no sound emerged. Her tongue couldn't form words. Her brain felt like so much melted butter.

Uberon's heavy eyelids lowered even further and his mouth stretched in a satisfied smile. He took the butcher knife from the counter and slashed his thumb. A hiss escaped his teeth as the steel burned his flesh.

"Open," he commanded as he brought the bleeding digit to her mouth.

Feeling helpless to resist, Corinne opened her mouth just enough for him to slide his thumb inside. Her lips closed over the knuckle and her mouth suddenly exulted in the strangely sweet and spicy effervescence that filled it. She sucked and swallowed, basic instinct taking over. Heat fizzed through her body and made her clit tingle. She shivered again as erotic pleasure rippled through her.

That feeling had to be better than sex.

"Not even close," he murmured as though he'd caught her thought.

Before she could voice a retort, he leaned down and, pulling his thumb from her mouth and covered her lips with his. Inhaling deeply, she surged against him, rising to her toes and clutching at his shoulders with both hands, desperate for more, more, more. A low chuckle of triumph and satisfaction floated on the sultry summer air, and the deposed Unseelie king slanted his mouth over hers. Without breaking the kiss, he dipped a shoulder to scoop an arm underneath her thighs. He straightened, holding her body in his arms.

"Accept me," he whispered, his wet lips moving against hers.

She reached up and wrapped a hand around the back of his head, fingers tangling in the long, coarse silk of his black hair, and tugged, lost in the passion he aroused in her.

"I need your words," he insisted, his voice guttural with the effort to allow her the freedom to choose him.

"*Yes*," Corinne moaned in reply.

Triumph surged. Uberon slanted his mouth across hers again, deepening the kiss to sweep the hot, wet velvet of her mouth with his tongue. She moaned deep in her throat and stroked her tongue against his, demanding her own taste of him as he carried her to her bedroom and, more importantly, the bed that awaited them. A whisper of his will made their clothes vanish as he lowered her to the mattress. Corinne mewled as he dragged his lips along the pristine line of her jaw to the sensitive, tender skin behind her earlobe where he paused to nibble and suckle. She undulated beneath him, hands alternately clenching the defined, lean muscles of his upper arms and shoulders and smoothing across the satiny skin marred by the occasional scar of a long-ago injury.

She would learn that such scars indicated nearly mortal injuries, for nothing short of lethal could leave such an enduring mark on his silver-engraved hide.

Uberon wedged a knee between her legs and made a place for himself there. Kneeling between her legs—which had the added advantage of opening her to his gaze and touch—he bent over Corinne and cupped the side of her head with one large hand and stroked her silky skin with the other. She sighed as his warm hand caressed her and gasped when he cupped the soft weight of her breast.

Corinne thought she'd never felt anything so delicious as the gentle kneading of her breast until Uberon's thumb swiped across the rosy, beaded tip. Without conscious thought, she arched into his touch in nonverbal demand for ... for ... she wasn't quite sure for what. Oh, she knew what sex was. No modern woman could avoid that, especially one who enjoyed reading romance novels. She knew that climax lurked beyond what she had already experienced, but she could not imagine anything feeling better than Uberon's touch upon her skin, Uberon's kisses, the heat of his body hovering over hers.

Dimly, she realized that she moaned and mewled and whispered hoarse pleas for more. She bit off a yelp when his fingertip glided through the slick petals between her thighs. Her hips bucked, seeking more of that scintillating, exciting touch.

"So lovely," Uberon murmured as he stroked her thighs and feasted his eyes upon her sex. He slid backward and bent downward, inhaling deeply of her musk. He brought his hands inward and opened her with his thumbs. Her incoherent cry made him smile as another surge of triumph mingled with lust, affection, and a compulsion to claim this female as his for eternity. He slid his thumbs along the wet lips of her sex and, resting his forearms across her thighs to hold her captive, he moved forward and ran the flat of his tongue the length of her weeping slit.

"Uberon!" Corinne shrieked, eyes snapping wide open. She gasped as he feasted upon her, drawing more of her honey into his mouth until she began to strain toward what must have been the prize: an orgasm. She panted and writhed against his unbreakable hold as the unbearable pleasure intensified and coiled and ... then ... released.

Uberon continued to lick and suck as his mate crashed through her first orgasm. With ruthless determination, he focused on driving her into another climax. He inserted a long finger into her rippling channel and drew it out only to slide it back in, establishing a pattern that would be repeated once she was fully relaxed and prepared for him. He added a second finger into the tight, virginal passage and she moaned her pleasure. His fingertips found the barrier of her innocence, which inspired fierce feelings of possessiveness within him.

This female was untouched by any other male and *his*.

Corinne cried out, her voice breathless as he hurled her over the precipice of another orgasm. She shuddered helplessly against the waves of pleasure he forced her to endure. After a long moment, she twitched and moaned yet again.

"I can't move," came the muffled complaint.

He chuckled against her as he crawled up her body, pressing open-mouthed kisses to her belly and then her breasts, spending time to induce her to arching weakly against him as he used lips, teeth, and tongue to deepen the rosy color of her nipples and aureoles. He nibbled the elegant sweep of her collarbone and the tender skin of her graceful neck. Corinne could taste the lingering remnants of her essence on his lips and tongue and breath when he returned to kissing her mouth. She skimmed her hands down his body, but he captured them before they managed to stray very far. He raised her hands above her head and wrapped one hand around both her wrists. He chuckled into her mouth at her inarticulate protest even as his other hand returned to her core and stroked her again, his thumb focusing on her over-sensitive and throbbing clit. Her hips bucked against him again.

"Tell me you're mine," he ordered, his lips brushing over hers with each syllable.

"I'm yours," she said, the last word ending on a high-pitched keen as he slid his fingers inside her for the most delicious of intimate strokes. "I'm yours."

"By air and water and fire and earth, I claim thee," he rasped as he took hold of his rampant cock and settled the weeping tip at the entrance of her body. His hips flexed and he parted the slick folds.

Corinne gasped at the gentle intrusion. She gasped and panted as her body stretched, yielding to Uberon's heated possession. She winced and bit back a yelp of pain when he breached her maidenhead. Sweat beaded on his forehead and upper lip as he held himself still to allow the pain to fade and her body to accept his invasion.

Corinne breathed through her nose, unable to draw her attention away from the loss of her virginity. How could she when she felt full to bursting. Surely, he could go no more deeply inside her. With that erroneous assumption, she relaxed.

When he felt her muscles relax around him, Uberon drove forward, burying himself inside his mate's body. She cried out again at the unexpectedly deep occupation. He rolled his hips back slowly, giving her the chance to enjoy the slide of his flesh inside hers. She mewled. He pushed back in, taking care to avoid abrading the newly deflowered channel. He held her jade green gaze with his as he moved inside her body and watched as discomfort gave way to exquisite pleasure. He felt the tightening of her muscles around him and released her wrists. She left them where he'd held them. Uberon delved down to where their bodies joined and, with a delicate touch, strummed her swollen, sensitive clit. The manipulation was enough to shatter her, and she cried out a final time as her body convulsed beneath and around him. The spasms of her internal muscles triggered his own release. He pumped hard, the strokes fast and uncoordinated as his world boiled down to the sublime ejaculation of his seed inside his mate's body.

"By witness of the sun, voice of the wind, embrace of the water, and kiss of the flame, I claim you, body, mind, heart, and soul." He rasped the ancient words in an equally ancient tongue only few remembered and sealed the bond that forever melded her soul with his.

The connection of their souls clicked into place as his cock slowly deflated. Uberon felt his mate's weariness and gathered her to him, giving her the shelter of his body as she succumbed to the imperative of slumber.

"I will love thee for all time and endow thee with all my wealth and power that you might never suffer harm," he whispered. His breath lifted strands of her ginger tresses. With another whisper of will and power, he cleaned and refreshed their bodies. He did not want his mate waking in discomfort, her skin oily with old sweat and sticky from their passion. With a feeling of deep satisfaction, he closed his eyes and allowed himself to sleep, anticipating a more restful slumber than he'd enjoyed in many millennia.

He looked forward to returning home with his soul-bonded mate. Already amazing as a human, she'd make an incredible fae. With that thought, Uberon dipped into her mind and sent her into deep, deep sleep so that when he woke he could initiate her transformation and spare her the agony of it.

You vowed to allow her the choice, came the chastisement.

Uberon recognized the voice. *She accepted me.*

She did not understand what that meant.

She is mine, mine to possess, mine to care for.

Foolish fae. She won't thank you for what you do to her.

Foolish swift. She'll be happy. She'll have me, *and I will fill her heart, soul, mind, and body.* Uberon especially looked forward to innumerable hours enjoying her body and anticipated that she would enjoy his with equal relish.

The unicorn's derisive snort resounded inside Uberon's skull. *Arrogant fae. Bring her to the Deepwood when you return. We shall await you there.*

Fiery pain erupted upon Uberon's skin as the soul bond manifested itself in the emergence of black jewels amid the silver filigree tracing that proclaimed his rank and power and pure blood to any who knew how to read the intricate runes incorporated into the complex design. A whimper followed by a groan drew his attention back to his mate. She arched away from him in agony as the soul bond erupted from her human skin, manifesting as a wide collar that spread over her clavicles and across her shoulders. Black diamonds matching those on his markings caught the faint ambient light. Blood seeped from the broken skin and soaked into the linens. With a sigh, Uberon unwrapped his arms from around his mate and admired the mark of his possession emblazoned upon his mate's skin. Rising from Corinne's bed, he fetched a bowl of cool, clean water and a soft cloth. With gentle tenderness, he cleaned her skin.

Some things were best done by hand.

But he used his power to remove the wet bloodstains from the sheets and dry the fabric.

CHAPTER 6

Corinne stretched against the sheets, which felt deliciously cool and smooth against her skin. Muscles twinged with unaccustomed soreness, a mild ache that bespoke of vigorous nighttime activity. Her lips curled in a smile at the hazy memory of the loss of her virginity and the glory of the pleasure she'd experienced. If she'd known sex was *that* good, she would have cashed in her V-card years ago.

With sybaritic joy, she ran her palms down her body, from ribs to upper thighs. Her hand strayed to her mound and realization filtered through. She rubbed her skin, her bare, hairless skin.

"What the hell?" she muttered. She lifted the covers, which she now realized she did not recognize, and looked down her body. The glimpse encompassed the glitter of silver and gemstones that were *embedded* into her skin. Her hands flew up to her chest, sensitive fingertips running over the cool silver tracery and the faceted jewels that crawled up her throat.

"What the hell?" she muttered again.

Corinne sat up and flung the covers aside. In doing so, her long hair swished over her body. She grabbed a hank of her hair and sighed with relief that at least she hadn't lost her hair, even if she did not quite recognize the rest of her own body.

The gleam at her fingertips caught her eye as she examined

the hank of hair. A yelp of surprise burst from her mouth.

"I have claws!" she squeaked in sudden panic.

"Beloved," came the baritone endearment from behind her. She looked up, swiveling to see Uberon walk through a door she hadn't realized was there. He shrugged off a loose robe as he approached, his pale skin practically gleaming, his eyes burning with heat and desire, and his cock swollen and erect.

"What have you done to me?" she cried out and scrambled away from him.

"You accepted me," he replied and extended a hand—a clawed hand—toward her.

Corinne blinked. The intricate silver tattoos emblazoned across his chest and over his hips—which really weren't tattoos because that implied ink—was studded with black diamonds just like she now had on her skin. Fury ripped through her at his trickery and obvious expectation that she'd spread her legs and fall on his penis.

"I said yes to sex, not to ... to *this*!"

He halted beside the bed. "What did you think saying yes to me would entail, Corinne? I told you want I wanted."

She shook her head. "Are you mad? I did *not* agree to this."

At that last word she gestured to indicate her body. "I have *claws* now. And you had no right to shave or wax me ... oh, shit ... did you *drug* me, you bastard? And just where the hell are we?"

Uberon blinked, surprised by her ire. His hand fell back to his side. Perhaps the swifts had been correct in predicting her reaction to the transformation. However, surely she would calm down once he explained.

"I informed you that you would be transformed, that it was necessary for you to survive here."

Through gritted teeth she growled at him, "And just where in the hell is here?"

"At the moment, we're in the Erlking's castle. He has graciously granted us leave to reside here until you are recovered sufficiently to travel to my home."

"The Unseelie Court?" she snarled.

"No. There is no more Unseelie Court. We have territory far to the north bordering the Quol. We shall occupy that."

"No. Just ... no. And I want you to undo this."

"We cannot restore your humanity."

"What's this 'we' shit? *You* did this to me!"

With implacable determination indicating his struggle to remain calm, Uberon repeated, "You accepted me and all that such acceptance entailed."

"I rescind that acceptance."

"You cannot. We are bound soul to soul, heart to heart, mind to mind, and flesh to flesh." At the mention of flesh, his erection bobbed as though in emphasis.

"I am not getting near that," Corinne snapped, her gaze captured by the swollen appendage.

Uberon seated himself on the bed and reached across to grasp his mate's upper arm.

"Let me go!"

"My body craves yours and yours will crave mine," he said as he pulled her toward him. She yanked against his hold, but his ancient strength easily dominated hers. He saw the light of power flash in her jade green eyes and quelled it with a thought.

"You jerk!" she hissed at him as she struggled to free herself. She raised a hand to strike him, but he caught it with the quick reflexes of a master swordsman.

Now, with both of her arms in his grasp, he forced her down and crawled over her, wedging his knees between her legs.

"No!"

He bowed down and captured her mouth with his even as he lowered his hips to pin her beneath his greater size and weight.

Dread of rape seized Corinne and she panicked, throwing her entire body into the struggle for freedom. She did not notice that the press of Uberon's lips against hers was tender. She only recognized terror and the loss of choice.

When his mate did not subside in her thrashing about at his tender touch, Uberon drew back and dipped into her mind. What he saw there appalled him. She was his mate and she was supposed to yearn for his touch, his kiss, his possession of her body. She was supposed to ache for him and receive him with naught but joy and pleasure.

Her terror disturbed him.

He released her, and she shot off the bed and across the room where she cowered like a cornered animal. He rose, and she begged, "Don't. Please don't."

"My touch should give you nothing but joy and pleasure," he

said, his voice quiet with unaccustomed confusion. "I do not understand this. I will not harm you."

"You took away my choice. You were going to rape me."

The cold words coated his heart with ice.

"I have not abandoned all honor such as that," he snapped. He climbed off the bed and walked to where he could loom over her. "Do not besmirch me with the evils of human males. I am Uberon, a king of my race and one of the most powerful of my kind."

Corinne averted her gaze and sniffed.

With narrowed eyes and icy disdain, Uberon straightened to his full height and said, "My cock rises to none but you and my heart beats only for you, but I'll not beg. You will. And when you do, rest assured that I'll spare you no quarter and fuck you raw until you admit you belong to me."

With a slithering rustle, cloth and leather wrapped around his body. Fully clothed, Uberon stalked from the bedroom in a towering fury.

"Aw, shit," Corinne muttered and buried her face in her hands. She stayed in the corner for a moment until her limbs stopped trembling and she thought her legs would bear her weight. They felt shaky as she rose, but strong enough to do what she needed them to do. Leaning on the wall and then a bureau for stability, she explored the room and found clothing, none of it practical. Exquisite, floor length gowns, delicate sandals, silky shawls: all of it suited an idle lady of leisure, not a headlong flight into the great unknown of the Erlking's kingdom.

And just who was this Erlking anyway?

In a fit of pique, she focused her angry gaze on a glass figurine and focused her urge to incinerate it … nothing.

"Damn it!" she grumbled, realizing that Uberon had stifled her power well and good. She hoped his block would wear off, because she was going to leave his arrogant ass if she had to burn down her host's castle to do so.

A knock on the door—not the one through which Uberon had entered and exited—distracted her. She grabbed Uberon's robe off the floor where he'd left it and pulled it on. The hem dragged the floor.

"Who is it?"

The door opened and a pretty face peered in.

"Lord Uberon asked me to see to your welfare," the woman said.

"He didn't actually ask, did he?" Corinne could not help but stare at the intricate silver design and blood red gems embedded in the skin covering the woman's throat and exposed upper chest and shoulders. Her fingers skimmed over her own embellishment.

"He suggested it," the woman said with a grin. "Considering how angry he is, I thought it best to humor him."

Corinne felt a grin tug at her lips, so she pressed them together in a firm line of disapproval. When she felt she could keep control of herself, she said, "Again, who are you?"

The pretty woman sighed and extended her hand in a curiously familiar, *human* gesture. "I'm Oriel, the Erlking's mate."

Corinne took her hand and shook it briefly. "Oriel. And I'm Corinne."

"Oh, yes, I know. I also know you were once human, like me."

"Like you?"

"Gus kidnapped me and brought me here." She chuckled, even as Corinne's eyes widened at the plain name given to the apparently wealthy and assumedly powerful Erlking. "Let me tell you, it took months before I was ready to forgive him for that."

"So, you're saying I should forgive Uberon for what he did to me?"

"Oh, no. I think you should lead him a merry chase." Oriel giggled, her amber eyes twinkling with merriment. "But I've not come up here to discuss that." She gestured toward the wardrobe and bureau. "You'll find a bath through that door" —she pointed across the room— "and some soap, towels, and such. Avail yourself of the clothes in the wardrobe; they'll fit you. And when you're feeling more or less normal, step outside the room and someone will be waiting to lead you to the dining room. You must be hungry."

Corinne blinked in surprise and nodded. Yes, she was hungry.

Damn it.

She padded across the floor and passed through the indicated doorway. Sure enough, a shallow pool steamed. Colored mosaic tiles gleamed through the water, reminding her of photos she'd seen of Roman baths. Arranged on a ledge, cut crystal containers offered an array of fragrant oils and salts to season the bathwater. A small table held two thick, folded towels. A matching washcloth was draped over the edge of the pool. Corinne looked into the ceramic pots that sat on another small table beside the pool and, rubbing a dab of their contents between her thumb and forefinger, discerned that both held soap. Whether the soap doubled as shampoo could only be answered through empirical trial, she figured.

"Ahhh," she sighed as she sank into the pool, which was just deep enough to allow the water to cover her up to her shoulders while she sat on the mosaic bottom. The hot water relaxed and eased the lingering soreness of her body. After she soaked for several minutes, her belly rumbled, reminding her that she needed to eat.

After washing both her hair and body with the fragrant soap, Corinne wrapped the towel around her body and found a silver comb and silver-backed brush which she put to good use. She gaped in amazement when each stroke drawing the comb through her hair left behind dry, shining locks. Enjoying the feel of her loose hair sliding over her shoulders, she rummaged through a bureau and found a lightweight silk chemise trimmed with lace. She dropped the towel and slipped it on, then opened the wardrobe and selected a midnight blue gown that looked simple enough to manage without the assistance of a ladies maid. She adjusted the ties to fit her body and wondered if it would be gauche to request panties and a bra. Tilting her head to one side, she rather thought that, considering the style of the clothing, modern undergarments likely had no place in this strange, new world where Uberon had brought her.

Damn him.

She searched the room and found a pair of soft leather slippers that tied to adjust the fit. The thin, flexible soles put her in mind of ballet slippers and offered basic protection against the bare wood beneath her feet. Tucking a strand of hair behind her ear, she opened the bedroom door and peered into a corridor.

"My lady?" a high voice piped.

Corinne barely stifled a yelp of surprise and looked around to see who spoke.

"Down here, my lady."

She looked down to see a perfectly formed, miniature person

no taller than her waist.

"Oh, hello," she greeted with uncertain wariness.

The little person nodded and smiled. "Welcome to the Erlking's keep, my lady. Lady Oriel bids me lead you to the family dining room, if you will please follow me."

The servant nodded and glided up the corridor. Corinne hesitated, not entirely positive whether she ought to follow this unknown person. Her belly growled loudly and made the decision for her. The little person walked with surprising speed, despite the obviously short length of his legs. Corinne took a couple skipping steps to catch up. The servant halted in front of a tall, dark door on which a sigil had been carved and filled in with something red and shiny. At his touch, the door swung open.

With a curt bow, the servant gestured and said, "Please enter. They await you."

"They?" she murmured. Dread made her heart pound and her palms sweat.

She nodded her thanks and entered a well-appointed room, her gaze landing on the enormous man whose fierce glare caught and held hers. She took in the sight of his wild auburn hair, close-cropped beard and icy, calculating gaze.

"Enter," he barked, his voice not loud, although nonetheless reverberating.

Corinne's heart sank to her toes.

"Gus, you're terrifying the poor girl," Oriel's voice floated lightly on the air. Then the lovely woman entered Corinne's narrow field of vision and she smiled with welcome. "Come in, come in. I've managed to convert my ... husband, I guess you'd call him ... to an American style breakfast, so you mustn't allow yourself to go hungry."

"Mate," the big man corrected in a gruff tone. "We're mated, not married."

"Give her time to acclimate, my dear."

"It makes a difference, my love."

"Of course, it does. But she's not quite ready for all that it entails. On top of that, she's a bit put out with Uberon."

"She's his mate and belongs with him," Gus rumbled.

Oriel gave him a fond, tolerant smile and sighed. "Yes, darling, but there's a right way and a wrong way to go about establishing and sealing the soul bond. I'm convinced that

Uberon didn't quite bother to explain things as he should have."

The Erlking harrumphed and subsided, running the back of a knuckle over his mate's smooth cheek. Oriel's eyes fluttered closed and she leaned into the touch. Corinne blinked at the easygoing, domestic squabble, astounded that the petite, amiable woman held her own against the outsized man who looked like a fabled Scottish warrior. A stray thought crossed her mind: Did he wear a kilt?

"Aye, I've a fondness for Caledonia," he murmured, his fierce gaze locking with hers again.

Corinne's jaw dropped. A moment later, she summoned the wherewithal to close her mouth. Had he read her mind?

"Stop it, Gus. You're frightening her again." Oriel lightly tapped his burly upper arm and directed a smile at Corinne. "Come in, my dear. I can't say that Gus' bark is worse than his bite, but he means you no harm."

Feeling compelled, Corinne stepped further into the room.

"That deep blue looks magnificent on you," Oriel complimented. "Uberon chose well."

"*Uberon* chose this?" Corinne gasped and looked down at the graceful drape of the silk covering her body.

"Of course. He always did have excellent taste."

"But … how? When?" Corinne spluttered.

"Not all that long ago. I was surprised he waited as long as he did before taking you as his mate." Oriel tilted her head and observed with a mischievous glint in her eyes, "Fae males tend to be impatient."

"Impatient," Corinne echoed in a faint voice.

"Oh, yes. *Yes.*"

Corinne blinked, the second affirmation being more passionate that the discussion merited. The she noticed the subtle movement of the Erlking's arm muscles and realized what he was doing. *And Oriel doesn't seem to mind in the least*, a little voice in the back of her mind pointed out.

She averted her gaze and focused on the sideboard. Gesturing vaguely in the direction of food, she asked, "Shall I—?"

"Be seated. Guests do not serve themselves here," came the breathy response, followed by a soft moan. "Oh, Gus, *yes.*"

Cheeks flaming, Corinne took a seat at the opposite end of the table, not wanting to intrude any further than she had already. Hardly a second passed before a silent servant unobtrusively offered her the choice between tea or coffee. She considered the options and muttered, "Coffee. It's going to be a coffee day. I can feel it."

The servant's mouth quirked upward, flashing her a brief smile of amused commiseration. He poured the morning beverage and then inquired as to what she'd like from the buffet of breakfast items. Not entirely sure of her next meal, Corinne stocked up on French toast, eggs, and hash browns. She forced herself to eat at a normal pace and not watch as her hostess' olive complexion flushed and the air somehow resounded with the small, breathy sounds of orgasm delivered by her mate's surreptitious touch hidden beneath the table.

The subdued passion in the tableau across the table made her squirm, first with embarrassment, then with discomfort as her own, newly awakened body began to throb and tingle and *want*. She felt herself grow moist and knew a flush pinked her skin. With a small cough to clear her throat, Corinne focused on her food and almost wished Uberon were there to touch her as Gus touched Oriel.

Almost.

Damn him.

With her belly filled, Corinne rose and politely excused herself, trying not to watch as Gus licked his fingers clean with obvious relish. She hastened from the room and the suspicion that he'd bend Oriel over the table and fuck her senseless as soon as she departed.

"Fae are a sensual race," the halfling commented as the door closed behind Corinne. "We see no need to hide our pleasure."

"I—I'm not fae," Corinne protested, her voice faint.

"Yes, you are. You just don't know it yet." The little person who'd guided her to the family dining room gestured and added, "Follow me, my lady. Allow me to show you Lady Oriel's lily garden."

"Lily garden?" Corinne fell into step alongside the servant.

"Aye. The Erlking ordered it installed for her pleasure. It's a great favorite with visitors."

She considered that and thought that a lily garden made for a refreshing change of pace instead of the usual rose garden.

"Er ... do I need a shawl or something?"

"No, my lady. 'Tis the height of summer here and the weather is most fair."

Corinne didn't quite know how to respond to that, so she held her silence until the next question popped out before she could stop it. "Um, do you know where Uberon is?"

"His grace has departed and charged the Erlking with your protection and well-being during his absence."

"He left? Where?" After asking the question, Corinne realized that the location didn't matter, since she had no idea, really, where they were.

"He did not confide in me," the servant replied with mild equanimity. "I have been assigned to attend you and see to your comfort."

"Comfort," she parroted, her voice again faint with disbelief. Her tone sharpened with the next question: "What if I said it would comfort me to return home?"

"Then I would regret my failure to see to your comfort," came the unperturbed reply.

"Huh."

They walked in silence, turning down corridors and crossing rooms until Corinne was thoroughly lost. She gasped in awe when the halfling opened glass paned, double doors that led to a sunny garden. Heady fragrances of fertile loam, fresh water, and verdant growth filled the sun-warmed air.

"Have a seat, my lady, or wander the garden. I shall return with refreshments. Do you enjoy reading? Lady Oriel has many books from your world."

Turning back to face the halfling, Corinne nodded, wordless from the effect of her overwhelmed senses. Finally, she found her voice. "Er ... yes, I would enjoy something to read. D-does Lady Oriel have any tales of adventure?"

The halfling grinned. "Excellent, my lady. I'll return shortly."

Corinne nodded and wandered off to look more closely at the lush and varied lilies that displayed their glory to the open sky. She walked slowly down groomed, winding, gravel paths that took full advantage of the garden's cozy size and the bountiful variety of blooms and circled several shallow fountains graced by more kinds of water lilies than she imagined existed. When she returned to the stone bench the halfling indicated earlier, she saw a sweating pitcher of water, a glass, and a well-worn copy of

Harry Potter and the Sorcerer's Stone by J. K. Rowling.

Corinne threw her head back and laughed.

Giving her a quizzical look, the halfling took an affronted step backward. "Have I given offense, my lady?"

Corinne wiped her eyes with the backs of her hands and shook her head. "Ah, no. I'm sorry … um … I'm afraid I don't know your name."

"Luthhir, my lady."

She wiped the damp back of one hand against her skirt and held it out to shake. "I'm pleased to meet you, Luthhir. I'm Corinne."

The halfling's large eyes widened even more at the friendly gesture of equality and backed away another step, putting himself beyond her reach. Instead, he bowed. "Is the book not to your liking, my lady?"

"Oh, I saw the movie, several times in fact."

"Movie?"

"Um …" Corinne closed her eyes with belated understanding that this preindustrial world would no doubt not have such entertainments as movies. That led her to wonder why she automatically assumed this place in which she had been deposited met the qualifications of preindustrial. Just because she hadn't seen any factories or automobiles didn't mean that this world didn't have them. After all, one wouldn't expect to find machines in plain view inside the Erlking's fairytale castle which resembled a strange cross between a Gothic cathedral and something Mad King Ludwig of Bavaria might have commissioned with its soaring spires, vaulted ceilings, and flying buttresses.

"Nevermind," she finished weakly. "It's one of my favorite stories."

Luthhir's round face relaxed, his apple-cheeks plumping with a smile. "Then perhaps you wish to read something with which you are not familiar, a new tale?"

"Ah, yes, a new tale." Corinne grabbed onto that olive branch with a heady sense of relief. "That is, if you have anything written in English. I'm afraid I'm quite illiterate in other languages."

"Of course, my lady. Queen Oriel has many books. I shall fetch something else."

Chagrined that the little man would rush off to parts

unknown just to fulfill her whim, Corinne called out, "No, I'll make do with this one today." She gave him a smile of apology. "But thank you for the offer. I don't wish to be of any trouble."

"Oh, no, my lady. It's my pleasure to serve you," Luthor demurred with practiced good manners.

"Perhaps you'll teach me the way to the library so I can fetch my own books," she suggested. "That way you won't feel obligated to go scurrying hither and yon."

"'Tis my duty."

"I'm sure you have more important things to do than wait upon me."

"No, my lady. I was assigned to your care."

She sighed, realizing that she would not escape her pint-sized guardian. "Then I would greatly appreciate being shown to the library tomorrow. Now, please take a seat. You make me feel nervous standing at attention like that."

"You may wish to inquire of the castle if you are to stay here for an extended length of time."

"Inquire of the castle?" she echoed, bewildered as the halfling took a seat next to her and folded his hands in his lap. His small booted feet did not touch the ground. "What do you mean by that?"

"Aye." Luthhir patted the stone bench. "The castle is sentient. It knows who walks and resides within its grounds."

"Sentient?"

"Do you not have such structures where you come from?"

"Er ... no, we don't," she replied, thinking of the sophisticated security systems that viewed and tracked everyone who entered or exited any building protected by high-tech electronics. Of course, the buildings were not sentient, though she assumed the security personnel who watched the monitors most certainly fell under that category.

Except for the human radish who had manned the security desk in her freshman dormitory. Egad, what a moron. A creep, too.

With a little shake of her head to clear her mind of such memories which would certainly do her no good here, she picked up the book and opened it. Luthhir kept her silent company for several minutes, absently swinging his feet. Then he slid off the bench, collected the tray with the pitcher and glass of now-tepid water, and murmured something about bringing something cool to drink. Finally alone, Corinne sighed and continued to read.

CHAPTER 7

Days passed in lazy idleness turned into weeks, and then came the change of seasons. Oriel appointed herself Corinne's tutor and began teaching her the dominant language of the fae world in which her guest now lived. Corinne missed her family and wished she had some method to communicate with them, at least to let them know she had come to no true harm.

As she lay in bed one morning, she admired the refraction of early sunlight through the crystals of frost that rimed the glass panes and realized that of all the changes she had undergone, one had slipped her notice. With a gasp, she pressed her palms over her belly.

Could it be?

She groaned with dread. How could she have been so foolish as to not think that even a single night of wild monkey sex might leave her pregnant? With sudden energy, she left the bed and ran through her morning ablutions and dressed. Oriel noticed her wild eyes when Corinne joined them for breakfast.

"Whatever is the matter, my dear?"

"I ... I ... I think I'm pregnant," Corinne blurted in a hoarse voice.

The beautiful brunette tilted her head to one side, pondered the statement for a few seconds, then asked, "What makes you think that?"

Corinne's gaze darted to the Erlking who listened with unabashed interest. She blushed with embarrassment. "I—I just realized that I haven't had my period since I came here."

"Oh, is that all?" Oriel chuckled. "Fae biology doesn't work quite like human biology. Even if it did, no pregnancy would have survived the transformation from human to fae."

"I'm not fae, though."

"You most certainly are." She ran her fingertips lightly over the silver and gemstones adorning her smooth flesh. "The soul bond ensures it. Besides, nothing crosses the Erkling's borders unless invited, and it's quite rare for anything other than the fae to be invited. No human would stand a chance."

"I welcome few of the fae," Gus growled in his deep baritone.

"Yes, darling, you're quite reclusive, which does wonders for enhancing your reputation," Oriel placated as she reached over to pat his hand. She smiled at Corinne. "The transformation involves a great deal of magic and usually generates a terrible mess. It's best you don't try to remember the gory details."

Corinne's own fingertips traced the silver engraved into the skin exposed by the wide, scooped neckline of her gown. Surely, she would have remembered *that* little operation, wouldn't she?

"As time passes, you'll notice other changes. Some are less subtle than the cessation of former biological processes, some more so. It's different for everyone, or so I'm told."

"How many people do you know this has happened to?"

Oriel held up her hand and curled one finger for each person as she named them. "Catriona who is mated to Captain Thelan of the Seelie Court, Calista who is mated to Captain Falco of the Daimónio Refstófae, myself, and you."

Corinne blinked. Under Oriel's patient tutoring, she had begun to grasp the history of the fae realms and recognized the women—no, *females*—named. The fae did not style themselves as men or women, which they considered human terms and therefore pejorative. They were male or female and fae and preferred precision in their speech.

She had yet to hear Oriel's personal history. Perhaps Oriel wished to keep that private. Regardless, she knew she would not be so rude as to pry. After a moment's thought, she returned to the original subject.

"So, I'm not likely to be pregnant?"

"I'm afraid that's quite impossible."

Corinne decided to accept the other woman's assurance. She sighed.

"Why the heavy sigh?"

"I miss my family."

"Would you like to write a letter to them?"

"I don't think the U.S. Postal Service has a route here," Corinne pointed out with acidic irony.

"Of course not. But Gus can pop into the human realm and drop a letter into a mailbox for you."

The Erlking's fiery eyebrows met his hairline at this blithe declaration.

"And postage?"

"He'll drop it into your parent's mailbox at their home."

"Oh." She paused. "If you can go there, why can't I?"

"I misspoke. One of the native fae can perform this task. Those of us who are *adapted* to fae flesh are less *malleable*."

Corinne's mouth opened to ask for more detail, but closed without speaking because the details really didn't matter at that point. She had no idea how to get home even if she could. So, she nodded her acceptance and replied, "I'll write a letter today."

Giving her a sympathetic smile while the Erlking looked out a nearby window, Oriel said, "You are the youngest of us to have been claimed and with probably the most to have lived for. If you wish to write a letter to your family every so often, I shall ensure it is delivered. It is the least we can do."

"Thank you," Corinne murmured, thinking that, yes, considering she'd been ripped from her happy, simple lifestyle and her family, it was the *least* they could do.

The Erlking flashed her a glowering stare. Absorbed in her own resentful musing, she did not see it. Oriel rose from her seat and joined her mate by the window. She took his large hand in her small, delicate one and whispered into his mind, *Have pity on her. She did not ask to be mated, abducted, transformed, and then abandoned among strangers.*

Your compassion is your most beautiful trait, my beloved, he whispered along the mating bond as his hand curled around hers.

Not feeling hungry, Corinne excused herself and left the room.

"I'll have a tray sent to her quarters," Oriel said to no one in particular.

"After we have finished," the Erlking said as he drew his mate into his embrace.

She melted against him and sighed as he stroked her back and cupped her round posterior. He released her hand and wound her hair around his fist to pull her head back. Submitting to his dominance with easy delight, she opened her mouth for him, an invitation he accepted with predatory glee. As he ravished her mouth, he pulled her skirt up and walked her back toward the table. His lips did not leave hers when he lifted her onto the table and moved between her knees. Oriel clung to his shoulders and sighed as he stroked the satiny skin of her inner thighs, her skirt ruched over her hips like colorful waves. She mewled when he probed the slick delicate tissues at her core and mewled again when he jerked open the fall of his breeches to release the thick, long length of his erection. They both groaned as he sank into her body. She whimpered a little when he withdrew and then clutched at him when he pushed back in. Soon he established a deep, commanding rhythm that drove them both to climax without mercy.

Knees shaking with the weakness of spent passion, Gus braced his weight on his hands, palms flat on the table. He took great shuddering breaths as he pressed languid, still hungry kisses to his mate's slender neck and shoulder. Slowly, he sank to his knees and directed his tongue to the work of cleaning the evidence of their passion from between her thighs. His ministrations soon had her keening as another orgasm swept through her.

No bee's honey ever tasted so sweet.

With the cries and grunts of passion fading with distance, Corinne walked slowly along the path she had learned led to the library. As Luthhir taught her, she laid her palm on the stone wall next to the door frame and murmured a polite thank-you in the powerful-sounding language the halfling told her was the Old or High Tongue of the ancients. When he'd mentioned that one of those ancients had mated her, she had scoffed until Oriel confirmed it with the evidence of ancient scrolls.

A current of warm air swirled around her, a physical acceptance of her gratitude for leading her to her destination without detour. She patted the wall and crossed the threshold into the library. At one of the three desks, she found thick sheets of heavy paper, already sharpened quills, and a pot of black ink. She dipped the point into the ink and began with the customary salutation: "Dear Mom and Dad."

She had no idea what to write after that.

Deciding what details to convey and what her parents would believe took hours of careful pondering before committing the words to precious paper, because, yes, she did now live in a preindustrial world where such things as paper cost a lot of money. She knew history and its inconveniences. She'd nearly declared herself as a history major until one of the professors had discouraged it: "If you want to make a living doing something other than teaching history, then don't choose history. Business executives consider history only slightly more useful than philosophy or fine art, which is to say not at all."

So, she'd gone with English and found that the more lucrative choice would have been accounting. Too bad her mathematical skills ranged somewhere between dismal and nonexistent.

"Everyone thinks that girls who major in the humanities are looking for an MRS," her brother Peter commented when she bemoaned the paucity of paid internships for English majors.

"I'm not looking for a husband," she'd retorted and slapped his arm.

The modern world, she had learned, did not appreciate those whose skills and interests lay outside science, technology, engineering, and math. In the castle's immense library, she looked at the tall bookstacks, wooden shelves gleaming, their burdens carefully tended. Perhaps living in a world that appreciated an education such as hers made good sense, made a good fit for her.

She wished Uberon would return so she could kick his ass. Or at least chew him out. He deserved nothing less for dumping her on Oriel and Gus, who yet inspired unreasoning fear. He was one seriously scary dude. The word *dude* in her thoughts made her chuckle. The Erlking whose nickname was Gus—she still didn't now if that was short for Augustus or Augustine or something else—definitely gave out those "do not mess with me" vibes and had the muscles and weapons to enforce them. Uberon, she thought, did not have quite the hefty brawn as the Erlking, although his body exhibited no less than physical perfection on a somewhat leaner scale. In fact, she thought, not one of the fae whom she had encountered displayed anything less than perfect physical fitness and a sort of agelessness that at first glance appeared youthful, but at second glance was not. Looking into their eyes, meeting those ageless gazes, she readily believed that such folk lived centuries, if not millennia.

A Navy SEAL's thousand-yard stare had nothing on these people. She knew, because one of her brothers was a SEAL. And she had a cousin who'd gone into the Army to become—eventually—a Ranger. The extended family boasted two Green Berets, another SEAL, and one in the Air Force pararescue command.

With a sniff of self-pity, she folded the paper after assuring herself that the ink had dried. Using the Erlking's wax, she sealed the letter.

"I'll ensure its delivery, my lady," Luthhir's high voice piped up, startling her.

"I thought I was alone."

"You were," he said. "But I would be remiss in my duties if I did not keep watch over you."

Corinne pressed her lips together in a thin line before the request to be left alone—really alone—escaped her. Luthhir did not deserve her ire; he was only obeying his boss' orders. She inhaled and focused on releasing her annoyance on the exhale.

"Thank you, Luthhir. I'll head for the lily garden now, if no one minds."

"Let the garden soothe you, my lady."

She handed him the letter and rose to her feet. She followed him out of the library and then took the familiar path that led to the lily garden, except the castle deposited her elsewhere. The sharp scent of pine filled her nostrils. A chill breeze bit through the thin silk of her dress.

"Good afternoon, child," came a smooth, masculine tenor that sounded as though it emanated from a much larger-than-human chest.

Startled once again, Corinne gasped and whirled about. Then she gaped, jaw working with every word sticking in her throat. Gleaming like a pearl with subtle hints of color glinting over its milky hide, the unicorn walked around her as though taking her measure.

"Uberon cannot be faulted for his work," the beast murmured.

"What do you mean?" she asked, voice trembling even as his comment goaded her into reply.

"We cautioned him against attempting this on his own, but he insisted. We underestimated his skill and power. That could be dangerous, very dangerous." Its silvery eyes flared green like the flash of color in an opal.

"Who's *we*?"

The unicorn ignored her question and took a step toward her. She took a step backward.

"Allow me to give you a gift," the unicorn said as its heavy neck arched and its head bowed so that the lethal tip of his spiral ivory horn pointed at Corinne's torso.

She glanced behind her and took another careful step back. She raised a hand, slowly so as not to spook the dangerous beast, and said, "Um, that's really generous of you, but you need not give me anything."

The unicorn took a step forward. Corinne stepped backward again and yelped when something sharp pricked her behind the right shoulder blade.

"Stand still, child," came a velvety command in a deep, dark voice as the white unicorn minced forward and placed the point of its horn just beneath her left clavicle. "It's discourteous to refuse a gift."

"Er … what is this gift?" she squeaked and hated her voice for the indignity. She glanced back to see the midnight bulk of a black unicorn whose horn poked through the fabric of her dress. Where in the hell had those come from? How had they penetrated the castle's defensive walls? Pinned between the beasts' razor-pointed horns, she did not demand answers: she felt it best not to annoy them.

The white unicorn answered her question: "Uberon's transformation quelled you. We're going to unlock your power."

"You're going to what?"

Rather than answer with words, the unicorns pierced her flesh with their horns. Impaled, Corinne screamed as agony swept through her body, burning as though fire consumed her from within. As one, the unicorns pulled their horns from her flesh. Free from the skewering, the woman collapsed in an ungraceful heap. The white unicorn then lowered its dripping horn and touched her with its bloodied tip. Light flashed and pulsed over Corinne's body. The wounds closed, front and back, filling with intricate seals of opal and silver.

"I'll stand guard until she wakes," the black unicorn volunteered. "Won't Uberon—that insufferable, arrogant fool—be surprised?"

The dawn swift chuckled and turned on his heels to melt into the pine forest's gloom.

When Corinne's eyes fluttered open the dew had settled and soaked her clothes. With a groan, she picked herself off the ground and pressed the heels of her palm to her forehead.

"Follow me and I shall show you the herb for your headache."

Corinne shrieked and swirled about, her bleary eyes finally landing on the ebony shadow of a ... yes, damn it ... unicorn.

"Quit that!" she snapped and stamped her foot like a child. "I am tired of people sneaking up on me."

The beast tilted its elegantly chiseled head to one side and blinked its fiery eyes. "People, hm? Well, it's nice to know you don't consider us dumb beasts."

"Oh, please," she muttered and rubbed her eyes. "After what I've been through these past weeks—or has it been months?— there's little I'd *not* believe any more. Talking unicorns is the least of my problems."

The beast's curved ears pinned back. It took a step forward and leveled the lethal point of its spiral horn at her midsection. "Consider your words carefully, girl, when speaking to a swift."

She slapped the horn as though to bat it out of her way. "If you were going to kill me, you'd have done it by now." She fisted her damp skirts and shook the material. "Ugh. If you'll point me in the direction of the Erlking's castle, I'll leave you to your dignity."

The midnight swift's annoyance vanished and it chuckled. Swinging the horn away from her, it drew alongside her. "Mount, girl. I shall return you to the Erlking's castle."

"Damn good thing I grew up riding horses," she muttered as she gathered her skirts in one fist and grabbed a hank of mane at the unicorn's withers. She swung her leg and leaped. The unicorn grunted when she landed heavily on its back. Lips curling in a nasty little smile as she scooted into place, she said, "You could have helped, you know."

"Insolent girl."

"Snooty swift." She knew better than to insult the majestic beast by calling it a horse.

With a snort, the midnight swift launched into a smooth gallop, all consideration of the herb to treat her headache having faded. With old skill, Corinne moved with the smooth rocking of the fleet beast's stride as its cloven hooves skimmed over a landscape that almost looked familiar. However, she did not recognize many of the flowers and plants they passed. Nor did she fail to notice the bright silvery glow of the twin moons overhead.

The question of how the Erlking's sentient castle had directed her to a distant clearing in the forest miles from its stone and mortar stuttered against the weary resignation that she was not meant to know everything because some things simply could not be explained. They just were. Like her magic.

She now felt its resurgence within her, bright and hot and icy and *wild*.

How she had missed it!

Her delighted laughter rang with triumph as the midnight swift carried her back to the castle.

"The magic returns at a cost, girl," the unicorn cautioned.

"I don't care! It's back!" With a laugh of delight, she flung up an arm and released a shower of bright sparks. Who needed charcoal, sulfur, and potassium nitrate? She was her own personal sparkler.

"Don't say I didn't warn you."

His comment triggered a question she did not voice: *What price?*

The great beast slowed to a dignified walk and then halted at the tall rise of steps leading to the Erlking's imposing front portal. Having never seen the castle from the outside, Corinne gasped in awe.

"It's immense," she whispered.

"Aye. What else do you expect from a mountain?"

She snapped her jaws shut to prevent anything rude or

idiotic from spewing forth. Legs shaking, she slid off and landed on the pristine gravel with a grunt of pain. The instant she lifted her hand from the unicorn's hide, it shot forward and raced away with blinding speed on soundless hooves.

"How does he do that?" she wondered aloud, her voice a whisper. With no answer forthcoming, she gathered her still damp and very wrinkled skirts in her hands and climbed up the stairs. The muscles in her legs protested at every step.

"I have gotten so out of shape," she muttered to herself.

One of the great doors swung open on well-oiled hinges at her approach. Corinne looked up and gulped at her host's fierce expression.

"Where have you been, girl?"

Her temper snapped. "Your castle spat me out yonder in the forest where your unicorns—*unicorns!*—played fun and games with me until they decided to return me. I'm frickin' hungry, sore, and tired. Unless you're going to offer me a hot bath, supper, and a bedtime story, I'll get out of your way now."

The Erlking's eyes widened at the young woman's impertinence, then narrowed as she swept past him. His teeth clicked audibly as he fumed for a moment. Then he growled in a language Corinne had learned to recognize as the High Tongue, but did not understand beyond a few key phrases. A musty groan shivered through the great stone edifice in response.

"The castle will see you to your quarters," the Erlking growled and stomped away.

Corinne almost turned and ran after him, but then decided she'd not enjoy the exercise in futility. Her host had already disappeared into the castle's depths and it would doubtlessly lead her back to her chambers regardless of how many wrong turns she took, deliberately or not. She pinched the bridge of her nose and hoped that Luthhir would have something for the headache that throbbed inside her skull.

That fucking unicorn reneged on its offer of relief.

CHAPTER 8

She awoke in a sweat, her body pulsing with need and her nightgown twisted around her torso. With a grunt, Corinne rolled out of bed and padded across the room to the small table where Luthhir had left a pitcher of water and glass as he always did. She poured some water, took a long, slow gulp, and set the empty tumbler back on the table before taking the time to rearrange her nightgown properly around her body. When the cloth once again draped as it should, she could not make herself return to the bed and the all too vivid dreams of her passionate night with Uberon. Instead, she crawled onto the padded bench that served as a window seat and leaned her sweat-dampened forehead against the cool glass. Her breath fogged the pane as she exhaled.

"This isn't fair," she muttered and plucked at the loose bodice of the nightgown, borrowed from Oriel like all her clothing. The damp cloth clung to her clammy skin, which didn't improve her sour mood. "I am so frickin' tired of wearing borrowed clothing."

She cast a disgruntled glance at the dark hearth as the chilly air bit into her skin. She knew she should not complain about her accommodations; after all, her hosts deserved no blame for having taken care of her for all this time. Uberon had dumped her on their doorstep; their generosity deserved nothing but gratitude. But she was sick and tired of being grateful for circumstances over which she had no control. And she was cold, damn it.

With a little growl, she flicked her fingers at the hearth and fire burst into flame. She gasped, surprised by the response of her magic. Corinne's lips curled in a satisfied smile. Apparently, the unicorn hadn't lied when it spoke of unlocking her magic. With another exertion of focused will, she forced air through the damp fabric of her nightgown and dried it. A hint of light breaking through the window distracted her for a moment.

Dawn.

Well, there's no use in trying to go back to sleep now.

She sat in front of the hearth and held out her hands to the cheery fire's warmth to wait just a little while longer before she dressed for the day.

Luthhir gaped when he entered her room to find his mistress already dressed and poring over a book from her perch beside the tall window.

"Good morning, my lady," the halfling nonetheless greeted her with customary politeness.

"Hello, Luthhir. Is the rest of the household up then?"

"I suppose you awakened hungry this morning."

She tilted her head to one side and realized that, yes, she was hungry—hungrier than usual. Or perhaps she was hungry as per usual. The restoration of her magic must be consuming additional energy that made her hungrier than she'd been any morning since arriving in these fae lands. No wonder she'd never had trouble retaining a slender figure, she thought. The magic took a lot of energy to sustain.

Setting down the book, she rose from the window seat and gave Luthhir a mysterious smile. "Yes, I suppose I did."

The little man looked askance at her. "Word is that you kept company with the swifts last night."

Corinne shrugged. "They wanted to see me. Who am I to deny them?"

The halfling did not lose his suspicious look, but changed the subject. "Since you have readied yourself, I shall escort you to the breakfast room."

As per usual, she fell into step behind him. "Luthhir, I know the way by now. And if I didn't, the castle would make sure I got there."

"The castle took you elsewhere yesterday. The midnight swift carried you from the Great Forest."

"So, I'm to blame for the castle's collusion with the unicorns?"

"Of course, not, my lady. This is just highly irregular. The swifts ... er ... do not ... er ... favor the Erlking."

"I can't imagine why not," came the dry response.

Luthhir coughed delicately. "That's neither here nor there and I respectfully ask that you not mention I said anything about that to his majesty."

"Oh, you can count on my discretion," she assured him and wondered how she would use that little bit of leverage. "You know, Luthhir?"

"Aye, my lady?"

"I've been rather sedentary since arriving here. I think I'd like to go outside today."

"Which garden would you enjoy today?"

"No garden. I want to leave the castle, may take a trail ride."

Luthhir gasped. "You mustn't leave the grounds."

"Why not? Does the Erlking have bands of marauders lurking beyond the castle walls?"

"Of course, not. That's preposterous."

"Then why can't I take a hike or ride beyond the castle? How dangerous could it be?"

"Neither the Erlking nor his lady would tolerate any harm coming to you!"

"So, why can't I leave the castle?"

Luthhir's expression turned mutinous. "You'd best inquire of his majesty. I haven't the authority to permit you to leave."

"I didn't need anyone's *permission* last night," she muttered under her breath as the breakfast room door opened. Stepping into the room, she squared her shoulders and pasted a pleasant smile upon her face.

"Good morning, Oriel, Gus."

The Erlking glared at her. Oriel smiled and said coyly, "I heard you had an adventure last night."

"I met the unicorns, if that's what you mean," Corinne responded as she took a seat. Servants leaped into action and quickly brought her a heaping plate and poured her a cup of coffee. Corinne took an appreciative sip of the rich, fragrant brew and said, "One of these days you're going to tell me where you get this coffee."

"Don't try to distract me, young lady. Gus, of course, brings it to me from the Old World."

"You mean Europe?"

"No, silly, our former home: Planet Earth and mundane dimension."

"So, he makes regular trips?"

"No," the Erlking answered in a tone that brooked no further speculation as to his activities. "You shall not leave the castle again without proper escort."

Corinne set down her cup and flatted both palms on the tabletop. Leaning forward, she hissed, "I didn't exactly ask to be deposited in the Great Forest."

"Now, Gus," Oriel soothed, placing a slender hand on his forearm. His burly shoulders relaxed as though that simple touch really did soothe him like a shot of tranquilizer. "We cannot take her to task for the castle's decision to heed the unicorns' summons."

"Summons?" Corinne echoed.

"None dare ignore a summons from the denizens of the Deepwood," Oriel said without humor. Her sober tone held the other woman's rapt interest. "Except for perhaps the Unseelie king, the Erlking, and the archivist."

"Who's this archivist?" Corinne asked, allowing her focus to be distracted.

"A cousin of sorts," the Erlking answered. "We three are related, though the ties are ancient and distant."

"'Tis said that Gus, Uberon, and Enders—that's the archivist—are the oldest and most powerful fae in all this realm, except for the two unicorns." Oriel's voice rang with pride for her mate, the most feared warrior across many worlds. "Gus is the highest and final arbiter of justice."

"Judge, jury, and executioner?" Corinne hazarded a guess, wondering how corrupted that power had become.

"Don't look so doubtful, my dear. Gus leads the Wild Hunt. His prey is the guilty and only those who wish to risk their own destruction will call upon his justice."

"Is that justice why I'm not allowed outside the castle walls?" Corinne asked before her courage crumbled into dust.

"Partially," Oriel replied as her mate shoved back his chair and rose from the table. "There are those who resent his authority and would seek to usurp it. They also seek to harm him by harming those for whom he cares."

"So, you're a prisoner, too."

Oriel looked pained and averted her eyes.

"Cease," the Erlking snapped, the fierce glint in his eyes blazing into barely contained rage. "I am charged with your safety and you shall do nothing to imperil that."

Corinne's jaw dropped, but no words came forth.

"And if anything—*anything*—you do causes harm to my mate, then I will *crush* you with my bare fists. Her well-being is more important than anything to me."

Corinne's gaze locked on the clenching and unclenching of those massive, scarred fists and knew without a doubt he meant every word. She lowered her gaze. "I am sorry, sir. I did not mean to cause offense."

"Yes, you did."

She flinched at the bald statement and intuitively knew no excuse would suffice. "I am sorry. Please know that you have my gratitude; however, I chafe at being confined."

"A woman's independence is a rare thing in fae culture," Oriel empathized. "I forget that you have not had the centuries I have had to adjust."

"Centuries?" Corinne parroted in disbelief. "You look no older than I. Maybe even younger."

"Centuries. You are so very young."

"But, centuries ago women weren't all that independent either."

"Time moves differently between here and the Old World. What passes for centuries here may or may not pass for minutes or days there and millennia elsewhere."

"Now, I'm really confused."

"Eat your breakfast, Corinne. I can see that you have become unbearably restless and will do my best to help you work it off. Now—"

The forlorn cry of a horn reverberated through the castle.

Corinne watched, fascinated, as the Erlking's attention pricked like a wolf's, his focus going laser keen. The glint in his eyes flared and he left the room, long strides covering the distance seemingly without haste but demonstrating both speed and purpose. He brought his fingers to his lips and a shrill whistle pierced the air.

Oriel caught Corinne's silent curiosity and answered the unspoken questions. "The Erlking's justice has been summoned. He must go."

"How long?"

Oriel shrugged. "It varies. He might return within a day or weeks. I have yet to hear of the guilty eluding the Wild Hunt longer than one cycle of the moons."

"And when he catches the criminal?"

Oriel shuddered with delicate distaste. In the distance beyond the mullioned windows rose savage howls. "Do not ask and pray you never witness the justice of the Wild Hunt."

Corinne nodded, realizing that the Hunt had only one gory outcome. No, she did not want to witness that. However, she could not help but ask, "What happens if the accused is actually innocent?"

Oriel looked a little ill at that, but she still answered. "Then the accuser meets the Erlking's justice."

The younger woman realized that, in the fae lands' highest court, there were no appeals. She nodded and bent her head to choke down her breakfast.

Later that day she found herself once again in her hostess' lily garden with a book on her lap and the soothing sound of trickling water mixing with the soft music of a breeze soughing through the branches of an ornamental shade tree. Small orange petals drifted from the tree's fading flowers and caught in her hair and the fabric of her gown. She looked up, squinting into the sun's glare, and thought that she'd never known trees to bloom in late summer or early autumn, but here they did. The pretty display put her in mind of spring and beckoned her to forget that winter was coming.

"Winter is coming," she murmured and grinned to herself. "You've been reading too much George R. R. Martin, my girl."

"Oh, you've read his work?" Oriel inquired as she sat on the marble bench next to her, carrying a book in her own delicate hand. "He's one of my favorite authors."

Corinne held herself still, letting the surprise of the other woman's unannounced arrival wash through her. Apparently *everyone* in this place had mastered the art of sneaking up on people. Holding a hand up to shade her eyes, she replied, "I'm surprised you have."

"Gus indulges me," Oriel chuckled. "Every so often he storms the bookstores and returns with sacks full of books. He hasn't quite gotten the hang of online ordering though."

"I'm not the most technically savvy person either," Corinne said. "Before I came here, I didn't even have a cell phone because there was no reception where I lived. Having one wouldn't have made much sense."

She paused, then asked, "How long have you been here that you've heard of online bookstores?"

"Remember what I said about time not moving equally among dimensions?"

Corinne nodded.

Oriel smiled and said, "I'd venture to say that we're probably contemporaries back on Earth, but that Gus found me and brought me back here somewhere between five hundred and a thousand years ago fae time."

"Fae time," Corinne echoed.

"I can't go back, either, so Gus does his best to bring me back the bits about home I loved. I'm sure Uberon will do the same for you.

Corinne snorted. "I can't imagine Uberon dancing attendance on me like that."

Oriel's smile faded. "Don't discount the strength of the soul bond between mates. We females get the best of it, I'm quite sure."

"I don't see how." Corinne gestured to the garden surrounding them. "Not that this isn't lovely, but you're stuck here. Even a gilded cage is still a cage."

"I felt much the same as you do when Gus first claimed me. I chafed at the restrictions. But then one day I did go wandering and I was abducted. I *saw* what my being in peril did to Gus and it wasn't something I ever wanted to see again. He puts my welfare above everything. He will fulfill my slightest whim if I only whisper it into the air."

"But he … he … he treats you like a … a blow-up doll."

Oriel's laughter rang, bouncing off the courtyard walls. "Oh, Corinne, do you not see that I revel in his touch? Gus is a predator, a very sensual predator. He wallows in the chase; he needs it."

"But, don't you find it degrading to have him groping you practically in 'public?'"

"You're very sheltered and, unfortunately, Gus seldom entertains. The fae are a sensual people. They protect their females with a dedication that makes Navy SEALs look like little boys playing at cops and robbers. And when they unleash that sensuality, it's utterly glorious. Fae males are extremely jealous of their mates."

"There's more to a relationship than sex."

"Of course. Gus will do anything to keep me happy. I try not to take undue advantage of that, because I love him and want his happiness. So, we both compromise a bit."

"You compromised everything."

"I gave up a life that really wasn't much to crow about. Once I got over myself and realized the depth and strength of Gus' devotion—which I'd done absolutely nothing to earn, by the way—I finally understood the power I have over him. He's likely the most feared male in all the fae realms and some others beyond those. Yet, I've but to pout like a spoiled brat and he'll turn himself inside out to make me smile again."

"He treats you like a pet."

"He treats me like his most precious treasure," Oriel corrected in a matter-of-fact voice. Turning her face toward the sun, she said, "You can't go back, Corinne. Stop wishing for what you will never have and make the best of what you've been given. You'll be glad you did."

Corinne rose from the bench and paced. "Uberon stole my freedom. He took away my rights."

"Yes, yes, you're an American citizen and you have rights," Oriel dismissed the familiar rant. "I've heard it all before. Hell, I've said it all before. You know what? It does no good. Gus will have your letters delivered to reassure your family that you're in good hands and well cared for."

"Well cared for?"

"It's not like we keep you in a cold damp cell and feed you spoiled gruel and stale bread."

Corinne blushed with embarrassment as she smoothed her hands over the fine, smooth fabric of her blue skirt. She pressed her lips against a nasty retort and a bolt of lightning cracked overhead, though no cloud marred the bright blue sky.

"I have magic," she said.

"That's nice," Oriel replied with utter disinterest.

"That doesn't make you nervous? You don't think I'm weird?"

Oriel laughed. "Oh, you're most definitely weird. We all are here. It's rather like the mysterious Isle of Misfits. But your elemental powers aren't the be-all and end-all of power here. I met Calista, the witchbreed mate to Falco, Captain of the High Guard of the eastern fae. They call their country Daimónagi which, loosely translated, means something like land of liquid demons. It sounds dreadful, doesn't it? But she's a lovely female, diffident and kind. And I've met Catriona, who's mated to Thelan, Captain of the Seelie Palace Guard. She's older than you, Calista, or me, but you'd never know it to see her. I heard from Enders that she drove Thelan up a wall until she finally realized there was no going back. Their daughter Daniellisande is mated to Enders. She's totally fun, a good friend."

Corinne listened and said nothing, but something of her incredulity must have shown on her expression.

"But my words don't convince you. I daresay Uberon made a hash of it, didn't explain everything to you, didn't make sure you understood that he had as little choice as you."

"What do you mean he had as little choice as I?"

Oriel held her gaze with a sober expression. "These males give their hearts and souls but once. I've heard that the purest of highborn Seelie Court fae males can bond with two females, but there aren't sufficient females to go around to double us up like that."

"Dear Lord, Uberon isn't planning on sharing me, is he?"

"What have you been reading?" Oriel gasped. "No, he won't share you. Let me tell you a little secret: these males of ours barely get along without killing each other. Only an extremely rigid code of honor enables them to endure the presence of other males. If a male violates that code of honor, he risks his life."

"Sounds like a grim way to live."

"It can be. Males outnumber females by at least half. Many never encounter their mates. Others take mates for whom they feel affection, but don't love and then must live up to the expectations of the mating bond. Those who lose hope sometimes abandon honor and attempt to steal a female. Justice is swift and lethal. Others become reckless and court death through insane courage."

"You make them sound worthy of pity."

"When you think of it, they are. They've built up a culture that practically glorifies death in a blazing spectacle. They hold themselves to impossible standards. They are hard, unforgiving creatures and rely upon us females to soften their bleak existence."

Corinne blinked as she mulled over her hostess' words. Slowly, she said, "You mean women are the civilizing influence here."

"That's close enough," Oriel approved. "Try to give Uberon the benefit of the doubt. He'd not have done what he did if he weren't compelled by the mating bond."

"He stalked me," Corinne murmured.

"He what?"

"He stalked me. I knew he—well, not him, precisely, but someone—was following me for days before he finally introduced himself to me. Then he stayed with me, but hardly spoke a word."

"He stayed with you?"

"Yeah. It was strange. He shadowed me like a bodyguard, helped around the cabin."

Corinne's eyes boggled. "He showed tremendous self-control. Amazing."

"Self-control?"

She shook her head. "Gus took one look at me, determined I was his fated mate, knocked me out, and brought me here. It took all of about fifteen seconds, I think. And you got days. Wow."

Corinne realized her jaw had dropped and closed it with an audible click of teeth. "You mean he saw you and took you and that was that?"

"Well, I did give him hell after I'd stopped being terrified of him."

"I should hope so."

Oriel chuckled. "I still give him hell every so often, just to remind him I can. The make-up sex is phenomenal."

Corinne squeezed her eyes shut. "Too much information, Oriel."

Her hostess patted her on the arm, then rose with the unread book still clutched in her hand. "Think on what we've discussed. If you're going to attain any level of contentment here, you must first accept what is. You're fae now and we're immortal. Eternity's a long, long time to be bitter and resentful."

Corinne nodded and watched Oriel glide toward the tall gate that separated the lily garden from the rest of the castle grounds. She picked up her book again and sat back down on the bench. She opened the book, but could not concentrate on the printed page. She looked around, taking in the beautiful flowers in their colorful profusion and the serene ponds with their sturdy pads topped by flowers emitting spicy fragrances. Bees and hummingbirds hovered over the blossoms. Butterflies fluttered their colorful wings as they hopped between plants in no discernible pattern. Overhead, a bird sang its trilling song from wherever it perched amid the petal-shedding tree.

It was a lovely cage, but a cage just the same.

She could not help but wonder whether Uberon would allow her more freedom and then cringed at the concept of being allowed anything.

"I am independent," she whispered. "I am a thinking, rational person and not a prized pet to be kept on a leash."

But the words did not sound so strident aloud as they did in her mind.

Corinne closed the book and set it down in her lap again. Had it really been only the night before she'd met the black and white unicorns in the heart of the Great Forest? What had Gus called it? Oh, yes, the Deepwood.

Separating the two syllables into their discrete words made her flush as a rush of lust surged through her body. Deep. Oh, how wonderful Uberon had felt when he'd sank so deeply inside her body! Wood. The memory of that massive erection sparked another shiver of desire.

"You have a dirty mind," she chided herself.

But that didn't quell her memory of the fiery passion he'd shown her, nor stop her from remembering the intense pleasure of it.

"I lived without it for most of my life. It's no big deal to do so again."

As though the reignition of her magic also lit the coals of her libido, she could not help but recall every touch, every kiss, every murmured word of praise and beauty. She felt her breasts grow full and heavy, the nipples tightening and pressing visibly against the cloth of her bodice. She felt her belly flutter and zings of pleasure streak down her thighs, which quivered with each bolt of sexy electricity. Heat pooled, as did moisture. She took a deep breath in yet one more effort to calm her flesh and caught the scent of her arousal, musky and rich.

I need you. The plea formed and broadcast before she could stop it. The aching honesty of it deepened her flush.

Do you accept me? came the reply, straight into her mind. It startled her.

Corinne examined the nuances of that response before answering. She felt the promise of it, the bone-deep devotion. Could she accept the same sacrifice as Oriel in exchange for undeniable pleasure and protection?

I won't be kept in a cage.

She felt more than heard a low dark chuckle of triumph and knew he thought he'd won.

You'll have as much freedom as I can allow.

Not good enough. No one tells me where or when I come and go. No one tells me with whom I may associate or not. No one treats me like a pampered dog.

You will accept my guidance.

But I make the decision whether to follow that guidance.

I require your obedience.

No. She caught herself before responding with something blatantly rude and offensive, like "Go fuck yourself" or "Over my dead body."

Apparently, though, he caught the stifled rudeness and took offense anyway. *I will command you.*

Command all you want. I never promised obedience. I'm not your fucking submissive.

His dark chuckle rippled through her mind, dashing away those hazy imaginings of a spanking bench and St. Andrew's cross.

Giving you pain is not my intention.

Good thing, because I'm not willing to do anything like that. It's degrading.

A sudden sensation of fullness made her gasp and look down.

Beneath the tranquil fabric of her skirt, her thighs quivered, but nothing visible accounted for the delicious feeling of something long and hard moving slowly in her body. She moaned and tilted her hips.

I give you pleasure, my sweet. And you will receive me with joy.

Her body tightened, nearly ready to melt beneath the heat of an orgasm, but then the invisible cock vanished as though it had never been and left her aching and yearning for release.

I return tonight. Beg me and I will fill you.

"That was a dirty trick," she muttered and squirmed on the bench.

You are mine and I am yours. Any male who touches you will die at my hand.

You're a frickin' caveman.

Actually, he was older—far older—than any cave man, but he saw no need to belabor that point. He needed her to accept him. She'd not release her soul into his keeping otherwise, which left them both vulnerable.

I have prepared our castle, carved of my own demesne where you may roam freely, and staffed for your every comfort. You have only to accept me and all that entails.

And just how big is this demesne?

You'll never see walls barring your passage.

No walls, she thought. That sounded promising. She turned over his words. He'd once vowed never to lie to her. "You'll never see walls" did not mean the absence of walls, she finally reasoned. Fencing, she concluded. He'd probably erected prison fencing topped by razor wire around his estate.

I'll not confine you by such crude means. No fence will bar your passage.

She analyzed his words, his tone, and detected no falsehood. She felt the delicious swipe of his phantom thumbs over her sensitive breasts. Of course, nothing showed beyond her physical reaction.

"You don't play fair."

That dark, triumphant chuckle filled her mind again. Corinne shivered, though the air inside the walled garden was warm.

CHAPTER 9

Corinne, Oriel, and the Erlking had just sat down to supper when Uberon strode into the vast dining hall. His long black cloak unfurled behind him as though directed by computer generated imaging for best dramatic effect. His leather boots made no sound on the stone floor. His unbound hair flared behind him with as much drama as his cloak. Watching his approach, Corinne's breath caught in her throat. She blinked. She'd forgotten he was so insanely handsome.

Then she gasped. As though in recognition of her soul-bonded mate, the tattoo of silver and gemstones in her skin suddenly flared with intense heat. A flicker of pain flashed across Uberon's fierce expression as recognition and magic raced through the coordinating silver and jewels embedded in his hide.

"Sit and dine," the Erlking invited, gesturing grandly with one hand and setting the heavy palm of his other on the delicate slope of Oriel's shoulder.

"My thanks," Uberon replied and took a seat next to Corinne. A servant rushed with a basin of water and towel. The mighty fae made quick use of them. "It's been a long and arduous journey."

Trying to be unobtrusive, Corinne inhaled. She frowned. Although he appeared not to have refreshed himself from at least a day's hard travel, he certainly did not smell dirty or sweaty. He smelled of pine and moss and fresh air. How odd. The sidelong glance he gave her indicated without words that he knew what she did … and that it amused him.

Her body, of course, responded to his proximity and his scent with embarrassing clarity. She squirmed, just a little, and blushed at Oriel's sly grin. She should have known that nothing she did would miss the uncanny awareness these people had.

Oriel clapped her hands and servants leaped into action, filling plates and goblets. Corinne glanced at Uberon who appeared to focus on his food and the conversation held with Gus, a conversation she missed because she'd allowed herself to be distracted.

Uberon's hand on her thigh. Stroking. Squeezing. Moving slowly, inevitably upward. She took a hurried sip of water and glanced at Oriel, whose focus had also turned inward. No doubt because Gus was fondling her beneath the table. He seemed to do that a lot. And she seemed to enjoy it.

Distracted and unable to keep track of time, Corinne looked up with dazed eyes at the invisible pulse that suddenly filled the air. Her eyes widened with realization when her gaze landed upon the flushed expression of satisfaction that curled her hostess' lips. Suddenly, Corinne wanted that same satiated smile for herself. Envy sprouted and grew, and she decided that what was good for the gander was also good for the goose. She reached down and grasped the hard muscle on top of Uberon's long thigh and squeezed.

"You play with fire, beloved."

She opened the palm of her other hand and a flame sputtered into existence and danced on the bare skin. "That's fire. Remember?"

She moved the hand beneath the table to the long, thick ridge of his arousal and stroked.

"Out," Uberon barked.

Ordered from his own dining hall, the Erlking laughed and hoisted his mate over his shoulder. With a light smack on her posterior, he strode from the room as the servants disappeared. Before the doors had shut, Corinne found herself bent over the table with her skirts tossed over her hips.

Bending low over his mate, Uberon growled into her ear, "Will you receive me?"

Gulping, she nodded and wriggled her hips.

He ground his groin against her, the rub of fabric rough against her heated skin. "I need your words."

"Yes," she gasped.

Somehow in that brief second, he'd managed to free himself from the confines of his trousers. He plunged inside her before the hiss of her acceptance faded into the air. Corinne squealed at the sudden invasion and then moaned as he started thrusting. He grasped one of her hands and drew it forward, then reached to do the same to the other. He held both in his grip as his other hand clamped over her bare hip to hold her right where he wanted her as he rocked in and out of her body. She mewled at the slap of his scrotum against her sensitive, swollen clitoris. With a growl, he pressed even more deeply into her, his cock rubbing against that internal bundle of nerves that intensified the pleasure. The hand at her hip loosened and slid around to strum her clit like a master guitarist with his favorite instrument. Corinne keened, the sound high and thin as she contracted around him and under him.

As climax crashed through his mate's body, the silver chased into her skin and the black diamonds flared with arcane brilliance. His lips peeled back with savage satisfaction at the sight as he continued to pound into her and drive her back to orgasm with ruthless determination.

"You're mine," he growled in the High Tongue of his distant youth. "Only mine. Always mine."

His nostrils flared as he took in the scent of her hot passion spilling over his cock and then running down her legs. He reveled in the fragrance of the sweet, sweet sweat that misted her flushed skin. He ground himself as deeply inside her as he could go, relishing the stranglehold of the hot, wet silk of her inner passage and the incoherent cries of pleasure she could not stifle. Soon, too soon, he burned with the need for release.

"Who owns you?" he snarled into her ear as his hips beat a rapid tattoo against the pliant flesh of her ass.

"Uberon!" she wailed as he pinched her clitoris and sent her soaring into dark brilliance. The clutch and ripple of her body cracked his steely control and he shattered, too, erupting in a fiery flash of burning black diamonds and glowing silver.

Corinne sagged, every muscle melted into useless goo. A whimper slid from her throat even as her mate slid from her body. She lay bent over the table in a postcoital daze that permitted neither organized thought or coordinated movement as Uberon stroked her backside, his fingers slipping through the wet folds of her sex and causing her to shudder helplessly at the sensation. She felt him lean over her, saw the shadow of his body before feeling the featherlight stroke of his fingertips along the back of her neck.

"Can you stand?" he whispered as his fingers toyed with the fine hairs at her nape.

"I don't think so," she groaned.

"No matter, beloved." His soft, satisfied chuckle gusted past her ear as she felt her skirts being drawn back over her hips and backside. "I can carry you."

With an ease that Corinne really didn't want to contemplate, he turned her over and cradled her against his broad chest. She felt the edge of a leather strap and realized that he still wore his cloak. Of course, she still wore her dress. And slippers.

Her head lolled against his shoulder as he covered the distance from the dining hall to her room with strong, sure steps.

"Never doubt me," he commanded. "I am yours as much as you are mine."

"You abandoned me," she muttered.

"Augustus agreed to your care while I secured our new home," he explained, an odd gesture for one who had not needed to explain himself in too many millennia to contemplate.

"So, that's his name, Augustus," Corinne murmured.

"That's one of his names," Uberon corrected.

"What are your other names?"

His lips curled in a small smile, because his clever mate immediately made the connection. "It has been so long that none except the Erlking and the archivist remember my family names. They only know Uberon and that is all you need to know."

She sighed, deciding not to pick that fight. She also decided there was no way she was going to call him something like "master" or "your Majesty."

"Nor would I demand it of you," he said, catching her thoughts. "You are mine to serve, mine to honor, mine to cherish."

The old-fashioned sentiment of his words warmed her heart.

"Mine to fuck."

The crude words sent a thrill of pleasure through her body. Her nipples peaked and her core heated. Embarrassed by her body's blatant reaction to the male's overwhelming sexuality, Corinne buried her face against his shoulder.

"Ready a bath," the Unseelie king ordered in a crisp voice as he crossed the threshold of his mate's chamber.

"Aye, your Majesty," came Luthhir's piping reply. "Shall I lay out a gown for later?"

"She won't need it," Uberon answered as he settled his mate onto the bed. "We leave in the morning."

"What?" Corinne gasped in surprise. "But you just got back!"

"And I have carved a new kingdom from the Quol. I must return to defend it."

"The Quol? A new kingdom?"

"The Quol?" Luthhir gasped. "Surely, the Quol is too dangerous for Lady Corinne?"

Uberon sent a hard glare toward the halfling who quailed beneath the fulminating glint of power. "Do you doubt my ability to protect my mate?"

"Of course not," the halfling replied with haste. "You are, of course, the Unseelie king."

Uberon's lips drew back from his sharp teeth as he corrected, "No longer the Unseelie king, but the Quoliálfur king."

"The Quoli are uncivilized," Luthhir protested in a weak tone.

"And I have recruited a sizeable population from among the former Unseelie Court as well as some Daimónagi who decided not to stay after the fall of its fortress." His smile sharpened. "I've rock trolls, djinni, pixies, and dwarves pledging their fealty to me, even a few intrepid humans, witchbreed, and gargoyles."

"Did you get angels and mermaids, too?"

"No, but I have allied with a tribe of vodnicci. In exchange for clearing their waters of Quoli intrusion, they will swear fealty to me."

"What do you offer them that no one else does?" Corinne whispered in awe, for in her weeks of intense study, no fae history had shown any ruler able to ally multiple races. The Daimónio Refstófae came close.

"Opportunity," Uberon replied succinctly. "I allow them to make their own fates without regard to ancestry and they will serve me. They will fight and even die for me."

Corinne blinked, realizing that the concept of social and economic mobility remained foreign to most of the fae and human realms in this strange world. She also noticed that Uberon made no mention whatsoever of democracy or voting. She pressed her lips together so as not to question him in front of Luthhir. Already she understood that doing so caused offense and offered insult.

"The bath is ready, my lord."

"Good. Leave us."

"Aye, my lord. I shall bring a tray shortly."

"Leave it over there," Uberon ordered with a curt flick of his fingers.

The halfling servant nodded and departed as the former Unseelie king turned his intense focus upon his mate. He blinked and her clothes vanished in a wisp of smoke.

"In the water with you," he said as he shrugged off his clothing.

Corinne's eyes narrowed, but she said nothing. His expression said more clearly than words that he would override any objection—with brute force if he deemed it necessary. With a spark of defiance, she put an extra swing in her sway as she walked to the anteroom where Luthhir had filled the tub with hot water. As she sank into the steaming depths, Uberon suddenly manifested under her, gripping her thighs and guiding her downward progress so that she impaled herself on his erection. She yelped as he filled her and brought up his knees to spread her legs wide open and force her to lean back against his chest.

She opened her mouth, but no sound came out as he lathered a washcloth and gently scrubbed her skin as though they merely shared the water and he was not buried deeply inside her body. His cock moved within her with the bodily shifting necessary to bathe until she began to writhe around his pulsing flesh. She gasped when he lifted her off and turned her around so they slid against each other, chest to chest while he washed her back and his chest. He tasted her skin as he bathed her, the washcloth following open-mouthed kisses and sumptuous strokes of his tongue. He pinched and rolled her nipples, soothing the tender peaks with the wet warmth of the freshly soaked washcloth. He held her when she convulsed in his arms. The hard muscles of his legs bulged as he rose to his feet and stepped from the tub with his mate cradled against him.

Corinne lay limp and helpless on a thick bath mat as he patted her skin dry with a soft, fluffy towel and keened when he showed her how well he multitasked, running the towel over his own skin as he feasted upon her sex until she convulsed again in unbearable pleasure.

Uberon carried his mate to the bed as waves of pleasure shuddered through her body. A quick glance informed him that the halfling servant had delivered a tray as promised. He wondered for a brief moment if the halfling would consider leaving the Erlking's employ to serve Corinne in his recently established kingdom. The thought dissolved as he lay his mate on the bed and climbed between her legs to ensure that he imprinted himself upon her body, mind, and soul throughout the long night.

Corinne felt like a gibbering idiot when her eyes opened to the golden light of midmorning. She groaned, every muscle sore and the flesh between her thighs swollen and tender. She felt well-used and the thought of that use teased a satisfied smile from her mouth.

"A bath awaits you, my lady," Luthhir announced, pulling a dress from the wardrobe that looked sturdier than anything she'd worn since arriving in the Erlking's demesne.

"Thank you," she murmured drawing on a wrapper. Her lips felt numb and clumsy, her tongue thick, her mouth dry.

"I set a mug of tea beside the tub, my lady."

"Marry me," she murmured with utmost gratitude.

Luthhir shook his head and grinned as she hobbled past on wobbly legs and unsteady feet. Really, the female said the oddest things, but he found charm in her strange phrases and quaint mannerisms. He glanced at her again and thought that the newly self-appointed Quoliálfur king showed true inspiration, endurance, and skill. The lady's cries of pleasure had rung throughout that wing of the castle until nearly dawn.

He did not doubt that her untried flesh ached.

Nor did he doubt that she'd soon enjoy a repeat of the previous night's passion.

And enjoy it she would.

None doubted fae sexual prowess, especially in the elder of their kind. In his centuries of service to the Erlking, Luthhir had witnessed more than one foolish human woman throw herself at a fae male in search of fabled pleasure. "Elfshot" the humans called it when one of their females tasted fae passion and eschewed their own kind ever more.

Stupid humans. Did they not realize that fae males did not take fragile humans to mate?

Luthhir snorted and ignored the evidence of his master's mate. Lady Oriel had long since relinquished what was left of her humanity; she was all fae now and a lovely one at that with hair the rich color of fertile loam and eyes the deep, warm, golden brown of amber. He had to admit that he liked the variety in coloring these former humans brought to the fae. Why, it was said the moon-born had eyes like amethysts.

He rather liked the jade green eyes of Lady Corinne, softer than emerald, gleaming instead of sparkling.

When he deemed the lady had soaked long enough, he knocked on the door and called, "The Erlking and Lady Oriel request your presence in the breakfast room."

He heard a splash and a heavy sigh, then her response, "I'll be out in a few minutes. If Uberon comes up to fetch me, tell him to cool his jets."

Luthhir did not know what jets were, but he did know he'd utter no such impertinence to the formidable ancient. Instead, he busied himself with the finishing touches on packing the lady's belongings.

In good time, Corinne emerged pink and moist and a little less stiff.

"I haven't seen this dress before," she remarked as she pulled on a comfortable cotton chemise.

"Lord Uberon ordered it. You need something sturdy for travel."

Corinne looked at the hem of the dress, which ended a few inches above her ankles. The short length would make walking easier than a hem that dragged the ground. Cleaner, too.

Luthhir placed a narrow roll of fabric on the bed and pointed toward a pair of boots. "Stockings, my lady, to prevent chafing. The garter belt is is to your left."

"Oh." Since she hadn't worn socks since arriving in the Erlking's lands—and she'd never worn actual stockings, only pantyhose—she paused and examined the garments for a moment in curiosity. Corinne unrolled one of the stockings and struggled for a moment to get the seam running straight up the back of her leg. She pulled up the garter belt and then turned and twisted to tie the garters, muttering, "I never thought I'd miss pantyhose."

Hoisting the hem of her skirt and chemise over her knees, she bent down to pull on the new boots. She inhaled with relief at the soft brown leather that surrounded her feet, ankles, and calves. The boots fit perfectly without pinching. Standing, she bounced on her toes and decided the soles were thick enough to protect her feet, but not so thick or stiff as to make walking a chore.

"Will I do?"

"Allow me to confine your hair, my lady."

"Of course," she replied and sat still while Luthhir's deft fingers smoothed her hair and wove it into a complicated braid threaded through with olive green and dull gold ribbons that matched her dress and the cloak she suddenly noticed was draped over the chair. When had that appeared?

"There are gloves in the pockets of your cloak," the halfling said as he gave her hair a final pat. "Join your mate. I'll convey your pack to the front entry."

What pack? The question remained unvoiced.

Acting on impulse and affection, Corinne twirled around and wrapped her arms around the startled servant. "Thank you for all you've done, Luthhir. I'll miss you."

The halfling stiffened in her embrace, then relaxed and returned her hug with awkward affection. "It's been a pleasure to serve you, my lady. I shall miss you, too."

She startled him further by kissing his smooth cheek before releasing him to join her mate and their hosts.

Conversation in the breakfast room stopped when Corinne entered.

"Good morning, my dear," Oriel greeted with a smile of affection. "It's a lovely day to begin a journey."

"Hello," Corinne greeted as Uberon rose from his chair and joined her at the door. He wrapped an arm around her shoulders and pulled her to him for a carnal, spine-tingling, toe-curling kiss. She panted when he broke the passionate connection and did not protest when he led her to a chair. She sat and blinked as he filled a plate for her and set it in front of her.

"You play dirty," she muttered when her mind started working again.

"Shall I bend you over the table before we leave?" he murmured back.

"Uberon!" she squeaked and blushed.

He chuckled. "Eat, beloved. We've a long way to travel."

"Since you've commanded the loyalty of some of the Daimónio Refstófae, will you fly?" the Erlking inquired.

"No. None of the highborn accepted my offer. Why should they? They have no lack of power or opportunity."

"Then you're stuck with low caste fae."

"The low caste fae followed me to the Unseelie Court," Uberon reminded him. "We held a kingdom that generations of Seelie kings could not conquer until that damned Enders and the moon-born joined forces."

"Your son had a good deal to do with that."

"Marog. He grew prideful and entitled."

"Your son?" Corinne echoed. "You said he died."

"Aye, he died of his own hubris."

"A mountain fell on him," the Erlking explained. He shook his head. "Don't let Enders into your new fortress. Every time a mountain falls, he's involved."

"Fortress?" Corrine's faint echo rose high as she thought of the centuries it took to build the great cathedrals of Europe. The Unseeling Court had fallen less than five hundred years ago, if her reckoning of recent fae history was accurate. "How could you have had time to build a fortress?"

"I called to the mountain and its spirit acquiesced."

She blinked, not understanding and not entirely sure she ought to ask for an explanation that she doubted she would understand. Oriel made a comment Corrine did not catch, so she focused on her breakfast while the conversation washed over her.

She'd get answers later.

The sun sat high in the sky when she took her last look at the Erlking's castle. Uberon hoisted her into the saddle of a tall, well-built horse with a pale golden hide that shimmered like pearl.

"It looks like an Akhal Teke," she commented as Uberon swung into the saddle of an even taller, fiery bay. The bay shook its black mane and stomped one heavy hoof.

"Not even close," he replied.

Corinne looked back at Oriel and Gus and waved, having already thanked them for their gracious hospitality before Uberon grabbed her hand and led her outside. She looked back at Uberon and nodded, blinking away sudden tears. She'd miss them.

The bay leaped forward and Corinne's palfrey followed with smooth, fleet strides. She quickly settled into the horse's rhythm and turned her face toward the sun for a long moment before gazing at the new world around her.

She rather thought it looked like Switzerland—not that she'd ever been there—but with warmer temperatures. Touches of red, gold, and purple testified to the onset of autumn. The sharp scent of pine blew down on cool alpine breezes to fill her lungs with exhilaration.

"It's beautiful here," she exclaimed.

"Aye, Gus wrought well."

She closed her mouth and pondered the implications of that short statement. Looking around some more, she thought she ... oh, no, she did recognize that bent tree trunk.

"I've been here before."

"Aye, Gus informed me. I'll have to speak to the swifts about that."

"They didn't harm me."

"No, but they could have. They were careless with you."

Another thought struck her. "You seem to be about the only one who doesn't hold them in deepest respect or even fear."

Uberon's dark chuckle didn't reassure her. "I know them too well."

That was probably another answer she didn't want.

"From what I've heard, those unicorns are like gods."

"Aye."

"And your lack of fear implies you're as powerful as they."

He neither confirmed nor denied that supposition.

"If so, then you're practically a god, too," Corinne concluded as each word dripped off her tongue.

"So long as you worship none but me with your body, I will be your god," he said.

Her eyes narrowed. "You realize that's blasphemous."

He shrugged. He did not believe as she did, but neither would he dismiss her faith. She would cling to it or relinquish it as she needed. "You will find no churches, temples, mosques, or synagogues in fae lands, although you may find shrines to honor ancestors and powerful spirits."

She nodded and wondered if a request to build a shrine or even a small chapel would be amiss. After all, if he could build a fortress from a mountain in mere months, then surely he could build a personal chapel in which she could pray. She put the idea in the back of her mind for later attention.

They rode, mostly in companionable silence. The fae horses stepped lightly over brick roads and dirt paths, across grassy meadows and through dappled forests. Beneath the towering canopy of deciduous and coniferous trees, even the call of birds seemed muted and hushed. Corinne's breath caught in her chest when she saw the white flash of a deer's tail and the white and brown striped hide of something large and graceful flitting through the brush. Shadowy movement accompanied by the mottled hide of a leopard caught her eye and she urged her mount closer to Uberon's.

"Uh, Uberon?"

"I see it, beloved. It recognizes me and will not attack."

"It *recognizes* you?"

"Aye. Beasts sense power and have intelligence enough not to confront it."

"I hear a subtle condemnation for humans in that statement, don't I?"

He said nothing, which served as sufficient confirmation as far as Corinne was concerned.

"I thought so."

"I killed a man who would have preyed upon you," he then said. "No bear, no lynx, no badger in your state park approached you, but a man with evil in his mind and heart ignored your power. He laid his trap and reveled in his plan to hurt you."

"I would have protected myself."

"Perhaps, if you were conscious when he took your body."

"What do you mean?"

"He intended to drug you, rape you, perhaps kill you. He did not see your power, only your beauty and his obsession."

"So, you killed him."

"Aye. Even if he had not targeted you, I would have killed him for the evil he visited upon other women, even young girls."

Corinne shivered with dread. How could she not have known evil stalked her? She'd known for days that Uberon stalked her. She wanted to ask how such a predator could have escaped law enforcement, but knew that very clever criminals could do just that and did more frequently than anyone wanted to consider. She remembered writing a blog article on famous unsolved murders and knew that many other, not-so-famous crimes remained unsolved.

"Do not fret, beloved. I protected you then, I shall protect you forever more."

She believed him and wondered if her special talents, which seemed so amazing back home, amounted to little more than party tricks among the fae.

They stopped for the night at an inn that reminded Corinne of a medieval bed and breakfast, if folks in the Middle Ages had such things. The innkeeper and his wife—mate?—greeted them with wary respect and prompt service.

"My boy will take good care of your fine horses, my lord," the innkeeper promised as an adolescent boy loped toward them to take the reins.

Corinne's knees buckled as she slid from the saddle.

"I've got you," Uberon said softly as he caught her about the waist and held her close. He directed his silver gaze toward the innkeeper who flinched. "A moment, good sir, while my mate gathers her strength."

The man—no, *male*—bowed, his white hair falling forward to reveal the pointed tips of his long ears. Corinne blinked, then realized the open collar of his shirt revealed a thin band of copper engraved into the skin around his throat. She glanced at the innkeeper's mate and saw the female wore a matching collar.

"Seelie fae, lower House," Uberon murmured into her ear. "A mated pair with the blessing of children."

Her gloved finger tips touched the silver and black diamonds peeking from the collar of her cloak.

"Aye, they know us for highborn, though they do not yet suspect who I am."

"And if they did?" Corinne asked, not entirely sure she wanted to know the answer to that question either.

"They'd fear for their lives," he answered in a flat tone.

Corinne felt a moment's sympathy for her mate whom nearly everyone feared, whether he deserved their terror or not.

"Do not pity me, beloved. I am not kind and seldom merciful."

She sighed and held her tongue because she did not know what to say.

"Can you stand now?"

His arm around her loosened and Corinne's legs held steady.

"Yes, I think so."

"Good." Uberon again looked at the innkeeper who turned pale under the former Unseelie king's icy regard.

"You ... you are Unseelie," the innkeeper's mate stammered, her hand rising to her throat.

"No longer Unseelie," Uberon said. "My mate and I journey to a new home."

The innkeeper glanced at the direction from which they had come. "You do not appear Daimónio Refstófae and the Erlking permits no highborn fae permanent residence in his territory."

"Do you serve me willingly or not?" Uberon asked, his voice low and menacing.

The innkeeper's mate pressed her lips together in a thin line of fearful disapproval and she tugged on the innkeeper's sleeve in silent plea to say nothing more that might give offense. But the male drew himself to his full height and summoned his courage.

"Vow you visit no ill upon us and I shall serve you willingly."

Uberon nodded once. "I intend no ill toward you or yours. I merely seek a good meal and a good night's rest for myself and my mate. Visit no malice upon me or mine and your safety and well-being are guaranteed until I depart."

"Welcome, my lord."

The innkeeper bowed and his mate curtsied before leading them into their home. Uberon ordered a hot bath to be followed by a hot meal as their hosts' son carried up their saddlebags. Corinne bit her tongue against a groan of discomfort as she climbed a tall flight of stairs to the chamber assigned to them. Uberon murmured that he would give her a moment of privacy while he set wards to ensure the inn's protection. She nodded, looked around the room, and sniffed. Other than the lingering odor of wood smoke, the place smelled clean. She glanced at the bed and decided to take no chances.

Corinne flattened her palm against the mattress and released a cascade of electric pulses to zap any vermin living within the straw ticking or the bed linens. The chamber door opened to admit the boy with three more young males who carried in a wooden tub. For a moment she wondered why a wooden tub, then shook her head at herself. The fae avoided iron. They wouldn't subject their delicate skin to the caustic burn of a steel tub.

The boys each bowed to her before slipping away on booted feet to soon return with buckets filled with steaming water. In steady succession they filled the tub until the last boy brought up an armful of folded towels and a cake of soap.

"Summon us when you are ready and we'll remove the bath, my lady," the oldest boy said before they all tromped from the room to give her privacy.

Corinne rummaged through the saddlebags that had hung from her palfrey's saddle and pulled out a lightweight wrapper. Setting it close to the tub, she stripped and got into the water. The polished surface of the wood offered no splinters, so she relaxed. After a few minutes, she washed, then stood to rinse her body from a bucket of cool water that made her gasp as its tepid contents contrasted with the luxurious warmth of the water in the tub. She made use of a towel and got to work washing her hair.

"My lady? I have a tray for you," the innkeeper's mate called through the door as Corinne rubbed her wet hair with a towel.

"Come on in and thank you," Corinne replied as she tied the belt on the wrapper to make sure she remained modestly attired.

The female entered, bearing a large wooden tray which she set down on a small table next to the hearth.

"Have you seen my husband?" Corinne asked.

The female's delicate eyebrows flew upward at the human term. "Ah, he's in the common room, my lady."

"Swilling beer, no doubt," Corinne muttered and imagined he'd insist upon his marital rights after having enjoyed himself in the common room while she remained alone and hidden from all but the briefest of personal interaction. She much preferred solitude when self-imposed. And her body ached, too, from the previous night's passion and the day's long ride.

"Enjoying a tankard," the female corrected in a prim tone.

"We produce a fine ale here."

Corinne sighed and bit back an apology. "Please have a fresh bath brought up here for him and let him know. Thank you."

"Aye, my lady."

The innkeeper's mate left. The four young males returned, emptied the tub, and refilled it with fresh water while Corinne ate her dinner. She moved to the narrow balcony and took a seat as Uberon entered the room to avail himself of the bath his mate ordered for him. He looked through the glass-paned doors at her and watched for a moment as she gazed over the unfamiliar terrain. His sweeping gaze did not miss the stiff set of her shoulders and the way she refused to look back at him. He wondered at her apparent ire as he stripped his clothes and sank into the hot water with a sigh. He decided to leave her to the privacy of her thoughts for the next little while.

When he finished his bath, he opened the balcony door and beckoned her to come back indoors. She obeyed, but he could see reluctance in every movement.

"Lie down, beloved."

Her mouth thinned, but she obeyed, knowing she had not the brute strength to defy him. He let the towel wrapped around his hips fall and climbed into bed with her. She lay stiff and unyielding within his embrace as he molded his body around hers and pressed the hard ridge of his erection against her bottom. Despite his vast power, he was merely male and subject to the physical reactions of masculinity.

"Sleep, Corinne. Rest." He felt surprise ripple through her, caught the astonishment and relief in her thoughts. Pressing a kiss to the top of her head, he said, "I am not such a brute as to insist upon my rights when you are stiff and sore. Rest and heal, beloved."

She relaxed and he knew he'd guessed correctly the reason for her reluctance.

"It is my duty and honor to care for your well-being," he whispered. "Trust in me."

Exhausted from the day's hard travel and succumbing to the lure of a full belly and a warm bed, Corinne allowed herself to trust in the powerful male who held her in his embrace and sleep without fear or worry. Uberon lay awake for a good long while as he fought his base nature to plunder the warm, pliant flesh of his mate. He could make it good for her, ensure he brought her intense pleasure. However, he knew she ached, that her delicate tissues were sore. She needed time to heal before he took his pleasure from her again.

Her flesh would be healed come morning. Though she was newly fae, she recovered as quickly as any of them.

CHAPTER 10

Heavy warmth rolled through Corinne's body and a long moan slid from her mouth as her eyelids fluttered open. She felt her spine undulate and her hips roll in unconscious demand as her mindless hands clutched at the tangle of long, ebony hair that spilled over her opened thighs. Her lungs heaved a deep breath as another wave of pleasure washed over her.

Uberon looked up from between her legs and wiped the wetness of his own saliva and her juices from his face with the back of one muscled forearm. He smiled a particularly vicious smile and said, "Good morning."

"Ahhh..." was all Corinne could manage, because he surged up her body and sank the hard, eager length of his cock into her even as he captured her mouth with his.

She tasted her passion on his lips and tongue. She felt the slide of his abdomen against her belly and breasts. His thickly muscled thighs wedged hers wide apart to accommodate the surge of his hips as he slid in and out of her body. Perspiration bloomed over her skin, reducing the friction between their bodies.

Lifting his head, Uberon locked her gaze with his and held it as he savored the joy of loving her, taking pride and pleasure in the rosy flush of her skin beneath and around the bejeweled silver of the soul bond adorning her beauty. He bowed his head to nuzzle her neck. Her hands swept over the deep, wide, intricate filigree and black diamonds that graced his own skin. Then her hands skimmed upward and traced the delicate outline of his pointed ears.

"Ah!" he grunted and his hips snapped into hers as the touch zinged straight to his testicles. She moaned and giggled, a breathless sound combined, and fondled his ears again. He bucked helplessly.

"I do believe I found your weakness," she whispered, her words panted in time with each hard thrust. She giggled again and rubbed the sensitive, erogenous zone of his ear tips.

"Beware how you exploit that weakness," he growled and drilled his cock into her, the fast, hard slap of their flesh adding its own urgency as he felt her body tighten around him. He edged a hand between them and his thumb found her clitoris with unerring accuracy. He pressed the bundle of nerves even as she tickled his ears again.

"Corinne!" he shouted as his seed boiled up from tight, heavy balls and filled her in hot, violent spurts even as she cried out his name and bucked helplessly beneath him.

Uberon collapsed on top of his mate and could not find his strength to roll aside even as his hips twitched with the aftershocks of a sudden climax. He exhaled and pressed slow kisses to the juncture of her neck and shoulder as her fingers idly traced mindless patterns on the back of his shoulders.

Finally, she said, "Uberon, you're heavy."

He propped himself on his elbows and grinned at her as she took a deep breath. "You need breakfast. We've a long ride today."

Corinne grimaced at the thought of another day spent in the saddle. "Do we have to?"

He pressed a lingering kiss to her mouth and answered, "Yes. I must secure the safety of my kingdom, else the Quol will reclaim its territory and swallow my subjects."

"I don't understand. Do you mean the Quoli will attack?"

He flexed his hips, driving his semi-aroused cock into her relaxed body. She gasped, then moaned as aftershocks of her recent orgasm sparked, causing the manifested her soul bond to flash. He knew he would never tire of seeing that, of *feeling* that.

"The Quoli attack. They always attack. They are mindless

hunger, insatiable and strong. Mogren, king of the Seelie Court stations the strongest fae Houses at the northern borders of his territory to beat back Quoli encroachment. If they fail, the jungle will spread and the Quoli will decimate the population."

"You speak as if the Quoli and the jungle—the Quol, I presume—are one and the same."

He rolled aside, regretting the necessity of leaving the hot, wet silk of her and promised himself that he would lock her in a bed with him for days at the earliest opportunity. They would mate until both exhausted their energy and perhaps she conceived his baby.

The idea of creating a child made his cock stiffen again.

But now was not the time.

He would better guide another child than he had Marog, he vowed.

"They are intimately connected," he said, ignoring the carnal demand of his cock. "The Quoli do not exist without the Quol and the obverse is also true. The jungle is deadly, teeming with poisonous creatures and carnivorous plants. It has flowers that lure the unwary to sleep and then use their roots to draw them underground where they penetrate the flesh and drink their victims' blood. Trees eject deadly thorns that paralyze and liquefy the victim's flesh and bones which then provide the fertile pot in which its seeds grow. The few animals that reside in the Quol are even deadlier."

"And you're taking me there? That doesn't sound like a good effort at looking after my well being."

"I cleared what territory I wanted and set wards to hold the Quol back from reclaiming that land. My people are establishing their Houses and estates, building a capital city. They cannot defend against the Quoli and establish a civilization at the same time; therefore, I must return with all haste and defend my people."

"But you're one man..."

"Beloved, I am no mere man." He drew her hand to his still-hard cock.

"Well, you're no 'mere' anything by my guess," she retorted in a dry tone, even as her hand wrapped around him and lightly squeezed. Uberon's eyes rolled back and moaned. She squeezed him again and, since he'd put her hand there, stroke the sticky length. Then, because she wanted—at least once—to take the initiative, she crawled over him and put her mouth on him.

"Corinne!" he gasped as his hand cupped her head.

She raised her eyes to meet his heavy-lidded gaze as she sucked the fat tip of his penis into her mouth. His body stiffened as he resisted the compulsion to thrust while she explored him with artless enthusiasm. A new bloom of perspiration turned his skin slick. He twined his fingers in her tangled hair.

"I'm going to come," he warned her, his voice raspy with the effort not to overwhelm her.

She hummed a response. The vibrations wrenched a cry from him as he abandoned control and ejaculated.

Wiping his seed from her face, she murmured though the musky, salty, *wild* taste of him clinging to her tongue, "I need to wash."

Uberon waved a languid hand at the tub which remained in the room because the innkeeper had not wanted to disturb the former Unseelie king's rest. "The water is ready."

"It's cold and dirty," Corinne protested.

"No, it's not. The water is fresh and hot."

Casting him a glance of doubt, she climbed from the bed and padded to the tub where, as he stated, clear, fresh water steamed in readiness.

"How?"

He smiled and said, "One of the benefits of having mated me."

"Vain brute."

"Tease me again and I'll fuck you until you can't stand, much less walk."

The threat—promise?—made her blood stir with excitement, but she knew that additional bedroom activity needed to wait. She climbed into the tub and wasted no time in an indulgent soak. Rising from the bed, Uberon exerted a whisper of will to refresh his body and clothing. He directed a drop of power to his mate's clothing, ensuring she would wear fresh garb.

"I liked the ribbons plaited in your hair yesterday," he said as she sectioned her wet hair into three hanks and began weaving them into a simple braid.

"I have no idea how Luthhir did that, so you'll have to be satisfied with my poor effort."

"Perhaps Luthhir will join us after we've settled into our new home."

"Do you really think he'd leave the Erlking's employ or that the Erlking would allow him to leave?"

"Gus holds none to his service by force. He did that once with the midnight swift and nearly died for the insult."

Corinne realized her mouth gaped open and shut it with an audible click of her teeth. She coughed. "He enslaved the black unicorn?"

"Not for long," Uberon replied with a small smile. "He was much younger then, and frequently stupid and impressed with his own consequence. I helped cure him of that."

"And yet he still speaks to you."

"He eventually realized that I saved his unworthy hide when the swift would have killed him for his offense. The swifts never quite forgave me for interfering."

Questions crowded Corinne's tongue, but she gave voice to no more of them. She had more than enough to think upon. She tied the end of her braid and rose from the stool situated in front of the vanity.

"Let's eat. I'm famished."

Uberon ran the back of one finger down the curve of her cheek in a small, intimate gesture of affection that melted her heart. "Of course, beloved."

She smiled at him and glanced at their belongings strewn about the room. "We'll need to repack before we leave."

"The innkeeper will do that. The horses will be made ready for us when we've finished our breakfast."

"It seems weird that you're accorded so much power, yet you have to ride a horse to get from one place to another. Or walk on your own two feet," she remarked as they walked down the staircase to the common room.

"We all have our limitations," he replied with equanimity and said nothing about Marog's ill-fated capture of the white dragon and the subsequent enmity of all dragons toward his House and lineage. Had his son restrained himself, Uberon might have persuaded a flight of dragons to relocate to his new kingdom.

The boy's foolishness and greed had caused so many problems.

"Why was your kingdom called the Unseelie Court?" Corinne

asked as they seated themselves at a table and waited for their hostess to bring them food and drink.

"Mogren's grandfather, or perhaps great grandfather—I can't remember which—was the Seelie king. We disagreed on a number of key points and I rebelled against his authority. Those who followed me suffered exile with me. We were labeled Unseelie because we were no longer considered Seelie. After a while, the term stuck and I no longer cared."

"Unseelie. Not Seelie," Corinne murmured to herself.

"Exactly."

She lifted her gaze and met his, surprised by the old, lingering pain in those silver depths. "You cannot define something by stating what it is not."

Uberon shrugged, the old arguments and ancient hurts having long since lost their ability to shatter his peace of mind. "The Unseelie Court was broken and is now being absorbed into the Seelie Court, so all who choose to remain will once again be known as Seelie."

"You said some of them agreed to follow you."

"I did. They chafe at the constraints of the Seelie Court."

Corinne tilted her head to one side and said, "That sounds an awful lot like you believe in the unalienable rights of life, liberty, and the pursuit of happiness."

Uberon's eyes widened with surprise and his laughter rang out, utterly startling the innkeeper who never thought to see nor hear, in his lifetime, humor from the normally dour and stern Unseelie king. He wondered whom the deposed king planned to exterminate and hoped his name did not feature in that surely extensive list. The innkeeper kept his gaze averted and continued to wipe down the countertop, ignored by his formidable guest and the Unseelie female.

"Aye, beloved. Not all human constructs deserve fear and loathing."

"Nice to be of service," came the dry retort.

He leaned forward and nuzzled her ear and said, "Remember, beloved, you are no longer human, but fae. And I will take great delight in demonstrating the fae pursuit of happiness tonight."

Corinne could not repress the shiver of thrilled anticipation that tingled throughout her body.

When they finished their meal, the horses waited for them, saddlebags packed as Uberon had promised. Corinne looked at him, raising one finely arched eyebrow. He responded with a sly smile that made the innkeeper clutch at his chest while his other fist clamped around the overpayment of silver coins received for accommodations and meals.

The innkeeper sighed with relief when his customers rode away and hoped he would never see them again. His heart just couldn't take the stress.

"You know you terrified that poor man back there," Corinne commented once they were well beyond earshot.

"I know," Uberon replied. "To most fae, I'm a monster."

"Well, parts of you are monstrous," she teased, feeling strangely at ease with him and reveling in his amused chuckle. "But, despite being rather overbearing, I wouldn't say you're the humanoid equivalent of Godzilla."

He didn't understand the pop culture reference, but got the gist. "I'm no tame pussycat, beloved. I have done and will do horrendous things as I deem necessary."

"What have you done?"

"Read the histories, my dear."

"I have, several of them at least. Oriel insisted I understand your background as much as I was able." She shrugged. "But history's written by the victor. I learned that much in college."

"My love, I *wrote* some of those histories you read."

"No way."

"You still don't believe me to be an ancient as I claim?"

She laughed. "Look at you. You can't be more than your mid-thirties, if even that. Men just—"

"I am no man," he interrupted gently. "Men are human and they live short, brutish lives. I am far more than a man and so are you."

"But—"

"Believe me. If you believe nothing else, believe me fully male, but not a man."

Her cheeks flooded with color, because she fully acknowledged his potent masculinity. She'd not read a book nor listened to another woman's tale that could compare to the overwhelming sense of utter possession when he surrounded her with his body and sheathed his flesh inside hers.

They lapsed into companionable silence, the conversation picking up when either had some observation to make. Accustomed to spending the better portion of her day in contemplative silence, Corinne did not resent the quiet hours. For his part, Uberon appreciated his mate's comfort with silence. Marog's mother had detested silence and filled it with her chatter, a habit that took centuries to learn to accept. He filled the millennia since her death with quiet study and research until coming across a solitary human woman on one of his research expeditions. He'd felt the bolt of recognition and confirmed it with the oracle.

Uberon enjoyed pointing out the significant landmarks they passed and relating their history and importance. He alerted her when a phoenix soared overhead and delighted in her awestruck wonder. He smiled with delight when she caught a wild animal hiding in the grass or brush as they rode.

At night, he took care of his mate as his fae nature compelled him and did not resent her insistence on helping care for the horses and set their campsites. He watched as she relearned to control her augmented powers, enhanced in a world that did not surround her with iron. He allowed her to ignite their campfires and sweep away a rainstorm. He watched without criticism as she manipulated the earth to swallow the sharp, uncomfortable stones that would have disturbed their rest.

Every night he cradled her within the shelter of his body. They sat before the small campfire, her back resting against his chest, while he recited the old tales that likely no one but he, Gus, and Enders remembered. He held her in his arms while they slept after setting wards around their small campsite.

"Do not cross the circle until I release it," he warned her the first night they spent in the open.

She raised an eyebrow and waited for him to explain. He appreciated the quiet inquiry and rewarded her unvoiced curiosity by tossing a pebble over the circle he'd drawn. The pebble flashed, smoked, and disintegrated.

"Got it," she said with a nod and said nothing about being confined or trapped, because she knew he set the wards to protect her. She felt that purity of purpose; Uberon had no intention of doing anything beyond preserving her safety and well-being.

Every night she felt the evidence of his desire press against her, though he restrained himself.

"I am no unthinking animal," he whispered in her ear. "I will not ravage you in the wild like some beast."

Corinne did not know whether to be grateful or regretful for his restrain, for she found herself missing the heady passion of his possession. She decided to be grateful, because she wasn't sure she wanted to get naked with him when she felt grubby from travel, even though Uberon made sure her body and clothing remained fresh and clean. It just wasn't the same as a hot bath and a good scrubbing.

On the ninth day when they crossed the border into the territory encompassed by the Seelie Court, she felt her skin prickle and tingle.

"The Veil," Uberson informed her. "Think of it as the ward guarding the whole of the Seelie Court, rather like the wards I set around our campsites."

"It must take an awful lot of energy to sustain this."

"Every citizen of the Seelie Court contributes a tiny percentage of his energy to its maintenance." He looked around, shrugged, and said nothing about the ward he set to protect his kingdom from the Quol. "Enders set it at the request of the Seelie king after I split from the Seelie Court. He wanted it to repel my re-entry into his lands."

"It didn't work, obviously."

"Not against me. I know Enders and his weaves too well, as he knows me and mine. However, the Veil works well for deterring the invasion of others. Humans cannot cross the Veil without protection."

"What about the vodnicci, trolls, pixies, dwarves, and djinni?"

"Don't forget angels," he quipped. "Anything with fae blood may pass, but their passage is noted. None enters the Seelie Court without the king's awareness."

"Not even you?"

"Especially not I."

Corinne lapsed into silence, content with her thoughts. Eventually, she asked, "When will we have the luxury of a bed, a hot bath, and a meal not cooked over a campfire?"

"Tonight," Uberon replied in his quiet way. His eyes glinted and he raised his chin, directing his piercing gaze into the distance. "Riders come."

Surprised, Corinne peered into the distance and saw ... nothing. "How do you know that?"

"Well developed senses. Keep your mount's shoulder at my horse's hip."

"I'm not helpless, Uberon."

"Then you may have the privilege of saving me should the need arise."

"Hah. I can't imagine you cowering before anyone." *Or anything.*

They continued riding at the same steady pace for a little while longer before Corinne's senses prickled with awareness. She probed as delicately as she could to determine whether the oncoming riders meant good or ill, but she discerned nothing.

A chill swept over her as a shadow passed. She wondered for a second whether a cloud or large bird passed overhead until she looked skyward.

"That's ... that's ..." she stammered, eyes wide and heart racing with fear as the horse she rode danced and jigged with the urge to flee as fast as its hooves could go.

"A dragon," Uberon said in a flat tone. "This may not go well."

The shadow passed over them again. The dragon roared, further frightening the horses. Corinne struggled to keep her mount from bolting.

"That's enough. Land and be civil," Uberon snapped, his voice at a conversational volume, but his tone brooking no defiance.

Corinne maneuvered her horse into position as ordered by her mate and watched the dragon circle overhead. She heard the beat of leathery wings and the hissing breath of the great beast as it landed nearby. Trying to remain unobtrusive, she gathered her power and prepared to release it at an instant's notice.

Uberon drew his mount to a halt and nodded at the dragon and its rider. The Dragon Rider nodded in acknowledgement. The dragon displayed its teeth in obvious threat.

"Can he control that thing?" Corinne whispered, her voice squeaking in barely contained terror.

"Dragons are intelligent creatures. It bonds with its Rider."

Corinne heard the capitalization of the word and realized that "Rider" served as much a title as a description. She continued to examine the legendary lizard standing close enough to roast them if it sneezed. Distracted, she missed the quiet arrival of the riders of whose approach Uberon had warned her.

"Greetings, Captain," Uberon spoke first, his tone cool and calm.

Corinne's head whipped around to take in the tall, beautiful male who sat with easy grace upon a black steed. Thin, pale braids adorned with colored feathers framed his chiseled face. Two more fae sat on their horses to either side of him.

"My lord," the one addressed as Captain acknowledged. "What brings you to the Seelie Court?"

"Just passing through, Captain Thelan. How fares your mate?"

The captain's expression darkened with icy rage. "She is no concern of yours, my lord."

"It's called being polite," Uberon replied with bland insult. "You should try it some time."

With an effort, the captain of the Seelie Palace Guard controlled himself. "You're lucky I didn't claim the Erlking's justice."

"You would have perished had you done so, because I did nothing to harm the moon-born." Uberon needed a moment to master his own emotion. He continued in a calm tone, "And you took your revenge upon my son and my people."

"As was my right."

"My people offered no offense."

"They are Unseelie."

"Since when is the status of being not-Seelie deemed an offense worthy of execution?"

"Uberon, you're picking a fight," Corinne warned in an undertone. "Quit it."

Captain Thelan's eyes widened and he suddenly laughed. "Has the mighty Unseelie king been brought to heel by a female?"

"Don't even go there, you jerk," Corinne growled under her breath.

Captain Thelan raised an eyebrow of palest gold at her comment. He blinked, then laughed again.

"You mated a human."

"As did the Erlking and you. Captain Falco of the Daimónio Refstófae High Guard mated a witchbreed. What of it?"

The Seelie captain shook his head, bemused and not willing

to answer. Instead he returned to his original line of questioning. "What brings you here, my lord?"

"Just passing through."

"No, my lord, I do not believe you. You do nothing without very good reason and passing through is no good reason to trespass upon enemy territory."

"I am not your enemy, Captain. I never was. I am taking my mate to Donshae where we shall catch a ship and depart from Mogren's territory."

"Where do you go from Donshae?"

"Really, Captain, what business is it of yours where I go once I depart? It's enough to know that I intend no harm and have no desire to linger."

"No, it is not enough to know. I insist you tell me your plans."

"Or?"

Thelan jutted his square chin at the seething dragon. "Goji'Rahn really wants to roast you."

Uberon's expression relaxed into a small, supercilious smile. "Do you really think one dragon can overcome me?"

"I'd be interested in finding out."

"Will you two quit it?" Corinne blurted, having lost patience with the veiled and not-so-veiled threats and posturing. "Look, Captain, we're not staying here. We're going home. If traveling through your country is such a crime, then arrest us."

"You've a spitfire there, my lord," Thelan commented with a chuckle.

"I've had just about enough of your condescending attitude," Corinne hissed and raised a hand. Blue fire glowed around her closed fist.

"Very pretty," Thelan said and dismissed her show of power.

Corinne blinked in surprise. The fire flickered out and she lowered her hand, wondering how her display had not impressed him. Had she shown that to anyone back in her old world, that someone would have fled screaming in terror.

"Nevermind him, beloved. He always was an arrogant little prick," Uberon murmured as he reached over to pat her leg.

"Before you two goad each other into a fight that I'll have to stop," one of the two riders interjected with dry annoyance, "King Mogren extends his invitation to meet with him."

Uberon bowed, not a deep bow, but more than a curt nod,

and replied, "Of course, Enders. Run along and tell him my mate and I are happy to accept his most gracious invitation. We'll stay for supper."

The archivist's upper lip curled, but he bit back a sneering retort. Instead he said, "You're determined to give offense, aren't you, Uberon?"

"I get so few opportunities these days to entertain myself," came the deposed Unseelie king's bland reply.

Enders slanted a calculating glance at Corinne and replied, "I'd say you're getting more than ever before."

Corinne's cheeks flamed. Uberon's already pale complexion turned white his expression from supercilious to icy. "You were never my better, Enders. Offend my mate again and I'll skewer you."

"Will you quit goading them?" Corinne whispered, reaching over to pinch Uberon's leg. "You're going to get us killed."

"Anything for you, beloved," he murmured in reply, catching her hand and drawing it to his lips. He kissed the back of her knuckles, all the while keeping his keen gaze on the archivist and the captain, whom he deemed a threat greater than the dragon and its Rider. Releasing her hand, he looked at the captain and said, "Lead the way, my lord. It's been a long while since I spoke with Mogren. How's the boy doing?"

"All grown up now," Thelan replied in a bland tone as he turned his horse around.

The other two riders fell in alongside him. Corinne heard the snap of the dragon's wings and felt the whoosh of air as it launched into the air.

"You really enjoy needling people, don't you?" she hissed at her mate.

"Thelan's so stuffy I can't resist."

"They could have killed us."

"The only one who has a chance of killing us is Enders and he's too concerned with saving everyone to engage in the wholesale destruction a war between us would cause."

"Well, of course he wouldn't risk needless casualties. Who would?"

Uberon speared her with a cool glance, sweeping aside the naive idealism of her youth. "He's not ruthless. I am."

Corinne blinked in confusion. Uberon had only shown her

the softer side of his personality, but this icy stranger who spoke of decimating entire populations frightened her. "Uberon?"

"You are my mate and keeper of my soul, such as it is, and I will always protect you. You hold my heart, too, withered and useless as it may be. But never forget, beloved, what I am." He leaned toward her. "I am darkness manifest, Unseelie."

"Darkness does not mean evil," she insisted with quiet determination.

"Not always," he agreed, but the mild tone did not deceive her. "Do not mistake me for sweetness and light. You are that for me, my salvation if you will."

"Can there be salvation for an immortal?" she flung back at him, stung by his words and apparent rejection.

"We shall see, won't we?"

They followed the archivist, the Captain of the Palace Guard, and another guard to a vast, sprawling palace that put Corinne in mind of a city unto itself. Gazing around her, she saw the dark smudge of a forest stretching along the eastern horizon and wondered if that forest were part of the Great Forest that touched upon the Erlking's lands.

Yes, it is. It is our forest and it protects the heart of this world, the Deepwood.

She blinked, wondering where that comment came from, because she did not recognize the flavor of the speaker's mental voice inside her brain.

"Welcome to the Seelie Court, my lady," Captain Thelan announced, his voice thrumming with pride.

She could see why. The enormous, sprawling edifice was magnificent, walls of golden stone towering above them, dragons soaring overhead, and the lively sounds of a thriving population spilling over the protective walls surrounding the fae community.

"Their Majesties King Mogren and Queen Cenise await you in the Great Hall."

"We're to be greeted with all due pomp and circumstance, hm?" Corinne muttered, impressed in spite of herself. She looked to Thelan and asked, "Do you think they would allow us the opportunity to refresh ourselves first?"

"No," he replied. "They bid you present yourselves immediately."

She thought that inconsiderate, but held her tongue. Well, if they didn't appreciate travel-stained, hungry, and tired visitors, then they should have allowed them a respite before commanding their presence.

She missed living in a democratic republic.

You will not appear to disadvantage, beloved.

Corinne gave Uberon a grateful smile, although she wasn't quite sure what he was going to do. Perhaps he merely meant to give her courage, meaning that he found her always presentable—which acted as a balm to her doubts.

In due time, their mounts' hooves clattered on paved ground. Tall, elegant residents paused in their activities to watch in haughty silence as the small party rode past. The dragon and its Rider swooped around to land in another area. More uniformed guards dashed forward to take the reins of their horses.

"Your belongings will be taken to the quarters the chatelaine assigns you," Thelan said as a raven-haired female trotted toward them and called out his name.

"The moon-born," Uberon murmured as the petite female launched herself into Thelan's arms and he caught her, his expression brightening with a smile that turned his icy beauty into something warm, dazzling, and altogether too gorgeous for words. Corinne blinked and turned to look at her own mate, whose more roughly hewn features did not blind with sheer masculine perfection. Perhaps his ancient age gave him that gravitas or softened the sharp edges of handsome masculinity, but she found his features less painful to contemplate.

She wondered if it were odd that she found Uberon's dark beauty comfortable, while the brilliant, sharp beauty of the captain of the Seelie Court's Palace Guard practically repelled her.

It's an effect of the soul bond, Uberon explained, mind to mind. *Now take my hand, for I shall not be separated from you until I am assured of your safety and continued good health.*

She wondered if his worry were excessive, but obeyed his simple request. The warmth of his strong hand enveloping hers transferred some good measure of comfort and reassurance. Surely, nothing ill could happen while Uberon held her.

"Follow me, my lord," the other guard beckoned as Thelan allowed his mate to lead him away.

Corinne glanced at the raven-haired beauty, who looked back at her and winked. Eyes wide, she gaped.

"The moon-born is no meek and proper fae female," Uberon said in an undertone as he responded with a grave nod. Catriona might not hold him in any affection, but neither did she blame him for the detestable actions of his son. He found some measure of relief and ease in that, though he would never have admitted it.

"Her eyes ... they're purple," Corinne breathed in amazement.

"Astonishing and lovely, aren't they?" Uberon agreed. "Though I prefer the softness of your jade eyes."

"Swamp muck green," she corrected in a dry tone.

"Jade," he insisted, "without the hard sharpness of emerald and the muddy overtones of swamp muck. They are beautiful, soothing, and magnificent."

His compliments made the breath catch in her throat.

"You are lovely beyond compare," he murmured. "And my opinion is the only one that matters."

Her cheeks flushed a lovely rosy color as she directed her gaze at the scuffed toes of her boots. However, she remembered her father reassuring her mother in much the same way to her mother's eternal gratitude and delight. Perhaps that is what all devoted husbands did.

I am more than a mere husband and you are more than a mere wife.

She nodded, because no mere spouse would pick up her thoughts like that. For the first time, she truly acknowledged the depth and the strength of the soul bond between mates and recognized it as stronger and more enduring than any sacramental vow or legal contract.

"Look up and meet the challenge of their eyes, beloved. You are mated to the Quoliálfur king," he murmured. "You are the Quoliálfur queen now and you shall bow before none."

Since she didn't think that news of a new fae kingdom somewhere far away in this mysterious Quol had spread beyond a mere handful of people, Uberon's admonition failed to reassure her. Corinne gave him a quick smile and tried not to gawk at the uniformity of the people she passed as they walked across the courtyard through a set of massive stone portals intricately carved from stone and so cleverly hung that a child could push them open without straining. She and Uberon followed their guide down a long, wide corridor with guards standing at attention at regular intervals. Caught in looking at their surroundings, she did not hear her mate whisper a greeting in the Old Tongue and did not notice the curl of warm air that slid over them in silent welcome.

"Are there no humans here?" she finally asked, keeping her voice low once she understood the reason for the uniformity of the populace within the magnificent, sprawling palace.

"Humans in the Seelie Court?" Uberon scoffed, keeping his voice low and quiet as well. "Until only a few centuries ago, no humans existed here at all."

She frowned. "What about Catriona and Oriel? And me?"

"They have long since relinquished their humanity; they are fully fae as are you," he said. He took a breath and asked in a suspiciously casual tone, "Have you heard of the Bermuda Triangle?"

"Of course. What about it?"

"There are places where dimensions and worlds rub closely together such that sometimes they overlap."

"You're telling me the Bermuda Triangle is one of those places?"

He nodded. "Such overlapping occurs irregularly and unpredictably and acts as a portal for whatever it catches. For instance in your world, a ship called the *USS Wasp* was lost in 1814 in the Bermuda Triangle. The crew and passengers washed up on the continent's southeastern shores and soon assimilated into the existing population there. Fyrgia and Nymmur arose from survivors of the shipwrecks captured by such portals."

She blinked and wondered if those humans had progressed in terms of art, philosophy, politics, and technology as had Earth.

"No," he answered. "Women on such ships were uncommon, so those who did arrive quickly found themselves in high demand as breeding stock. The prettiest ones commanded the highest prices."

"They *sold* the women?"

"Women were chattel already with little or no rights then; why should landing in new territory change that?" he shot back with cold logic. "Few of those vessels carried books: gold, jewels, porcelain, spices, sugar, but not books."

"But ... but disappearances continued into the twentieth century. What about those people and the more modern ideas they brought with them?"

"They had little impact," Uberon answered. "Perhaps in small pockets of communities, small settlements, you'll find more enlightened attitudes, but I've not come across any. The diversity of cultures is one of the reasons I have enjoyed visiting your old world."

"You probably didn't seek them out either," Corinne grumbled, thinking that he could have at least offered to teach them.

"You're correct," he admitted without remorse. "The humans who landed in this world and developed their own cultures hold the fae in suspicion, if not outright contempt. I saw no reason to seek them out. I tried once; they did not welcome me."

"But, couldn't you have—"

"Forced them? Aye, I could. But I allowed them their choice. Humans so often choose poorly."

"Bide here, my lord, my lady," their guide bade them, coming to a halt for a second before walking through another doorway with tall wooden doors set with gleaming silver panels.

"Ah, the throne room," Uberon murmured.

"I thought we were to be taken to the Great Hall."

"The Great Hall serves as a throne room. This is where their majesties give audience to their subjects."

"So, they're treating us like subjects."

"I admire a clever female."

She scowled at his faint smirk, even though the compliment pleased her.

One of the tall doors swung open slowly as though weighted by millennia of petitioners' expectations. A magnificently garbed major domo stood before them and looked down his long, straight nose.

"How shall I announce you, my lord?"

"Their Majesties, King Uberon and Queen Corinne of the Quoliálfur."

The major domo's pale eyebrows shot upward and disappeared into his hairline. "There is no Queen of the Quoliálfur."

Uberon's smile could have graced a great white shark. "There is now."

The major domo swallowed nervously and rapped his staff twice on the marble floor. The sound reverberated in the enormous space.

"Their Majesties King Uberon and Queen Corinne of the Quoliálfur approach."

"Rest your fingertips atop my forearm," Uberon instructed, holding up his arm, which Corinne abruptly noticed was freshly encased in a black leather vambrace chased in silver. A quick glance at him had her gaping in astonishment, for his chest, shoulders, torso, and back were bare but for the bejeweled silver filigree embedded in his skin. She ran her gaze down where a heavy black leather belt topped a black leather battle kilt. She'd thought Liam Neeson could rock a kilt, but … oh, my!

Corinne placed her fingertips on his forearm and noticed that misty green silk wrapped her arm. Silver lace draped over her wrist and dripped from the cuff. She glanced down and saw not her travel-worn clothes, but an elegant gown finer than anything she had ever worn. With her free hand, she touched the heavy weight that pressed upon her head and realized that her hair had been cleaned and coiled into an elaborate arrangement and topped by a what felt like an intricately fashioned crown. A light current of cool air wafted over her and she realized that most of the silver and black diamonds embedded in her skin were on display.

She returned her gaze to Uberon, his powerful stride propelling him down the length of the Great Hall like an evil fairy king bent on lending the full weight of his influence and lineage to this meeting with the Seelie King. His long black hair hung free, a straight fall of ebony extending nearly to his waist. Two thin, intricate plaits pulled the hair away from his face and descended, caught at intervals with knots of silver. A short-pronged crown graced his head.

When the hell had this happened? How the hell had this happened?

"You bow to no one," he whispered the reminder.

Corinne scrambled to keep up.

"Your Majesty," the obviously tall, elegant, and insanely handsome—were all these people too beautiful for words?—king greeted Uberson with a polite murmur and a cool nod. "What brings you to the Seelie Court?"

"I accompany my queen to our new home," Uberon replied with an answering nod of recognition, one king to another.

"I have not heard of this Quoliálfur."

"It's recently established," Uberon replied. "I have carved out a new kingdom from the Quol and my castle awaits."

"Castle?"

"Aye. This one recognizes me, as well it should since I had a hand in the creation of it. Ask it and it shall confirm that a new castle has emerged from a mountain."

Corinne concentrated on keeping her mouth closed, rather than agape like an imbecile, as the Seelie king spoke in that powerful, fluid language she had sufficient education to know was the Old Tongue, even if she did not understand what he said. The immense edifice rumbled, speech manifesting aloud in the sighing of wind through passageways and the grinding of stone. The Seelie king turned his attention back to Uberon, though his queen's attention never left their royal guests.

"You have spoken no falsehood," King Mogren acknowledged. "What do you intend for what remains of the Unseelie Court?"

"Those who wish to be assimilated into the Seelie Court may remain to subject themselves to your rule. Those who do not have already relocated."

Mogren nodded. "I wondered at the depopulation of the Unseelie Court. This serves as explanation."

"I've had a few centuries to work on it." Uberson shrugged as though stealing away a sizeable population and relocating them to form a new nation carved from a hostile territory were a minor accomplishment.

Corinne blinked. Perhaps for Uberon it was. She blinked again, realizing that "a few centuries" counted as recent to these people.

"And who is this at your side, Uberon?"

Uberon brought his mate's hand to his mouth and lightly kissed the back of her knuckles. Lowering her hand, yet not relinquishing it, he replied, "May I present to you my mate, Corinne?"

She heard whispers of "soul-bonded" from onlookers

scattered throughout the room.

"We wondered how you fared when your first mate passed."

"We were mated, but not soul-bonded," Uberon replied in answer to the unasked and impertinent question. "But I have found my destined mate and I am well pleased with her." He gave her hand a light squeeze. "And I dare hope she is well pleased with me."

Titters of amusement raced around the room. Corinne blushed.

"Unseelie?" the Seelie queen inquired.

"Human," Corinne replied with a slight snarl roughening her voice.

Whispered exclamations of "moon-born" rose in the air.

"Dark moon," Uberon said, the syllables sharp as shattered glass. "Given immortality by *my* power."

Stunned silence met his pronouncement of strength and superior power. Corinne pressed her lips together, more than a little irritated to have been used as the trump card in this pissing contest. She resented being presented as a trophy, a sort of example of Uberon's might and an indirect threat of the power the Seelie Court faced should they cross him.

That wasn't nice or necessary.

It was absolutely necessary, beloved. You are mine in every way and they will now respect that. Otherwise, I would find myself in a war with the Seelie Court for Marog's attempt to usurp the bond between Catriona and Thelan. I could have forcibly stopped it, but did not.

They still blame you for your son's actions? Ludicrous. You cannot be responsible for the actions of someone else. She paused, then snapped, *I am my own.*

His indulgent chuckle in her mind infuriated her. *The moment you accepted my claim, when you received me inside your body, you agreed to become mine in body, soul, heart, and mind. The transformation confers power; it must for the individual's survival. Mogren sees your power and does not like it, especially not bound to me.*

Despite not really understanding the implication of her decision, she knew ignorance gave her no defense. Ignorance did not excuse her, despite any wish otherwise.

Could someone really usurp the soul bond?

Uberon did not answer her unspoken question. She pondered that a moment longer and decided that he wouldn't have mentioned it if it had not been a possibility. She chewed on her lower lip as she imagined—rather easily—him taking on the entire Seelie Court, flashing sword in hand like some sort of uber-Aragorn ... but even more deadly and infinitely sexier.

Really, she had to stop thinking in terms of Hollywood movies and overactive hormones, especially since she was certain she'd never see another movie and she was angry enough to make Uberon sleep on the proverbial sofa for years to come.

Lost in her thoughts, she did not hear the remainder of the conversation and gasped, startled when a cool hand touched hers. She looked up into the brilliant eyes of Queen Cenise.

"Overbearing, aren't they?" she murmured with a small smile. "Catriona was much like you when she arrived. I enjoy her company very much; she has become a good friend. I would enjoy the pleasure of your company tomorrow morning in my solar."

Corinne blinked, not really knowing what to say.

Alliances may be forged by queens, Uberon whispered into her brain even as he returned verbal tit for tat with the Seelie king.

Jeez, why don't you guys just whip 'em out and get it over with?

Because when I "whip" mine out, it will seek you.

You're annoying me, Uberon. I'm mad at you.

I know and will tease you from your ill humor.

Corinne wanted to growl with exasperation and smack him upside the head. Instead, she glanced back at the queen whose knowing expression encouraged her to feel that she had, perhaps, found a friend. She pasted a smile on her face and said aloud, "Thank you for the gracious invitation. I'm honored to accept."

CHAPTER 11

After a bit more posturing between kings and trading not-so-veiled threats, the audience ended. Courtiers hung back, either not daring to commit offense or not desiring to sully themselves through association with the deposed Unseelie king. However, four palace guards approached at their king's summons, two to lead Uberon somewhere and two who more or less ordered Corinne to accompany them somewhere else.

At least they did not lead her to the dungeons, because a palace like this surely had dungeons. Instead, the two guards led her to a pleasant, sunlit room where several ladies gathered, including one whose appearance tickled Corinne's memory. That female rose from her chair and approached to greet the new arrival. The others drew back, pulling their skirts closer around them as though the sweep of Corinne's hem against their clothes would transfer some dread contagion. She heard whispers of "Unseelie" and "cursed" and "unclean" around her. The power within her flared, hot and dangerous, darkening her green eyes with a fiery glint and causing the black diamonds on her body and in her crown to pulse.

"Hello! You must be Lady Corinne. I'm Lady Daniellisande, daughter of Lady Catriona and mated to Lord Enders."

"Enders," Corinne murmured, then the memory of the austere beauty of the male whom Uberon seemed to accord at least some respect. The flare of power calmed and, though she did not know it, the other ladies in the room breathed a collective sigh of relief. "He accompanied us here."

"Aye," Daniellisande replied with a smile. "And he was none too happy about it, either."

"Why? We've never done anything to him."

"You? No, you haven't. But Enders and Uberon have a long and troubled history of which not even I know the whole." She grinned. "One of these days, those two are going to meet in the arena and beat each other to a pulp. Males do seem to need to do that to settle issues between them, don't they?"

Corinne sighed. "Yeah, they do. I have five brothers—all older—and they're never so happy as when they're beating the hell out of each other."

The raven-haired beauty's eyebrows rose at Corinne's blunt language, but she chuckled all the same.

"Five brothers? Really? How marvelous!"

"I didn't fear much in the way of bullies," Corinne admitted. "But they're all a little overprotective and overbearing."

"My mother is Catriona, called the moon-born. She was once human. Growing up, she told me stories of the children she raised during that period of her life. I can hardly imagine it. Enders and I have not yet been blessed with a child, though I know he longs for one as much as I."

Corinne blinked at this openness from the stranger who drew her to sit with her on a sunny window bench. She ventured, not really knowing how to respond, "I haven't seen many children since I've been here."

"And you won't," Daniellisande replied with a little moue of sorrow. "It makes sense if one thinks about it. Immortals who reproduced like humankind would soon overpopulate the world. Therefore, we have few children and those are doubly precious to us for their rarity."

Corinne could understand that and nodded. Now that the subject had been broached, she began counting and realized that she'd not had a period in ... well, not since she arrived. But she wasn't pregnant. At least, she didn't think so. She looked at her new friend and, with more than a touch of embarrassment, asked, "Do fae women have ... er ... menstrual cycles?"

"You mean monthly bleeding like human females?"

Daniellisande tilted her head to one side as she considered what she knew on the topic. "No. I believe it is nature's way of limiting our reproductive capacity. However, I am sure I would not like to experience these menstrual cycles as I have heard them described."

She leaned forward. "Mama explained them to me when I was quite young, thinking that I would need to have such knowledge in preparation of feminine maturity. She was mistaken, but I remember pitying the human girls who had so little control over their own bodies. What was it like for you? I assume you are sufficiently mature to have experienced that biological process?"

Corinne's expression turned wry and she replied in a dry tone, "You could say that. My … er … courses started when I was only ten years old. My father was horrified. My mother took it in stride and showed me what to do. No one ever told me about the cramps though. God, those were awful."

"Cramps? Please explain. I have concluded that such a biological process would be inconvenient and, well, messy, but I did not know it could be painful, too."

Corinne wondered how much this apparently very young woman—female—knew about reproduction and decided to go for broke. "You know that a woman's uterus contracts to push out the baby?"

"Of course." Daniellisande leaned back and waited for more information.

"Well, for many girls, the uterus contracts when they have their monthly bleeding. The contractions are painful, sometimes extremely painful."

"Oh, those poor dears. Do they outgrow this pain?"

"I didn't."

"I never knew human females endured such misery simply due to biology." The black-haired female gazed out the window. "Perhaps I should be grateful to be fae and not envy human females their reproductive capacity."

"Mom always said each of her children was a gift worth any amount of pain."

Daniellisande reached over to pat Corinne's hand. "I am sure she meant it with all her heart."

"I hear you've found a new friend," a new voice interrupted.

Corinne looked at the female joining them and realized she was the one who'd rushed into the courtyard to greet Captain Thelan.

"Hello, Mama," Daniellisande greeted, rising to her feet to embrace a woman who appeared young enough to be her twin. "Your reunion with Papa went well?"

"It always does, my dear. Now make room for me so I can pry into this one's knowledge of the world I left behind."

Corinne's eyes blinked in rapid succession as she realized that she faced the fabled moon-born, soul-bonded mate to Captain Thelan of the Seelie Palace Guard. But hadn't Catriona been assimilated into fae culture for at least two or three centuries? Maybe more? Corinne's confusion must have shown on her face.

"Time between the realms is fluid," she replied, using the same words as had Oriel, the soul-bonded mate to the fearsome Erlking. She leveled her violet gaze at Corinne and asked, "Who was president when Uberon brought you over?"

Before Corinne could answer, the collection of ladies in the room squealed in awe and fright, some going so far as to swoon as the door swung open and Uberon stepped into the room.

"Blithering idiots," she heard Catriona mutter under her breath.

His gaze instantly locked onto Corinne, like an arrow sinking into its target. Corinne's mouth opened, her expression going slack as she took in the barbaric magnificence of his crowned, bare-chested glory. He extended his hand toward her and said, "We leave. Now."

Corinne rose slowly to her feet and stammered, "But the queen—?"

"Ought to be relieved of the imbecile she mated," Uberon grunted. "Come with me."

She could not help but look at Catriona and Daniellisande. Both ladies shrugged their shoulders and said nothing, although their expressions offered only a mere hint of sympathy. Corinne sighed, knowing that she'd not get that comfortable bed, hot bath, and good meal she wanted. She also knew better than to cause a scene in potentially hazardous territory. Except, perhaps, for the moon-born and the archivist's mate, she had no friends in that room. So, she walked toward Uberon and obliged him by placing her palm in his.

As soon as their hands touched, she felt the immense rage within him seeking an outlet. Her gaze flew upward and he met her eyes.

"I will not harm *you*," he murmured under his breath. "But if we do not leave, then I may level this palace to the ground and all who reside within it."

She nodded and allowed him to draw her from the room.

"Give the queen my regrets!" she called out.

Catriona and her daughter nodded.

The door slammed.

"Foolish, bigoted imbeciles," Uberon muttered as he practically marched through the corridors.

"Uberon, what happened?" Corinne's breathless question reminded him to slow his pace so she could keep up.

"That pissant of a Seelie king attempted to force me to ally with him as his *vassal*."

Corinne knew Uberon's attitude toward the expectation that he bow or kneel to anyone.

"How could he force you to do anything?"

"First, he attempted to secure exclusive trade agreements. Then he offered to send a guard to escort us and then occupy my kingdom—a guard answerable to him. Then he threatened to hold you hostage."

"Oh, dear."

His teeth flashed in a savage smile. "He's lucky I did not decapitate him right there."

She swallowed a lump of nervous worry. "Uberon, what did you do?"

"He still lives."

Well, *that* doesn't bode well. Corinne shut up, figuring she really didn't want to know more at that point. Perhaps later, when they'd outdistanced the Seelie army which was surely hunting for them. Another question occurred to her and she blurted it before thinking better of doing so.

"How are we going to get out of here?"

"I'll commandeer a dragon if necessary."

"The dragons don't like you."

"They hate me. They know I did not capture one of their kind, but they also know I did nothing to stop it or set it free."

The old quotation from Edmund Burke came to Corinne's mind: "All that is necessary for the triumph of evil is for good men to do nothing." She shuddered. How did one, even someone as powerful as Uberon, commandeer a dragon?

They exited a door Catriona did not remember and passed into dwindling sunshine. A white dragon, its scales gleaming like opals, snorted. It turned a dark eye toward them and lowered its serpentine neck so that its massive head held level with the fae.

Mount, Unseelie king.

"You!" Uberon blurted, his surprise astonishing Corinne who thought nothing could surprise her ancient mate. His eyes narrowed. "Why should you assist us?"

My Rider begs this favor of me. The mighty lizard's scaly lip peeled back from fearsome teeth. *And you shall owe her and all my kind a favor now.*

Uberon nodded and said, "Done." He glanced at Corinne and added, "Follow me."

Gathering the delicate fabric of her skirts, she clambered up the dragon's surprisingly warm hide to take a seat at the great lizard's withers. She wrapped her arms around Uberon's waist and buried her face into the strong muscles of his back. The dragon's wings snapped out and she flinched. The beast hissed, sparks of liquid fire spraying as it ran a few steps before leaping into the air. Those mighty wings beat the air, the sound deafening to Corinne's ears as her body flexed and coiled with the movement of the immense body beneath her.

Where to, Unseelie king?

"Quoliálfur."

The Quol is vast.

"Do you know Donshae?"

The northernmost port at the edge of Ursai territory where the Seelie Veil meets the Quol.

"Aye. Fly us there. I will not ask you to penetrate the Quol itself."

You would spare a dragon?

"The Quol and the Quoli will not spare you, and I have no desire to rend the moon-born's second soul by destroying her dragon."

You are brave, Unseelie king, to defy the hunger of the Quol and to imply I belong to the moon-born.

"Aye, you do belong to each other. Tell me, dragon, do you share her fae or her human soul?"

None of your business.

Listening to the exchange, Corinne wondered whether she, too, had two souls, one human and one fae? If so, what did that mean and how would it affect her and, possibly, Uberon?

CHAPTER 12

If Corinne had felt a bit peckish when they fled the Seelie Court, she was absolutely ravenous when the white dragon landed near Donshae. Behind the concealment of a merchant's warehouse, Uberon and Corinne dismounted.

"Remember your obligation," the white dragon reminded the Quoliálfur king.

"Aye," Uberon said with a curt nod. "Use my debt to you wisely."

Immense, leathery wings snapped out as the great beast spat a single gout of liquid flame. Uberon turned his back on the dragon, took Corinne's hand, and began walking toward the city. She noticed that, some time during the flight, her sturdy travel costume had replaced the fine silk gown and crown. Garbed in black leather trousers and shirt with a black wool cloak swirling around him, Uberon would have disappeared into the darkness but for the pale gleam of skin and the silver knots caught in his hair. Corinne's own hair had fallen and hung in a wild tangle. She spared a thought for the difficult task of combing the tangles free even as every muscle in her body trembled with sore weariness and her belly rumbled with hunger.

She shivered, although the night was not particularly chill. Still, Uberon noticed and transferred his cloak to her, draping the pre-warmed weight over her shoulders.

"Aren't you cold?" she asked as she drew the cloak more tightly around her body.

"Not at all," he replied and reached for her hand again.

She took it and let him guide her, if only because she had no idea where they were or where he was going. He'd pledged to protect her and she would hold him to that. Her annoyance with him took second place to pragmatic need. Damn it, she was *tired* of traveling and sleeping on the ground. She knew her peevishness unreasonable and childish, yet she could not quell it. Sometimes a woman simply needed her comforts.

She heard music and singing—mostly off-key, which indicated varying levels of inebriation. She heard thumping and shouts, the smacks of fists on flesh or on wood. She heard the occasional squeal or moan. Foul scents assaulted her nose: refuse, inferior cooking, rotten food, spoiled wine, spilled beer, fish. Over it all came the roar of the tide and the scent of saltwater.

Corinne sighed. She supposed harbor towns were the same everywhere, filled with sailors and merchants and whores.

"Donshae used to be a nice fishing village," Uberon commented. "I can't quite remember how long ago that was, exactly."

Corinne didn't answer. Her stomach's growling increased in volume.

"Ah, here."

Uberon ducked through a door, tugging his mate with him. She collided with him, her face landing between his shoulder blades. With a muttered apology, she took a half-step back and blinked at the dull light gleaming yellow through a haze of smoke and body odor. Corinne did her best not to meet any patron's eyes straight on, but to just let her gaze slide anonymously over the crowd.

"Well, if it ain't tall, dark, and handsome," cackled a blowsy looking serving wench whose endowments overflowed the low neckline of her loose bodice. "What brings you back?"

Corinne peered around Uberon's broad, solid form and noticed the serving wench was human. Had they left the Seelie Court's territory? She hadn't felt the tingle of the Veil, but then perhaps the rush and roar of cold air upon the dragon's back had obscured it.

Donshae lies just beyond the Veil. It serves all nations, all races. It's a fascinating place.

She didn't respond, being more concerned with filling her empty stomach and getting some much-needed rest than with the trading center's demographics.

Aloud, Uberon answered the tavern's employee. "I need a table and supper for two. Then a private room."

The wench's eyes narrowed as she noticed the cloaked female standing closely behind her customer. "Agrikko don't allow no private whores. You got an itch, you use one o' the girls here."

"She is my mate," Uberon corrected, his quiet voice cutting through the din and smoke. "And she is due respect."

"Aye, m'lord," the wench snapped with a quick bob. "I'll lead you to Agrikko's best table. I assume you got coin to pay for it and the room."

"Aye."

Corinne followed the tug on her hand as she watched the woman's broad hips sway. Conversation among the patrons died as Uberon wove through the tables and no hands dared dart out to pinch or grab the female trailing behind him. She heard mutters of "fae" and "Unseelie" as she passed through the multicultural throng. She saw sharp, pointed teeth and bi-colored hair on some, deeply red skin combined with black or gold hair on others, and the normal and familiar range of features on humans. She saw pointed ears, rounded ears, and furred ears placed like animal ears. She saw some of the platinum blond, narrow-framed features of the fae and even a table populated by six halflings, their large eyes and broad faces giving them a deceptive air of childlike innocence. Most of the different races segregated themselves from the others.

Practically weaving with exhaustion, Corinne almost didn't notice when Uberon stopped walking.

"Sit here," he said and guided her into a chair that had her tucked away in a corner with her back to the rough-hewn wall. He took the chair next to her, ensuring that his shadow fell over her to add a smidgen more concealment. He removed his gloves.

The serving wench returned shortly to slam heavy mugs of ale on the marginally clean tabletop. "I'll be back with yer stew, m'lord."

"Thank you," he replied with grave courtesy. Before Corinne could reach for the mug's handle, he covered its mouth and dipped in a bare finger. Corinne fancied she heard a faint whisper, but knew that couldn't be true because the crowd's noise level kicked back up once the king took his seat without smiting any unfortunate onlookers.

He removed his hand from the mug and said, "It's safe to drink."

She nodded and hoisted the heavy tankard to her mouth for a sip. Although not as cold as she would have preferred, the ale was surprisingly good. She took another swallow, then set it down. Best to get some food in her belly before drinking any more and having the alcohol go straight to her head.

"Do they know who you are?" she whispered.

"They know I am fae and highborn as well. They need know nothing more than that."

She nodded, suspecting that knowledge of his identity would send patrons fleeing in terror. After all, that had already happened at one establishment where they paused for a meal and someone had guessed Uberon's identity. She did not miss the pained look in his eyes, though she doubted anyone else noticed it.

What, she thought, must it be like to be so feared that the mere mention of one's name caused terror and panic? The magnitude of his loneliness gnawed at her.

Heavy bowls of thick pottery landed on the table, filled with the rich savory aroma of fish stew and accompanied by a steaming loaf of fresh bread. Although her belly rumbled loudly with eagerness, Corinne waited until Uberon pronounced the food safe to eat before diving in.

"This is actually quite good," she complimented with surprise.

"The ambiance leaves a bit to be desired, but the innkeeper's wife cooks well," Uberon replied. "She will likely have some kind of fruit tart if you've room for it."

Corinne nodded and doubted whether she'd have room for it, for the bowls were large and filled to heaping.

"I shouldn't be surprised by the bouillabaisse, but I guess I was expecting something more like beef."

"I doubt one will find many cattle this far north and this close to the Quol."

"Venison?"

His lips curled in a small smile of indulgence. "No one with any sense goes hunting in the Quol. The jungle is more likely to eat them instead."

She shuddered and said no more on that topic. Instead, she asked, "What keeps the Quoli from invading the town?"

"Tall walls and strong wards."

"Ah." She took a few more bites of bread and stew, another swallow of beer. "I don't suppose there's a chance of a bath here?"

"No, not here. But I'll make sure you have wash water."

"All right."

He understood her sigh of acceptance, if not enthusiasm, even as he understood her preference for a real bath rather than the sweep of magic that refreshed her skin and clothing. He liked that sensual preference; it responded well to his touch. He reached over and tucked a stray lock of hair behind her ear.

"Allow me to brush your hair tonight."

"Do we even have a brush?" She pursed her lips, not relishing the thought of borrowing a brush from one of the "girls" working in the tavern.

"We have everything we need," he assured her.

They finished their supper and the serving wench brought them fruit tarts, liberally drenched in a sweet, spicy glaze that made Corinne moan with gustatory pleasure. Uberon enjoyed the tart, too, though his mate's moan made his cock swell.

He left silver coins on the table and allowed the serving wench to lead them to a room at the far end of the balcony. With his hand resting possessively at the small of Corinne's back as she walked ahead of him, he saw her cheeks flame at the carnal noises emanating from behind the doors they passed. He enjoyed that blushing reaction and hoped she never got so jaded that the delightful blush disappeared.

Upon entering the room at the end of the balcony, he held up a gold coin. The wench's eyes gleamed with avarice and she reached for it. He snatched it back.

"Wash water, hot and lots of it, with soap and towels. We'll need clean linens on the bed, too."

The wench's mouth thinned at the demands, but she nodded, bobbed a curtsey, and promised to have everything requested in short order.

"Do not touch anything yet, beloved," he murmured and sent a pulse of power through the room.

"What was that?"

"Just killing vermin and removing the bed linens."

She shuddered. "Oh my God, you mean—"

"Lice? Fleas? Bedbugs? Of course. This inn is frequented by sailors on shore leave who are more interested in food, drink, and women than in bathing. Neither does the innkeeper insist upon cleanliness. I daresay the bed linens have not been changed in months."

She shuddered again at the very thought of lying on sheets soiled many times over. "Do you think the … er … bugs will return?"

"After we leave," he assured her. "Do not doubt my protection, my dear."

She sighed in relief, having assumed that "protection" only encompassed the sort of things bodyguards prevented.

"As least you'll never have to take a bullet for me."

"Humans remain inventive in ways to kill."

She nodded knowing that many Bermuda Triangle transports arrived well after the invention of gunpowder and firearms.

"Do … does the fae … er … discourage firearms?"

"Our magic has little or no effect upon iron or anything made of iron," he admitted with admirable candor. "Humans experiment and they know this weakness of ours; therefore, we do what we can to cause their mechanisms to fail."

"People learn from their failures," she said slowly, thinking aloud. "They improve their techniques, refine their knowledge."

"Aye."

"The fae won't be able to hold technology at bay forever."

"True."

"What do you think will happen then?"

"Humans will either comply with the restrictions we place upon them or the fae will annihilate them."

"I get the feeling that humans aren't well tolerated to begin with."

"Your instincts are correct. Yet, the humans managed to carve two sizeable kingdoms from formerly fae territories. If the humans' technology proves intractable, then we may well find ourselves allying with trolls who fear no bullets and have not the intelligence to fear cannons."

"Trolls," she repeated faintly.

"And djinni. We consider them a treacherous folk, yet they can manipulate sand and small particles of silicone to foul the works of any mechanism. The vodnici manipulate water. Allied with the djinni, steel mechanisms will rust overnight and turn inoperable. Not even the most advanced human forges can manufacture an army's worth of firearms that quickly."

"Unless they learned from Henry Ford," she murmured as the serving wench returned with a knock on the door.

Accompanied by another servant, the two women each set down two buckets filled with steaming water.

"That's all the hot water we've got unless you wish to wait. By that time the buckets will have cooled off," she said.

"That will be sufficient."

She bobbed another curtsey. "Good, m'lord. Then I'll be back with soap and towels."

He held up the gold coin for her to see. "And this shall be waiting for your kind assistance."

She nodded, bobbed, and departed, the other woman whispering about collecting her share of that gold coin.

"I have to ask."

"Yes, beloved?"

"Where did the money come from?"

"I pulled it from my vault."

She shook her head, neither understanding nor quite believing him. "And the dress? And crown? Don't tell me you've got a wardrobe stashed in this vault of yours."

"I have not," he admitted. "But I do have a store of exquisite fabrics and laces and jewels and I command them to manifest and form as I need."

"You can do that, but you can't fly?"

"We all have our limitations."

Corinne laughed. She couldn't help it. Caught by her amusement, Uberon smiled, a rare expression of joy that made the breath catch in her throat. Her laughter faded and swelled into something else, something powerful. She could not blink, could not speak. Her gaze flickered to the fall of his trousers and the bulge straining against the supple leather.

"Wash now or later?" he murmured.

Her mouth opened, but no sound emerged as she felt invisible flames flicker over the surface of her skin, kissing her with heat and desire. She watched as his clothing dissolved into nothingness, leaving him fully nude for her admiration. He lifted his arms and spread them to receive her.

"Uberon," she whispered and flung herself across the room into his embrace.

CHAPTER 13

In the darkness of the hours before dawn, Uberon propped himself up on one elbow while Corinne slept and ran his hand in light strokes over her still tangled hair. His fingertips moved from the silk of her hair to the satin of her skin, trailing over her shoulder. She sighed and snuggled in more closely to his warm body. Her soul shined so brightly. It cast its brilliance into his dark soul, imbuing him with a sense of goodness and purity that he wasn't sure he had ever possessed. Not knowing to whom he prayed, one of the three most ancient fae in that world sent silent thanks to the heavens for the gift of his mate.

The desire to be worthy of her inspired him to be a finer version of himself.

Wouldn't Enders have had a hearty laugh at that?

The last of his generation had succumbed to the soul-bond and turned him into a besotted nincompoop.

His hand stilled, settling over the flare of her hip, fingers aching to slide a bit further and delve into her honeyed sweetness. But the days of rigorous travel had wearied her and she needed rest. The tightness in his chest relaxed at the knowledge that he gave her what she needed. Providing for his mate meant more than simply ensuring adequate food, shelter, and clothing. It encompassed caring for her *every* need. Fulfillment of that imperative satisfied something deep inside him, a heretofore unrealized need, a yearning, gaping void he'd not previously understood because he'd never known there was anything different.

He spared a moment to remember Marog's mother, whom he'd mated because doing so had been mutually advantageous to them both. Like all their kind, she was beautiful, unexceptional in a species for which beauty was as common as five fingers and five toes on each hand and foot. He remembered her as kind and cool-natured, if not particularly compassionate. The kindness resulted from a keen awareness of position and reputation and obligation. She'd bitterly resented the split from the Seelie Court and never allowed him to forget his fault in heaping the misery of exile upon her.

Uberon did not particularly miss her when she died with an iron blade in her heart, even though honor and mild affection demanded retribution which he had visited upon her murderer with swift and brutal vengeance. Centuries had passed before the djinni ventured into that corner of their territory again, and centuries more before the first intrepid souls dared to settle there once again. Legends of his curse still rose occasionally among the older djinni.

If something ripped Corinne from his life, he would decimate the world in his rage and grief.

He never knew anything could be so precious to him as this once-human female.

Uberon drew his mate closer to his body, curling around her as though to shelter her with his own flesh from all danger. He inhaled deeply of the mingled fragrance of their skin and the lingering musk of passion. He ignored the press of his eager cock between the sweet globes of her ass, though he was sure he could slide inside her body while she slept and obtain release again. Her body would receive him. However, he refused to use her like that because she meant more—so much more—to him than service as a receptacle for his libido.

He lay there and listened to the occasional thud of booted footsteps and the rasp of slippered soles against the rough planks of the balcony floor. He listened to the squeak of hinges beginning to corrode from the always salty air when a whore's customer finished his business and departed. His keen ears heard the feigned sounds of delight from those same whores who knew being better actresses meant earning better bonuses from their customers. He heard the stifled squeal of pain as one customer used a woman too roughly. Feeling magnanimous, Uberon sent a thread of power toward that room. The whore's vagina suddenly grew sharp teeth and the man abusing her lost his manhood with a strangled scream of horror—strangled because an invisible cord tightened around his throat until he lost consciousness.

She'd likely lose her job, but no one would believe that a woman's body so well-used by so many men could do the damage one customer would surely accuse her of. Uberon's own strong, white teeth gleamed in the darkness as the warm, coppery scent of blood added its odor to the miasma of smells that filled the tavern.

The whole sordid transaction gave justification to his contempt for humans. No other species so condoned ill use of an entire gender as did humanity. The superiority of the fae lay not only in their power, but in their protection of the weakest of their species. He pressed a kiss to the fragrant tangle of Corinne's hair. Her abilities made her a goddess among insects when compared to humans, though the strength of most fae dwarfed hers. Corinne's real power lay in her power over him.

His ears pricked at the sudden absence of sound as heavy footsteps stopped in front of the door to their room. Whispers in a rude human language he'd not bothered to learn filtered through the door. He needed no linguistic expertise to understand the hiss of steel sliding from a leather scabbard.

Stupid humans thought to rob a wealthy fae lord.

Uberon eased from the bed, careful not to disturb his slumbering mate. A flicker of thought garbed him in supple black leather. His gloved hand curled around the hilt of his favorite sword, a long, deceptively slender blade with edges so keen they sliced through steel like butter. Unfortunately, the corrosive taint of steel would pit the blade and dull the edge, but a whetstone could repair the damage.

He held his other hand up, ready to fling raw power at the other human whose greasy stench seeped under the door. He crossed the room on silent feet and positioned himself near the door.

The latch jiggled and clicked. The door opened barely the

span of a hand's breadth. Uberon aimed for the shadow lurking just beyond.

One of the men murmured something. The door opened wider. A short, stocky man sidled through, a slightly taller, and gaunt man creeped in right behind him. He grunted when he collided with the first man who stopped abruptly when Uberon's blade kissed the skin of his neck.

"Give me one reason I shouldn't kill you," Uberon said, his tone pitched low so as not to disturb his mate's rest.

"We don't want no trouble, my lord," the skinny man answered in the common trade tongue, his voice heavily accented.

"Then you shouldn't have gone looking for it." Uberon withdrew his sword and slid it into its scabbard. His lips peeled back to display his teeth. The two burglars mistook it for a smile.

The shoulder of the heavier of the two men shifted. Uberon read the intent in his beady eyes. He inhaled sharply, his chest expanding. The two men gasped, but could draw in no air from the vacuum that surrounded them. They clutched at their throats, the heavier man dropping his dagger which landed without a sound because sound could not travel through a vacuum. Uberon watched dispassionately as the lack of air worked its deadly effect.

Having efficiently dispatched the would-be burglars, he exhaled, releasing the air he withheld from the two intruders. A nudge of his booted toe resulted in no response from the corpses, so he unleashed his will and the bodies disintegrated into small piles of coarse, greasy ash.

Another flicker of will restored his nakedness as he padded back to the bed and rejoined his mate. He curled his body around hers and flung a light net of wards around the perimeter of the room in case some other stupid, avaricious human decided to relieve the wealthy fae lord of what belonged to him.

Corinne continued to sleep and recuperate from the exhaustion of travel and vigorous rounds of lovemaking. The wards muted the sounds filtering through the thin walls, a secondary benefit that allowed Uberon to close his eyes and indulge in some sleep himself.

He woke as weak light passed through the dirty window panes and cast the room in dull shadow. He cleaned and clothed himself and set the water in the buckets to scalding, for his mate would wish to wash the conventional way before they continued their journey. He opened the window and peered through. Below him the city began to awaken. Across the topography of rooftops, he saw sails billow as ships headed out on the morning tide to catch fish and carry cargo. A fresh salty breeze swirled through the opening, sweeping away the faintly acrid odor of death and dissolution.

Corinne stirred, absently reached for him, an unconscious gesture that warmed his cold heart, stirred his icy blood, and brightened his blackened soul. Leaving the window open, he walked back to the bed and sat on the edge of the mattress.

Running the back of one finger down her smooth cheek, he said, "Awaken, beloved. We've far to travel today."

Her eyes fluttered open and she stretched. The blanket slipped down to reveal plump, ruby-tipped breasts. Unable to resist their temptation, he leaned down and kissed one. She moaned and arched beneath him. He obeyed the inarticulate demand and suckled, working the hard tip with his tongue and reveling in the sweetness of her flesh.

"Uberon," she sighed and twined her fingers in his hair.

Uberon decided a delay would do no harm and, naked once again, pushed the blanket down and crawled over her. Her thighs parted for him as he took his place between her legs. He relished her soft sounds of pleasure as he transferred his attention to the other breast and skimmed a hand down her body, tracing random patterns into the soft skin. She undulated beneath him, her hips tilting to welcome his invasion. Corinne sighed, then moaned, as he sank into her body, already wet and eager to be possessed.

Her mate lifted his head, his silver eyes locking with hers as his hips snapped back and forth in a ruthless rhythm that made her breasts jiggle and her blood sing. She reached up to cradle his face between her palms and his pace slowed, grew gentle, the fiery passion soothed by her mere touch. He groaned and closed his eyes, their bodies now surging and ebbing like the rolling tides, the climb to orgasm just as inevitable.

Corinne cried out, a high, thin sound as her muscles convulsed around him and her limbs could do no more than clutch at him to hold him close. Uberon groaned and ground his hips into her, burying himself as deeply as he could as his own release emptied into her body.

"Now I really need a bath," she muttered and unclenched her hands from his upper arms.

The Quoliálfur king pressed a tender, sensual kiss to her mouth and replied as he brushed back a tendril of tangled hair, "You shall have one."

Pulling from her body, which made her utter that little whimper that never failed to delight him, he directed his will toward the buckets of steaming water. As she pulled herself into a sitting position, Corinne gaped as the buckets reformed and expanded into a tub. The water they held swelled in volume to fill the newly fashioned vessel.

"Bathe, beloved," he said, turning to face her as his own skin glowed fresh and clean and supple black leather wrapped around his body. "I shall ensure we have breakfast and then check on our mounts."

Corinne tilted her head and gave him a puzzled glance as she rose from the bed and evidence of their passion trickled down her thighs. "The horses are back at the Seelie palace."

"They'll have arrived by now, unencumbered by riders."

"How?" she asked, lifting a leg to climb into the tub.

"They're not really horses."

"Do I want to know?"

"Probably not right now."

She sighed. "But you will tell me? Later?"

"I will tell you," he agreed. "After we're on our way."

"Uberon?"

He paused at the door. "Yes, beloved?"

"Is it possible for you to check and see whether Gus delivered the letters I wrote to my family?"

He nodded, both regretting that she missed them so much and grateful that her kind and generous heart had not forgotten them. Her concern boded well for her future as the mother of any children they might have. The image in his mind of his mate ripe and round with his child made his cock swell with renewed enthusiasm and a burning desire to fuck her well and often. Perhaps she might give him a precious daughter.

"I'll check," he promised and passed through the door, taking care to shield her from the view of any passersby who might look through the doorway.

Getting his body under control, he strode the length of the balcony and down the staircase. A bleary-eyed wench lifted her head to acknowledge him as he entered the common room.

"I shall return with my mate shortly. We require your best breakfast."

She nodded and returned her attention to wiping down tables with a dirty rag. He changed direction and headed for the stable yard where their mounts waited in disdainful silence. An hostler approached the gleaming golden steed, only to dodge a striking hoof.

"You made it," Uberon greeted them. "Good. Any troubles?"

The black horse lifted its nose and cast a cold glare at him.

"Yes, yes, our leavetaking was abrupt and rude. However, I could not tolerate any threat to my mate. I apologize for the substandard accommodations and the inconsiderate treatment."

The golden horse snorted in grudging acceptance of his apology. The black horse turned its head aside in clear dismissal.

"Mind your manners," Uberon warned. "Or would you prefer to forfeit your release?"

Blowing forcefully through its flared, velvety nostrils, the black horse arched its neck and lowered its head in submission.

"Good," the fae lord said with mild satisfaction. "I'll see that you receive an extra ration of grain and fresh water before we head out."

He turned and walked away, the two horses following him to the utter astonishment of the two hostlers who watched. The hostlers flinched when Uberon turned to face them.

"See that my mounts receive your best grain and as much fresh water as they will drink. They have traveled long and hard to rejoin me here and deserve the reward."

"Them's vicious animals, my lord," the younger of the two hostlers remarked, lip curling in a sneer.

"They'll mind their manners now, provided you treat them gently."

The hostler shrugged and lifted a halter to slide over an equine head. The golden horse raised its head and took a step back.

"Behave," Uberon snapped.

The golden horse lowered its head and allowed itself to be

caught while the older hostler approached the black horse. That beast held still while the hostler tugged a halter over its large head. Both horses meekly followed the hostlers into the small stable where Uberon made sure they received what he promised them.

When he returned to the room at the end of the balcony, Corinne had finished her bath and sat on the bed, a towel wrapped around her body while she painstakingly struggled with combing the tangles from her hair.

"I'm ready to cut this mess off," she muttered with frustration.

"Allow me to comb your hair. I didn't get to do that last night," he said and sat down beside her.

She hesitated, then handed him the comb. He repositioned her so that she sat with her back to him. He swept her wet hair aside and pressed kisses to the nape of her neck and the back of each shoulder. Goose pimples rose on her skin and she shivered as pleasure rippled through her.

"Do not cut your hair. It is your crowning glory, as though you carried the sunset within every strand," he said as he stroked the tresses which began to loosen beneath his touch. He ran the comb through her hair, right behind his fingers. After only a couple of passes, the comb traveled freely through the long, wavy locks.

"Shall I braid it?" he inquired, setting the comb aside.

"Please."

His fingers deftly manipulated her hair, weaving it into a complicated plait threaded through with glossy black and green ribbons that hadn't existed until he decided he wanted to embellish her hair.

"Now, a habit to match," he murmured as he eased the towel from Corinne's body. The sight of her exposed flesh had its predictable effect on him, but he concentrated on other business. After all, he'd told her, he was no unreasoning animal unable to control himself. "Stand, beloved."

She stood, feeling a little self-conscious although she did not know why, especially after the vigorous activity of the mating bed. She supposed "marriage bed" wasn't quite accurate.

A breath later, she felt the touch of fine fabric against her skin. She looked down to see herself clothed in a silvery green riding habit that resembled no historical style to which she could put an era of fashion. However, from her vantage point, it certainly looked elegant. She lifted the skirt just enough to peek at the soft leather boots that encased her feet.

"You know, this is really pretty, but pants would be more practical."

"Not if I'm going to fuck you again in the next few hours."

And, just like that, her core heated and moistened and her nipples beaded and visibly pressed against the bodice of her dress. Apparently, her libido liked when he talked dirty.

This is embarrassing.

Uberon held out his arm and she placed her fingertips on his forearm. He murmured as they walked from the room, "You're mine. Do not be ashamed to show it."

"I don't think anybody could miss that."

"Good. Let them witness and gnash their teeth with envy."

"You can be a real jerk, you know that?"

"It's good to be me," came the dry response.

She laughed and her amusement cheered Uberon to no end.

By the twin moons, he *loved* this female.

The wench slid plates heaped with thick slices of buttered bread, boiled eggs, strips of fried meat, and scoops of shredded vegetables, some of which were pickled. Corinne didn't question the food too closely, sure that she probably did not want to know the source of some of those meats and vegetables. She tasted everything on her plate and ate what appealed.

"Milk? But you said there were no cows around here," she commented when peering into the heavy earthenware mug beside her plate.

"Goat's milk," he guessed as he brought a mug of ale to his mouth. "If you don't like it, we'll see if they have some juice."

She nodded, not looking forward to the option of quaffing heavy, dark ale with her breakfast. Corinne took a sip of the warm goat's milk and wrinkled her nose at the musty flavor. She coughed.

"Um, no. It might work for cheese, but ... no. Just no."

Uberon nodded and signaled at the serving wench. She approached, her expression wary.

"Somethin' not to yer likin', milord?"

"Have you any fruit juice?" Uberon inquired, affecting a

pleasant demeanor that didn't quite convince the wench if her still-wary expression told the truth.

"We got duku," the woman replied. "I can have the cook squeeze it for yer."

"That will do nicely," the fae lord replied. "Be sure to bring some honey, too, just in case the duku isn't ripe."

The wench nodded and retreated to the kitchen.

"What's duku?" Corinne asked.

"It's a tropical fruit that tastes something like grapefruit."

She pursed her lips and nodded. She preferred grapefruit-flavored juice to the strong, musty goat's milk. She wondered how he knew about grapefruit, but then reconsidered asking. Some things really weren't that important. Besides, he'd mentioned previous trips to her old world, so the idea of his being exposed to grapefruit during those visits made sense.

The wench returned soon with an earthenware tumbler filled with watered-down duku juice. She waited a moment for the fae lord's nod of approval, which he did not offer until his mate had tasted the juice and indicated her acceptance, before attending to her other duties.

"Thanks, U—"

"How much for the wench?" came a raspy demand from behind Uberon.

Corinne choked on her juice and looked at her mate, who turned around with icy deliberation to face a tall, burly male with deeply coppery red skin and thick black hair caught in a queue at the nape of his neck.

"My *mate* is not for sale," Uberon replied, every syllable sharper than broken glass.

"How much for just a candlemark? She looks clean. Young. *Fresh.*"

Corinne felt power gather with her outrage. Bracing her hands on the tabletop, she pushed upward. "Look, moron—"

"Leave or die," Uberon snapped.

The interloper dared put his hand on her, though the touch offered no overt violence.

"Hands off," Corinne snarled as she wrenched her arm from his light grasp. She leveled a blast of fire, which he shrugged off and absorbed as though she'd done nothing more than blow a puff of air at him.

"Fire's useless against a djinn," the male said with a grin displaying brilliant white teeth. "But I'll enjoy showing you."

Corinne raised her other hand to launch another blast of power at him, but Uberon forestalled her with a mere finger laid upon her upper arm.

"You made your choice," he said, and unleashed his cold fury. The djinn gasped as his skin purpled, then went blue and hard. It cracked as the liquids within his body froze and expanded. The sharp inhalation of breath ended with a crackling rattle as his lungs froze.

"Uberon?"

"Yes, beloved?"

"You've killed him."

"Aye." Now frozen solid, the djinn began to crumble into tiny shards of ice.

Corinne averted her gaze and gulped air to quell the sudden need to vomit. "He's ... he's ..."

Her mate turned his face toward her, icy silver eyes meeting hers. She shivered at the utter lack of humanity in his face. She gulped again. This formidable male who made her body sing and who cared for her needs with such diligent tenderness had just killed a man—male?—who dared insult her. Corinne wondered about this powerful male's value system, then realized in truth that not only was he not human, he also subscribed to an alien code of honor she might never understand.

"Have you finished eating?"

She blinked and gaped in shock at his dispassionate tone. She glanced back at her plate and the thought of eating anything else churned her stomach. Corinne shook her head, unable to verbalize an answer.

Uberon correctly interpreted her horrified expression. He extended his hand and said, "Come. We must be on our way."

Corinne blinked and obeyed, putting her palm to his out of newly formed habit if for no other reason. Despite the cold brutality she had just witnessed, she trusted him. Uberon would not harm her.

Uberon kept his grasp loose and gentle, knowing that his defense of her honor had frightened her. She'd become accustomed to the harsh code of honor to which the fae subscribed, the strict necessity a fae male obeyed to protect his fragile mate, regardless of whether she actually was fragile. She followed him, stepping with careful delicacy so as not to tread upon any of the rapidly thawing pellets of the offensive djinni male. Uberon tossed a silver coin on the table in payment of the food and the task of cleaning the detritus of dead djinn.

"Stop!" a deep voice commanded as the fae lord led his mate through the doorway toward the stable yard.

Uberon halted, repressing a small sigh of annoyance. He partially turned to look at who dared command him and raised an eyebrow in inquiry.

"I'm the sheriff of Donshae and you're accused of murder, my lord," the male said with grim determination. "Release the female and come with me. You're under arrest."

Uberon did not blink. Instead, he gave the interfering male an opportunity to live. "The djinn insulted my mate. I am within my rights to defend her honor."

The male pressed his lips together and exhaled a gusty breath through his nose. "My lord, we have laws and make no exception for race."

Corinne squeezed Uberon's hand and he acquiesced to her unspoken demand for mercy.

"No one places a hand upon my mate without her assent. That male did and received justice for the insult. Delay us no further."

The sheriff's expression darkened. "Not even a fae lord is above our law, sir."

Corinne felt Uberon grow still and knew that the sheriff's life grew immeasurably short.

"Sir, the man accosted me. My husband ... er ... *mate* defended me. Surely, you would not persecute him for that?"

Uberon's heart quivered and warmed at her defense of him, her small attempt to spare him retribution from the law. He gave her hand a light squeeze and let his ire dissolve.

"Quiet, female," the sheriff ordered. "This does not concern you."

"What? Of course, this concerns me! I was the one the djinn accosted."

"He discounts you as nothing more than my chattel," Uberon murmured in explanation. "You have no rights here."

Fury swelled within Corinne's heart, making the swirling

design and black diamonds glow. The sheriff averted his eyes against the brilliant glare from above the modest neckline of her riding habit.

She took a step toward him and hissed, "I'll show you what dumb chattel can do."

"Control your female, my lord. She won't like what happens otherwise."

"Ooooh!" she screeched.

"My lady is powerful in her own right, Sheriff," Uberon replied with freezing calm, still keeping firm hold of Corinne's hand. "She does not *require* my protection, though she has it."

"Nonetheless, you're under arrest for the murder of Ibi Abdeel Elzawad, captain of the *Wind Scarab*."

"The crew of the *Wind Scarab* will have to find a new captain. I'm not going anywhere with you."

The sheriff gestured and six deputies emerged from concealment. No surprise showed on Uberon's face.

"We can do this the easy way or the hard way."

"Or we can not do this at all," Uberon replied and unleashed his will. The six deputies suddenly clutched at their throats as the air around them disappeared. "Step aside or let your men die. It's your choice."

"Release them from your deviltry, fae!"

"Drop your charges and vow not to pursue us."

The sheriff watched in horror as his men turned bluish from a lack of air. With begrudging concession, he accepted defeat, unwilling to sacrifice half his deputies. "Go then, and do not return."

"Gladly," Uberon replied and released his will. Air rushed back into the six separate vacuums with a series of loud cracking noises. He crooked a finger at the hostler who stood beneath the eaves of the stable, reins in hand and face pale with dread. "You'll not see us again in your lifetime."

The sheriff opened his mouth and Corinne interrupted before he could speak. "If you don't want that lifetime to end now, you'll hold your tongue, mister."

The sheriff's mouth snapped shut as the hostler led the horses forward. The fae lord and his lady mounted their steeds, settling into finely crafted saddles. His eyes glittered with impotent outrage at having been so easily bested in front of a mere woman. By a mere woman.

"The fae have long memories," Uberon warned as his large black destrier drew alongside the sheriff. "And anything with human blood has a short life. Save your life and your justice for those who merit it."

The black destrier launched forward with a mighty heave of its burly haunches. The golden palfrey followed close behind. The sheriff turned around slowly, his traumatized deputies gathering around him, to watch the formidable Unseelie fae lord and his Unseelie mate ride north toward the harbor's shore.

"Are you going after them?" one of the deputies inquired, rubbing at his throat.

"No. He won't be back."

"You can't be sure of that."

"Fae don't lie. They don't have to."

CHAPTER 14

Uberon felt his mate's discomfort as they rode. Skimming her thoughts and emotions he observed her reaction to a new understanding of her dependency upon him. She struggled with the concept of limited—or nonexistent—rights and privileges, far different than what she was accustomed to. In many ways, his world imposed greater burdens and expectations upon its females than did hers.

"Am I really your property?" she asked in a small, uncertain voice.

He answered as honestly as he could without causing Corinne additional and unnecessary distress. "You are mine, but I do not consider you chattel. I would never see you as mere property."

She favored him with a small smile of gratitude, but did not accept his evasion. "That doesn't answer my question, Uberon. Am I chattel?"

"Donshae is a free city in that it vows allegiance to no one nation. It is governed by a council of men who decide the laws that benefit them. It benefits them to relegate females to chattel."

"How does it benefit them?" she cried.

He raised an eyebrow in silent reminder of her own world's history, of the cultures in which women still petitioned and fought for basic rights as thinking, feeling human beings. Corinne sighed in defeat and guessed she ought to be grateful that Uberon was more considerate of her.

"I don't want your gratitude," he said, his voice guttural and rough.

Her gaze flew to him, tall and elegant in the saddle as the horses moved swiftly, steadily, tirelessly.

"I want *you*. I want everything you are and, in return, I give you all that I am." He glanced at her, held her gaze for a long, intense moment. "Our souls are merged. I could no more desecrate you than myself."

She nodded, knowing that much about the arrogant and proud Unseelie king. She also supposed that the exchange of everything of herself for everything of himself was rather uneven. He was larger than life. Legendary. So much *more*.

Not for the first time in her short life, Corinne felt inadequate.

"Never."

She glanced at him again.

He thumped a fist against his muscled chest. "Fate does not pair the souls of unequal mates. You complete me. You are light to my darkness, compassion to my cruelty. I give you strength, you give me softness. We complement each other."

He opened his mind and pulled her in, so she could *see* the truth of his words, his conviction. She gasped and tears welled in her eyes.

"I do not want your gratitude," he repeated.

"And I cannot help but give it to you," she sniffled. "All my life I tagged in someone else's footsteps. I was never as strong, as fast, or as clever as my brothers. I earned a degree my family does not value because they see no good purpose in it. I began a career that they don't understand and which offered no consistency, no security."

She sniffled and took a moment to bring herself under control.

"I'm the family failure, the screw-up, the impractical one."

"And yet they love you," he countered.

"They do," she acknowledged. "But they don't understand me."

"I do."

She sniffled again and nodded. "I think you do, Uberon.

Usually."

He chuckled and reached across the space between their horses to cup her cheek for a tender second. "A little mystery is always good, eh?"

"Just a little."

Her small smile felt like the appearance of the sun after a storm. His success in reassuring her, easing her emotional pain, swelled his heart and his pride. He raised his hand and pointed ahead.

"See the three-masted ship?"

Corinne shaded her eyes and peered into the distance. She barely made out the hazy shape floating on the horizon. "Yes."

"That is a private wharf. Donshae does not own it, although the merchant who does lives in the city. We will embark there."

"Embark. We're going on a ship?"

"It's the safest way to Quoliálfur without a dragon to fly us there, and few dragons will fly near the Quol. I will not risk you to the Quol."

She nodded, certain that she did not care to go anywhere that deterred dragons. "No objections here."

She paused as another thought occurred to her.

"Um, Uberon?"

"Yes, beloved?"

"This sounds stupid, but what about sea monsters?"

"Sea monsters?"

She blushed, which made him smile. "Yeah, you know, large, ravenous creatures that live in the sea. I mean, there are dragons here, unicorns, a lot of other creatures I'm sure I haven't yet encountered. Why not the Loch Ness Monster and its sisters?"

"The Loch Ness Monster is a freshwater beast," he replied. Corinne's eyes bugged. *Was he serious? Or joking?* "Yes, we have ocean dwelling creatures here that you might label as sea monsters."

"Please don't tell me you have kraken."

"They prefer tropical waters."

"We're in a tropical area." She gestured at the dark, hungry jungle lurking in the opposite horizon.

"So we are."

"Uberon." Her voice carried a thread of warning.

He chuckled, unable to remember if he'd ever had so much

fun before taking this fiery female as his mate.

"I shall protect you, even from sea monsters."

"I'll hold you to that," she grumbled. "If your adventures get me killed, I'll haunt you."

He grinned at her and she shook her head at the absurdity.

"Uberon?"

"Yes, beloved?"

"If that wharf is privately owned and not part of Donshae, does it share the city's protection against the Quol?"

He approved of her astute question. "The merchant is an old acquaintance of mine. His property and family fall under my protection."

She frowned. "Is the Unseelie Court near here then?"

"No, it's far south, south of Seelie territory. This continent cools the further south one travels, warms as one goes north."

"Southern Hemisphere," Corinne murmured to herself.

"Indeed."

Her brow wrinkled with thought. "How did the king of a country far to the south come to place a merchant and his family in the far north under his protection?"

Again, Uberon approved of and delighted in her keen mind and curious nature. "He—or, rather, his family over several generations—procured specimens and material objects for my studies."

The image of a sort of wild-eyed mad scientist wearing wizard's robes such as might have been designed for a Hollywood movie popped into her mind. "You conducted experiments?"

"I did."

"On what?"

"A multitude of things. I collected tomes and learned scholars and rare objects. I studied and experimented to fill the emptiness. It sufficed then, but no longer."

"But you haven't given up your studying?"

"No. I remain curious about the true nature of things and enjoy understanding their secrets."

"So, basically, you are a scientist."

"No, because I know magic is real. A true scientist considers *magic* a term for something we simply don't understand. I understand the science behind your world's radio broadcast, although you'll find no such thing here and most folk would consider it magic. But I also access and manipulate a force beyond mere energy with nothing more than my will: that is magic."

"It sounds as though anyone could perform magical feats if only they understood how to access and manipulate that force."

"Theoretically, that's possible," he agreed, his tone mild. "Not so much in practice. Power such as you and I possess arises from the soul and is sparked by divinity."

"You're saying that we're essentially gods."

"To humans, aye, we would be if we so desired it."

"And have you?"

"Desired godhood? I? No. Others have succumbed to the lure of worship. Most of your world's pagan gods and goddesses are fae who succumbed to the lure of human adoration. I do not need to be worshipped."

Only loved, she thought, which made him essentially no different than anyone else. Another disturbing though came to her. "What about God?"

"God as in Yahweh or Allah?"

"Yes. God. Is He real?"

"I have seen no concrete evidence that convinces me your God is real; however, neither will I dismiss the possibility. After all, according to the modern humans of your world, I am neither possible nor real."

"Do you see your role here as that of a god?"

"Not at all. I am Uberon, king of the Quoliálfur, formerly king of the Unseelie Court, one of the three most ancient of my kind and whose lineage has been lost to time. I know who I am and that identity does not concern itself with occupation as some sort of benevolent overseer of my world."

"Just your kingdom."

He nodded to acknowledge the point. "Aye. But I do not watch over my subjects' lives and evaluate their every action. I leave them free to live as they see fit, provided they do not violate my laws or infringe upon the freedom of others."

"That's rather enlightened of you."

"I'm a hip, modern sort of king," came the bland reply.

Once again, Uberon's dry humor made her laugh. When she finished chuckling, she noticed they'd arrived at the wharf. *How did we get here so quickly?* She looked at Uberon, who said nothing. She thought that, perhaps, he did not see her glance of bewilderment, then dismissed that thought. Uberon noticed *everything*. Corinne told herself that answers would be forthcoming; she just had to exercise patience.

Her palfrey followed his destrier onto the heavy wooden planks. Sailors and stevedores paused in their tasks to watch the newcomers with suspicious eyes. Uberon dismounted and, not looking at his mate, said in a low tone, "Remain mounted. Should it be necessary, your horse will convey you to safety."

"Do you expect danger?" she asked, also keeping her voice quiet.

"Always."

"Ooookay."

"What do ye want, milord?" a sailor inquired as he approached, his accent as rough as his appearance. His pale eyes lingered with greedy calculation upon the red-haired female accompanying the black-haired, Unseelie male.

"Please summon Master Merogis. Tell him Lord Nochnaya and his mate are here."

Ignoring the female's surprised expression, the sailor raised his eyebrows at the word *summon*. However, he shrugged and replied, "He'll be informed. Is he expecting you?"

"I doubt it."

"Then he'll not appreciate being summoned like some lackey."

Uberon looked down his nose at the insolent sailor and his upper lip curled in a sneer. "Appreciate it or not, he'll come. Now do as I bid you."

"We're free men here, Lord Nochnaya."

Uberon said nothing. He simply leveled his icy silver glare at the man who averted his eyes first. The sailor muttered imprecations under his breath about the undeserved haughtiness of snooty fae lords and departed to carry out that same fae lord's bidding. Let Master Merogis deal with him, he growled to himself, the heavily accented words reaching Uberon's keen ears.

Uberon cared nothing for the man's opinion. He listened to make sure the man mentioned nothing regarding capture of his mate. Glancing around at the seamen and workers populating the wharf, he knew they hungered for soft female flesh with a greed that debased whatever pretenses they held to civilization. Uberon would not tolerate a single rough, dirty finger laid upon Corinne. If Merogis did not arrive soon, those sea monsters lurking beneath the waves would eat well this day.

With the black horse on one side of Corinne and Uberon on the other, Corinne thought herself well-protected. She had her own tricks, too, which she doubted those grubby sailors and stevedores suspected. Still, their predatory focus and lustful avarice made the tiny hairs at the back of her neck prickle. She doubted neither the danger around them nor Uberon's protection, and hoped her mate could conclude their business without killing the ship's crew.

"Why did you give the name Nochnaya?" she whispered.

"The Merogis line have always known me as such."

"I don't understand."

He consented to explain. "They have done business with a wealthy fae lord among a clientele consisting of wealthy noblemen. Did they know they dealt with *me*, then they'd either disappear altogether and have nothing to do with my business, or they would cower in gibbering fear. I prefer to transact business with people who retain their wits in my presence."

"Oh." Once again, she intuited a sense of deep loneliness within him.

They waited in a tense standoff, both sides keeping watch on each other. The tropical sun beat down upon them. Corinne felt sweat trickle between her breasts and down her spine, despite the lightweight habit she wore. She mused to herself that she should have asked for a hat, something lightweight with a broad brim.

She kept glancing at Uberon, who stood within arm's length—his arm's length—alert and ready for danger. He looked like a sophisticated barbarian king. She wrinkled her nose at her own fanciful oxymoron.

"Lord Nochnaya!" called a man walking toward them. Or waddling. The ocean breeze caught the loose, colorful silks draped around his rotund body, and they flapped like pennants. Corinne blinked and tried to maintain her composure when she noticed that the long toes of his shoes curled up and over with golden tassels dangling from the tips. The wind tossed a matching tassel dangling from the bright green fez that somehow stayed firmly affixed to the top of the man's head.

Uberon raised his hand in silent recognition and murmured so that only Corinne could hear, "He's ridiculous, but very, very smart. Don't underestimate him."

"Lord Nochnaya," Fidor Merogis greeted again with a broad smile plumping his heavy jowls and making raisin-like eyes nearly disappear within his broad, round face. "I did not expect you. Welcome!"

Uberon bowed, although not as deeply as Fidor Merogis did. "It's good to see you, Master Merogis. I had not anticipated sailing north again so soon, but plans change."

"That they do," the merchant replied, his eyes looking over the fair female form perched atop a fine golden palfrey. "And who is this accompanying you, my lord?"

"Congratulate me, Master Merogis, for I have found my mate."

The fat man's eyes widened with surprise and, perhaps, a smidgen of disappointment. An educated man, he knew that this fae female was forbidden to him, the males of his extended family, and the rough men who worked for him, hungry though they might be for the taste and touch of a woman's body. "This is an auspicious occasion, Lord Nochnaya! You must allow me to host you tonight. We shall have a feast in honor of your nuptials."

"We would be honored to enjoy your gracious hospitality and my lady would certainly enjoy some feminine company for a few hours. I hope your lady wives are in good health?"

"Aye, and my daughters are ready to be married. Fine girls they are, healthy and obedient. They'll bear a man many sons and give him pleasure for many years. I've merely to find the men worthy of them who can pay the bride price."

Corinne's eyes narrowed and she pressed her lips together in a thin line of disapproval. She reminded herself she had not the right to criticize another culture. The reminder failed to calm her ire on those women's behalf. Then she thought that if she were to be sequestered with this male chauvinist pig's wives and daughters, then she might subvert their inculcation with a few pointed suggestions. She did not consider whether igniting the women's discontent with their lot might sentence them to misery, only that they deserved to know they had value beyond their capacity to breed sons and warm a man's bed.

She remembered reading a book about the consequences of a country cursed by an offended witch and smiled to herself. Men received the curse—that women on the island nation would bear only sons—with joy until a second generation passed and they had no women. She wondered if she could somehow effect such a curse upon Donshae and this fat merchant's compound. If not, perhaps Uberon could.

You are devious.

I'm furious. Will you do it?

Perhaps. I shall ask if his people would prefer that their women bear them sons instead of daughters and let them suffer the consequences of their preference.

I knew I liked you.

"Hand your mounts over to my men," Master Merogis instructed as he led the way toward shore and his sprawling house beyond. His guests followed close behind. "They'll take good care of the beasts. And follow me inside. The courtyard is cool and refreshing. I conduct all of my business there."

Master Merogis waved his hand in a gesture to encompass the expansive manse. "Your bride will be glad of a cool bath, I'm sure. Women like to be refreshed before we fuck them to a hot, sweaty mess, eh?"

The merchant chuckled. Uberon did not. Merogis took no offense, because his guest had never before demonstrated a sense of humor. Lord Nochnaya paid generously in gold, which made him a client due all obsequious consideration and indulgence. It was too bad he'd never managed to interest the wealthy fae lord in one of his daughters. The familial connection could have been exploited for great profit and power. He spared no more thought nor regret mourning what had never been. There was no profit in it.

Stepping beneath a pergola shrouded by a blooming, fragrant vine dropped the temperature several degrees. Corinne breathed a sigh of relief. Uberon glanced at her and frowned with concern. She wiped her sweaty forehead with the back of a forearm and gave him a reassuring smile while looking at him garbed in leather and looking unaffected by the sweltering tropical heat. Damn him.

Shorts, tee shirt, and sandals would be a hell of a lot more comfortable than this dress in this heat and humidity.

And they would scandalize the entire city.
Could you at least see your way to allowing me short sleeves?
I'll see what I can do.
Thanks.

They walked into the merchant's home, thick walls holding in coolness and cleverly placed windows catching refreshing breezes. Corinne heaved another sigh of relief and appreciation. The three of them halted, with their host summoning a servant to lead her to the women's quarters. She glanced at Uberon with no small degree of trepidation before following the servant.

"Master Merogis, it would please me greatly to have my mate join us for the evening meal," Uberon said.

The merchant's brow creased, then smoothed. "But, of course! You fae are much attached to your womenfolk, and I understand the imperative not to allow such fair beauty to hide from your eyes any longer than necessary." He clapped his hands as though having come up with a grand idea. "I shall bid my own wives to join me at supper. Then your lady wife will not feel bereft of suitable company while we dine and discuss business."

"A most elegant solution," Uberon agreed. "Indeed, I dislike to be parted from my mate."

"My wives will hardly be able to contain their excitement," Merogis predicted, rubbing his hands together. His eyes roved over the tall fae with the chiseled, handsome face and physical beauty the merchant knew better than to aspire to. He made up for his lack of good looks and athleticism with a keen mind and superior business sense which had enabled him to amass the fortune necessary to purchase highborn wives of outstanding beauty. He hoped his wives would repay this social treat with a bedroom enthusiasm they normally lacked. They obeyed, but they went no further than that. Their disinterest and veiled contempt pricked at his pride.

Beneath the expansive bulge of his belly, his cock twitched even as he entertained the faint hope that his wealthy client would consent to sharing his fresh and lovely mate. Merogis had never sampled a fae female, and having one so close made his fingertips itch. He wondered if Uberon would accept an evening's swap of his wives for a few hours with his mate. Hope died a swift and inevitable death as his mind reminded his body that fae males did not share their mates. Ever.

To suggest such a swap, even for a single evening, would insult his wealthiest client. And the fae had some strange talents. Not that Merogis put much stock in wild, surely exaggerated tales of fae magic; but, living so close to the Quol and the weird, frightening occurrences that happened near its boundary, he did not discount that the fae lord enjoying his hospitality possessed arcane skills he did not.

No, he told himself, he would satiate his appetites on his wives and merely indulge in the pretense that the body he plowed belonged to the fae female. Life was safer that way and more likely to continue. The fae lord wore that sword at his hip with an ease that bespoke of intimate familiarity. Master Fidor Merogis knew a seasoned warrior when he saw one.

CHAPTER 15

Seven dark-eyed women and one barely adolescent girl looked up at Corinne's arrival. Two of the women exhibited the softened jaw lines and crow's feet of maturity. The other four looked at least a generation younger. All six women and the girl lounged like colorful water lilies on large cushions scattered like lily pads across a deep blue tiled floor, their bare feet adorned with bejeweled toe rings and ankle cuffs. One of the women snapped a command to which a flutter of drab cloth responded, alerting Corinne to the unobtrusive presence of a serving girl.

She looked at the servant fetch a tray and carafe of deep ruby liquid. The woman beckoned to Corinne with a gesture and called to her in cascading, liquid syllables. Corinne blinked, not understanding the words, but knowing what that gesture meant. The other mature woman rose gracefully from her cushion and smiled, offering a gap-toothed display testifying to a diet of too many sweets and poor dental hygiene. Her voice lisped a little as she spoke in halting words.

"'Allo. You ... honored ... guest."

Corinne smiled back and murmured, "Thank you."

The woman walked around her, eyeing her with a critical gaze. "Eat. Bathe. We ... have ... curtains."

Corinne blinked and smothered a chuckle, because she found the incorrect word surprisingly apt. Thin, vibrantly colored silks drifted about the woman's plump body like sheers ruffled by a summer breeze. The woman nodded and murmured to herself and reached out to touch the ginger locks escaping from the visitor's complicated plait. She rubbed the thick silk between her thumb and forefinger as though surprised at the texture and lack of heat.

In her liquid tongue she rattled off what Corinne supposed were instructions. The mature women identified themselves as the mothers of the girls in order of descending age: Sin'halissar, Sin'clannad, Ari'valia, Ari'dongharad, and Han'al. While the three older girls looked to be in their mid to late teens, the younger two still radiated the innocence of childhood. Fidor Merogis' statement that all of his daughters were ready to be wed churned Corinne's stomach. The serving girl nodded and bowed and hurried off to do her mistress' bidding. The woman took Corinne's hand and led her to a plump cushion.

"I speak ... good ... no?"

"Er ... yes. You speak very well," Corinne agreed, reminding herself that she knew not a single word of the woman's native language and was in no position to disparage another's command of a language she herself was still learning to master. Thank goodness Uberon usually spoke to her in English rather than the common trade tongue of this world that Oriel insisted she learn. *With mastery of the common trade tongue, you can make yourself understood almost anywhere on the continent.*

The woman beamed with pride. "I teach ... girls."

"That's good," Corinne replied with obvious sincerity, since she could see that these women led very restricted, limited lives. They surely welcomed anything that broadened their education.

"Come. Eat."

The woman gestured at the cushion and Corinne sat, although she doubted she displayed the grace of these ladies who spent their lives perfecting indolence. While the other middle-aged woman looked on, Corinne picked an unfamiliar morsel of food with her fingers and bit into it. Flavor exploded on her tongue and her eyes widened with surprise.

She supposed she ought not to be surprised. In a culture that restricted women's lives so severely, they would master the culinary arts. As she chewed, she decided to speak to Uberon about how fae women—*females*—conducted their lives. Her experience in the Erlking's castle and limited time in the Seelie Court indicated that fae females had little in the way of occupation; but, she admitted, her exposure to them had been brief. She did, however, remember seeing female guards, so at least they had that avenue of occupation.

One of the young women approached and gestured to another of the small dishes. Corinne tried something else, choked on the spicy heat, and grabbed a goblet to drain it. The younger ladies laughed at their prank. Even the older women smirked.

"They try to kill you with their food," her brother Samuel once told her after returning from overseas deployment. "Even your allies."

She now understood what he meant.

She nibbled on the assortment of foods offered, all of it bite-sized and made for eating without utensils. She refilled the goblet and drank its potent contents in moderation. When Corinne had consumed her fill—and her head buzzed from the alcohol—the ladies drew her to her feet and led her to another chamber. Eager, bejeweled hands quickly divested her of clothes and pulled her into a large, cool fountain. The women gasped at the fae soul bond embedded in her skin, their inquisitive fingers tracing the intricate patterns of silver and black diamonds.

"Ouch! Stop that!" Corinne yelped when someone attempted to pry a diamond loose with a sharp fingernail. After a muttered apology, laughter and comments she did not understand flowed as the ladies bathed her and bathed with her.

Corinne felt thoroughly violated afterward.

Her hostesses chattered and debated among themselves as servants brought out a bewildering array of silks and jewels until finally Corinne found herself draped in filmy shades of blue and her wrists and ankles bedecked with layers of delicate gold chains dripping with blue stones. She looked and felt positively barbaric.

The older ladies fluttered and giggled as they, too, dressed in their finest garb. When a male servant knocked at the door to the women's quarters, they assumed meek, sober expressions and directed their eyes to the floor. The servant glared at Corinne who dared meet his gaze.

They followed him down a long, airy corridor. A refreshing breeze blew through intricately carved stone screens, cooling the passageway. Corrine's mind drifted into contemplation of the skilled craftsmanship needed to manufacture those screens and wondered if their host had imported the panels or the stoneworkers

The servant stopped at a doorway curtained by floor-to-ceiling beads which clacked as the ocean breeze wafted through the long strands. He barked a command and the ladies pushed through. They stumbled to a halt, mouths gaping and eyes flashing when Uberon rose from his bank of cushions to acknowledge the females.

"Mmmm," the woman who taught the trade tongue to her daughters hummed her appreciation of the kilted, bare-chested fae lord who extended his hand toward his mate. She licked her lips and made it clear without words that she envied their guest her good fortune in having such a well-formed, handsome husband.

Even though she agreed, Corinne's cheeks burned with embarrassment at the other woman's obvious and lustful appreciation of her mate. It reminded her too much of the fawning, drooling looks directed at her brothers when they stopped by the college dormitory. She did not know whether her brothers ever accepted the blatant invitations; she did not want to know.

"Come, sit with me," Uberon said.

Corinne stepped forward, conscious of the other women's envy as she did so. Fidor Merogis barked a command at his two wives, obviously disgruntled by their distraction with the fae lord's physical beauty. The women scurried forward to take their places at each of his flanks. Merogis' meaty hands immediately grabbed and squeezed a breast on each woman. From their strained looks, he didn't bother with a gentle touch.

"Cruel bastard," Corinne muttered under her breath as she sat on a cushion beside Uberon.

"Do not interfere," Uberon warned. "They will suffer the consequences."

Corinne huffed her disapproval.

"Your woman is obedient," Merogis observed with approval and a greedy glint in his eyes. "Do the Unseelie females look like this one? I would pay a ship's hold of gold for such a rare beauty."

"My mate is unique and has no equal," Uberon replied. He

shook his head. "I recommend you do not approach any fae with such an offer. Our females are few and precious to us."

Servants approached carrying platters heaped with food. Savory fragrances wafted from the steaming rice, herbed vegetables, and spiced meat.

"Follow their lead," Uberon murmured in Corinne's ear as Merogis' two wives moved to fill a plate for him. He spoke in English, the light accent sexy and distinctive. "Draw no more attention to yourself than necessary. Our host may attempt something and it's best to lull him into a sense of false security."

"I'd set fire to stone before I'd let him take me."

"I know and I would add my fire to yours. But the women don't deserve to suffer for their master's perfidy and greed."

Corinne had to agree.

"I do not recognize this rude tongue your woman speaks," Merogis said in the common trade tongue as his wives fed him from their fingers.

Uberon answered in the same language as one of the women held a golden goblet to the merchant's fleshy lips. "My mate comes from beyond the Unseelie Court. Her soul called to mine."

"A woman's soul? Has a woman such a thing?" Merogis laughed. "They are sweet to look at and good to fuck, but of little use otherwise except for the bearing of sons. And no man wishes to jeopardize the formation of his son, which requires a man to have multiple wives to slake his needs."

Oh, I really do want to curse this pig!

Uberon's chuckle reverberated inside her mind. Corinne felt no recriminations, no disapproval. She plucked a meatball from the closest platter and held it to his lips. He chewed.

"Excellent."

Corinne ate a meatball and agreed.

Merogis turned the conversation to matters of trade, negotiating to secure exclusivity on supplying the royal court of the Quoliálfur in what was sure to be a long-standing, lucrative trade agreement. Uberon met the wily merchant's negotiation with an utter refusal to promise the profitable trade deals Merogis so clearly desired. As the males ate and conversed, the merchant's wives chatted quietly with each other while tending to their master. They lapsed into resentful silence when he offered the Quoliálfur king all five of his daughters in exchange for exclusive trade contracts.

"While your offer is most generous," the fae king replied as he stroked a hand down his mate's red hair, "I neither need nor want another female."

"A virile man like you? How could you not need multiple women?" The merchant's eyes gleamed as they roamed over the sculpted muscles. His gaze shifted to run up and down the fae king's mate. "A single woman who can satisfy the appetite of a man like you must be insatiable."

"Fae mates crave only each other," Uberon replied.

Reviewing the conversation between the merchant and the king, Corinne had an idea. *Offer him gold for his daughters.*

Did you not—

I heard you and appreciate it. Really, I do. But if we take these girls, then we can give them an education, a better life.

What will they do with that education? What careers could they take that would allow them to retain their dignity?

Your kingdom is new. Why not open opportunities for women? Like your homeland?

Yes, but without taking a few hundred years to do so. She huffed. *Uberon, you're the king. Make a law.*

Not even a king can override culture.

Perhaps not all at once, but you can decree that women not be denied the same education and opportunities as men. Let these girls be the vanguard of that.

Have you asked them whether they wish to be the vanguard of anything?

She huffed again, hating his cool logic. *I can barely communicate with them. Only one of the women speaks more than a few words of the common language, and I don't speak their native tongue.*

Stroking a fingertip along her jaw, Uberon said in English, "If these girls give their consent, then I shall buy them and see them educated and employed in Quoliálfur."

Merogis clapped his hands, which set his jowls to jiggling. Three women clothed in little more than strategically draped chains strutted through the beaded entrance. A flautist and drummer followed them in and took their places in a corner of the room. Skirling music set the three women to dancing, which involved much rolling of hips and shaking of bosoms and tossing of hair. The merchant watched with rapt attention as he pulled one of his wives into his lap. He growled a command and she opened the front of his robes. At another command, she bent over his lap and took his soft penis into her mouth.

"I can't believe this," Corinne murmured and averted her eyes. "Even when Gus was touching Oriel right in front of me, he protected her. He didn't lust over some dancer and use her to get his rocks off."

"That, beloved, is one distinction between human and fae."

"No," Corinne argued with a stubborn shake of her head. "My father would never treat my mother like that."

Uberon conceded the point.

"Lord Nochnaya, show me how a fae female pleases her master," Merogis beckoned, then groaned with pleasure as his fat hands clenched the woman's hair and pushed her head into his groin. Corinne flinched at the sound of the woman gagging.

Uberon directed a cold, silver gaze at the man who forced the woman to swallow him. "Some things we fae keep private. But I would be grateful to be excused so that I might enjoy my mate's company without distraction."

Merogis licked his lips and nodded, a wave of his thick hand granting consent. Uberon rose to his feet, drawing Corinne up with him. He bowed and, taking his mate's hand in his, departed for the sumptuous chamber the merchant had assigned him.

Corinne spent the night in Uberon's arms; but, after their host's postprandial display and the gagging sounds echoing in her ears, she found no enthusiasm for conjugal relations. The fae king said nothing, he merely gathered her close to his body and urged her to sleep without fear.

She awoke alone, wrapped in a thin wool blanket.

After taking some time to remember her location, she washed and dressed in her cleaned riding habit. Corinne stepped into the hallway and looked both ways. The coast was clear.

She glanced back at the door to the room, then again in both directions down the corridor. Making a decision, she walked.

Where are you?

Negotiating with Merogis.

She inhaled with anticipation. *The girls?*

Aye. Your compassion and idealism spark the better part of me.

Where are you?

At the wharf.

Corinne tore off at a run, startling the servants she passed. Sailors swiveled around to watch as her booted feet thumped down the wooden planks. She saw the merchant's brightly colored robes flapping in the wind and Uberon's long black hair unfurling like a flag. Standing in a cluster of fearful uncertainty, Merogis' daughters alternately watched the two men and looked at the waiting ship as they conversed in quiet tones.

Though he did not raise his head to acknowledge her, Uberon extended his hand toward her. Corinne skidded to a stop and grabbed his hand, willingly allowing him to reel her in and tuck her close to his side. He bent down to press a kiss into her hair and returned his piercing gaze to Mergosis.

"You are indulgent," the merchant commented. "Women require strictness, else they make trouble."

"They are now my trouble," Uberon reminded him with a shark's smile. "Have their belongings brought aboard, along with my horses and packs."

Merogis shook his head. "Lord Nochnaya, you purchased the girls, nothing more. I consider myself generous in allowing them to go with the clothes on their backs."

At Corinne's outraged gasp, Uberon tightened his hold on his mate, signaling to her to let him take care of the situation. He lifted his gaze to take in the merchant's prosperous compound. Looking back down at Merogis, he said, "What a pity it would be if the wards protecting your estate were to fail. The Quol has no mercy for its prey."

Merogis' swarthy skin turned ashen.

"I should think such a doting father would wish his daughters to be comfortable with their familiar possessions around them."

"A father with valuable daughters commands a high bride price to ensure they live in comfort," Merogis retorted.

"Ah, but I've already paid and have the bill of sale in hand."

"A bill of sale for female flesh and nothing more."

A haunting cry echoed from the distance where the dark jungle lurked. Sailors paused in their work to make signs against evil or murmur silent prayers for their safety. Fidor Merogis glanced toward his home.

"The wards remain viable at my will," Uberon said. "Your daughters deserve the comfort of their belongings."

"They own nothing. They were my property and property cannot itself own other property."

"Do not allow your greed to destroy you."

"The wards have stood for over two centuries and no exiled fae lord is strong enough to dismantle them. You have what you paid for, Lord Nochnaya. Please take your cargo and go."

Uberon nodded. "Come, beloved. The girls will need your support."

Corinne clenched her jaw, knowing that Merogis had just sealed his doom and that of many others. A sailor led the two horses up the gangplank, another following behind carrying saddles and saddlebags. Two more sailors herded the girls onto the ship. The girls cast frightened looks at their father waddling back up the wharf, barking orders as he went and not once turning back to bid them goodbye.

"They're better off without him," Corinne said. "But I feel sorry for their mothers."

"They'll not mourn for long."

"You mean they'll die? You'd actually let the wards fall?"

"Beloved, if a king does not keep his word, then he loses his authority."

"But that fat jerk doesn't know you're a king!"

"He knows I am highborn fae and that is sufficient."

"But what about all the other people here?"

"If they're smart, they'll sail off before the Quoli overrun the compound."

Corinne shuddered and gripped the railing so hard her knuckles turned white. "They'll all die."

"Aye."

"And Merogis won't lift a finger to save them."

"No."

"You can—"

"I can, but I shall not."

Tears glistened in Corinne's eyes as she looked at the towering male who treated her with such tenderness and generosity, and yet condemned a veritable village to death. This, she realized once more, was the Unseelie king, a fae whose icy heart struck fear into thousands of generations of people.

Over the snap of sails, the creak of wood, and the splash of water, she heard thin, high shrieks of triumph as the wards protecting the merchant's compound cracked beneath the pressure of the Quol's mindless hunger and the withdrawal of will and energy that created and sustained them. Corinne could not bear to ask when the wards would crumble and the mysterious Quoli would swarm toward the water to reclaim their territory.

The ship's captain approached the fae lord to confer with him. They spoke in low tones and in the captain's native tongue which Corinne did not understand. She did, however, examine him covertly and determined from his orange and purple hair and pointed teeth that he was either not human or perhaps only partially human.

"What is he?" she finally asked, her voice subdued.

"Maltani. On the continent, they are more commonly called witchbreed."

"Not fae?"

"Remotely fae. The Maltani emerged as an amalgamation of races that interbred over thousands of years to eventually become a distinct species."

She nodded, not knowing how to respond or even if a response was needed.

"Come, beloved, let's show the girls to their cabin."

Corinne blinked, startled by the abrupt shift back to the Uberon she knew and loved. Yes, *loved*.

CHAPTER 16

The girls clustered around Corinne as Uberon led them to their cabin, large enough for two portholes to let in fresh air. Subdued in the presence of the wealthy male who'd purchased them from their father, they maintained a fearful quiet.

I wish there were a way I could learn their native tongue quickly.

You have but to ask.

Corinne's eyes widened with astonishment. *Can you—will you—give that gift of their speech?*

Of course.

Corinne thought there was no "of course" about it. *Then will you? Please?*

She felt invisible fingers stroking inside her brain as though rifling through mental files. More invisible fingers stroke elsewhere, making her squirm as her libido sparked and hummed like a well-tuned car under the hands of a skilled mechanic.

You're playing dirty.

You like it.

Well, she couldn't very well deny that and wondered if she and Uberon had a separate, private cabin.

Of course, we do. I plan to ravish you properly tonight.

A shudder of desire rippled through her even as a headache

pressed against her skull. She supposed that the sudden dumping of knowledge would strain the capacity of her mind. At least that explanation made sense.

Uberon's arm wrapped around her, drawing her back to his front. He bent down and nibbled at her earlobe and whispered, "Listen and speak. You will understand and be understood."

"Did you just—?"

"Every living language I know you now command," he said. "And I shall take great pleasure in fucking you in every one of those languages."

Corinne wanted to moan as arousal slicked her thighs. Uberon nipped her neck and straightened. She sighed and gathered her composure and wits, although the girls who watched with wide, knowing eyes did not misunderstand the interaction between the handsome fae lord and his exotic looking mate.

"This is your room," she said, carefully enunciating the unfamiliar sounds and syllables as she pushed open the cabin door. "No crew are permitted in here while you occupy the room, so you must take responsibility for keeping it clean."

The girls' disappointed expressions declared more loudly than words that they had expected servants to wait upon them. However, they nodded their understanding.

"Report the presence of any crew member in this room to me or Lord Nochnaya."

The girls nodded.

"Bide here until we give you leave to wander the ship."

The girls nodded.

"And do not enter the crew's quarters."

The girls nodded, a couple of them looking shocked at the admonition. Surely, they needed no such warning. Corinne wasn't inclined to take that chance. The girls were at an age of curiosity and some of those sailors were attractive.

You will not approach the sailors yourself, beloved.

I haven't the least desire to form anything but the most casual acquaintance with any other male, she reassured him as the image of him above her and driving into her body flashed through her mind. She squirmed again.

Good.

Uberon then escorted her to the well-appointed cabin she

would share with him.

"Whom have we displaced?"

"The first mate."

"Oh." She almost wished she hadn't known that, but neither was she so generous as to relinquish the little privacy she could claim on the ship. "How long is this voyage?"

"If the weather holds fair, three days," Uberon answered. "I will have some food brought to you while I confer with the captain. Stay in the cabin until I ensure the crew understands my requirements for polite behavior."

"Do you really think—"

"Any male who insults you dies," he said, his tone brooking neither argument nor forgiveness, an indication that any female would likely face the same dire fate, although he did not say as much. After all, he had condemned the girls' mothers and the female servants to death by withdrawing his power from the wards that shielded the Fidor Merogis' compound from Quoli invasion.

Corinne hoped the innocents died quickly. She hated the thought of their prolonged suffering. She also wondered why Fidor Merogis hadn't taken the threat of the withdrawal of the wards more seriously.

He does not understand or believe that I set them and I maintain them.

She averted her eyes, unable to meet Uberon's cold, implacable gaze. She remembered seeing much the same look in her oldest brothers' eyes when they found their true loves, although Uberon packed a much bigger punch than any mere human ever could. He slid a fingertip under her chin and lifted her face toward his.

"Corinne, do not turn from me."

"I can't handle the ... the casual cruelty," she confessed.

"I cannot—nor will I try to—alter my basic nature, beloved. I am fàe, one of the three most ancient of my kind. I have witnessed and performed things you cannot imagine, yet I bend for you."

She closed her eyes and understood that any expectation that Uberon deny his deepest self was doomed to failure. He could not change what he was any more than she could change her own nature. Yet the impending doom facing innocents pierced her tender heart, and she could not help but mourn them before they even knew they were sentenced to cruel, harsh deaths. Tears welled up and she blinked them back, though she did not beg him to reconsider, to reverse the action he considered just and deserved according to the rigid code of honor to which he held himself.

"Ah, Corinne, your tears shatter my heart," he murmured as he gathered her close, cupping the back of her head with his palm. "You cannot save everyone, nor can I."

She nodded, though his tenderness broke her resolve not to cry and she sobbed into his shirt. The sharp pattering of small objects hitting the wooden floor of the ship distracted her. Hiccupping, she wiped her eyes and, looking down, saw the gleam of tiny beads scattered over the rough planking.

"Tears," Uberon said softly. "Fae tears crystallize when shed. They are more valuable than diamonds."

He cupped his hand, holding it out, and the tiny, winking crystals rose from the floor to gather in his open palm. With his other hand, he withdrew a handkerchief from thin air and deposited the small, glittering pile onto the fine cloth and twisted it tightly so not a single crystal escaped. He pressed the makeshift pouch into Corinne's palm.

"These are yours. Use them as you will."

"Tears," she echoed, her voice faint.

"Aye. And yours. Humans don't know their origin, for we guard that secret."

She nodded, understanding why. She'd seen *Pirates of the Caribbean: On Stranger Tides* with its lore of mermaids, the power of their tears, and the disgusting lengths to which men would go to extract those tears. Men, her father and brothers had long warned her, were not to be trusted. Except for them, of course. Because they only had her best interests at heart.

She looked at the wad of cloth in her hand and, for just a second, considered offering her tears to Uberon in payment for restoring the failing ward. Almost immediately, she reconsidered. She knew he would refuse.

Wealth did not motivate Uberon.

She briefly considered withholding her favors unless he complied with her wishes and discarded that, too. She refused such dishonesty. Besides a kiss from Uberon, a stroke, and she'd fall back and spread her legs and beg for him to make love to her. No, betting on her ability to resist his persuasion ... well, she decided not to be quite that stupid. How could she persuade him, she wondered and came back to the answer she had earlier: she could not. Nor would she.

The circuitous path of her thoughts tormented her.

Uberon held his silence as his mate worked through her thoughts. He could not remember ever having been as young as she, as idealistic, or as innocent. Those qualities shined brilliantly as diamonds to his eyes and he cherished them. Yet he would not be manipulated. He was once the Unseelie king and now claimed a new throne as the Quoliálfur king. He was *king*.

With almost unbearable tenderness, he pressed a kiss to his mate's head and bade her wait for him in the cabin. She nodded, barely noticing when the door closed behind him. She opened the wad of cloth in her hand and spilled the crystallized tears into her palm. Stirring them with the tip of her index finger, she murmured in stunned acceptance, "I am not human."

Lifting her head, she looked toward the porthole and inhaled deeply of the salty breeze blowing in off the ocean.

"Was I ever really human?"

Perhaps her conversion to fully fae met some sort of prophecy or destiny lost to her family's history. Perhaps some distant grandmother had once been fae and found herself trapped on Earth. Perhaps ... but she did not know and speculation answered nothing. She reviewed what she did know: her mother's mother had possessed the same arcane, elemental abilities as she, although her grandmother had hidden them. She had not discussed them except to admonish her granddaughter to master them and then use them sparingly and only when unobserved. Raised on a diet of paranormal romances on television and the movies, she took such warnings to heart.

Corinne huffed a soft, bitter laugh. How gullible she'd been. How ready to follow and obey the words of others. The unicorns had unlocked the power bound during her conversion to fae flesh. Being fae strengthened her power, made her formidable in her own right—even if she could not hope to match the vast strength and power of her mate. She wondered if her power would grow as the years passed. Surely, Uberon had not always been so strong?

She heaved a sigh and poured the tears back into the handkerchief. Knotting it to keep the crystals secure, she set it aside and rose to her feet. Her soft boots shuffled against the wood floor as she crossed the room to gaze out the porthole. This room, she noticed was smaller than the one given to the girls. Had they commandeered the captain's cabin? Surely not.

Corinne watched the churn of waves as the ship cut through the blue-green water. She inhaled the fresh scent of the ocean air and gasped when a whale rose from the surf and breached, crashing with a mighty splash. Then another rose and fell and slapped the water with its broad tail. She watched, entranced, barely noticing when the cabin boy entered the room and set down a tray of bread, cheese, fruit, and a bottle of wine. Belatedly noticing his arrival, she murmured an absent-minded thank-you as he let himself out.

Her stomach growled, reminding her she'd not eaten yet that day. Obeying the demand of her empty belly, she picked up a wedge of cheese, a hunk a bread, and a piece of whole fruit she did not recognize and carried them to the porthole to watch and wait while she ate.

"Did you see them?" she asked when the cabin door opened again and every sense she possessed told her that Uberon had entered the room, even though she did not look in his direction.

"The whales? I did. Magnificent, aren't they?"

She nodded. "I think I like them much better than dragons."

"They're not so short-tempered," Uberon agreed and sat beside her.

"You mean you haven't given them grave offense."

"No, I haven't. They have long memories, whales do, for all that they do not speak.

Corinne wondered what whales would say if they did speak. She did not realize she posed the question aloud until Uberon answered.

"I daresay they'd tell long, involved stories and have deep philosophical discussions."

She turned to face him and smiled. "Perhaps they're poets."

"Perhaps they are. For all that I have lived, I do not know everything of this world. I suspect the whales could teach me."

Corinne looked into his eyes and saw nothing but love for her reflected in them. Well, love tempered with the glint of passion. She lifted a hand to cup his cheek and he turned his face into her palm as though begging her forgiveness for his cruelty, for his very nature. Raising her other hand, she cradled his face and pressed her lips against his in a chaste, closed-mouthed kiss. His mouth yielded to hers and she kissed him again, deepening the touch.

"Corinne," he breathed against her lips.

She kissed him again, letting her palms slide down to the supple leather of his shirt and lower to the fall of his breeches. Nimble fingers unlaced the closure and opened the flap, exposing him to her feathery touches as she continued to kiss him. She nibbled at the corner of his mouth, then the cleft of his chin. She pressed soft kisses to the strong column of his neck and tasted the salt of his skin with darting licks of her tongue. His heart thumped, strong and heavy as she worked her way downward, sliding lips and tongue over the fluttering pulse at the base of his throat, to the strong, elegant stretch of his collarbone.

"Corinne," he moaned as her hands wrapped around his thick, pulsing length, the muscles in his thighs bunching with the effort to hold his body still for her gentle, teasing exploration.

He hissed when she bent down and rubbed her cheek against his erection. She nuzzled him, inhaling the musky scent of him. He hissed again when she lapped at the broad head, flattening her tongue to swipe the moisture dribbling from the sensitive tip. She held the white fluid on her tongue for a moment, savoring the taste of his essence: musky, salty, *wild*.

Uberon's hand trembled as he lifted it and settled it over her hair with the lightest touch so as not to compel or impede. He wanted no reminder of the sordid scene with Merogis and his unfortunate wife.

"Corinne," he breathed again when her mouth engulfed the bulbous tip of him and her tongue stroked the sensitive flesh. His entire body trembled as she explored him, yet he made no move to control her nor to plunge his eager cock down her throat. Instead, he let their garments dissolve into nothingness, leaving their bodies bare to the tropical heat and the ocean breeze. He inhaled, scenting the spicy musk of his mate's arousal.

Corinne feasted. She could describe it no other way. She wallowed in the textures of his body, the tastes. She shuddered when he skimmed her skin and hair with hands that left trails of fire in their wake, heated sensations that made her core ache and pulse and her thighs relax and spread as she continued to touch, kiss, and lick.

"I'm going to come," he warned as she slurped the head of his cock and fondled his balls, drawn up close to his body and heavy with seed.

"I want to swallow you," she murmured, then lowered her mouth over him and sucked hard, cheeks hollowing.

Uberon groaned as she pulled the ecstasy from his body and could not help the small shifting of his hips as he ejaculated down her throat. She swallowed, the working of her mouth and tongue drawing out his orgasm until he fell quiescent beneath her and she finally released him.

His chest heaved as he drew her up. Still gentle, still controlled, he captured her mouth with his and tasted himself. His semi-hard cock again swelled, harder than ever. Yet despite the urge to plunge into her body, he stroked her skin, palmed her breasts, and began his own slow, sensual exploration of his mate's delectable flesh.

Corinne could not summon the strict control Uberon commanded; she writhed beneath him where he positioned her on the bed. She moaned and mewled as he touched and kissed and tasted every inch of her, relishing the flavor of her ruby nipples and driving her to a boneless, quivering mess of need so that by the time he slid inside her body, she could do nothing but welcome the invasion and receive him with all the joy in her heart.

He thrust with long, slow strokes, ensuring she felt the drag of every inch of his flesh moving through hers. She ignited, her body bathing him in its sweet, musky cream as he continued to stroke in and out, sparking aftershocks that soon built in intensity to yet another orgasm that crashed through her. She panted and could not resist—not that she wanted to—when he turned her over and repositioned her, drawing her ass upwards while her shoulders rested upon the mattress. From behind, he plunged into her body, rocking with purpose as need took command. His balls swung with the hard, fast rhythm, slapping her her clit every time he bottomed out inside her body, hips digging into the fleshy mounds of her buttocks.

Uberon finally relinquished all control and grunted as he

exploded inside her, filling his mate with all that he was, all that he could give her. His sweating chest pressed against her back as his lungs heaved deep, rasping breaths and he buried his face in the crook of her neck and shoulder. He kept hold of her as she shuddered helplessly, bent over his arm while his seed trickled down her trembling thighs.

"I love you," she whispered as they sank to the mattress.

"I love you, too," he murmured, drawing her into the shelter of his embrace, not withdrawing from her body because his cock had other ideas. She gasped and he chuckled, a dark, velvety sound as he hardened inside her. Uberon slid his hand down to lift her leg while he slid in and out of her channel with slow, languid rolls of his hips. The continued stimulation launched her into another series of small tremors that quickly built into a soft rolling orgasm which ended on a long, sated sigh.

Drained of energy and drenched with sweat, Corinne drifted off to sleep while Uberon held her and pondered deep thoughts.

The ship would arrive at Quoliálfur within three days if the wind held steady and the weather held fair. He needed to figure out what to do with Merogis' five daughters, one of whom was too young to be married off. He had no doubt that the competition to win the hands of the pretty girls and ally with the Quoliálfur king would be stiff.

Considering his mate's propensity to find similarities in circumstances to Hollywood movies, Uberon supposed that she'd liken Quoliálfur to those frontier towns where the men outnumbered the women and were desperate for wives. He rather thought that men in those towns hadn't so much wanted wives as they wanted soft, feminine bodies to fuck. Yet, the imbalance of fae males to females increased in Quoliálfur. The non-fae species who had settled in his new land—not so new if one were as short-lived as humans—also found themselves with a shortage of females. Precious few dwarves, Maltani, or gargoyles had journeyed north, but Quoliálfur enjoyed a healthy share of halflings, pixies, and djinni as well as the dominant fae races. He also had some Winterei, an ancient mixture of human, jotunn, and fae that, like the Maltani, had evolved as its own race. His kingdom represented a rather worldly collection of races who had agreed to live peacefully among each other in exchange for the opportunities he offered.

Really, he supposed that what he offered as king of Quoliálfur differed little from his beloved mate's native country. Perhaps those belligerent, contradictory humans had some use after all.

He stroked a hand over Corinne's hair, relishing the feel of the silken strands beneath his palm, and told himself that he'd acquired the best humanity had to offer and made her even better by transforming her to fae. No doubt she would reach the same conclusion after a century or ten.

CHAPTER 17

Corinne spent much of the next three days with Merogis' daughters. They all nodded and smiled at her when she spoke to them of education, training, and careers, but she could tell none of them believed a word she said.

"I will teach you how to read and write," she promised.

"Why would we need to know that?" the oldest asked. Corinne guessed she was seventeen or eighteen years old. The girl shrugged with resigned fatalism. "We will spread our legs and bear the sons of the men to whom your master gives us. If he does not beat us, we shall be grateful for his kindness."

Corinne tugged on her braid. "There is more to life than that."

The youngest, whom she now knew was merely eleven years old, shook her head and replied, "Not for us."

"But I am giving you that opportunity to do more, to *be* more."

"No, you are not. Your master humors you," the middle girl said with a perception beyond her years.

"He's not my master," she muttered for the umpteenth time. The girls rolled their eyes in silent disbelief. Corinne raised her eyes to the sky and counted to ten, then twenty, then thirty to control her fraying temper and muttered under her breath, "God, give me patience."

She knew she could not expect the girls to disregard everything they had been taught, to dismiss the evidence of their very lives. Yet their refusal to entertain any other notion that a different fate lay waiting for them merely to grasp it exasperated her.

"You have a kind heart," one of the girls said, daring to lay a hand on the fae lady's arm. "But we know our fate, even if you do not."

The girl glanced at Uberon standing near the bow, long hair blowing in the wind like a shining, black banner. She looked back at Corinne. "He will find us husbands and he may even secure their promises to treat us well. But he has no interest in us beyond his kindness to you."

Corinne's shoulders sagged. She could not deny the girl's wise words, even if they disheartened her.

"I cannot teach when they are not willing to learn," she complained as she lay in Uberon's arms while the twin moons rose high over the horizon and their gleam outshined the stars.

"The older girls, perhaps not," he agreed, taking care to keep his tone mild and neutral. "But the younger may yet be convinced."

"What do fae women do?"

"Many fae females hold occupations, but their occupation ceases when they are mated. They then turn their attention and energies to managing their mates' lands and businesses and, if they are so fortunate, their children."

"What about the other races?"

"I do not know of any race in this world that allows females the same freedom and latitude as that which you enjoyed."

"Humph."

"Neither do they labor under the same responsibilities and expectations."

She snorted.

Uberon rolled over and pinned her beneath his weight. He tilted his hips, sinking his cock into her still wet and sensitive folds, even as he grasped her hands and drew them above her head where he imprisoned her wrists in the gentle, unbreakable grasp of one hand. "And is this life you lead so awful?"

Corinne could only gasp and then moan. A moment later she lost the capacity to think and speak and had no focus other than the heady pleasure her mate lavished upon her body.

On the afternoon of the third day, the cabin boy perched in the crow's nest cried out, "Land ho!"

Corinne and the girls rushed to the starboard side of the ship for their first glimpse of their new home. As the ship plowed through the waves, they saw colorful buildings of wood and stone rise in stately spires from a steep, rocky coastline. The sight reminded Corinne of a fairytale version of the Amalfi Coast. Or at least the photographs she'd seen of that region. The city looked freshly washed, as though from a recent rain. A hint of lemon danced on the ocean wind, as though the sea itself coveted the citrus scent for its own delight.

The ship headed for a tiny harbor. Stone cliffs rose sheer and tall around the sheltered water. The laughs and shouts of fishermen, vendors hawking their merchandise, and children playing echoed off the rock.

"How does one get up there? Do people here fly?" the girls inquired as they looked up, up, up at the buildings clinging to the steep hills facing the sea.

"We climb a lot of stairs," Uberon murmured in response.

The girls gasped, startled and embarrassed. He gave them a look of tolerance, knowing their experience limited.

"When we dock, I shall lead you to your new home. Follow no one but me."

They nodded. Corinne, too, because she hadn't the faintest idea where he planned to take them.

"I do not wish to leave," the oldest of the girls murmured, daring to lift her gaze to his. Her sisters gasped at her audacity. "I ... I like the ship."

"I think it's the first mate you like, more than the ship," he corrected in a dry tone.

Corinne's jaw dropped. What had she missed?

The girl's cheeks flushed a dusky red, but she did not deny the fae lord's words.

"Lord Nochnaya," another sister began in a fearful tone, ready to plead for her sister's forgiveness.

"Your Majesty," he corrected, his voice crisp. "You shall properly address me as Your Majesty or King Uberon."

The oldest girl turned pale, realizing she had spoken out of turn to a king.

Certain he had their rapt attention, he continued, "You will follow me to your new home." He nodded at the oldest girl. "If the first mate truly wishes to claim you as his mate, then he may come and pay court to you like a proper gentleman and steal no more kisses in dark corners."

Corinne's eyes widened at the realization of just how much she had missed.

I guess I'm not the vigilant chaperone I thought I was.
The girl is clever and besotted.

"My lord," the first mate called as he approached, having heard that last sentence. "The ship sails out again as soon as she is provisioned, probably tomorrow. I cannot remain behind to pay court to Sin'halissar."

"Almost I think better of you," Uberon said, slitting his silver eyes. The Maltani first mate barely flinched. "The ship remains in port until the dark moon. She flies a new banner now."

"Master Fidor Merogis owns this ship."

"Master Merogis is dead and his warehouses destroyed."

"How do you know this?"

"Word comes on the wind. The wards around the compound fell and the Quoli swept in to reclaim that which they had lost."

The sailors overhearing the conversation flinched. Several looked ill. A few turned away to conceal their grief. None of them questioned the fae lord, because all of them knew fae did not lie. They also knew this fae commanded vast power.

The Maltani gaped, then whispered hoarsely, "Did any survive?"

"No."

"Mother," one of the girls whined as she sank to her knees in tears.

The girl's grief failed to distract Uberon's attention. Leveling an icy glance at the witchbreed sailor, he said, "Present yourself at the Quoliálfur castle tomorrow morning if you wish to pay court to Sin'halissar and take her to wife."

"Mate," the first mate dared to correct.

Uberon blinked, almost a nod of approval. "Mate, then. Almost I think better of you."

He turned away to oversee the docking of the ship and confer with the captain.

"Look!" the youngest girl exclaimed and pointed toward the

pennant flapping at the top of the mast above the crow's nest.

Corinne and her sisters looked. The ship no longer flew the green and gold flag of Merogis' ownership. It flew the black and silver colors of the former Unseelie Court and the current Quoliálfur king: two silver crescent moons on a black field. Corinne wondered if the Jolly Roger would have been more appropriate, but said nothing.

They all fly my banner now.

Uberon called to them and they went to him. They followed him down the gangplank and wobbled on legs accustomed to traversing the pitch and roll of a ship's deck. None made any complaint as they followed him, picking up their skirts and gawping at the shining city draped with flowering vines and window boxes overflowing with colorful blooms. The strong scent of citrus flavored the air.

They climbed. And climbed. And climbed. Even Uberon breathed heavily as they neared the castle at the top. The hot afternoon sunshine bounced off the light gray walls which appeared to glitter faintly from the flecks of mica embedded in the granite. Tall portals of dense, heavily figured wood swung open at their approach.

"Your Majesty," a servant intoned as he bowed to his king. "Welcome home."

"Golsat, this is my mate, Queen Corinne," Uberon said, taking his beloved's hand in his and raising her fingers to his lips.

The servant's brow furrowed, but he said nothing impolite. After bowing deeply to the new queen, he waited for the rest of the introductions. Uberon did not disappoint him.

"These females are the daughters of Fidor Merogis, the merchant. He has perished, and I have taken charge of the girls. They are to be treated as honored guests."

The major domo nodded in understanding. He bowed to them and said, "My ladies, please follow me. I shall show you to your new quarters."

The girls paused and looked to Corinne for reassurance.

"It's all right," she said, putting her trust in Uberon's introduction of her has his queen. "You're safe here."

The five girls followed Golsat. Corinne looked at Uberon and said, "He's not—"

"No, he's not fae. He's a gargoyle."

"A gargoyle," she echoed.

"One of the few creatures that can take on a Quoli and win."

"Good Lord. And what other creatures can take on the Quoli and win?"

"Dragons, gryphons, basilisks, ice drakes, firebirds, but usually only singly. And I."

"And you?"

He ran the back of one finger down her soft cheek. "Haven't you realized by now that, except perhaps for the Erlking, I'm the most dangerous thing in this world?"

She shivered, but not with fear, as the liquid heat gathering between her thighs indicated. She, the young woman who had resented the overprotective, overbearing attitudes of her badass brothers, had given her heart, soul, mind, and body to the biggest badass across multiple dimensions.

And she was not sorry for it.

Uberon's nostrils flared, catching the heady scent of her arousal. Taking her hand, he led her inside the castle to find a room where he could fuck her in privacy. If anyone in the castle entertained any doubt as to their king's claim to having taken a mate, the muffled sounds filtering from the red drawing room dispelled those doubts.

Spilling his seed inside Corinne's body, the Quoliálfur king anticipated with glee the prospect of introducing his mate to every room in the castle in just such a manner. The castle had a lot of rooms. And shadowed corners. And cozy alcoves. And sheltered courtyards. And even some thermal springs.

Welcome, Uberon and Uberon's mate.

"What was that?" Corinne mumbled, blinking in dazed surprise.

Still lodged deeply inside her body, Uberon replied, "'Tis the castle welcoming us."

She heaved a breath and remembered the Erklking's fortress. "It's sentient, isn't it?"

"Aye."

"And you built it, didn't you?"

"I raised it from the mountain." He shared the memory of the castle's creation with her so she finally understood exactly what he meant.

"Fuck."

"I thought you'd never ask," he murmured and began thrusting again.

CHAPTER 18

Damned good thing I learned cursive, Corinne remarked silently as she scribbled notes with an old-fashioned quill pen that needed ink every five seconds. Or less. She chewed on her lower lip and wondered if Uberon would consider introducing his people to ballpoint pens. Or pencils. Even a pencil would be an improvement.

Perched on a stool at what she thought of as a small drafting table and which Uberon called a secretary, Corinne recorded the proceedings of the royal audience. She ignored the curious glances petitioners and courtiers cast toward her as she listened and learned. She disliked being cast as the secretary, and quickly realized that *scribe* served as a better title.

Few commoners can read or write, Uberon informed her. *Many rely upon memory. Therefore, it's important to accurately record what happens.*

She nodded her understanding and wondered whatever happened to the old truism that the victor wrote the history. The Quoliálfur king merely raised an eyebrow at her, but otherwise did not respond. She wanted to complain about the injustice of being relegated to scribe when she'd rather manage by Uberon's side; however, she also realized she needed to learn the culture and acquire at least a general understanding of the laws before she could even pretend to be worthy of that responsibility. So, she listened and wrote, the scratch of the quill pen on parchment strangely satisfying in a way that pecking away at a keyboard was not.

She wondered if Uberon would mind her snatching some paper and writing her stories.

Of course, not. Everything I have is yours.

Warmth suffused her, because her mind immediately went to that hard, thick, long appendage that he'd given her not so many hours ago and vowed again was for her use and hers alone.

I like the way you think.

Of course he did, the big, handsome horndog.

His deep, velvety chuckle reverberated in her mind.

You know, you never did tell me what happened to the horses.

The horses?

Yeah, the big black and palomino animals that we rode all those days and miles—remember them? I didn't see them loaded onto or off of the ship.

They did not accompany us here. I released them from service and sent them home.

You sent innocent, domesticated animals free without someone to care for them?

Uberon's velvety chuckle rippled through her mind. *They're not simple horses, beloved, but demons pressed into service and well able to take care of themselves.*

"Demons?" she squeaked aloud in mingled surprise and horror.

Raised voices distracted her attention and she looked up from the desk.

"Your Majesty, we heard you brought back women. We want them. We're willing to pay good gold."

She turned her face toward the tall doorway and the group of men—males—standing there. One held up a leather sack filled with what she assumed was gold coins.

Uberon raised his icy silver gaze at them, then returned his attention to the petitioner in front of him and said, "I will send guards to your estate to see whether the wards have failed or whether it is merely wild animals that have killed unsecured livestock."

"I know it's those filthy Quoli," the man protested.

"Quoli would not stop at killing a few goats," Uberon replied with chilling certainty and a wave of his hand.

The man's expression darkened, but he moved aside to make way for the rude newcomers' approach. One of the group latched his gaze upon Corinne. She blinked, and he licked his lips suggestively.

"Rumor spreads fast," Uberon murmured. With a gesture, he told them, "Speak freely."

Their leader nodded, took a second to gather his courage, and then spoke, "We've hardly any women here but whores and hags that used to be whores. We've all used 'em and make no apology for it. But we want something more. We want to establish families, found our own Houses."

Another chimed in: "We're the wealthiest males in Quoliálfur. We've worked hard and feel the press of years. We want sons to inherit our good fortune."

"Why not daughters?" Corinne murmured under her breath as she dutifully recorded the petition. "Why can't they inherit?"

Uberon, for all intents and purposes, ignored the comment and said, "And what if you should get daughters upon a woman?"

The man who fixed his attention upon Corinne answered, "Then we'll get good bride prices for them."

"And should your daughters not care for the husbands you choose?" Uberon prompted.

The man shrugged. "No matter. They'll spread their legs and bear sons regardless."

Corinne ground her molars with the effort to hold her silence at the boor's callous words.

"My mate would see you go forever without a woman for that sentiment," Uberon stated, his voice low, smooth, conversational, and all the more frightening for it.

"Your mate?" the leader echoed with a furtive glance toward Corinne.

"Aye. *Mine*." Uberon rose from a throne made of exotic wood from Quoli trees and the cleaned bones of Quoli natives. He speared the man with a sharp glare. "I'm inclined to agree with her."

"You won't stop me from taking a wife, Your Majesty," the man said, squaring his shoulders.

The others in the group took a step away from him, lest they, too, be burned in the forthcoming blast they believed inevitable.

He glared at them, then redirected his gaze to his king.

"No, I won't stop you from taking a wife as long as you gain the woman's consent," Uberon replied mildly. "However, I will not tolerate mistreatment. Our mates are too precious to harm."

"Women are plentiful, just not here."

"Then go. Live where women are plentiful." Uberon paused, then added, "That's an order. Master Orifelgany, you are no longer welcome in *my* kingdom. I expect your departure by dawn tomorrow."

The man gasped and spluttered in protest. "What about—? I cannot!"

Uberon ignored him and leveled his gaze at the other males in the group. "The females here are not for sale. Go, before I lose my patience with all of you."

The men backed away several steps, then turned and hurried out of the audience hall. Uberon extended his hand toward Corinne. She rose from her stool, obeying the silent summons. She disliked the peremptory gesture and expectation of her obedience, but she also understood this was neither the place nor time to assert her independence and undermine his authority.

"We are finished for today," Uberon announced.

"Your Majesty?" a courtier called out. "Who is this wo— female?"

"Bow to your queen who is called Corinne. Obey her as you do me."

Everyone in the audience hall bowed. No females other than Corinne occupied the space, which emphasized the paucity of mates for the worthier males in Quoliálfur. She fisted her cold hand in the folds of her silk skirt and began to understand the enormity of responsibility thrust upon Uberon's shoulders for having agreed to purchase Merogis' daughters.

"My lord," a Maltani male stepped forward and bowed. "You bade me present myself today."

"Aye, I did. Follow me."

The ship's first mate gaped for a brief moment, then schooled his expression to quiet pride and confidence. From the periphery of her vision, Corinne watched him stride toward them with the rolling gait of a seafaring man. She followed the light pull of Uberon's hand clasping hers and accompanied him to a formal drawing room where she took a seat beside her mate.

"Fetch Sin'halissar, please," she bade Golsat.

The gargoyle bowed and departed, his stride surprisingly light and agile. When the door closed behind him, Uberon directed his piercing glare at the sailor and spoke, "What makes you worthy of Sin'halissar?"

The first mate retained his calm. "I long for a family and have the means to support one. I have plans to captain my own ship within a year, which will bring both wealth and prestige upon my family."

"You are Maltani. Sin'halissar is human," Uberon pointed out.

"Aye," the male replied with a nod. "We Maltani are sufficiently fae to bind our souls. Her life will be tied to mine."

"How old are you?"

"I am a bit over a century and have been sailing for most of that. My mate will have a long life."

"You exile yourself by mating outside your own species."

The Maltani nodded. "I know. I have but a distant cousin or two remaining on Maltan, and we were never close. I have no home there."

"Why do you want to marry Sin'halissar?" Corinne inquired.

The Maltani sailor met her gaze and said in a quiet tone that rang of sincerity, "My heart beats only for her."

"The *Sea Hart* is yours," Uberon said. "Treat her and her crew well, and she will provide you and your family with a good life."

The sailor's eyes widened. "My lord! The *Sea Hart* belongs to Master Orifelgany."

"Not any longer. She flies my banner. You shall also have his estate."

Having an inkling of what just happened, Corinne asked, "What if Master Orifelgany attempts to take his ship back?"

"Then the crew will kill him."

The door opened and Sin'halisssar ducked under Golsat's heavy arm. Eyes widening with surprise and delight, she exclaimed, "Hibr!"

Uberon rose to his feet and Corinne followed suit. He said, "We shall give you a moment of privacy to discuss your plans."

He walked across the room, Corinne tagging close behind. Exiting through another door and entering a different room, she asked, "Why didn't you interrogate him further? How can you be sure he means to treat her well?"

She found herself backed against a wall, naked. Uberon lifted her, positioned her legs around his naked hips, and pressed his nose to the juncture of her neck and shoulder. He inhaled of her scent and notched his erect and eager cock within her tender folds.

"Uberon."

The Quoliálfur king licked her skin and growled low in his throat. Her core turned liquid with heat and desire.

"Uberon."

"He said his heart beat only for her. No Maltani would state such unless he has found his heart's mate," he explained as he slowly pushed up into her body.

"Then he—?" she attempted to ask, but the words ended on a moan as Uberon filled her. She wound her hands up and around the strong column of his neck.

"Not like us. Never like us. *Nothing* is like us," he declared as his hips pumped.

Corinne's eyes rolled back as he thrust into her hard and fast, her body responding to the impromptu ravishing with heady pleasure. She moaned and melted into him, her mouth opening and yielding to his claim.

She did not know how long their fast and fierce coupling lasted, but she did know that Uberon had easily wrenched two orgasms from her before he released his own climax. He carried her to a chaise lounge where he deposited her, suddenly cleaned and clothed. However, her passion-befuddled brain hardly recognized his words when he promised to return after escorting Hibr from the castle.

Entering the room on bejeweled feet, Sin'hallisar sat on a chair beside the chaise lounge and whispered a grateful thank-you before asking, "Do you think I shall enjoy Hibr's bed?"

Corinne summoned her scattered wits and responded, "I hope you will. If he harms you, you must inform me."

The girl bestowed a soft, besotted smile upon her benefactress and said, "I do not think he will hurt me."

"For what it's worth—and that's quite a lot, I should think— neither does Uberon."

"Do you know the bride price his majesty will demand for me?"

Corinne shook her head. "No clue. I'm not even sure he'll demand a bride price."

"Of course, he will," the girl scoffed with a gentle snort. "He paid my father gold and he will wish to recoup his loss and perhaps make a profit."

"I don't think Uberon's all that interested in filthy lucre."

"What?"

"Money."

"Oh. You do have odd turns of phrase. Where are you from, my lady?"

"Nowhere you've ever heard of," Corinne replied and averted her gaze to blink back sudden tears of homesickness.

"You miss your home?"

She nodded. "Desperately sometimes."

"I do not miss mine," Sin'halissar stated. "I am glad that his majesty purchased us and brought us here. Otherwise I should not have met Hibr. Father would have sold me to the first man who offered sufficient coin."

Corinne said nothing.

The girl huffed a bitter laugh. "Actually, he did, and the gold did him no good."

The two females lapsed into silence. After a long moment, Sin'halissar asked, "Will you tell me about your home?"

Glad to have the opportunity to reminisce and refresh her childhood home and her family in her mind, Corinne obliged.

Sin'halissar laughed. "Fluffy white crystals falling from the clouds? Surely this cannot be true?"

"Oh, snow can be beautiful. It's trite to say so, but it really covers everything like a blanket. When the sun shines after a snowfall, the snow sparkles like millions and millions of tiny diamonds."

"It sounds glorious."

"It doesn't stay that way for long. Soon it turns gray and brown with dirt and then it's just a nasty, icy mush. I don't much like the cold anyway."

"Please describe this cold to me. What is it like?"

Corinne thought for a moment how she would describe cold, wintry weather to someone who had only known tropical heat. "Have you ever put her hand in water so cold that you could not stand it for long?"

"A merchant once brought ice packed in sawdust. Father allowed us to sample some from a block before he sold the rest. My teeth chattered!"

"Think of that cold and make it even colder."

"Surely, that is not possible?"

"It's very possible. Anyway, think of a cold so cold that it burns your skin. In order to protect yourself when going outside, you must wear layers of heavy clothes and boots."

"Even the women?"

"Even the women."

Sin'halissar shook her head and smiled. "You come from a very strange land. I am glad his majesty claimed you and brought you here."

"You have no idea."

"Your Majesty?" rumbled the major domo's deep voice as he opened the door. "His majesty bade me escort you to dine with him." The gargoyle nodded at the betrothed girl. "Your sisters await you, miss." His eyes twinkled within the cool stone of his craggy face. "I think his majesty would appreciate the rescue."

Corinne chuckled and jumped from the chaise lounge, every step reminding her of the passionate interlude not long before. Sin'halissar followed close behind and muttered about the cold stone beneath her bare soles. Corinne reached out to brush her fingers along the stone wall.

"Will you warm the stone beneath the girls' feet until they have been properly shod?" she whispered in the fae High Tongue Uberon had implanted into her mind.

A gasp followed by a small sigh of relief soon announced the results of her request.

"Thank you," Corinne whispered into the air and felt a cool current curl around her and brush her cheek before dissolving.

"You meet the castle's approval," Golsat rumbled.

"I do?" Corinne wondered if the castle spoke to him, too.

"Stone speaks to stone, my lady," he answered her unspoken question. "The castle shelters all who live within it and it notes those who also give shelter."

She mulled over the odd turn of phrase and decided that the castle apparently liked people who cared for other people. She raised her hand again to let her fingertips slide over the stone walls in silent benediction.

The gargoyle paused beside a door and opened it. "Ladies."

Corinne and Sin'halissar passed through, Golsat following behind. The younger woman's sisters clustered at one end of a long table where Uberon sat, chattering like a flock of birds. He looked up at their arrival and smiled with obvious relief. Corinne giggled, seeing the cold and mighty fae king disconcerted by a bevy of human girls. Sin'halissar rushed to sit next to the nearest sister and whispered loudly, "Lady Corinne made the stone heat beneath my feet!"

"Did she use a spell?" Han'al, the youngest of the human girls, inquired.

"No, she asked the castle to make your sister more comfortable," Golsat replied as he smoothed the girl's hair away from her face.

What the hell's he doing touching her? She's just a child!

She is his mate. He recognized her when she stepped foot within the castle.

She's not anyone's mate. She's only eleven.

Servants approached with platters of food and began serving portions.

He will wait until she comes of age to claim her.

And if she doesn't want to be claimed?

She will. Her heart bonds with him already.

How is that supposed to work? He's ... he's made of stone!

Gargoyles shift to flesh to mate.

I ... I ... no, I think I don't want to know. He won't hurt her, will he? Corinne shook her head at a servant's offer of some sort of mashed vegetable concoction that smelled sour.

Even I would think twice about hurting anything under a gargoyle's protection. Nothing will harm that girl as long as Golsat lives.

Er ... how long will he live?

I believe the indigenous peoples of your homeland have a saying: only the rocks and the wind live forever. Uberon took a sip of his wine.

And Han'al? Corinne took a bite of a gamey meat and wondered if she ought to have a word with the chef about soaking wild game in milk to tame the strong flavor. Then she remembered the lack of cattle and wondered if soaking in goat's milk would have the same effect.

She will … transform.

Like me?

Similar.

Corinne swallowed, took a sip from her goblet, and suddenly craved a sweet iced tea. With lemon. *I don't like that she has no choice.*

She never expected a choice, he reminded her.

The girls continued to chatter about the luxury of their accommodations, the promise of a seamstress to sew new clothing for them, and the tutor Golsat had hired. Corinne glanced at the gargoyle and wondered when he had time to hire a tutor for the girls. Then she wondered why he had done so, because the girls had shown little interest in acquiring an education. Had Uberon ordered it?

Golsat would prefer his mate educated, and he cannot accomplish that without extending the same opportunity to her sisters, too.

Corinne nodded her approval, pleased with the girls' apparent acceptance of an education. She hadn't really looked forward to trying to teach the girls when she knew so little about their world herself.

The Merogis daughters discussed their oldest sister's impending nuptials, what to wear for a Maltani mating ceremony, and whether Sin'halissar would live aboard the new captain's ship or whether she would remain on dry land.

"I would sail with Hibr," she answered with a shy blush. "At least until the children come."

Uberon made no pronouncement, but Corinne guessed he'd have a word with Hibr and strongly recommend that the Maltani bring his mate aboard with him.

With the oldest sister's future settled, the next sister speculated about her prospects and bemoaned her lack of acquaintances. Amid the clink of silverware against fine porcelain, she theorized that, if King Uberon were not going to claim her himself and allow her the choice of a husband, then she needed to meet people.

"And you shall," he reassured her. "After you have a new wardrobe."

"But how, Your Majesty?"

Uberon pinched the bridge of his nose and then gave the girl a pained smile. "I shall hold a ball."

"A ball?" the girls echoed in confusion.

"A ball!" Corinne exclaimed with amazement. *But you ...*

I detest balls. But they work well for introducing young ladies to eligible gentlemen.

Will we have to hire a dancing master?

Fuck. He sighed. *Yes.*

"Do you know how to dance, Uberon?" Corinne asked.

"Any dances I remember have been lost to history," he admitted. Turning to Golsat, he said, "Send word and hire a dancing master and we'll need musicians, too, who know the latest tunes."

Golsat nodded. "And whom shall you invite, my lord?"

"The respectable, unmated and unmarried males of Quoliálfur." Uberon paused, recalling that his kingdom had few such worthy individuals. His face took on a pained expression. "Then, if the girls who are of marriageable age do not find their mates, we shall hold another ball and invite eligible males from abroad. We shall do this once a year until all the girls are settled."

Corinne's eyes widened at this peremptory change in her plans.

Your plans are not their plans, beloved. You want them to have choice and they choose a traditional future.

She bowed her head and accepted the truth of his reminder.

CHAPTER 19

Preparation for the ball took months. Invitations were written and sent to their destinations on outbound ships and then overland to individual recipients. Time passed while responses slowly traveled to Quoliálfur, with more than expected accepting the opportunity to form an alliance with the reclusive fae king. Responses indicated estimated arrival dates, which required additional time to allow for the transportation of suitors and their entourages. Corinne put those long months of waiting to good use, ordering wardrobes sewn for the girls and hiring tutors to educate them.

Corinne continued serving as the court scribe in the mornings and working on arranging the ball in the afternoons. Uberon gladly dumped the planning into her lap and assigned Golsat to assist. The hulking gargoyle kept a watchful eye on all the girls, especially the youngest sister, only reluctantly leaving her in the care of the tutors he and Corinne hired to teach the girls mathematics, history, science, geography, reading, writing, and dancing. Corinne attended the lessons, too, stating that being new to this world she needed to learn as much as she could about it.

Uberon, however, refused to allow the dancing master to instruct his mate personally, which resulted in him taking dancing lessons, too. The instructor flinched every time that silver gaze landed on him, especially after his handsome, flirtatious assistant ignored the king's warning to keep his wandering hands to himself and palmed one girl's ass. The resulting withered claw covered in scaly black hide functioned perfectly well, but drew shudders of horror and distaste.

"A woman will never accept him with that—that—deformity," the dancing master complained on behalf of his traumatized assistant.

"Then he shouldn't have groped my ward," Corinne replied.

When he pronounced the king, queen, and her ladies-in-waiting, as he termed them, proficient in the latest dances, he took his leave from Quoliálfur with a casket of gold and a personal vow never to return.

The other tutors learned from that young man's mishap and adjusted their instructional techniques to avoid rapping knuckles for impertinent behavior or addressing the girls with any disrespect whatsoever. The very concept of correcting errors in the queen's work made them tremble with fear despite the queen's reassurance that she expected such correction.

"They're terrified of you," she complained at dinner.

"Good." He lifted his goblet and drank.

The five sisters, however, quickly lost their fear of Uberon, especially once they understood they were under his protection, not being held for his exploitation. They teased him, joked about him, pestered him, and frequently sent him stalking from the room pinching the bridge of his nose and muttering dire imprecations about ill-bred, impertinent girls. Corinne just laughed, knowing he would not harm them for all their silliness. She enjoyed seeing them bloom as much as she enjoyed watching the formidable male turn indulgent and avuncular in their presence. She knew he'd never admit to having developed a fondness for the human girls.

Amid the arrival and departure and service of tutors and instructors, the seamstress arrived, accompanied by six assistants and a dozen trunks filled with bolts of fabric and buttery soft leathers, and muttering about the filthy, humid heat and the filthy tropical insects and the filthy, lustful sailors who pressed their dishonorable attentions upon the innocent young women in her charge. Uberon leaned down and whispered in Corinne's ear, "The blonde is pregnant."

"How do you know that?" she whispered back.

"I can smell it on her."

Her eyes widened. "No? Really?"

He gave her that faint little smile that never failed to arouse her and replied, "Perhaps."

Her expression twisted with annoyance. "I'm not stupid, Uberon. Tell me."

He held his mysterious little smile and said nothing.

"I'll fake my orgasms," she threatened.

"No, you won't," he whispered and nuzzled her neck.

She shivered.

The five sisters giggled and whispered as the seamstress draped fabrics over them and sketched designs that made the best of their figures. Uberon did not allow either her or her assistants to ply their trade upon his mate. He insisted upon creating gowns in exquisite fabrics and elegant designs that showcased Corinne's exotic coloring and the soul bond's manifestation of silver and black diamonds.

The seamstress and her assistants measured, cut, and sewed with focused diligence, creating entire wardrobes for the five girls and those few respectable women who would attend the ball in company with their courtier spouses.

Finally, a few weeks before the ball, guests began to arrive from most of the kingdoms receiving invitations. After morning audiences, Uberon retreated to the recesses of his castle to avoid them. Golsat stepped in and assigned guards, which included two more gargoyles who kept alert, stony gazes as cold and hard as granite upon the goings-on within the castle. One of them accompanied Corinne at all times, even standing guard over her during morning audiences.

A whispered word to the castle secured its unique protection. Corridors developed dead ends and circled around to dump wandering guests in the places they started. The private rooms occupied by the king, queen, and their wards disappeared: no door led to them that any trespassing visitor could find. By clever manipulation of rooms, doors, and hallways, the castle kept all visitors confined to the area Uberon designated for their use.

When unable to retreat physically, Uberon affected the cold, remote, haughty personality of the feared and dangerous

Unseelie king that parents around the world still used to threaten their unruly children into obedience. Corinne considered discussing his aloof behavior, but decided against it after slitted eyes focusing on one overly fawning cavalier sent the unctuous man scurrying back to a departing ship.

Two days before the ball, a ship from Fyrgia disgorged its cargo on the the narrow shore. Sitting in her official drawing room, decorated in silver, lavender, and dark green at Uberon's orders to complement her coloring, Corinne received the newest visitor.

"The Honorable Cedric Oyochea, heir to the Baron of Burrel of Fyrgia," the latest suitor for a favored ward of the Quoliálfur king introduced himself.

"You've come far," Corinne replied from the throne with Golsat standing guard beside her. She took pleasure from the recent geography lessons in knowing exactly how far the man had traveled. "Welcome to Quoliálfur."

"When may I meet the ladies?"

"Only three are of marriageable age and one of them is already betrothed," she replied without answering his question. "We'll be holding the wedding soon and all our honored guests are invited to attend."

The human nobleman nodded, but his expression congealed into disappointment followed by determination.

The parade of hopeful suitors, never more than a trickle of guests, concluded with the Honorable Cedric Oyochea's arrival. Corinne drafted Hibr into service as an escort for the sisters, ensuring that he not only spent time with his betrothed, but that he never saw her alone. The day before the grand ball, Uberon, Corinne, and their guests gathered in the Maltani temple the newly minted captain's ex-patriot countrymen had built over a century ago.

Tropical flowers bedecked the temple and released their sweet, heady fragrances into the sultry air. Wearing a toga trimmed with gold embroidery, Hibr met his bride-to-be at the dais, and they joined hands beneath the oculus. An elderly Maltani with floor-length gray hair wearing a drapery of red stone beads met the captain's steady gaze. Then he turned his gaze to the human bride. Falling upon her lifetime of training, she fixed her gaze on her bare toes. Jeweled bands encircled her throat, wrists, and ankles, gleaming through the sheer, filmy layers of fabric drifting about her body like a cloud. At the elder's quietly murmured command, Hibr took Sin'halissar's hands in his. He murmured something indistinct and the girl lifted her gaze to his. She gave him a shy smile, eyes shining. Hibr returned her smile with an expression of sure approval and a slow nod.

The elder, having schooled his expression to neutrality at the sailor's willingness to exile himself from his homeland by mating outside his race, raised his face and hands toward the sky and began praying in a sing-song voice beseeching the gods for blessings upon Hibr and his heart's true mate, the human female Sin'halissar. As the elder spoke, the light streaming through the oculus brightened. Captivated by the light, Corinne reached for Uberon's hand, grasped it, and squeezed. The bright white light flared, then shattered into countless glowing shards of crystal brilliance as the crescendo of the elder's prayer crested on a triumphant shout. The glittering powder settled on the guests gathered within the temple dusting them with the arcane blessing.

The bride and groom raised their joined hands. The elder pulled out a short-bladed knife and severed long locks of hair from Hibr and Sin'halissar. He deftly braided the strands into a long, thin cord and tied it around their wrists. With his gnarled hands hovering over their bound wrists, the elder murmured holy incantations. The cord began to smoke. The acrid scent of burnt hair singed the nostrils of every person in the small temple. Having been coached by her betrothed, Sin'halissar endured the pain of the burning cord by biting the inside of her cheek until blood filled her mouth. Sweat beaded on her face and trickled down her back. Hibr's bi-colored hair, darkened with sweat, dragged against the coarse weave of his toga as he turned his face to glare at the elder. His lips peeled back from his pointed teeth and he growled, "Finish this."

Showing no remorse for having delayed this bonding of souls between Maltani and human, and the pain that delay inflicted, the elder lifted his upper lip in a sneer that did not interrupt the slowly spoken incantations issuing from his mouth. Watching the proceedings and hearing the whimpers that Sin-halissar could not stifle, Corinne decided she'd had enough. Toeing off a shoe, she set her bare foot against the naked stone of the temple's floor and felt the slow shudder of connection with the foot of the mountain from which Uberon's castle had been carved. She begged the mountain for a favor and it obliged.

The elder hissed as the stone beneath his own bare feet flared white with sudden volcanic heat. He looked up and noticed the queen glaring at him. Her own upper lip curled in a silent sneer and she bared her teeth at him.

What hurt you do to her, I will do to you tenfold.

The Maltani elder hissed as the thickly calloused soles of his feet began to sizzle on the hot rock. Locked within the ritual, he could not abandon it. The incantations flew from his lips as he hastened to finish the mating ritual that bound Hibr's life and soul to Sin'halissar's.

The elder's concluding shout vibrated with anger and pain. Two Maltani rushed forward to carry the lamed elder from the temple as the last ashes from the burning cord drifted to the temple floor. Uberon called for a healer, who detached himself from the crowd to tend to the newlyweds' burns before tending to the elder's injury. Corinne slipped her shoe back on and smiled with grim satisfaction.

"We gather in the great hall of Castle Quoliálfur for the wedding feast!" Corinne proclaimed, having been informed beforehand that the bride and groom would retreat to a private place to consummate their union. She thought they would head for the captain's cabin on the *Sea Hart* which had returned to her new berth just days before.

A company of Quoliálfur guards directed the procession of guests following Uberon and Corinne to the great hall. Golsat and the handful of other gargoyles who served Uberon closed ranks around the bride's sisters, keeping them safe on the march back to the castle. The king and queen occupied the head table. The bride's sisters took their seats at another table flanked by the forbidding gargoyles. The guests seated themselves, gawked at the king's wards, and gossiped among themselves.

In a corner, musicians played spritely music for the festive occasion. Servants carried in platters of hot and cold foods and pitchers of wine. The fragrances of food and perfumes and flowers and sweat mingled into a heavy, pungent miasma that affected Corinne's appetite for the worse. However, she made a successful pretense toward eating and, like a good hostess, ensured that everyone ate their fill.

With windows thrown open to catch the cool night breeze blowing off the ocean, Corinne placed her hands in Uberon's to lead the dancing. Noticing his mate's flagging endurance, he transferred the duties of host to Golsat and excused Corinne and himself for the night.

"Thank you," she murmured with sincere gratitude. They reached their quarters and she crossed the bedchamber to lean out of an open window and take deep gulps of fresh air to settle her churning stomach. "I hadn't realized how badly people smell."

"Immersion bathing presents a difficulty for many," Uberon reminded her. "Most must make do with washing from basins."

She shuddered with a modern woman's distaste. "I'm glad the castle has hot springs."

"The castle takes great care to pamper you," Uberon observed as he came up behind her and ran his hands over her bare shoulders and the delicate sweep of her collar bones. "It keeps your skin soft. Smooth. Glowing."

She exhaled and felt her knees soften as he bent down to press sweet, sweet kisses to the satiny skin revealed by the gown in which Uberon had clothed her.

She'd gasped when it first wrapped around her, clinging snugly to her body from the flare of her hips to the fullness of her breasts. "You can practically see my nipples!" she had exclaimed, even though she knew Uberon selected the fabric and color to frame the intricate whorls and curlicues and lines and curves of the soul bond made manifest.

Now that she leaned against him, her back to his front, at the window overlooking a sheer drop down the mountainside, her mate pushed down the revealing bodice of her gown. Head resting against his chest, she heard the strong thump of his heart and the catch of his breath when he slid his hands beneath the soft mounds to support their delicate weight. Her knees began to melt as he rubbed the sensitive nipples, bringing them to hard points that begged to be rolled and plucked. Uberon obliged and moisture, hot and sweet, soaked her thighs.

"Uberon," she moaned, arching into his touch and reaching up to bring his mouth to hers. He leaned over her, his long hair cloaking pale, ruby-tipped skin from view as he drew her away from the window. Pressing his lips to hers, he continued to fondle his mate's breasts as the scent of her arousal wreathed him. A flicker of his will dissolved their clothing into nothingness. He swept Corinne into his arms and carried her to the bed where he continued to kiss, lick, and caress until she wept with the desperate yearning to be claimed.

"Mine," he whispered as he slid inside her sensitive body. Already he felt the ripple and clutch of her inner muscles as she slipped headlong into the first orgasm he would give her that night. *"Mine."*

"Yours," she agreed on a sigh that hitched as he drove her to another climax on the heels of the first. "Uberon!"

"My beloved. Forever."

The heat and discomfort of the party forgotten beneath the pure pleasure of her mate's touch and the refreshing waft of night air, Corinne accepted and received her mate's passionate claim with joy.

CHAPTER 20

The festivities lasted ten days, during which Corinne dove into a crash course in learning how to be a hostess. Golsat assisted, for which he earned her everlasting gratitude. She and the two eligible Merogis daughters accompanied a cohort of suitors eager either to acquire a lovely young wife, an assumed alliance with the Quoliálfur king, or the young woman's generous dowry. Or all three.

For their part, the two sisters followed their strict training and conducted themselves with demure modesty. Swathed from neck to toes in loose, colorful silks, they offered their swains no teasing glimpses of skin. Golsat's fierce glare caught many of those same suitors' gazes lingering upon the creamy expanse of branded skin exposed by the outfits worn by their hostess. A couple bolder, less prudent men suggested that the queen visit them.

Both suffered immediate consequences, their genitalia withering and turning black and putrid, an odiferous rot that removed them from the gene pool. They left in haste and disgrace to endure the ignominy of failure. Although Corinne protested her innocence regarding the cruel retaliation, the remaining suitors kept a very polite and respectful distance from her thereafter.

Except for the Honorable Cedric Oyochea. He alone dared ask

the queen to dance at the grand ball held two nights prior to the culmination of the event. He lifted his arrogant gaze to meet the king's pale icy eyes after he bowed to the queen and asked for her hand in a dance.

"It's just a dance, Uberon," she whispered. "He can't do anything too obnoxious with you watching."

Uberon nodded, his reluctance evident. Corinne placed her hand in the nobleman's and he led her to the dance floor. They took their positions and proceeded through the steps of the stately dance. Oyochea maintained a correct and respectful distance and his hands never wandered inappropriately. Every word he uttered upheld punctilious civility, although his heated gaze flickered to the tempting display of cleavage and the soul bond manifested in silver and black diamonds sprawling across her skin.

"Your Majesty, your beauty outshines your wards tonight," Master Oyochea complimented with a greasy smile, gaze dipping to the creamy expanse of silver-chased, jewel-encrusted skin rising above the low neckline of her bodice.

"Thank you," Corinne murmured in polite response, but without returning his smile. Because civility dictated she continue the conversation, she said, "I am pleased at the turnout for the ball."

Oyochea nodded. "Misses Sin'clannad and Ari'valia are radiant and most desirable, especially being favored of His Majesty."

The steps of the dance separated them, which gave Corinne a few precious seconds to think of a response that would not offend. When the steps brought them back together, she said, "That favor ensures the girls' welfare. They are dear to us."

"And it shows," the courtier remarked. "You have them well-guarded."

"Most of the palace guard is dedicated to their protection," Corinne admitted.

The dance steps separated them again. When they came back together, he agreed with her: "Such treasures should be well-protected. Do they not have younger sisters?"

"Yes." Corinne's hackles raised as a frisson of warning tingled down her spine. "They're confined to their quarters tonight."

The courtier simply smiled again and commented, "I am sure

they will become beauties like their older sisters, and just as valuable to the king."

The set ended. Oyochea returned her to Uberon's side with a deep bow and a supercilious smile. Corinne gave him a gracious nod, heeding her mate's warning that she was not to bow (or curtsey) to anyone. The nobleman turned on his heel to await his turn to take one of the Merogis girls on the dance floor.

Corinne wiped her palms on her skirt. She felt soiled for having touched her hand to that man's. Turning to Uberon, Corinne said in an undertone, "There's something off about that guy."

Uberon placed his hand over hers and answered, "I cannot read his thoughts. 'Tis most unusual, although I have come across a handful of humans whose minds did not yield readily to me."

"Do you think, perhaps, he has other abilities?"

"Possibly. He bears watching."

Corinne agreed.

Oyochea solicited her hand for two more dances. Nothing in his overt behavior drew suspicion, but her instincts trilled warnings that raised her hackles. She kept an eagle eye on the two young ladies whom she chaperoned. Though she noticed blatant flirting by various gentlemen with the two girls, the girls conducted themselves with restrained decorum. The palace guards stationed about the ballroom and other public rooms ensured nothing untoward occurred. Corinne mulled over the courtier's comments and delicate probing regarding the younger sisters and wondered about the security of the family's private rooms. Even the castle's machinations could be circumvented by someone devious and determined enough.

"Uberon, can you ward the door to the girls' room?" she asked.

He nodded. "Certainly, beloved. None shall pass through the door, except the girls and their maids."

"Thank you. That will keep the lecher out if he tries to compromise one of my girls."

A faint smile graced Uberon's expression as he contemplated his mate's protectiveness toward the girls. She would make a good mother if they were ever so blessed. Regardless, he would enjoy the effort of procreation and ensure that she did, too.

The clock chimed and Uberon stood. The musicians lay down

their instruments. Everyone turned to stare at the imposing king.

"Thank you, everyone, for joining us tonight. I hope you enjoyed yourselves. Tomorrow morning, I shall confer with Sin'clannad and Ari'valia as to their preferences. Selected gentlemen will then be invited to private interviews with them, at which time you may offer your proposals or bid them goodbye."

You don't really care whether they enjoyed themselves, Corinne accused him, a small grin playing about her lips.

No, but even I can observe polite civilities.

She chuckled aloud, keeping the sound soft and quiet.

Two gargoyles detached themselves from their posts and flanked the girls, who obediently allowed their guards to escort them to their room to retire for the rest of the night.

"Make sure none but the girls enter or exit their quarters," Corinne reminded the guards, never suspecting that such strictly raised, obedient, *traditional* young ladies would jeopardize their reputations and marriage prospects by venturing out with a man, especially a man whom they did not know.

"Aye, my lady."

Once the girls had left the ballroom, Corinne rose and placed her fingertips upon Uberon's forearm. He inclined his head in a regal nod to acknowledge his guests and then escorted his mate to their chambers, leaving the servants to ensure guests returned to their rooms in orderly fashion.

Corinne rolled her shoulders and heaved a sigh. "I never would have guessed how exhausting this was."

"Do you regret it, my dear?" he asked as he loosened the lacing of her gown.

"No. Saving them was the right thing to do, even if they chose a path different than what I intended."

Bending down, he pressed a kiss to the top of her shoulder. She shivered and sighed.

"No. They deserve the choice." She shivered again as her mate eased the bodice of her gown down and his warm hands cupped the soft, tender weight of her breasts. "Uberon, you know what that does to me."

"Why do you think I do it?" he retorted with a low chuckle. "You looked so lovely tonight. I hated all those lustful gazes upon you."

She huffed a soft breath. "You're the one who insists on displaying practically my entire chest."

"They need to see the mating mark in its full glory. They need to know you are claimed. You are *mine*."

"The nonhuman males have no interest in me," she observed. "It's almost as if the … collar … repels them."

He nodded and ran light kisses along the top of her other shoulder. "As it should. But it does not work that way on human males."

Her head rolled aside to bare her flesh to him. "Men allow themselves to be governed by honor, not necessarily instinct."

"Or not."

"Or not," she agreed, her voice catching as Uberon's hand skillfully manipulated the now aching flesh of her breasts. She arched her back to press her breasts more fully into his touch. She squirmed as liquid heat blossomed between her thighs. "Uberon, I need you."

He smiled against her skin, pleased and satisfied with her reaction to his touch.

"You shall have me," he vowed, his voice guttural with need. Their clothes vanished at his thought and he scooped her into his arms. She squealed when he dropped her on the bed and gasped when he pounced, caging her beneath him. His eyes glowed, bright, hot, molten. He crushed his mouth to hers and roughly shoved her legs apart. The blatant admiration of their guests had aggravated his animal desire to protect and possess his mate. Now, alone in the privacy of their quarters, he could not resist the imperative to claim her yet again and make sure she knew to whom she belonged.

"I cannot be gentle," he warned her, the words thick and rasping.

Corinne's green eyes darkened and she lifted her hips, notching the head of his erection between her already wet and swollen folds. With a little growl of her own, she impaled himself upon him, making Uberon gasp at the sudden aggression and her claiming of him. An answering growl erupted from his chest and he took command of their coupling, pounding into her with a fierce intensity that held neither tenderness nor gentleness.

When morning broke, Corinne stretched and grimaced at the unexpected tenderness of her well-used body. She could not repress the indulgent smile that stretched across her face. Uberon was always passionate, but memory of the intensity of the night before turned her bones to jelly. She shuddered as her body heated up with anticipation. She knew without looking, however, that she lay alone in the big bed. The king of Quoliálfur would not neglect his duty just to swive his mate one more time.

Even if she wished he had.

With a sigh of regret and a groan of soreness, she rose from bed and noticed a single flower draped across the pillow.

"Oh, Uberon," she sighed and brought the lavish violet bloom to her nose to inhale the spicy fragrance. "How utterly romantic."

"My lady," came the soft voice of her maid.

Corinne turned her head toward the pixie female. "Yes?"

"Lord Uberon bade me inform you when you woke that your bath is prepared."

"Ah. Thank you."

The pixie moved to the tall wardrobe and opened it, pulling out a deceptively simple gown of deep violet. "And he bids you wear this today."

"Of course," she replied as she walked to the anteroom where, indeed, a hot bath scented like the flower Uberon had left for her waited. She sank with a moan of pleasure into the hot water and allowed herself a few minutes to soak before washing. The pixie returned.

"I'm to wash your hair and dress it," she said.

Corinne murmured her acquiescence and leaned her head back. The maid worked with brisk efficiency. After rinsing, Corinne rose from the bath and dried herself with a towel before slipping on the purple dress. Looking at herself in the mirror, she gasped. The deep, jewel-like color of the dress darkened her jade green eyes and made her ivory skin glow. Gold and ivory lace frothed at the cuffs, while the neckline ran straight from one shoulder to the other, covering up much of the embedded pectoral. Material skimmed her body, flaring gently at the hips to cascade in smooth folds to the floor. The maid drew a girdle of flat gold and ivory links around her waist, fastened it, and let it drape low over her hips, the dangling ends designed to swing with every swaying stride. The pixie then fastened long, narrow chains along the belt, the ends terminating in black diamonds to form a sort of overskirt that emphasized the natural sway of her hips.

"My lord does admire your form," the pixie murmured.

Corinne nodded and wondered if he dressed her so in an ploy to inspire the jealousy that had led to the previous night's almost violent passion. A thrill ran through her body at the thought. Perhaps that wasn't such a bad idea.

She emerged from the royal chambers into subdued chaos. Corinne grabbed the arm of a scurrying servant and demanded, "What's going on?"

"Ari'dongharad has disappeared," the servant blurted, then turned pale with dread at the pure fury suffusing her mistress.

Corinne's intuition cast blame upon a certain smarmy courtier.

"That *bastard*. I never thought someone would go for one of the younger girls," Corinne growled, her hand tightening on the servant's arm, the sharp claws poking through his sleeve and drawing beads of blood. The pixie cringed.

"Oh, sorry."

She released her hold and pinned the servant with her jade glare. "Where are Sin'clannad and Ari'valia?"

"The king has confined all the girls to their quarters under the watch of the gargoyles."

"Good. Where is the king?"

"In the library, my lady."

"Have someone bring me tea in the library. I'm going there to discuss killing a kidnapper."

The chains on her skirt swished and clinked as she strode to the library where Uberon glared out the window, fuming. He did not turn around when she entered.

"Who's not accounted for?" Corinne asked.

"Oyochea," Uberon replied.

Corinne was not surprised. "Can you trace him?"

"I cannot sense the cur. Nor can I sense Ari'dongharad. He must be shielding her."

She opened her mouth, then closed it as an idea came to her. "We cannot track him through a mental connection, but what about dogs?"

"Dogs?"

"Like bloodhounds. Tracking dogs. Are there any here?"

"No, we have no dogs. They do not thrive this close to the

Quol." Finally, Uberon turned to face her, his expression set in sharp, deadly purpose. "But the hellhounds will find him."

"Hellhounds?"

He nodded. "I have summoned the Erlking. That bastard will not escape the Erlking's justice."

"And Ari'dongharad?"

"He will find her and bring her back to us."

Deprived of a target for her rage, Corinne looked out the window. After a moment's thought, she asked, "Which ship is missing?"

"None of them."

"None? Did Oyochea take Ari'dongharad overland?"

"As best I can determine." His expression turned bleak, betraying his fondness for the child. "If he took her through the Quol ..."

He shook his head, not wanting to finish the gloomy thought, but his mate insisted.

"What will happen if he takes her through the Quol, Uberon?"

The king took a deep breath and marshaled his thoughts. "The Quol is perilous, toxic. None who pass through remain unharmed or unchanged. Most who venture into the jungle die."

"Why would Oyochea venture into certain death and take his captive with him?"

He shook his head. "Either he does not believe or understand the Quol's danger or he has some sort of protection from it."

Corinne opened her mouth to ask another question that Uberon probably couldn't answer. Before the words left her tongue, a scream reverberated in the castle and the library door slammed open. Startled, Corine yelped and wondered how Gus had arrived so quickly. She blinked and realized this was not Gus, fond and doting mate of her friend Oriel, but the feared and powerful Erlking, the ultimate arbiter of justice in that world.

"Speak," the Erlking commanded from behind the frightening visor of his black helm as a dozen large dogs with red eyes and bared teeth streamed into the room and circled around him, restless with bloodlust.

Uberon spoke, the description terse and his voice thrumming with impotent rage.

"A child?" the Erlking clarified.

"Aye, naught but fifteen summers."

"I'll find him, but the girl may not be alive," the Erlking warned. "Bring something she wore close to her skin."

"I'll get it," Corinne volunteered and dashed to fetch the child's shift. The castle shifted, shortening the distance to bring her to the girls' room more quickly than usual. Skidding to a stop, she burst into the room. The gargoyles instantly leveled their halberds at her.

"I need Ari'dongharad's shift, a nightgown, something she wore against her skin that has not been laundered."

Her face stained with tears and taut with worry, Ari'valia retrieved an item of clothing and thrust the wadded cloth into the queen's hands.

"Thank you," Corinne murmured. "How did he get to her?"

"A ... a servant lured her from the room," Han'al, the youngest girl and beloved of Golsat, answered. "He said ... he said he wished her to carry a message to Sin'clannad."

Golsat snarled. The girls' eyes widened and she seemed to shrink within herself.

"Golsat, you're frightening her," Corinne chided in a gentle tone.

The gargoyle turned his pointy-toothed snarl aside and glared at Corinne. She drew herself up as tall as she could and her palms tingled with power. Wind suddenly whipped around the room. Fae queen and gargoyle stared at each other. The gargoyle lowered his gaze first.

"Find that servant," she hissed. "I want to speak to him."

"Too late," Golsat replied with dark satisfaction.

"Did he escape?"

"No." The gargoyle's lips peeled back to show long, deadly fangs.

Corinne nodded, understanding that the guard had taken their bloodthirsty vengeance upon the servant guilty of either treachery or gullibility. She whirled about and ran back to the library where the Erlking and his hellhounds waited to launch the Wild Hunt. He snatched the wadded cloth from her hands and tossed it to the hounds. They snarled and snapped and slavered and shredded the cloth as they inhaled the child's scent. One hound tilted its head skyward and let loose a chilling howl that the others picked up.

The Erlking and the former Unseelie king exchanged silent

looks. The Erlking nodded and uttered a terse, one-word command. The hellhounds raced from the room and the world's ultimate arbiter of justice followed, keeping stride with them without straining.

"He'll find her," Uberon said in a quiet voice.

"But will she be alive?"

"If not, he'll bring back her body."

"This is …" Corinne's voice died away. She sank into a chair and leaned her head into her hands. "Oh, I can't focus on suitors and courtship now."

A hand settled gently on her shoulder. "I have instructed the servants to delay the proceedings in light of last night's treachery."

An ashen-faced servant entered the room bearing a tray in trembling hands. Uberon nodded his thanks and did not inquire as to the servant's distress. Between his own rage, the palace guard's need to redeem themselves of their failure, and the Erlking's visit, everyone feared for his or her life.

The servant scurried away to attempt to convince an equally trepidatious coworker to fetch the tray when the king and queen were finished.

When the door latched behind the servant, Uberon felt desire surge through him. He recognized it as a physical imperative to reaffirm life, to seek reassurance and pleasure in the face of anxiety and anticipated sorrow. However, he needed no arcane ability to understand that his mate experienced no reciprocal arousal. Nor would he force his attentions upon her.

Every step painful, he walked around Corinne and sat in a chair facing her. He wrapped his hands around hers, rubbing the wetness of her tears with the pads of his thumbs before they hardened to crystal and fell. She raised teary eyes to his bleak expression.

"I'm so scared for her, Uberon."

"I know, beloved. I, too, am fond of the little baggage."

She smiled, but her lower lip and chin trembled. "Why? Why take her? She's so young?"

"In human terms, she's old enough to wed and secure a royal alliance."

"I hate this. I *hate* this." Her voice cracked and she trembled with a potent mix of rage and sorrow.

"Oh, Corinne," he murmured and pulled her into his embrace. Stroking her unbound hair as she sobbed into his shirt, he murmured indistinct reassurances that he did not himself believe. With a sigh, he rested his cheek against the top of her head as her sobs dwindled into rough hiccups.

"Uberon, you're ... you're ..."

"Yes," he replied, clenching his jaw as she cupped the thick bulge pressing against his leather pants.

She lifted her wet eyes to look at him. "Take me."

"You do not want that," he denied through gritted teeth.

She gave him a firm squeeze through the supple leather and he hissed.

"I do. Now fuck me."

With a growl, he curled the curved tips of his claws over the neckline of her bodice. "You don't mean it."

"Fuck me."

Silk ripped as his claws tore through it. With a growl he pulled her to the floor and ripped open the fall of his trousers. Another hard yank jerked the shreds of her dress from her body and broke the belt. Uberon grunted and drove into his mate's body with a hard thrust. She, too, grunted and the sound excited him. The rapid slap of skin on skin and their deep grunts filled the room until Uberon's hoarse shout accompanied cathartic ejaculation. Corinne panted and moaned as his hot seed coated her inner walls. His finger delved into her folds, the thumb strumming her clit with ruthless purpose. A moment later she convulsed around him, under him, as he drove her into climax.

Uberon rolled to the side, pulling his mate with him. Lying on a priceless carpet, he curled around Corinne and buried his face in her hair and wept. Neither of them heeded the hardened tears that scattered across the floor.

CHAPTER 21

Waiting never felt so horrible as it did throughout the rest of that day and into the night. Bowing to the demands of kingship, Uberon took care of the necessity of administering the operation of his kingdom. Corinne, too, attempted to distract her worried mind by keeping busy. They cut the daily audience short, citing ruling privilege. Meals passed in tense quiet with little conversation, the clink of silverware against porcelain the only noise breaking the silence. The three remaining sisters took their midday meal with Uberon and Corinne, although their conversation remained subdued.

The day dwindled into evening. The two sisters' suitors cooled their heels in drawing rooms where they played cards and board games and engaged in desultory discourse. Coins exchanged hands with wins and gossip made the rounds. Under the grim chaperonage of four gargoyles, Sin'clannad and Ari'valia spent a few hours in quiet conversation with their suitors.

The entire company had just sat down to supper when the doors flung open and the Erlking strode through carrying a child in his arms. Blood, mud, and other unidentified substances spattered and stained his armor and garments.

"Ari'dongharad!" Corinne cried and toppled her chair as she jumped to her feet and ran toward the formidable Erlking even as the hellhounds streamed around him.

The Erlking paused to let Corinne examine the girl, then advanced to the table.

"Did you find him?" Uberon asked, his voice hoarse, first gazing upon the girl's limp body and then into the cold fire of his cousin's eyes.

"She received justice," the Erlking replied.

"And Oyochea?"

"What is left of him feeds the Quol."

Corinne noticed the hellhounds' bloodstained jaws and thought there must not be much left of the dastardly nobleman. She felt neither regret nor sorrow for the nobleman's doom. She raised her arms. "I'll take her now."

The Erlking's fiery glare softened. "My Lady Corinne, the child has been harmed."

"Did he—?" Corinne couldn't bear to say it.

The Erlking shook his head. "No, not that. But the Quol ... it is poisonous. The girl has been affected by its malignity."

"Will she get better?"

He shrugged and looked at Uberon, who shook his head because he, too, could not promise that the child would recover from her exposure to the jungle's toxic environment. Who knew what poisonous fumes the girl had breathed, what venom bloodthirsty insects and plants had injected through her skin, what diseases or toxins she had unknowingly ingested with a simple gulp of water? Seeing the silent exchange, Corinne's expression congealed into determination.

"No, she will *not* die," the queen vowed. "Uberon, summon the best healer. Please."

"No healer can counteract the Quol," the king said with a sad shake of his head.

"No! I refuse to accept that there is nothing we can do."

"She is human, beloved. She does not have the ... endurance ... to survive."

"Then transform her!"

"I cannot."

"You *will* not."

He bowed his head and then raised it again, eyes flat and inscrutable. "No, I will not. To do so would be to bind my soul to hers as I am bound to you. Do you relinquish the soul bond?"

Her eyes widened. "I didn't think that was possible."

"If you want to exchange your life for hers, give her your position as my mate, then I cannot deny you."

Corinne swallowed and averted her gaze, ashamed at her reluctance to take such a drastic step that would, as far as she understood, cost her her own life, a sacrifice she had no desire to make. "Is there any other way?"

Uberon looked over the stunned and quietly watching crowd of guests. "If there be any fae here who would bind his soul to this child and take her to mate when she comes of age, then I will settle upon him a title, land, and riches." His eyes narrowed with threat. "And I will watch over you to ensure Ari'dongharad's well being."

A black-haired djinn stood and bowed. "I am of noble blood, but a younger son with six brothers who would inherit before me. I would be titled in my own right and remain here in Quoliálfur. I revere my dam and sisters; they have been my joy. This girl would suffer no harm from me."

"Will you bind your soul to hers?"

The djinn nodded. "I will set my fire to her blood, breathe my wind into her lungs, and plant my sand within her heart."

"He is djinni," someone protested in a guttural hiss. "Djinni cannot be trusted."

Uberon cast his icy gaze upon the dwarf who objected to the alliance. "And would you give this child your stone and gold and gems in exchange for her life and loyalty?"

"She's a child!"

"And she'll soon outgrow you!" another guest jested, lip curling in a sneer.

The djinn directed an earnest gaze toward the king of Quoliálfur. "I shall not exercise my conjugal rights until the girl is mature."

"Not until she's at least eighteen and not without her consent," Corinne snapped.

"Agreed."

"And you will swear fealty to me and serve as my loyal subject," Uberon added.

"Agreed."

"To the chapel," the king ordered.

"We have a chapel?" Corinne echoed faintly, not having come across such a facility in her months in the Quoliálfur castle.

"It's more of a prayer room," Sin'clannad murmured, leaning close to the queen.

"I wonder why I did not know about it?"

"Perhaps because his Majesty answers all your prayers?" the young woman shot back with a naughty smile.

Corinne blushed. She shook off the distraction as Uberon gestured for her, Gus, and the djinni suitor to follow him. Flanking Sin'clannad, Ari'valia, and the youngest sister, Han'al, Golsat and three more gargoyles accompanied the family party to a small chapel tucked away in the depths of the mountain castle. Candles flared upon their entrance, their dead wicks glowing brightly at Uberon's command. Three pillars clustered near a shrine depicting a pearl-crowned, golden, nude madonna holding a sheaf of wheat in one hand and a small sickle in the other and kneeling before a trident and iridescent fish scaled in mother of pearl. The queen goggled at the mixed symbolism and said nothing.

Then she noticed the wide, shallow bowls resting upon each of the pillars. One bowl appeared to be made of tortoiseshell and contained sand. Fire burned in a second bowl made of red glass. A sky blue bowl of some thin, fragile material she could not identify held a shifting pile of tiny white crystals that reminded her of nothing so much as snowflakes. But that could not be, because snow could not endure the tropical heat.

The Erlking laid the girl down at the base of the three pillars. He took a step backward, bowed, and departed without another word, surrounded by the eerily silent hellhounds.

Corinne knelt beside the child. Someone—she did not see who—pressed a damp cloth into her hand. With the tenderness of a mother, she wiped the girl's ashen face, her tears crystallizing and bouncing off the girl's skin and the damp washcloth.

The djinn approached and glanced down at the pretty girl to whom he would bind his future and share his life force in exchange for status and wealth. He glanced at Uberon who captured his gaze with his own.

"I know the djinni ritual. Do not think to deceive me."

The djinni suitor nodded his understanding and replied in his own sibilant language, "This is sacred to my people. I would not debase it with falsehood."

Uberon nodded and, with a gesture of his hand, said, "Proceed."

The djinni nodded once and bowed his head. He murmured in his native language, calling upon the elements of the desert: sand, wind, fire. They answered him. He took the red bowl and broke it apart with his bare hands. The sharp edges sliced through his skin, yet he did not interrupt his chanting. The fire leaped from the shards to sizzle within his blood. He placed his bloody hands upon the girl's bare arms and smeared his blood over her. The fire leaped from his skin to hers. The child cried out and bucked against the searing pain, but the djinni's strong grasp held her in place.

Corinne surged forward to stop the torture, but Uberon held her back.

"No, he must do this," he whispered into her ear.

"He's hurting her!" she hissed.

"'Tis a djinni ritual not meant for humans."

"I swear—"

"If Ari'dongharad survives this, then she will live a long life until her mate dies."

"I hate this," Corinne muttered.

"I know."

The djinni took the tortoiseshell bowl in his hands and drizzled sand into his palm. Still chanting in that sibilant tongue, he rubbed the fine sand over his heart, the sharp grains turning the skin raw as he ground them in. He ripped open the bodice of the girl's soiled and tattered dress and did the same to her with a handful of fresh sand from the bowl. The sand then flared and both djinni and human screamed with pain as the grains liquified and formed into a stylized sun over their hearts.

Corinne blinked in mingled amazement and horror. The lines and curves looked like spun glass, but they flexed with the living resilience of skin.

"Fascinating," Uberon murmured under his breath.

Breathing heavily, the djinn resumed chanting, his voice hoarse. He brought down the third bowl. Holding it to his face, he inhaled deeply. The chanted ritual hissed from his mouth as he set down the bowl and tilted the girl's head back. He bent down as though giving her mouth-to-mouth resuscitation and forcefully exhaled the tiny crystals into her lungs. The girl's eyes flew open and her back arched. She pressed her tiny hands against the djinn's chest to shove him away, but he would not permit her to escape until he had shared the whole of his breath with her.

Fully deflating his lungs, he released her and toppled over as the enchantment settled into place, sealed by blood, breath, and flesh. The child rolled aside and coughed and wept, trying to escape the male who had given her the means to survive the Quoli taint.

Corinne caught her in her arms, rocking back and forth as she hugged the girl to her body. She wept, tears crystallizing and pattering when they hit the stone floor. Uberon whispered a curt order to the gargoyles. One of them hoisted the djinni male over his shoulder and carried him off to recover in comfort; the other three escorted the Merogis sisters to their room.

"Here, give her to me. She's too heavy for you to carry," he said, touching Corinne's shoulder.

She nodded, her face tear-stained, and allowed Uberon to take the girl into his arms.

"I'm glad to have you back," he breathed over the child as he cradled her against his chest. "Rest now. You will recover."

Ari'dongharad blinked, gave a small nod, and leaned her head against him in utter trust. With a rattling breath, she lapsed into a natural, restorative slumber.

Three girls claimed, he thought to himself, and neither of them the two marriageable prospects for whom he had endured this entire circus of socializing and dances. He vowed to get the remaining two young ladies settled as quickly as possible.

Not unless they agree, came his mate's acid response even as she directed servants to tend to her ward's djinni mate to ensure his full recovery now that he shared the girl's burden of the jungle's toxicity.

They have the choice, he agreed with a mental sigh and hoped they would agree soon. He was heartily tired of these ambitious guests who courted his wards for no other reason than the anticipation of what financial benefits and political advantages such a connection to the king of Quoliálfur would confer upon them.

The next several days passed in a flurry of interviews and tête-à-têtes as nervous suitors vied for the hands of the remaining two wards while Ari'dongharad and the djinn slowly recovered. Mindful of the gargoyles' stony glares and the fate of the Fyrgian nobleman who dared abscond with one of the girls, half of the men decided that no estate, castle, or hoard of gold was worth living under the gimlet eye of the Quoliálfur king and certain horrible doom if something untoward should befall the lucky man's bride. Ships flying the Quoliálfur flag departed, carrying passengers relieved to have escaped a dire fate as the king's titular sons-in-law.

Ari'valia made her choice from among the gentlemen who remained.

"I don't like him," Corinne whispered after listening to the interview between the swain and Uberon. "He's smarmy."

"He will not be faithful to her," Uberon said with the certainty of one who beheld the man's deepest thoughts.

"She doesn't deserve a philanderer."

"No, and I shall not approve the match."

Corinne chewed her bottom lip in worry. "Do you think she'll sneak out to see him?"

Uberon slanted a knowing glance at her and said, "I'll make sure of it."

"What do you have planned?"

"Disillusionment."

That evening, Ari'valia chattered with excitement about her supposed husband-to-be, extolling his virtues.

"I'm not convinced he's worthy of you," Corinne said. "In fact, I think you can make a much better choice."

Ari'valia's expression turned mulish. "He is very handsome and well-spoken. He is my choice."

"I don't like him."

"You are already wed," the girl argued in a peevish tone. "Why would you deny me my future."

"I do not want you to see him," Corinne said, not allowing the girl to dissuade her. "I forbid it."

Ari'valia pressed her lips together in a thin, angry line and focused on her plate while her sisters picked up the conversation, turning it to less volatile topics. Unaware of being manipulated, the girl retired to her room early after persuading a servant to carry a message to the disapproved gentleman. Uberson surreptitiously intercepted the message and ordered the servant to say nothing or suffer dire consequences. The threat worked, and the servant found other occupation far from Ari'valia's suitor.

Corinne nearly gaped in awe at the subtlety of Uberon's power as he directed the girl's inclination toward disobedience. Her awe morphed into nasty suspicion.

"Did you ever manipulate me like that?" she whispered as they lay in wait for Ari'valia to sneak out of the girls' bedchamber.

"No, beloved, never," he replied, sincerity ringing from every syllable. "I told you before that I prize free will. I may act to persuade you, but I will never rob you of your will."

She nodded, her own instincts corroborating the truth of his words. "Look, there she is."

Uberon wrapped them in a cloak of darkness to hide them as they followed the foolish young woman to the gentleman's room. They waited while she eased the door open and peered inside. He was not there. Determined to have that particular man, she set off to find him, unaware of the dangerous shadow following her.

She found him in a tavern with a wench on his lap and one palm squeezing a large, pendulous breast while the other held a half-empty mug of ale to his mouth which spouted such genteel sentiments as how he would enjoy swiving the Merogis girl until she grew fat with his heir.

"Then I shall return to you, my lovely beast," he crowed and pressed a slobbering kiss to the flesh exposed by the wench's low bodice. "And I shall make you forget all those other men."

Raucous laughter and crude jeers followed that pronouncement, which incited the inebriated man to yank open his trousers and expose his generous endowment for all to admire. The wench cooed and wrapped her rough, work worn hands around the dangling organ.

"Put it in your mouth," he demanded while the crowd egged them on with cries of "Suck! Suck!"

Cowering in an unobtrusive corner and shielded by her guardian's power, Ari'valia did not protest when Corinne took her hand and said, "You've seen enough. Let's go."

"I thought he loved me," Ari'valia whimpered in shame.

"He enjoys your beauty and your obedience, but he does not love you," Uberon said as he sped them back to the castle.

"Why did you not tell me?" she wailed as embarrassment caught up with her.

"Because we hoped you would see his true nature yourself."

"I do not wish to marry," the girl grumbled.

"Of course, you do. But you need not choose a husband now," Uberon reassured her as they walked through the corridor leading to the girls' bedchamber.

"They are all promised, except for me."

"Oh?" Corinne prompted.

"Yes, Sin'halissar has her sailor. Sin'clannad has decided upon the soldier from Nymmur. Han'al is going to marry Golsat; she told me so. Ari'dongharad is now bound to that djinn."

"The warrior from Nymmur is honorable," Uberon murmured. "I shall approve that match."

Corinne put her hands on Ari'valia's shoulders and held her facing her. "You need not marry if you do not find a worthy man who values you. If you but say the word, I will authorize your education and have you trained for a career."

"You would have me work as a servant?" The girl drew back in horrified offense.

"I would have you make something useful of your life."

The girl's expression turned mulish again.

Recognizing that the conversation had ended, Corinne bade her goodnight and watched her retreat into the innocent safety of her room.

Sin'clannad wed her choice the next day. The rest of the suitors departed the day after that.

CHAPTER 22

Corinne stood by Uberon's side, shielding her eyes against the glaring sun with her hand as they waited for the arrival of a trading ship. The black pennant flapped in the stiff breeze which felt wonderful as it cut through her skirts and molded the fabric to her legs. Uberon's long, black hair streamed away from his head like a banner in echo of that pennant bearing two silver crescents upon a black field.

She absently noted the creak of heavy wood, the shouts of sailors, and the other sounds of maritime industry as rolling waves slapped at the piers jutting from the wharf and the hulls of the ships moored there.

"What is it?" she asked as her mate's body stiffened. "What does the wind bring?"

"A human. A man from your old world."

"How do you know? How do you think he got here?"

"All in due time, beloved. For now, we wait."

The ship's sails billowed and snapped as it tacked across the water. She could hear the captain shout orders and saw sailors scramble like ants as they manhandled the sails. A turntable released and the anchor dropped on its thick heavy iron chain. A fine shudder ran through Uberon as the concentration of caustic iron bit at his mind and body. Corinne gasped, not expecting the sizzle of pain.

"What's that?"

"Iron," he replied as cool relief oozed over her. "You've grown sensitive to it more quickly than I anticipated."

"Iron?" she parroted. Then realizing he had shielded her from the iron's taint, she murmured, "Thanks."

He responded with a slight nod as he watched a longboat lower from the ship to the water. Manned by eight sailors at the oars, the boat cut through the water, heading straight for the pier. Corinne shifted from foot to foot, impatient with the wait. Eventually, though, the boat pulled up to the pier. One of the forward oarsmen threw a rope, which someone on the pier caught and deftly wrapped around a post. Someone else lowered a rope ladder with wooden rungs.

"Who commands the ship?" Uberon asked, bending over to address the officer who snapped orders to the oarsmen.

"Captain Irganteen, my lord," the officer replied, his white hair tossed by the wind and revealing pointed ears.

"Your Majesty," Uberon corrected.

The officer's fae eyes widened and he gulped, then remembered to bow, a tricky maneuver in the rocking longboat.

"Come on dock and tell me what you have," Uberon commanded.

"Aye, Your Majesty."

The oarsmen rolled over a large, bulky shape wrapped in a canvas sail that Corinne had no doubt they would want replaced. With practiced teamwork, the sailors hoisted the cumbersome package to the dock. A groan emanated from it upon landing roughly upon the wooden planks. The fae officer scrambled up the ladder with nimble agility. He turned copper colored eyes toward the female who met his gaze without humility or modesty. He blinked at her bold regard. Her nostrils flared, catching his scent. He sniffed and caught her scent mingled with that of the male who watched the silent exchange with predatory attention.

The officer blinked, dismissed the mated female, and said, "I remember the last rift between the worlds. It's open again."

"Aye," Uberon replied. "I suspected as much. Were there others?"

The officer shook his head. "Six total, all dead but this one. Will you close it?"

"What makes you think I have that power?"

The fae officer grinned and replied, "Because you did the last time."

Uberon's silver eyes narrowed to slits as his gaze honed-in on the thin copper collar encircling the fae's bare throat. "And what do you know of it?"

"My younger brother was there."

"What House are you?"

"Not an important one, else I'd not be sailing the seas with these ruffians," the fae replied as he squared his shoulders. He looked down at the human fully wrapped and constrained within a sheet of canvas and at the Unseelie queen who approached the bundle with curiosity and insufficient caution. He bowed. "By your leave, Your Majesty?"

"Go. Finish your voyage. Inform your captain that I shall reward him and all the crew for bringing this refugee to Quoliálfur. Spread the word among my fleet that all such refugees are to be rescued and treated as honored guests and brought here. I shall recompense any loss of profit due to interrupted trade."

Summarily dismissed, the fae officer bowed and returned to the boat.

Uberon turned his attention to Corinne, who squatted beside the refugee and tugged at the canvass covering his head.

"Why did they wrap him like this?"

"Probably to save him from blistering under the sun."

"They could have treated him better than this," she grumbled.

"And they will henceforth. As it is, he is lucky they did not leave him to drown."

"And why would they?" She pulled the heavy fabric from the man's bearded, sunburnt face and gasped.

"Samuel!" she shrieked. Her nose wrinkled at the stench of unwashed, putrid flesh. "It's Samuel!"

Irrational, jealous rage surged through Uberon and he focused on exerting control and calm, rather than obliterating this filthy, damaged human who seemed to have some sort of claim on his mate's affections. With a deep breath, he asked, "How do you know him, Corinne?"

She raised eyes shining with tears to him and announced,

"He's my brother."

Uberon closed his eyes in a slow blink and congratulated himself for not having succumbed to that insane impulse to reduce the rescued man to a greasy smear. His sweet Corinne would never have forgiven that.

"Then I am doubly pleased he found his way to our shores," he said and raised his hand in silent summons. The gesture brought pounding feet attached to six males presenting themselves for service.

"Fetch something on which to carry this man and transport him to the castle. Be careful with him."

The volunteers nodded and ran off to find something they could use as a stretcher. Uberon and Corinne remained beside the unconscious man until he was shifted onto a litter and strapped to it to ensure he would not roll off as they toted him up the steep mountainside into the castle's cool interior.

Once inside the castle, two gargoyles took the litter and followed the queen to a luxurious guest chamber. Curious, the Merogis sisters—except for Ari'Dongharad who yet remained abed recovering from her excursion into the Quol—followed, chattering speculations and broaching questions. Corinne sent servants scrambling for basins of water, rags and soap, to clean the man's damaged body.

"You must leave us to this work, Your Majesty, Lady Ari'valia," a senior maid said. "'Tis not proper for you to be here for this."

Worried, but truly having no desire to see her brother naked, Corinne bowed to the servant's admonition and excused herself.

"I will help," Ari'valia volunteered. She met Corinne's gaze and seemed to perceive something that no one other than Uberon had. "He is important to you, isn't he?"

"He's my brother," Corinne whispered. "I don't know how he got here, but we must nurse him back to health."

Overhearing the queen, the maid interjected in a crisp tone, "Then leave us to get him cleaned up. We must treat his wounds. Lady Ari'valia may return later to assist in his convalescence."

Wrapping her arm around Ari'valia's shoulders, Corinne left the room. The door closed behind them with a decisive *click* of the latch.

"He will recover. Urmentrüd is an experienced nurse. She is

whom the human guards and sailors seek when they suffer injuries," Sin'clannad reassured her as she and the other sisters gathered around the queen.

Corinne nodded and found a bench nearby on which to sit and wait until the servants permitted her back inside the room with her brother.

She felt as though she waited countless hours; however, she knew better. She leaped up from the bench when the door opened and rushed inside the room at the healer's approving nod. Thoroughly bathed, his body no longer exuded the foul stench of infection and unwashed skin. His short, ash blonde hair had been shorn to a velvety fuzz upon his scalp. Neat white bandages wrapped around his arms and torso. Sharp herbal scents wafted from them, telling of the healing salves and unguents used to treat his wounds and fight infection.

Corinne pulled a chair next to the bed and took a seat. With exquisite care, she took her brother's limp hand in hers and held it. She whispered, the words breaking, "Samuel, it's me, Corinne. You're safe now. Please wake up. You're safe now."

She did not know how long she sat by her brother's side until the king himself entered the room.

"I can't leave him alone," she protested.

"Ari'valia will keep him company," he assured her.

"But he doesn't know her. She's a stranger to him."

"No male minds waking to a pretty girl beside him," he said.

Corinne gave in, accepting the truth of that pronouncement. Ari'valia took the vacated chair and grasped Samuel's big, rough hand in her small, soft ones. She promised, "I will have you notified of any change."

Corinne nodded and allowed Uberon to lead her to supper.

A week passed during which Samuel burned with fever, thrashing and shouting in delirium. The fever abated as his body's own defenses and the strengthening, antiseptic herbal medicines forced down his throat and used to treat the extensive wounds on his body fought to keep him alive and restore him to health. Corinne spent uncounted hours at his bedside, assisting as she was able, from bathing his skin with cool, wet cloths to drawing cool currents of air from the castle's depths into the room to relieve the heat of his fever.

Finally, the fever broke and he slept a natural sleep. Corinne wept with relief, not protesting when Uberon picked her up and carried her to bed where he wrapped his body around hers and held her within the warmth of his love and protection.

On the eighth day, Samuel's eyelids fluttered open. Instinct and training held him still as he waited for his blurry vision to clear and he took in what information he could with his other senses.

"Samuel?"

Ah, he recognized that voice. But his mouth and throat felt too dry to utter a single syllable.

A slim, strong arm slid under his head to lift him just enough for a cup to dribble a trickle of cool, herbal tasting water past his slack lips. He swallowed. In came another dribble. He swallowed again, taking pleasure in the way the cold tea soothed his throat.

"More," he whispered, his voice hoarse and rusty, as the cup was withdrawn.

"Only water now," came a soft reply from that voice he recognized. Another cup pressed to his lips and drizzled a bit of untainted water into his mouth. He swallowed.

"Thanks," he muttered and fell back asleep.

When next Samuel awoke, his vision cleared to reveal a young woman, maybe sixteen or seventeen years old with dark hair and large brown eyes like a doe. The girl helped prop him up to drink several swallows of pure water. She said something in a language he neither recognized nor understood: it wasn't Arabic, Russian, Japanese, Spanish, French, or German. The consonants were sharp and the vowels short and flat, not unpleasant to the ear.

The girl held up a bowl and a spoon and mimicked eating. He nodded his agreement. The girl barked an order and a burly servant that looked more like stone than flesh and blood entered. Samuel cursed his weakness, because he could neither defend the girl nor himself from the hulking creature. However, the creature paid him no more heed than a piece of furniture as he hoisted Samuel into a sitting position propped up by extra pillows the pretty girl stuffed behind his back.

"Corinne?" he asked, hoping that the girl would recognize the name, because he swore that he'd seen and heard his sister in this strange place, this place from where he would rescue her, come hell or high water.

The girl beamed and repeated, "Corinne." She pointed toward the door to let him know that someone named Corinne did exist beyond that door. Or maybe *Corinne* meant *outhouse* in her language. He did not know.

The girl pointed to herself. "Ari'valia." She pressed a fingertip to his chest, bare except for the bandages, and said, "Samuel."

He thought her accent charming. Then he realized she had correctly identified his name.

"Yes. Samuel," he said and managed a weak smile.

The girl nodded, touched that slender finger to her breastbone, and repeated, "Ari'valia."

"Ari'valia," he repeated obediently.

She nodded and smiled and held up the bowl, that lesson having concluded in favor of feeding him. Samuel attempted to raise his arms, but the muscles trembled and his bones felt as though they were magnetically affixed to the bed. He opened his mouth and let the pretty girl spoonfeed him like a baby. It was better than starving.

Soon thereafter, he drifted off to sleep again.

When he awoke next, Corinne sat beside him.

"You're awake!"

"Corinne," he whispered, blinking with a potent mixture of relief and disbelief. His bleary eyes took in the fine silk of her strange costume. "How?"

The corner of her mouth crooked up and she said, "We're not in Kansas anymore, Toto."

"I never did like that movie," he grated. "Where are we? How do we get out of here? Mom and Dad have been frantic with worry."

"You eat. I'll talk."

He nodded, knowing he didn't have the strength to do anything but comply. She held a spoonful of some sort of porridge to his mouth and began speaking.

"We're in Quoliálfur," she began. "It's in an ... an alternate dimension."

Samuel frowned in obvious disbelief and worry that his baby sister had somehow been brainwashed.

"I know what you're thinking, Sam. I'm not crazy or on drugs or anything like that. For now, you'll just have to take my word for it."

He sighed and opened his mouth for another spoonful of the bland, pasty substance.

"I'm ... married, I guess you could say, to the king of Quoliálfur. He's good to me."

Samuel's eyes narrowed with suspicion, because "good" might have been relative in comparison to torment.

"He loves me and I love him."

"Marriages can be dissolved, Corinne. I'll get you out of here."

Setting aside the bowl of porridge, she sighed and unbuttoned the high neck of her gown.

"Corinne, I don't want to see—" he protested.

She cut him off as she pulled the fabric open to expose the silver engraved in intricate patterns into her skin and the black diamonds sparkling among the design. "This marriage can't be dissolved."

"He did this to you?"

"*Magic* did this to me."

"There's no such thing as magic, Corinne. You always did take those old fairy tales too much to heart."

She held up her hand, palm flat and facing upward. A ball of flame popped into existence and danced on her skin without burning her. Then it winked out of existence. She turned her hand so the palm faced him and spread her fingers. With separate little pops, four small flames danced between her fingers and began to swirl around her hand in random patterns.

"There is such a thing as magic and we're caught in a fairy tale, Samuel. It took me a long time to accept that and I will give you as much time as I can for you to reach the same conclusion."

She picked up the bowl and spoon and resumed feeding him. "Do you know how you got here?"

"My team ... oh, God, my team," he groaned. "Are they here, too. Do you know where they are?"

She shook her head. "The sailors who brought you here said you were the only survivor. Where were you?"

Samuel leaned his head back against the pillows and struggled to contain the upswell of grief and rage that threatened to explode. After a long moment, he squashed the violent emotion and locked it down to enable him to speak.

"We were chasing traffickers about two hundred miles west-southwest of Bermuda, he began.

"The Bermuda Triangle?" his sister asked.

"In that area, I suppose," he answered. "Why? That stuff's all been debunked. There's no mystery to that area of the ocean."

She shrugged and said, "Continue. Please."

"My team and I were chasing traffickers and we were hit by a sudden squall. It came up from nowhere. One minute we were bouncing across the waves, and the next our boat was dead in the water and sinking."

"Oh, Samuel."

He closed his eyes against the hazy memories of his teammates one by one losing their strength and slipping, exhausted, beneath the waves. "I don't know how long we floated. Did anyone survive?"

"Just you. You were half-dead when we brought you in."

"I've got to get back to my CO."

"Sam, there is no going back." She averted her gaze to gather her thoughts, then looked back at him to lock eyes. "Coming here changes us. It's a one-way trip."

"I get that it's primitive here," he said, looking around as much as he was able. "But I'll get us out of here, Sis."

"I can't leave. I don't want to leave. My life is here with Uberon."

"What the hell kind of name is Uberon. Who the hell is he?"

"I shall excuse your ignorance just this once," came a cool, deep voice from the doorway.

Samuel's jaw snapped shut as the man he surmised had abducted his sister and brainwashed her entered the room looking like a costar in a *Lord of the Rings* movie. From his imposing height to his booted feet, the man looked absolutely, impossibly authentic.

"Never again speak to Corinne with disrespect or I'll kill you," the man threatened.

"Uberon, please, this is a huge adjustment for him," Samuel's sister pleaded. She looked at her brother. "Sam, watch what you say. Uberon's a bit protective."

"He *kidnapped* you."

"I gave myself to him and he … he …"

"I kept what was gifted to me." The tall, regal man turned weird, silver eyes with *vertical* pupils to Samuel and added, "Heed Corinne. She was your sister, but she is now and forever my *mate.*"

Samuel shook his head in weak denial. Corinne placed a hand on his shoulder. He met her gaze and realized with a sinking heart that her jade green eyes had no white sclera and the pupils were vertical, too. He glanced at her hand and swallowed uneasily at the sharp claws that curved from her fingertips. *Changed indeed.*

"Sam, we'll talk later. In the meantime, consider that you've been treated well here and that I am happy, truly happy, here."

Samuel leaned his head back against the pillows and accepted his circumstances ... for now.

CHAPTER 23

Corinne's brother recuperated with the speed and single-minded focus of an elite warrior, which he was. As soon as he was able to hobble around with a cane, she guided him to the small chapel where he knelt at in a pew, bowed his head, and prayed to a God he accused of abandoning him. He understood the irony of that, but didn't care. He watched his sister, lurking out of sight to see how Uberon treated her when not in his presence.

"The king dotes upon her and would never allow anything to harm her," a gravelly voice from behind him murmured.

Samuel spun about, surprised that something so huge and apparently made of animated stone could creep up behind him unnoticed. Neither his balance nor his strength being quite restored, he wobbled and tilted. A large silicone hand grasped his upper arm and steadied him. Samuel put his hand on the major domo's bare forearm and felt ... stone. Living stone. Cool, polished smooth, impenetrable.

"Y-y-you're ..."

"A gargoyle," Golsat replied. "Your concern for her Majesty does you credit, but there is no need."

The term *gargoyle* sank into Samuel's brain. His knees buckled. Golsat reacted quickly and hauled him to a bench.

"Now do you believe?" the major domo challenged.

"This ... this is ... impossible," Samuel muttered, shaking his head, fisting his hands on his knees.

"This is not your old world. My Lady Corinne has found her place here and so must you."

"I have to go back."

"There is no going back. Only a handful of fae have mastered the art of opening portals and traveling between worlds."

"He's one of them," Samuel said, jutting his unshaven chin toward the doorway of the room where Uberon and Corinne played cards with Ari'valia and Sin'clannad.

"Aye. But he'll not bend to your persuasion."

"He'll bend to hers."

"She will not go back. And he carries letters to your parents to ease their worry."

"So, that's where the letters come from," he murmured. With a sigh of defeat, Samuel bowed his head and admitted to being caught in a no-win situation. Golsat sat beside him in easy silence. The heavy wooden bench creaked beneath his weight.

"What am I going to do here?" Samuel wondered aloud. "I'm a Navy SEAL, but those skills mean nothing here."

"Oh, I wouldn't say that."

"What do you mean?"

"You are accustomed to being a strong man, yes? And you have the demeanor of a warrior."

"In my world, I am a warrior."

"Then you simply need a king to whom you will swear fealty."

"I'm no vassal or villein."

A sound rumbled from Golsat's deep chest. Samuel realized the gargoyle was chuckling.

"All here are vassals to Uberon, King of Quoliálfur. He is not the first king I have served, nor the most lenient, but he is just and honorable. You could do much worse than swear fealty to him."

"Did he put you up to this?"

Golsat frowned. "No one forces a gargoyle to do anything he does not wish to do. In my own way, I am just as powerful as he."

"Then why not rule your own kingdom?"

"Administration sucks."

Samuel gaped, eyebrows raised, then he laughed. "Corinne

taught you that expression, didn't she?"

Golsat favored him with a small smile. "She did. I find it apt on many occasions."

"So, if my understanding is correct, then Uberon is über magical." Samuel liked the pun. "Can you do what he does?"

"No. Magic has little or no effect on gargoyles. He can neither compel us nor deceive us with a glamor. Magic used against us will fail. It is a testament to his power that his castle does not crumble when we set foot in it."

"And why would the castle … oh, it's magic, too."

"King Uberon awakened the mountain and used its sentience to raise the castle. Because gargoyles are of stone, the mountain's magic is actually sympathetic to our resistance to magic."

Samuel scratched his head. "A sentient castle, huh?"

"Should the castle deign to acknowledge you, you will know it. It's quite fond of your sister."

Golsat rose to his bare feet, soles of stone not needing protection from grit or pebbles underneath. "When you are able, come to the arena. King Uberon has many warriors with whom you can spar. The exertion will benefit you."

Having much to think upon, Samuel started taking long walks. Soon he found himself accompanied by Ari'valia who easily kept pace with his slow stride. They amused each other by learning one another's languages. He found her a quick study, glad to see that a pampered, constrained life had not dulled the girl's wits.

As his strength and stamina grew, he found his way to the arena where burly men and men-like creatures lifted heavy weights, ran laps, and fought with blunted weapons. The quartermaster sized him up and handed him a breastplate, a pair of vambraces, and a saber.

Holding the weapon awkwardly, Samuel said, "A sword really isn't my kind of weapon."

"They don't have gunpowder here," Golsat said.

"Jesus H. Christ! How do you *do* that?" Samuel spun around. "And what do you know about gunpowder?"

The gargoyle favored him with an unperturbed look and answered, "The properties of gunpowder make it too volatile for practical use here, so King Uberon forebore to import it."

"This is ungodly primitive."

"By your technological standards, yes. But a good warrior adapts. Are you a good warrior, Samuel?"

"I'm fucking fantastic," the man growled through clenched jaws.

"Good, because I've been looking forward to testing you." Golsat held out his hand and the quartermaster placed a longsword in his palm. The gargoyle spun the heavy weapon with ease and delicacy.

"Let's go, Pebbles," Samuel muttered.

Golsat inclined his head and turned on his bare heel. Samuel followed him out as soon as the quartermaster helped him buckle on the breastplate and vambraces.

Under the glare of the tropical sun, the sand's heat traveled through the leather soles of Samuel's boots. He hefted the sword, testing its balance and weight.

"It's just a big knife," he told himself. "Think KA-BAR, just bigger."

That seemed to help.

"Attack when ready," Golsat invited as Samuel circled him. "You can't hurt me."

Samuel muttered imprecations about rock, paper, and scissors and lunged when the opportunity seemed ripe. The gargoyle moved with incredible lightness and speed, blocked the blow, and parried hard enough to knock the sword from the human's grip.

"Again."

Samuel picked up the sword and tried again. And again. And again. He quickly realized the gargoyle toyed with him, tested him. Experienced at combat, Samuel did not forsake his concentration to annoyance or anger, but used the emotions to strengthen him. However, his recent state as an invalid had taken a toll on his strength and stamina. All too soon, sweat streamed down his skin and plastered his short hair to his scalp. His lungs heaved like bellows. His muscles trembled with exhaustion. Samuel knew when to quit or risk relapse. He dropped the sword and shook his head. No, the sword bore no resemblance to his missing KA-BAR.

"No more."

"This afternoon you will spar hand-to-hand with Sin'clannad's husband. He is a fine, human warrior."

Samuel looked at the gargoyle without speaking and wondered how the heavy stone male could move with such lightness and agility and speed and endure the crushing heat of the sun. Then he remonstrated with himself for so readily accepting the new reality of animated stone and magic.

"Tomorrow morning, you shall meet me here to continue your instruction with the sword. You show promise, young Samuel."

Samuel nodded, sweat dripping from his chin, and thought, "Aye aye, Pebbles."

He knew better than to say that aloud. A good soldier or sailor recognized superior authority when it saw it.

He groaned as he bent down to retrieve the sword. Returning the blunted weapon and the dented, scratched armor to the quartermaster who directed him to the baths, Samuel took a moment to reflect on his progress. He did not notice the silver gaze that watched and evaluated him from a shaded spot in the arena seating.

"I hear you sparred in the arena today," Corinne commented at supper that evening.

Samuel looked up, as did the Merogis sisters.

"I did," he replied, rolling shoulders that ached from the afternoon bout with a human opponent. He resisted the urge to squirm under a disapproving gaze that looked altogether too much like their mother's. "Golsat invited me."

Her brow creased with worry. "Do you think you should engage in such strenuous activity so soon?"

Samuel relaxed, realizing that Corinne only fretted for his good health. "I need to exercise, Sis. Lying about won't rebuild my strength, and I don't want my skills to get rusty."

Doe eyes round with wonder and admiration, Ari'valia asked, "Are you a mighty warrior then?"

He smiled. "I'm a Navy SEAL, princess."

She frowned. "I am not a princess."

"It's a word of ... of ..."

"It's a term of endearment," Corinne explained in the girl's own language.

Ari'valia beamed at him. Corinne snickered.

Samuel began to meet Golsat every morning for continuing instruction in swordsmanship and found himself popular every afternoon for sparring in hand-to-hand combat. Even as he taught Uberon's soldiers the mixed martial arts he knew—a brutal combination of krav maga, the system, jiu-jitsu, taekwondo, karate, and kung fu—he learned from them. Focused on the sessions in the arena, he did not notice for some time the audience that gathered.

"He's quite good, isn't he?" Corinne murmured as she watched him parry Golsat's strike.

"He's a bit weak on the left." Uberon turned to face her disgruntled frown and grinned. "Yes, he's very good."

"Hah. Don't humor me. If you're such an expert, *you* go down there and spar with him."

Seeing an opportunity to impress his mate, Uberon agreed. "I'll arrange the match for tomorrow morning when he's rested and fresh."

"Humph."

He appreciated the sway of her hips as she walked away from him.

Sitting on his other side, Golsat murmured in a dry tone, "She's never seen you fight, has she?"

Uberon chuckled. "Either way, I win. She'll either be impressed with my prowess or she'll want to soothe my bruised ego."

Golsat laughed. "I look forward to the day when I can enjoy such attentions from my mate."

The king's humor disappeared. "That is not for several years yet."

"I can wait. Stone is patient."

The next morning brought packed seating, a rare overcast sky, and the delicious sight of the Quoliálfur king wearing nothing but a leather battle kilt. The locks of hair framing his face had been braided and pulled back. His towering figure of lean, defined muscle drew admiration from both male and female members of the audience. He held a long saber in a loose grip and waited for his young opponent.

Samuel allowed none of his surprise to show at the proud display of silver and black diamonds that draped across his opponent's chest, ran over his shoulders, and dipped low down his back. The clouds parted just enough to allow a ray of sunshine to envelope the imposing male and set the silver and jewels ablaze. Unaccustomed to seeing such a blatant display, the spectators buzzed with awe.

Uberon, did you do that?

Do what?

Part the clouds so you lit up like a Christmas tree. Corinne forebore to mention how the blatant display impressed her. Knowing her mate, he probably picked up on it anyway.

Do you have any idea how heavy clouds are?

Seated in the stands, Corinne sighed and accepted that Uberon had no intention of answering her question, which indicated that he probably manipulated the weather—but in whose favor?

He will not suffer defeat because the sun blinded him.

You're very sure he'll lose. My brother's a Navy SEAL. Do you know what that means?

I'm one of the three most powerful fae in this world with over a hundred thousand years of practice with the sword. Do you know what that means?

Don't kill him, Uberon. He's my brother.

I have no intention of killing him. But a little humiliation wouldn't go amiss.

"No armor?" Samuel, unaware of the mind-to-mind conversation between his sister and her mate, observed aloud as he checked the fit of the vambraces and greaves protecting his forearms and shins.

"I won't need it."

"Even a blunted sword will cut."

"Then I shall enjoy your sister's tender care." Uberon grinned with unadulterated male anticipation.

Samuel frowned, not liking the allusion of his sister's intimate relations with the intimidating man facing him. Or any man, really. He spat into the sand and said, "No magic."

"Of course, not." Uberon turned his body, raised his blade, and his other hand. "*En garde.*"

Samuel positioned himself.

"Attack when ready," the king invited.

Samuel waited a few seconds, gauging the king's stance, his hold on the sword, his attitude. Feeling he had the fae's measure, he struck.

With an ease that smacked of nonchalance, Uberon parried

the blow and taunted, "Is that the best you've got?"

"Just testing," Samuel answered. With economy of motion rather than fancy flourishes, the SEAL gave it his best. Within seconds, he realized that the fae toyed with him. None of his strikes landed anywhere near the smooth bare skin of his opponent whose sword licked in and out with blinding quickness and accuracy. Soon his body bore stinging nicks and welts from the blunted edge. Harder blows dented his armor and left bruises beneath. He redoubled his efforts to no avail.

Then the point of Uberon's blade hovered at his throat.

"Do you yield, Samuel?" the king inquired in an urbane tone.

Samuel swallowed, the bulge of his Adam's apple grazing the metal. His chest heaved with every harsh lungful of air. Recognizing the king outclassed him as a swordsman, he opened his fist and dropped the sword.

"I yield."

The sword's point withdrew and Uberon took a step back. "You've become quite good. Swear fealty to me."

"I gave my oath to serve my country."

"That vow means nothing here. You cannot return there, so you honor an oath that no longer has value."

Samuel lifted burning eyes to the king's and said, "I am a free man, no one's subject."

"You served one country and its laws. It is no longer your country. Why not serve Quoliálfur?"

"Who would be my commanding officer?"

"Golsat. He thinks you eminently suitable for the palace guard."

"To stand around all day in livery? I don't think so."

"Do you so despise the Swiss Guard in your world's Vatican City?"

"Of course not."

"Then consider my palace guard the same as that Swiss Guard. The palace guard are the elite warriors of Quoliálfur. I would entrust the safety of your sister—my *mate*—to the protection of none other than the best I have to offer."

Not really understanding the whole "mate" thing, Samuel bowed to destiny. "All right, then."

Uberon chuckled, the sound low and not cruel. "Not the most enthusiastic reception I could hope for, but it will do."

"I don't renege on my promises."

"I know," the king agreed, not mentioning that he'd dipped into Samuel's mind for such certainty.

"If I ever return to my world, that oath takes precedence."

"Of course."

"Then, yes, I'll swear loyalty to Quoliálfur."

Uberon did not miss the careful phrasing, but neither did he remark upon it. He had other incentives to bind the warrior to him. He looked into the stands, gaze drawn to his mate wearing deep gold silk. The Merogis sisters sat with her, the fabric of their colorful dresses rippling in the tropical breeze. Samuel's gaze followed the king's and he nodded in acknowledgment, but did not wave.

"You think yourself disgraced," Uberon commented.

"You beat me."

"I've had a lot more practice than you."

"You look younger than me."

"A benefit of immortal youth."

"That's absurd."

"If you say." Uberon looked up into the stands again, then back at Samuel. "Kneel."

"What?"

"Kneel. If you would swear fealty to Quoliálfur, then kneel."

Samuel nodded and, with a grunt, knelt. He clenched his jaw against the pain of sand grinding into the nicks on his knees and the stinging salt of sweat.

"Repeat after me."

Samuel nodded and repeated Uberon's words, "I promise on my faith that I will be faithful to the kingdom of Quoliálfur, now ruled by Uberon, King of Quoliálfur, and will observe my homage to him completely against all persons in good faith and without deceit."

"I accept your oath of loyalty and service," Uberon replied. "Thus you are bound to Quoliálfur and its crown by witness of the sky, the sea, the mountain, and all who live to hear it."

Samuel gasped as a feeling like a heavy cloak settled over his body, weighing him down. He felt the cooling, drying touch of a breeze then the slide of fine linen and leather over his skin.

"Rise, Lieutenant Samuel of the royal guard of Quoliálfur."

Samuel blinked, mind stuttering at the magic he'd just

experienced. From soiled, sweat-soaked, and mildly injured, he stood refreshed, healed, and clothed in a guard's uniform. A delighted squeal from the audience drew his attention.

"Ari'valia is yours, if you want to take her to wife."

Samuel's surprised gaze flew to Uberon's. He gulped, because he could not deny the desire he felt when he looked upon her. However, her youth contrasted sharply against his years and experience which rendered him older than his true age of thirty-two. "She's too young."

"She's of marriageable age and it appears she wants you."

"If I marry her, you know I won't leave her."

"I know. But she will make your life here much more enjoyable."

"If I have the chance to go home, I'll take her and Corinne with me."

That didn't phase the king either.

"If Ari'valia consents to accompany you, I will allow it; however, Corinne stays with me."

Samuel met the king's eyes, solid silver with slitted black pupils. He noted the elongated, pointy-tipped ears. He glanced aside at the obviously inhuman gargoyles with the dull gleam of their stone hides reflecting the sunshine. A good soldier or sailor learned one crucial lesson in service: embrace the suck. He'd always prided himself on being an excellent sailor, the best of the Navy SEALs. That mean he needed to embrace the suck, accept the circumstances, and adapt. Now.

Samuel looked back into the arena seating and knew that, even still in many cultures around the modern world, guardians settled young girls upon men without thought for those girls' preferences. He at least liked Ari'valia and she appeared to enjoy his company. Successful marriages throughout history had been based on less.

"Aye. I'll care for her."

"You shall wed tomorrow."

"Tomorrow?" Sam echoed, dismayed at the squeak in his voice.

"No need to waste time; you humans have so little of it," Uberon murmured. Then, to disconcert the man even more, he leaned forward and said, "You are what she needs."

"I feel like I'm robbing the cradle," Sam muttered.

Uberon ignored his misgivings. "You'll need a crest for the noble House you will establish."

Accepting his fate and adapting to it, Samuel smiled and thought of the eagle, anchor, and trident of the Navy SEALS. "I already have one."

CHAPTER 24

Corinne hugged her brother and the young woman who was now her sister. She looked at the other Merogis sisters and realized that the futures of each had been settled. She was no longer responsible for their well-being. The realization engendered mixed feelings of satisfaction and melancholy. She wondered if, perhaps, she would feel like that with her own children if she and Uberon ever had any. That thought led to whether he even wanted children, especially since he had lost his son.

"I will welcome and cherish any child we may have," he reassured her, although she'd said nothing. He cupped her shoulders, palms resting lightly upon her as the wedding party made their way to the great hall where the wedding banquet would be served.

"You're reading my thoughts again."

"Only those you broadcast."

She sighed and supposed she couldn't blame him for "overhearing" her loudest thoughts.

"I look forward to the procreation, whether we produce a child or not," he whispered into her ear. The warm, velvety timbre of his voice sent shivers of desire up and down her spine and well he knew it. He inhaled, nostrils flaring. "You're ready for me."

"Always," she murmured in agreement as his fingers tightened over her bare skin. Again, the gown he chose for her bared the extent of the soul bond made manifest. Upon seeing her exposed thusly, Samuel had pressed his lips together in a thin line of disapproval. He much preferred she dress more modestly, although he acknowledged that his opinion no longer held primary influence over her sartorial choices. She hadn't the courage to admit that her mate chose her gowns.

"She looks radiant," Corinne remarked, doing her best to ignore the slickness between her thighs.

Indeed, Ari'valia shone as brightly as carnival lights in her vividly colored, flowing silks and bedecked with the traditional wedding regalia of a wealthy merchant's daughter. The style put Corinne in mind of a barbarically amazing amalgamation of Indian and Chinese garb and accessories.

"In her parents' native country and tradition, the bride wears her dowry to signify her family's wealth as well as to show the groom's family that they have allied themselves to a family of good connection," Uberon explained.

"It was kind of you to settle that dowry upon her," Corinne replied, blinking at the gaudy magnificence of it. "And to help out Samuel, too."

A heavy cape of deep blue fell from her brother's broad shoulders, his newly established family crest embroidered in white and gold thread. His black leather boots gleamed. He cut a dashing figure in closely cut pants and shirt.

"Why gold instead of silver?" she asked.

"Humans prize gold," he replied, although fae silver did not tarnish. "It's a lingering preference from their history before falling through the portals."

Corinne nodded and wondered why Uberon had not offered to transform her brother to fae, although she decided not to ask him. She wasn't sure she really wanted to know the answer. Uberon knew of her question and kept his silence.

They followed the wedding guests, a much smaller party than had attended Sin'clannad's nuptial ceremony. The more intimate ceremony seemed to suit Ari'valia and Samuel better anyway.

"Your Majesty!" a page called out as he ran toward them. "Please, Your Majesty!"

Uberon turned to face the pimply-faced teen. "What is it, Zeffros?"

The boy hopped to a halt to avoid running headlong into his king. "An emissary from the Seelie Court is here. He requests your audience and says it's urgent."

"Give my apologies to your brother and Ari'valia," Uberon commanded, running his hand down his mate's back. He looked back at the page and snapped, "Golsat, to me."

The gargoyle immediately left off what he was doing to attend to his king. Together, they headed toward the audience room where the emissary from the Seelie Court waited.

As he walked toward duty, the king of Quoliálfur somehow assumed the icy, powerful mantle of the Unseelie king, a cold-blooded, cold-hearted, analytical being of immense power and neither compassionate nor caring. Watching his departure, Corinne shivered and understood just how he had held a continent in fear of him for tens of thousands of years.

Without wasting time or energy on pleasantries, Uberon's quiet question made the emissary wince and his already pale complexion lose even more color: "What is so urgent that I must neglect my mate's brother at his nuptials?"

The emissary summoned his courage and reminded himself that the Unseelie king had no reputation for killing messengers. At least, not yet. He withdrew a small scroll from a leather bag hanging from his shoulder and held it out. "A message from his majesty, King Mogren of the Seelie Court."

"You know its contents. Summarize."

"The Quoli have attacked and conquered the Lahn Ursai region."

"Did the Akh-sinh of the Lahn Ursai survive?"

The emissary shrugged. "We have no word. King Mogren has lost nigh on twenty Dragon Riders and half the Palace Guard. Captain Thelan was gravely injured."

"And the moon-born?"

"She remains at his side."

"What about Enders?"

"He ordered the retreat."

Uberon cursed under his breath, knowing that the archivist would not have ordered a retreat unless he was convinced they had no chance whatsoever of victory. After all, he and that uppity

Captain Thelan had invaded his castle to rescue the moon-born from Marog and practically decimated his own palace guard in doing so. Of course, they'd had the assistance of an enraged and ravenous dragon.

Stupid Marog. The greedy boy always wanted more than his due.

Already suspecting the answer, Uberon asked anyway: "What does Mogren ask of a king whom he does not recognize?"

The emissary's eyes squeezed shut at this delicate juncture, for he suspected the king of Quoliálfur held grudges and knew that he would not likely forgive the insult recently suffered. Opening his eyes, he flinched from the icy silver gaze and replied, "He requests military assistance from Quoliálfur."

"And what of the Daimónio Refstófae?"

"King Murcio's assistance is being solicited even as I speak with you now, Your Majesty."

"Mogren reneged on his offer to assist them in their time of need," Uberon said. "Why should I believe he will honor any obligation to a country he declines to recognize?"

The emissary gestured toward the scroll in the king's hand. "King Mogren officially acknowledges the nation of Quoliálfur and you as its rightful king."

Uberon nodded. "And guarantees against his duplicity? What of that?"

"I cannot speak for the king."

"Then why are you here, if not to speak for him?"

The emissary bowed, hoping the show of respect would assuage any harsh feelings the cold-natured fae might direct toward him. "King Uberon, I am charged with presenting the need of the Seelie Court to you and seeking your assistance. My authority extends no further."

"What else?"

"What?"

"If you are charged with the responsibility of securing my cooperation, then you are also authorized to make certain trades or concessions in order to appease me."

The emissary nodded. "I—I and my family are bidden to remain here as hostages."

"You *and* your family?"

"Aye. My mate and two children accompany me."

"Mogren must be desperate indeed to risk your mate and children."

"All of the Seelie Court is in need. The Quoli advance and we cannot stop them alone." He gestured vaguely to indicate Uberon's kingdom as a whole. "You are the only one who is known to have erected a barrier the Quoli cannot cross."

"What do I get out of this?"

"King Mogren is ready to transfer half the Seelie Court's treasury to—"

"I have no need of his wealth." It occured to Uberon to demand that the moon-born be made his subject, but he knew that request would not only meet refusal, but it would also hurt his mate and enrage his cousin. Enders was fond of the moon-born who was mother to his own mate. He cared little for the refusal, but had no desire to incur his mate's disgust or hatred. Enders' wrath would be annoying, probably damaging, and not worth the petty satisfaction of having offended Mogren.

He considered the dilemma, for the Seelie Court truly had nothing he wanted, except the patronage of the archivist. Looming over the nervous emissary, he said, "Return to the Seelie Court with your family. I have but one request: the archivist must agree to spend ninety days a year for the next millennia in Quoliálfur in service to me. His mate is welcome to accompany him and stay as our most honored guest."

The emissary gasped. "But—but the archivist is not a subject of the Seelie Court. King Mogren cannot command him."

"Those are my terms. Do not return unless you have his agreement." Uberon stated and turned on his heel. Golsat, who had remained silent through the exchange, followed close behind.

"Why request the archivist's presence?" the gargoyle asked once the doors closed behind them.

"He owes me."

A low buzz of speculation greeted his arrival in the great hall where the banquet continued in full swing. He took his seat next to Corinne, who leaned toward him and asked, "What was that about?"

"I'll tell you later."

She settled back in her chair and allowed the festivities to distract her until later when she lay hoarse and panting in

Uberon's embrace. He hadn't been kidding about enjoying the procreative part of their union.

Rolling over and idly toying with one small nipple on his hard chest, she took a moment's pleasure in the way it beaded in reaction to her touch and then asked, "So, what was that impromptu meeting all about?"

Uberon grinned and allowed his mate to lull him into divulging what she wanted to know. He would have done so anyway, but this was much more enjoyable. He ran his hand down her side, following the dip of her waist, the rounded flare of her hip, and back up again to stroke the plump softness of her breast. Two could play at that game. He hissed as her other hand grasped his still semi-aroused penis and began stroking it to fully turgid readiness.

"The Seelie Court wants our help," he replied, allowing his fingers to dip between her slender thighs already wet and slick with their combined fluids. She moaned and lightly squeezed his cock. He hissed again, his breath catching in his throat from the pleasure that streaked through him. "I declined their trade."

Fondling him, Corinne pondered his words for a moment made delicious by the touch of his fingers on her skin and between her legs. She managed to retain coherent thought, but realized her brain wouldn't hold out for long before it melted into sizzling pleasure. "What did you ask for instead?"

Uberon smiled at his mate's clever perception and ducked down to capture her mouth with his, claiming her with dominating strokes of his tongue. As he rolled her onto her back and nuzzled the delicate skin beneath her ear, he answered, "Mogren can't be trusted. I asked the archivist to agree to spend ninety days a year here for the next millennium."

Since her first and only experience with the king of the Seelie Court left a bad taste in her mouth, Corinne did not object to his characterization of the Seelie king. "Why would Enders agree to that?"

Uberon kissed a wandering path down her neck and spent several minutes worshipping her breasts with his mouth, reducing her mind to warm goo. He gave her the same answer he gave the emissary: "He owes me."

She clung to her mate as he journeyed down her body until he feasted upon her sex, hands twining in his long hair, nails dragging against his scalp. Her eyes rolled back as a climax crashed over her. She cried out when he surged forward and crushed his mouth to hers, sharing the combined taste of their earlier release as he drove into her again, filling her body, heart, and mind in ways that no romance novel ever adequately described.

She could only hope that Samuel gave his bride a smidgen of the pleasure Uberon gave her. If so, Ari'valia would be a satisfied woman.

CHAPTER 25

"You would hold me hostage?" Enders snarled at Uberon from across a small table in a sunny drawing room. It bore two tumblers of ice and a pitcher of iced tea, lightly sweetened and flavored with fresh lemon, for which the king had developed a fondness due to his mate's preference for the beverage. "How dare you?"

"Nonsense, Enders." Uberon waved his hand in a languidly dismissive gesture he knew would annoy the other fae. "I could use your insight, and I'd appreciate it if you would condescend to tutor my mate. She is still quite ignorant of our history and traditions. Besides, she quite likes Daniellisande."

"Insight, eh? You never needed that before."

"Not since the early years of the Unseelie Court," Uberon amended. "But I have a new laboratory here and find myself falling back into old habits. You bring a different and learned perspective that I will find useful."

Enders took a sip of his beverage and grimaced. "Ugh. What is this vile brew?"

"Corinne calls it iced tea. She's quite fond of it. Would you prefer ale?"

"Yes, I would, thank you. And how is your pretty mate?"

"She's well, thank you. And yours?"

The archivist's austere features softened. "Doing better. She miscarried last year."

Uberon nodded, appropriately solemn. "You have my condolences on the loss. Corinne has yet to conceive."

Enders raised an eyebrow and smirked. "But not for lack of trying."

"Of course not." Uberon took a sip and savored the refreshing flavor. Really, Earth did have some wonderful things. He wondered how well the cacao plants he imported on his last visit would fare in the climate and soil of Quoliálfur. His mate missed chocolate. The lemon, lime, orange, and grapefruit trees flourished. He considered where tea cultivars would grow best. Fetching tea from Earth grew tedious.

"Uberon."

The king blinked, surprised that he had allowed himself to be distracted from the topic at hand. He did not usually allow his mind to wander.

"Our mates do tend to affect us that way," the archivist commented with a trace a smugness in his voice.

"Another reason I need a sharp mind around here." Uberon bared his teeth. Enders did not mistake the expression for a smile. "Besides, you owe me."

"I owe you?"

"'Twas you and that damned Thelan who brought my castle to its figurative knees, who destroyed my kingdom for the Seelie Court to claim."

"Rather it was Marog who caused it. If he hadn't abducted Catriona, none of that would have happened."

"You could have retrieved her without destroying my castle and my kingdom."

Enders shrugged, not debating the point. He had his reasons for his actions and did not deign to justify them to anyone but himself. Or Daniellisande. But he'd not been mated to the moon-born's daughter when he did what his colleague accused him of doing.

"When I split from the Seelie Court, you did not support me," Uberon added.

"When you split from the Seelie Court and took a third of its population with you, I thought you were wrong. I still think you were wrong."

"So, destroying the Unseelie Court was your way of restoring order?"

Enders shrugged again, unwilling to apologize or justify his decisions. "You still haven't convinced me why I should agree to your demand."

"Maybe it's because I miss you. We were once as close as brothers."

"Hah. Not likely."

"Then perhaps I would like my mate to have a friend who is her equal."

"That's closer to the truth."

"Then because I ask it. You love the Seelie Court and its people. I have no care for them and its downfall to the Quoli will not disturb me. Refugees who wish to resettle here must swear fealty to me as they would if they settle in any other foreign nation." Uberon took another sip and bared his teeth. "I'm sure you don't want to see that happen."

"You always were a cold and calculating bastard."

"That's why you like me."

"I haven't liked you for a long, long time. But I do respect you, Uberon."

"Then we have an accord."

"Aye. I'll inform Mogren."

"Bring your lovely mate when you return. Corinne will be glad of her company."

Enders nodded. He paused, tilted his head to the side and asked, eyes burning with curiosity. "How did you carve out this kingdom from the Quol and hold it?"

Uberon took another sip and favored Enders with a genuine smile. "That's *my* secret."

CHAPTER 26

"I don't like it."

Uberon blinked and waited, because Corinne hadn't finished speaking yet. Shrill cries of seagulls filled the silence.

"I understand the need. I understand why you're going. But that doesn't mean I have to like it."

He nodded, understanding her sentiments. "Beloved, as long as I have lived, I have come across few entities that could be described as truly evil. The Quol comes close. It may not be pure evil, but it is pure hunger that consumes everything in its path. It does not love, cannot care. The spirit that animates it advances in the form of the Quoli. They dare not venture far beyond the jungle, but they are the force that spreads it. Where the Quoli go, so does the Quol."

She nodded, having nothing to say that would affect the outcome of their discussion. Uberon placed a finger under her chin and tipped her head back. He pressed a tender kiss upon her mouth, then straightened and held her gaze.

"I cannot, in good conscience, allow the Seelie Court to succumb to the Quol."

She sighed.

"I will take a small company of gargoyles and we shall accompany Enders to Lahn'Ursai. Daniellisande will remain here with you. Golsat will also remain to support and advise you as needed."

"He wouldn't leave Han'al anyway."

"Not likely," Uberon agreed.

Corinne clutched at his shirt with sudden desperation. "Promise me you'll come back."

"Nothing will keep me from returning to you. Nothing."

Uberon wrapped his arms around her, giving her what comfort he could. And she did take comfort in the ferocity of his promise, in his bright passion for her, in the absoluteness of their connection. She loved his sly humor and how the very humanity of her nature inspired him toward compassion.

She made him strive to be a better man, for all that he denied being a man. Because men were human and he was fully fae, fully male, fully *hers*.

The silver and diamonds embedded in her skin warmed.

What had his influence upon her yielded? Locked inside her own skin, her own mind, she could not discern any great difference. Perhaps that was good. Perhaps Uberon did not want her to change. Perhaps …

But no matter, she returned his hug, wrapping her arms tightly around him as though never to let him go.

She felt his lips against the top of her head, heard him inhale the scent of her and fix it upon his memory. She did the same, inhaling the fragrance of her mate—fresh, slightly musky, *wild*—and lifting her face upward for his kiss. Then he released her and she, perforce, let her arms fall to her sides.

"Rule in my stead, Corinne, my beloved. You are the queen of Quoliálfur."

She nodded, eyes filling with tears.

"You have listened and learned as scribe. Now it is time to put that knowledge to use."

She nodded again, wringing her hands.

"Listen to the wind. It will bring you word of me."

"And I will reply via return current," she vowed.

He smiled, giving her one of those rare expressions of love and joy. "You are stronger and more powerful than you realize. I am already proud of you and I know that you will make me prouder still."

"I love you, Uberon," she whispered, unable to control her voice beyond that without dissolving into tears.

"I love you, too."

"How very touching," a cool comment interrupted.

Uberon spun on his heel to confront whoever interrupted their private moment. Corinne peered around him and gasped.

"I know you."

The ebony unicorn nodded, its black spiral horn bobbing. The pearl unicorn walked up and took its place beside it.

"You didn't think we'd allow you to save the world without ensuring you had something to come back to, did you?"

"You're a bit far from your forest," Uberon responded in a dry tone.

"If you succeed, the Great Forest will extend even here."

"The forest goes where you go," Corinne murmured with sudden insight, seeing the reciprocity. The Quol consumed, the Great Forest nurtured.

"Clever girl, isn't she?" the white unicorn commented.

"If you must impose upon my hospitality, then see to it that you guard those whom I hold dear," Uberon said.

The midnight swift snorted with derision. "Presumptuous fae. We unlocked her power after you transformed her. We will not harm her."

The fae king's eyes narrowed. "I know you will not harm her, because I'd kill you if you did. You both know that I'm one of three who could succeed in that attempt."

"Your power has limits, fae."

"So does yours, beast."

"Quit!" Corinne snapped and stamped her foot like a child. "Stop bickering!"

The fae king and the two swifts turned to look at her with incredulous expressions.

She pushed at Uberon. "Go, before I refuse to let you leave and save the world."

She glared at the unicorns. "I will consider your words, but remember this is *my* kingdom and I rule here."

For the second time that day, Uberon smiled. And then he laughed at the swifts' stunned silence.

It was a wonderful image by which Corinne could remember Uberon as he walked up the gangplank and boarded the ship that would take him to the westernmost shores of the Seelie Court. From there he would travel to the vast region or *lahn* formerly held and governed by House Ursai, one of the most powerful houses in all the Seelie Court. There, he would meet both the archivist and anyone else Master Enders deemed important and suitable for beating back the ravenous Quoli and the dangerous jungle they left in their wake.

With Golsat standing protectively beside her, she watched the ship disappear over the horizon.

I am with you, came the whispered reassurance on a playful current of wind.

I will wait for you. Always.

CHAPTER 27

Years passed.

Corinne ruled Quoliálfur, tempering Golsat's cold, hard logic and pragmatism with mercy and compassion. She relied upon him, learned the customs and the traditions of the many peoples who populated Quoliálfur as well as the laws that Uberon had established during his reign. She repealed those she saw fit to eliminate and decreed those she deemed appropriate, using her own common sense as a gauge.

She founded a school, fulfilling one goal to see girls as well as boys educated and trained for useful careers. She lured guildmasters and scholars with gold and bludgeoned them with sweetness and threats until they relented and acceded to her demands to accept female students. To ensure that parents allowed their children to attend, she dug into the kingdom's deep coffers to pay the tuition of all students and recompense parents for the loss of wages contributed through child labor. After a couple of decades, the citizenry grew accustomed to seeing the country's youth make their way to school rather than to work. The educated populace then found their knowledge and skills in demand and took advantage of the expanded and often lucrative employment opportunities that came their way.

Messages from Uberon came sporadically, always on a current of wind and always short, sweet, and too damned vague to be reassuring. She replied each time, using skill taught and power liberated by the dawn and midnight swifts. She found it fascinating that neither of the unicorns understood how Uberon had carved his kingdom from the Quol or how he managed to keep it.

She rather liked that they did not know. It proved them something less than omnipotent or omniscient.

She watched as Han'al grew up and celebrated the claiming ceremony when Golsat officially proclaimed her his mate and merged his soul with hers, granting his flesh and blood mate the eternal youth enjoyed by many fae species. She enjoyed visits from Sin'halissar and Hibr and, eventually, their six children. She watched Samuel and Ari'valia grow old and produce a passel of children who then produced grandchildren. Sin'clannad followed her warrior husband back to Nymmur and never returned to Quoliálfur, although ships sometimes brought bundles of chatty letters. Ari'dongharad bore her djinni mate two children and perished in the attempt to deliver a third.

Corinne, like the fabled Penelope, wife of Odysseus of ancient Greek legend, found herself beset by suitors seeking to take the fae queen to wife and to rule over a wealthy, thriving kingdom. With Golsat at her side and confidence in her ability to protect herself, she did not fear abduction. Nonetheless, the princes and noblemen who vied for her hand annoyed her.

"I'd like to boot them into the ocean. Maybe a kraken would find them tasty," she griped one evening while dining with Samuel, Ari'valia and their adult children and three grandchildren. Uberon had been absent for almost thirty years.

"You know you can't do that," Samuel replied as he spooned a cold soup into his mouth. It reminded him somewhat of gazpacho, but without the tomato base. "That would be tantamount to declaring war on those countries."

"I know. That's the only reason that frog-faced jerk from Buleen still has his hand."

"You mean the fellow wearing the heavy bandage on his right hand?"

"That's the one."

"What did he do?"

Corinne's lips peeled back from her teeth in a gesture reminiscent of her mate and which made her seem purely fae. It never failed to startle her brother, whose shoulder-length hair now sported streaks of gray. That she did not age also convinced him that his sister had long since left humanity behind.

She grimaced. "What do you think that lecher did?"

Samuel sighed. "What did you do to him?"

"Let's just say that he'll have scars."

He fixed her with a stare that she returned without remorse. "You burned him, didn't you?"

"Third degree, Brother. He squealed like a stuck pig."

Samuel shook his head at his sister's bloodthirstiness, but could not say that he regretted her action. He would have chopped the man's hand off. She might be immortal, but she was still his sister.

When they finished supper, Corinne set her napkin aside and rose as she did every evening except during severe weather. "I'm headed to the wharf."

Samuel nodded, rose from his seat, kissed his wife, and accompanied the queen. It was his turn. The next night, Golsat had the honor of walking through the city to the wharf where Corinne would listen for word from Uberon.

"You haven't heard from him in weeks, Corinne," he pointed out. "Perhaps he—"

"No." She cut him off.

"You can't be sure he's still alive."

"Actually, I can," she said, voice firm with conviction.

"How?"

She ran her fingertips over the silver filigree and black diamonds adorning her neck and collar bones. She smoothed the skirt of her dress. Without Uberon present, she'd had to hire a seamstress to maintain her wardrobe. "The mate bond remains intact. Nothing but death will sever it."

When they reached the end of the pier that stretched the furthest into the bay, she stood still. Gulls shrieked overhead. Water slapped at wooden posts and hulls. Canvas sails and banners snapped in the wind. Raucous shouts and laughter rose above the din of loud conversation and fiddles playing sea shanties back on shore. The twin moons, Dennae and Fata, hid behind a thick layer of cloud cover. The smell of fish, tar, and other less savory odors hung on the air. Corinne waited, listening.

I am with you.
I wait for you. Always.

Her shoulders sagged with relief. She knew Uberon lived, but she did not know whether he thrived.

Watching his sister with concern, Samuel wrapped his arm around her shoulders and asked, "Is everything all right?"

She nodded. "He lives."

The former Navy SEAL wished he had sufficient reason—as well as strength and skill—to give his sister's husband a well-deserved whupping, but he understood the call of duty. An ugly suspicion presented itself to him, not for the first time.

"Are you sure you're doing the right thing by waiting for him? It's been a long, long time. Perhaps he—"

"No." Again she cut him off. She took a moment to compose herself, compelling herself to understand that humans did not have the certainty of the fae. "Fae are true to their mates. They cannot be otherwise."

Samuel suspected otherwise, but nodded and humored his sister.

They walked back to the castle. Samuel escorted her to her chambers, briefly conferred with the guards stationed at the entrance to the royal quarters, and then made his way to the large suite of rooms he shared with Ari'valia. She looked up from her embroidery and gave him a placid smile in greeting which did not quite conceal her worry.

"She pines for him," Ari'valia commented.

"Aye." He paced the room. "She's certain he's alive and faithful to her, certain he will return. But how can she be? Men are fickle. I did three tours of duty and infidelity was rampant. He's been over there for, what, thirty years—no way he kept his dick to himself."

"Have you been faithful to me all these years?" Ari'valia inquired, laying her embroidery in her lap.

"Of course, I have. I love you."

She sighed. "After all this time, you still do not understand. The fae are not like us. They are immortal. Thirty years is but a blink of an eye to an immortal. The king is at least a hundred thousand years old, perhaps two or three times that. The histories do not say because they are lost to us. Unlike we who are human and short-lived, he will not regard this time away from Corinne as extensive."

"Corinne's younger than I," he pointed out.

"By counting years, yes. But she will live thousands of years and she knows that. She sees the evidence of it every time she looks into her mirror."

"All right. But how can she be certain he's faithful to her?"

"Ari'dongharad once explained it to me like this: they share a soul which means they almost share a mind. They are connected in ways that time and space cannot affect. The king would no sooner hurt his queen than he would cut off his own leg with a rusty knife."

"It still seems strange."

"Aye, to humans it does. But they are not human. Uberon never was and Corinne barely remembers being so."

"What should we do? I don't like seeing her just fade away."

"We will find out where Uberon is and send a message. No doubt she assures him she is in fine health so as not to disturb him or distract him from his duties."

Samuel nodded. "I'll canvass the ships' crews tomorrow. Will you help me write letters? We'll need to send a letter with each ship."

"Gladly. She convinced the king to save me and my sisters; I am happy to save her."

With Golsat standing guard over the queen the next day as she entertained the daily audience of petitioners, claimants, plaintiffs, defendants, and suitors, Samuel handed the captain of each ship moored at the wharf a letter and a pouch of coins to pay for delivery. Those captains who flew the double crescent of Quoliálfur and prospered, vowed to deliver their letters should they come within a day's journey of the king's location. Those foreign captains who were less honorable or dependent upon Quoliálfur for their trade took the gold with little intent of seeking out the king who could beat back the Quol. Perhaps if they stumbled upon him while walking to a tavern, they might hand over the letters in their possession.

Then there was nothing to do but wait. If Corinne suspected her brother's activities, she gave no indication of it. Every evening she still made the trek to the end of the furthest pier jutting from the wharf to listen to the wind. Experienced seamen knew better than to accost the queen on her daily excursion.

Those who ignored the warnings of their wiser colleagues either died or suffered injury, for no male—human or otherwise—dared insult the queen more than once.

Golsat, Han'al, Ari'valia, and Samuel worried as she slowly faded. Each year she took less and less interest in ruling the kingdom, in her family, in anything beyond the daily walk to the end of the pier. She began taking long strolls through the city, not searching for anything in particular, which puzzled Samuel and the guards he assigned to shadow her. Finally admitting to the infirmity of age, Samuel relinquished that duty to those who had youth, energy, and strength. Corinne made no attempt to evade their watch; she simply wandered. She entered no shops and spoke to no one.

"She's gradually making her way to the border," a guard said, having pieced together the puzzle of the queen's seemingly aimless wandering.

"The border?" Golsat echoed in surprise and not a little worry.

"Perhaps you could ask her about it?" The guard cast a worried glance over his shoulder as the queen paid only desultory attention to the latest petitioner's request.

"Aye. I'll accompany her tomorrow."

The guard nodded, relieved to relinquish her protection to the nearly indestructible gargoyle.

Golsat wondered if the Quoli had somehow managed to connect with the queen, perhaps beckoned to her, summoned her to the border where where she could fall into their clutches and succumb to their hunger. Had they grown so strong in the king's absence? Had the king's magic weakened?

The next day Golsat followed her after she concluded the daily audience early. She walked without haste, seemingly in no particular direction, although the guard had correctly determined that her footsteps gradually drew her toward the jungle lurking to the east. She appeared not to realize where her feet drew her.

Curious, Golsat watched as she approached the border, which appeared to have crept forward overnight. Had the Quol taken advantage of Uberon's extended absence to encroach upon his kingdom? His eyes bulged as a thick plane of air appeared to solidify and warp and bulge. Eerie cries, howls, screams, and other less pleasant sounds emanated through the straining ward.

The queen advanced the ward and raised her arms. Power like waves of heat rippled from the earth and air, coalescing around her and tightening into a glowing ball of energy around her closed fists. The constant breeze blowing off the ocean ceased, adding its might to the draw of power. Golsat's jaw dropped in awe and fear as she took the final steps toward the flimsy border and punched it with those glowing fists. With a hiss and roar, the wards flared as though infused with lightning. The screaming and howling behind the border rose in an ear-splitting crescendo that made even the gargoyle wince in pain.

"Help me," Corinne whispered.

Golsat looked around and realized she did not speak to him.

"Tell me what to do."

The guard strained to hear the king's response, but heard nothing. The power she channeled pulsed, a heavy beat of deadly power that both strengthened and pushed the border backward. She walked slowly, visibly trembling, her thin leather shoes sinking into putrid puddles as clean, fresh air, unfiltered sunlight, and fae power corroded and dissolved the malicious, poisonous, jungle flora exposed by the retreating border. Her foot crunched the brittle skeleton of some animal, a sapling withered to a slimy mess, the caustic decay ate at the hems of her skirts.

The trembling of her body changed from thrumming with power to a desperate attempt to remain upright. Her hands fell to her sides and her spine and shoulders bowed beneath the weight of exhaustion.

"Thank you," she whispered, dizzy with the exercise of power.

She took another step forward.

"My lady, you should go no further," Golsat warned, daring to restrain her by placing his hand upon her arm.

She looked up in surprise, startled at the touch. She glanced down at her arm and Golsat snatched his hand back.

"Do you know how long it's been since someone touched me?" she whispered, her voice melancholy as she stared toward the eastern horizon. "None dares touch the queen."

"It's a lonely existence," Golsat agreed.

A single tear trickled down her cheek, the first he had seen. "I miss him."

"I know."

The tear hardened and fell to the reclaimed soil. "Why won't he come back?"

Golsat figured the question was rhetorical and needed no response from him. Instead, he kept his voice gentle and said, "Come, my lady. You should return to the castle."

She looked up at him again. "Can you contact him?"

Golsat shook his head, regretting the inability. He quite liked the queen. "Were you not speaking with the king?"

"No, the swifts. They do not know how to push back the Quol, but they do know how to restore a failing ward." She glanced skyward and squinted at the sun. "They promised me a price to pay for power. I have but made a small deposit. They say the soul bond will supply Uberon with access to my strength as he needs it."

She sighed and turned back toward the castle. Golsat blinked, realizing that the queen did indeed look diminished, the drain on her strength and energy constant. The gargoyle wondered if he might, however, get word to the Erlking or the archivist or even the unicorns. Surely, they would assist in reuniting Uberon with his mate. After returning to the castle and seeing Corinne to her chambers, he summoned the few gargoyles living in Quoliálfur.

"We must contact the king. The queen fades."

The gargoyles waited in stony silence, patient for the rest of the explanation.

"The queen pines for King Uberon. I will send each of you with a message of summons, one to the Erlking, one to the Deepwood, and one to Seelie Court."

"That leaves one behind," a fourth gargoyle pointed out the obvious.

"Aye. The queen's brother can no longer undertake his duties as her guard. His health declines."

"He is old for a human."

"Aye. I will have whichever one of you who wishes to serve with diligence and honor to guard the queen."

A gargoyle, a little taller and leaner than the others stepped forward. "I am not mated and have no family to protect. I will guard the queen in your stead."

Golsat almost smiled. "No, not in my stead, but alongside me."

The gargoyle nodded, accepting the mild correction. Golsat turned on his heel and returned to the castle, the other gargoyle following him.

No one noticed the three gargoyles taking flight early the next morning. They flew steadily, the hungry magic of the Quol sliding off them without effect.

Corinne, distracted by her elderly brother's confinement to his bed, did not seem to notice the change in her guard. She knelt beside Samuel's bed and held his hand, hardly daring to believe that this frail old man who struggled for breath was her brother. She remembered him tall, strong, handsome, and bursting with vitality. Glancing at Ari'valia, who now walked with a cane, she knew that her sister-in-law remembered him the same way.

Waking from a light doze, Samuel turned his head and blinked. With a weak smile, he said, "You look as pretty as the day I first woke up here."

She smiled, unable to reciprocate. Instead she gave his hand a light squeeze. "How do you feel? Are you up to eating anything?"

"No, I'm not hungry. Where is Ari'valia?"

Corinne wanted to cringe at her brother's querulous tone, but did not. Instead, she smiled and quietly departed as his wife took his hand and they conversed in low, whispered tones. His decrepitude appalled her and that shamed her.

"The fae have little tolerance for age and the decline it brings upon mortals," Golsat commented in a quiet voice as he fell into step beside Corinne.

"You've come to know me too well," she replied. "I don't know why his pending death surprises me so. It's natural and expected."

"For a human," he pointed out. "You have not been human in over fifty years."

"I was human for hardly a quarter century," she mused. "Then mated and transformed to fae. I'm not even sure how long I lived with Uberon before he abandoned me to save the world."

She sighed. "Surely, he has saved it by now?"

Golsat had no answer to give her.

CHAPTER 28

Samuel died.

Wan and pale, Corinne wept as flames consumed the pyre and its dearly departed offering to the gods. Or God. She wondered about that and prayed anyway, hoping that her brother would be reunited with the family from whom fate had torn him. And her. Corinne watched as the granite memorial she commissioned was erected, a plain cross engraved with the crest of the Navy SEALs and his name on the crossbeam.

No one dared chase after the crystallized tears scattered on the ground.

Returning to the castle, she trailed behind Ari'valia and her children, grandchildren, and great-grandchildren. She knew that the extended family had already decided that Ari'valia would move from the castle to live with one of them. Corinne dispatched two guards to ensure the old woman's protection until she died.

Bereft of her husband, Ari'valia died a week later. Corinne ordered her ashes interred next to Samuel's under the aegis of the granite cross. She looked across the brief span of rocky earth to Han'al, who leaned against her mate and sniffled with grief. Arm in arm, the two immortals walked back to the castle.

"I'm all that's left," Han'al whispered. "If it were not for Golsat, I would not wish to continue living."

Corinne nodded, understanding how the former mortal felt. Han'al and Golsat had yet to be blessed with children. "I will release Golsat if you ask it, so that you and he might relocate someplace where grief does not permeate the walls."

"Golsat will not break his vow to the king," she answered, although resentment warred with gratitude in her eyes.

"I will speak with Golsat."

"No," he replied without hesitation when she broached the idea at supper. The three gargoyles dispatched to contact the king had returned in ignominy, their missions failed. He refused to fail. "Until Lord Uberon releases me, I stay."

And that was that.

Still the years passed, the loneliness endured, and Corinne slowly withdrew. She dwindled from slender to gaunt and, except for occasional treks to the border to reinforce the protective wards that kept the kingdom safe from the Quol's encroachment, seldom left her quarters except to sit in a sheltered courtyard where the castle murmured to her. Every night she walked to the end of the furthest pier, except during storms, to listen for a word from Uberon. She listened to the wind and clung to the infrequent assurances it brought. She lost interest in her appearance, allowing her handmaid to dress her as the servant saw fit. She ate what was put on her plate, and too little of that for the two gargoyles' comfort.

CHAPTER 29

A letter arrived.

The seal remained unbroken, which Golsat considered a small miracle as he took it from the ship captain's hand with a word of thanks. He hoped it was from Uberon, but the seal dashed that hope. Instead, King Mogren of the Seelie Court wrote to declare that the Lahn'Ursai had been retaken and secured against the Quol. Finally. The Seelie Court owed its everlasting gratitude to King Uberon of Quoliálfur who had been injured in the effort to save an entire continent from the lethal incursion and would remain as Mogren's honored guest while he recuperated. The six gargoyles who had accompanied him had perished. Not even the stalwart strength and resistance of gargoyles could withstand the concerted focus of the ravenous Quol and the Quoli it sent against them.

Golsat raised his eyes to the sky to give thanks to whatever gods existed for the good news and to grieve for the loss of his comrades. Spreading his wings, he launched himself into the air and raced to the queen's preferred courtyard.

She lay on a stone bench in a shaded spot, lightly dozing. Yet the gargoyle's hard landing in the courtyard's tight confines did not startle her. She blinked slowly and pushed herself to a sitting position with equal deliberation.

"What is it, Golsat?"

He handed her the letter.

Corinne's hands trembled. She read the short missive twice, her heart beating at a rapid pace, her breath coming fast and shallow.

"Uberon," she whispered, then her eyes rolled back and she collapsed.

"My lady!" Golsat yelped and rushed forward to pick up her crumpled form. He carried her to her chambers where handmaids fluttered about her in useless distress. He ordered them from the royal quarters and summoned his mate.

"Watch over her," he begged Han'al. She is nearly as dear to me as you."

"I will," she replied.

Golsat canceled that day's audience, gruffly dismissing all petitioners, claimants, defendants, and others who sought royal favor or decision. He summoned the three gargoyles who had failed to deliver their letters and offered them a chance for redemption.

"Go to the Seelie Court to attend King Uberon," he ordered without indulging in explanation. "Accompany his return to Quoliálfur."

"What happened to his guard?" one asked.

"They perished."

Silence lay heavily upon them as each considered the might and peril required to kill six gargoyles. That the king lived impressed them beyond measure. The three gargoyles bade their families good-bye and took to the air, each carrying a missive from Golsat to Mogren.

CHAPTER 30

Corinne waited. The tropical sun beat down upon her, yet she did not feel its heat. Saltwater slapped at the pylons and the hulls of ships, waves crashing on the shore. The wind whipped at her clothing and tugged at her unbound hair. She squinted against the glare of sunlight sparkling on the surface of the ocean.

I come.

She heard and felt the weariness in his mental voice. Her own reply echoed the exhaustion of her soul, *I wait.*

The day wore on. Corinne refused all offers of food and drink, all exhortations to take her rest in the shade. She stood tall and gaunt at the end of the pier and waited. As the sun dipped low to paint the sky with violet, crimson, and orange, the tall masts of a ship poked above the horizon. The white and blue banner of the Seelie Court flew from the tallest mast.

Hurry.

Impatient, Corinne lifted her arms to summon the wind and bend it to her will. Where once she blew out candles and slammed doors, she called gusts from across the ocean to propel the ship through the water as quickly as the wood could withstand. She spoke to the element, commanded it with an authority and skill never before exercised. The gargoyles flanking her stared in amazement. The unicorns who taught her how to wield her increased power in the first decade after Uberon left would have been proud.

The clop and ring of hooves upon the wooden planks of the pier drew their attention. Golsat turned around to greet the dawn and midnight swifts. Both looked exhausted, as though they had galloped without rest for days.

"My lords," he said, bowing low and wondering how they knew to come. He did not question the means of their uncanny speed; unicorns could bend distance and time to their need. From their heaving, sweaty sides, that effort cost them dearly.

The unicorns spared him a brief glance, then turned their attention to the queen.

"Remember what we taught you," the midnight swift said. "Finesse is just as critical as brute power."

The two arcane beasts watched as she pulled in the ship to a rocking halt at the pier. Corinne lowered her arms and released control of the wind. Sailors shouted, springing into action to moor the vessel and extend the gangplank.

"The king first!" the ship's captain shouted.

The sun disappeared with an eerie flash of green light that left the sky clothed in darkness but for the distant twinkle of stars, neither moon visible. Corinne paid the sudden descent of night no heed as her gaze locked upon the ship from the Seelie Court.

She inhaled and swayed on her feet when the king appeared at the ship's railing. His face turned to her, his gaze finding hers without error or delay and holding it.

"Uberon," she breathed and raised one hand toward him.

His lips moved, but she could not hear what he said. No matter, she knew he uttered her name.

A light breeze lifted his long, unbound hair as he limped down the gangplank. His clothing hung on his gaunt frame, not withered from maltreatment or starvation, but worn by unceasing effort that cost him energy and strength. Golsat looked from his king to his queen and realized that a good portion of the energy Uberon had used had come from Corinne.

She walked toward him, each step slow and restrained. She looked at him with wide eyes as he grew near, taking in the lines of weariness engraved upon his face, the uneven stride, and two long streaks of silver, one just right of his widow's peak and the other at his right temple, breaking the solid black of his hair. She thought the silver made him look distinguished and wondered if he would heal from whatever injury caused the limp.

When his worn boot settled on the pier, Corinne flung herself into his arms with a cry: "Uberon!"

His arms wrapped around her as hers wrapped around him. The soul bond flared bright, the light temporarily blinding those who looked directly at it as the king and queen of Quoliálfur embraced. Even the unicorns averted their eyes from the sudden glare. The brilliant joy of reunion burned the crushing loneliness of separation to ash.

Uberon pulled away just far enough to look deeply into his mate's shining eyes. "You're so beautiful. I missed you more than my heart could bear."

"I missed you, too."

The simple words propelled them into another desperate embrace. He fisted his hand in her tangled hair to tilt her head back and slanted his mouth over hers. Their passion flared along with the soul bond. Energy crackled and sparked around them.

Finally lifting his head from hers, he swept her into his arms with a display of renewed strength and vigor. His silver eyes burned. Her jade eyes glowed.

"Uberon, we need to discuss—" the dawn swift began.

"Not now," the king replied, cutting off the words as he began walking toward shore, his stride now strong and even.

"Uberon!" the midnight swift barked.

The king and queen of Quoliálfur ignored them. They had more important things to do.

THANK YOU!

Please leave a review.

Thank you for reading *Daughter of the Dark Moon*, the third book in the Twin Moons Saga. I really hope you enjoyed it.

Like every other independently published author, I ask you to leave a review. If you have a particular question, concern, or comment about this story or any other of my books that you'd like to send directly to me, use the contact form on my website: www.henhousepublishing.com. I enjoy hearing from readers and will respond to your message.

About the Author

Holly Bargo is the author's pseudonym and really did exist. She lives on a hobby farm in southwest Ohio with her husband and a menagerie of very spoiled, four-legged beasties. They have two adult children, one a university student and the other in the military. We thank him for his service to our country.

Readers can contact the author through the Hen House Publishing website at www.henhousepublishing.com, where she also maintains a blog. Holly enjoys hearing from readers.